Let us sit upon the ground and tell
sad stories of the death of kings.

Richard III

CHAPTER I

As the door to the bedroom creaked, William Hardy stirred. For three days, he had been languishing in his quarters at the Hotel Pelikan in Sévignac, wrestling with a deadly fever. Several times he had almost succumbed to its soothing overtures but had somehow dragged himself back from the brink, crying out the name of his true love back in Kent. Now, as the hinges snapped from their wooden frame, he knew it was not the fever that would take him, but something, or rather someone, far more terrible.

Hardy turned his unshaven face towards the door just as a caped man slid into his bedchamber. He was the far side of forty years of age and carried a physician's case.

'Ah, there you are,' the visitor said, drawing near.

As he hauled his head from the sodden sheets, Hardy braced himself for a blow.

None came.

The cloaked man slowly sat down on a wooden chair beside his bed. The tricolour ribbon on his chest stood out like a wound. He looked at Hardy and smiled. 'Permit me to introduce myself,' he said, peeling off his silk gloves. 'I am Doctor Vacher.'

Hardy shuddered. 'I know who you are.'

The doctor removed his hat, revealing a shaved scalp. A pair of round silver-rimmed spectacles rested on the end of his nose, which protruded from his pale face like a crow's beak. 'This is my assistant, Ernest Masson,' he said, as a second man entered. He was younger than the bald man, and had greasy, thinning, dark brown hair.

'We work for Citizen Danton,' Masson said as he poured water into a copper ewer on the bedside table.

The doctor removed his glasses for a moment and rubbed the lenses with a silk, scented handkerchief. He looked around the shabby room as if to familiarize himself with its poverty. He then placed his spectacles delicately back on his nose before moving close to Hardy's face. 'Hmmm, the face of fever. Look here, Masson, his visage is pinched and his cheeks are hollow.'

'His eyes are sunken, too,' Masson added, trying to impress his master.

'It's nothing that cannot be cured with the help of a febrifuge,' the doctor said. 'However, I will be plain with you, Mister Hardy. I am not here to heal you. I am here to harm you.'

Hardy's hands began to tremble. He looked at Masson who had silently withdrawn a pistol from his coat and was pointing it towards him.

'We know what you're doing here in Brittany,' the doctor muttered as he opened his aging leather case, revealing a coil of glinting scalpels, knives, and a cleaver.

'The meddling William Pitt has sent you to offer support for an uprising led by the Marquis de La Rouërie,' Masson said, as the physician readied the instruments.

'I know of no such thing,' Hardy tried to protest.

'What you're going to tell us,' Masson continued, 'is what military forces the British intend to send, when they are going to arrive and where exactly they plan to land.'

The doctor wiped a small cleaver with a cleaning rag made of baize. 'You are going to do us the courtesy of providing information about de la Rouërie,' the doctor said. 'He and his men are hiding near Dinan. Tell us where.'

The physician placed the instrument on a white cloth and stood up. He stretched out his hands as Masson presented the ewer with the efficiency of a sacristan. The doctor dipped his fingers in the water and washed them methodically before wiping them down with a cloth.

Masson took a scalpel and turned it in the light of the lamp, studying its fleeting coruscation, before handing it to the doctor.

Hardy grasped the drenched sheets with his twitching fingers.

'Are you going to give us the information we need?' the doctor asked. 'Or am I going to have to use my surgical skills?'

Hardy looked at the wall opposite, fixing his attention on a poorly framed oil painting of the Brittany coast. He stared at waves breaking on the shore and for a moment remembered his own hometown on the shores of Kent. He lifted himself from his mattress and leaned towards the doctor. Hardy gazed for a moment into the man's jet-black pupils before clearing his throat, spitting brown saliva in the doctor's face. 'The only thing you're going to get from me,' Hardy whispered, 'is a fever.'

The doctor bucked like a startled mare before wiping the mucus off his face.

'You dog!' Masson shouted, smashing the pistol into Hardy's face and knocking a tooth from his jaw.

Hardy gasped and sank back into his sodden bed, his bloodied lips already beginning to swell.

Masson threw his full weight over Hardy's heaving chest and bound Hardy's bleeding mouth with a white cravat. 'No one will hear your whimpering now,' he whispered.

The doctor took the smallest scalpel from his surgeon's case and held it between his thumb and first finger, tilting it slightly as he admired its silver blade. Without warning, he moved with the celerity of a wolf and grabbed Hardy's right hand tightly. 'The more you tell us, the less you will lose,' he said, lifting the scalpel.

Hardy winced.

Masson pinned Hardy's hand to the wooden frame on the side of the bed.

The doctor slowly began an incision into the base of the little finger.

Hardy emitted a muffled scream as the bone snapped like a twig.

The doctor lifted the amputated finger and turned it in front of his dilated eyes.

Droplets of blood fell from the stump onto the floor.

The physician began again.

'Be reasonable, Hardy,' Masson said. 'The good doctor doesn't need to go on with this. You may even be able to use your hand again if you tell us what we need to know.'

'If you cooperate,' the doctor muttered, 'I will give you some antimonials for your fever and have you deported safely back to Britain. If you continue to be obstinate, I will have you shot. It's up to you. What's your decision?'

Hardy opened his eyes and beckoned with his head for his interrogators to come closer. Masson removed the scarf from Hardy's mouth. The two men bent expectantly over their prisoner as Hardy drew breath as if to confess. As Hardy's lips drew near to the doctor's face, he whispered. 'Go... to... hell.'

'I think you will be there before us,' the doctor growled as Masson whipped Hardy with the butt of the pistol, smashing the bridge of his nose and exposing the bone.

Hardy stared defiantly at the men as blood oozed from the wound.

'I think it is pointless asking anything else,' the doctor sighed. 'The English have a tedious habit of wanting to die rather than talk.'

Vacher took his handkerchief and wiped his gleaming scalp. He washed his hands, donned his black coat and grabbed his bag and hat. 'Take our prisoner downstairs,' he barked.

Masson dragged Hardy from the room to a horse and carriage outside. 'Get in,' he snapped, thrusting Hardy into the carriage.

'You have one more chance, Mister Hardy,' the doctor said. 'Tell us what we need to know and we'll send you back to England.'

'For King and country,' Hardy moaned.

'Very well,' the doctor replied.

The coach rattled and bumped along stony roads as the sun began rise. Every jolt caused Hardy to wince. He peered out of the open windows, gazing at scenes of misty copses, fallow fields and busy farmhouses, and as he did he inhaled the early morning air, taking his last deep draughts of life, devouring every scent.

In an hour the coach stopped at the gendarmerie. Vacher and Masson pulled their prisoner out onto the gravel street and ordered two soldiers standing by the door to take him inside. Hardy was pulled from the coach and dragged through the arched stone doorway into a large reception room. A long desk stood proudly in the middle of the room. The air was thick with tobacco smoke and reeked of cheap brandy.

'Sign here,' the doctor said, presenting Hardy with a document adorned by the blood red seal of the municipal authority in Rennes.

'What is it?' he asked, the blood still trickling down his face.

'It's your confession, stating that you are a British spy and that you're guilty of aiding the enemies of the French Republic.'

Hardy took it in his left hand and studied it for a moment in the light of a lamp. He examined the date at the top, January 12th 1793. 'How do you expect me to sign this?' he asked, raising his bandaged right hand.

'You will sign it with your left hand,' the doctor replied.

'I will not sign it at all.'

'Very well,' Masson took over. 'Guards!'

A musket butt was rammed into his back. Hardy stumbled as the soldiers pulled him to the backdoor of the police station. He was pushed into an untended yard where a tall wooden post was the only thing to break the bare earth. Without ceremony he was blindfolded and tethered to the stake.

Masson began to intone the offences with the indifference of a jaded priest. 'You have been charged and found guilty of assisting the enemies of the French Republic. Your sentence is death by firing squad, with immediate effect.'

'No court? No jury? No defence?' Hardy enquired. 'This must be France...'

'If you were a man of reason you would realize you have foregone your right to such things,' Masson retorted. 'Now would be a good time to pray, if you believe in such foolishness.'

Hardy peered blindly in front of him as the French agent's footsteps moved away. He shook his head from side to side but could sense nothing except the sound of men standing to attention and muskets being shouldered.

Hardy bowed his head. He began to pray out loud. 'Our Father, who art in heaven, hallowed be thy...'

The words were cut short by the sudden blast of muskets. Bullets tore into his chest as if cutting through ice. Hardy dropped like a sack, his blood-drenched shirt clinging tightly to his punctured torso, his body coming to rest as if kneeling before a king.

The doctor slowly walked towards the stake and touched the prisoner's neck, feeling for the carotid pulse. 'His heart is still beating,' he said.

Masson cocked a pistol and marched to the slumped body. He placed the end of the weapon at Hardy's temple. 'Not anymore,' he remarked as the weapon fired.

CHAPTER 2

Thomas Pryce, the newly inducted Vicar of St Leonard's Deal, stood before the gilded mirror in the hallway of his redbrick rectory. He ran his right hand through the waves of his raven hair then brushed down his short black jacket with both hands, adjusted his white clerical bands and stared for a moment into his eyes.

'How are you feeling, husband?' The words were spoken in French by a tall, elegant woman now standing beside him.

Pryce replied in the same language, speaking it effortlessly. 'Look at me, Eloise. I'm nearly thirty but I look ten years older.'

'The last few years have not been kind to us,' she said. 'But the doctors talk about this little town of Deal as an ideal place for souls like us to convalesce.'

'But there will be much work to be done,' Pryce said.

'It's your first day,' she whispered, holding his sagging shoulders and reaching up to kiss his neck. 'Be kind to yourself and let the sea air bring its healing.'

Pryce turned from the mirror and stroked his wife's chestnut hair.

'You are my compass,' he said.

'And you are mine,' Eloise replied, handing him a cape.

Pryce kissed her and then gathered the woolen cloak around his shoulders. He stooped to pick up a black bag with his prayer book, Bible, holy water and stole. He gripped the door handle and then inhaled deeply as he marched out of the porch onto the frosty path.

'Are you the new rector, sir?'

Pryce had just closed the garden gate and the voice came from a plump woman running towards him.

'I am. Is there anything wrong?'

11

'My husband sent me.' She said breathlessly. 'He humbly asks that you bless his new boat.'

'What's your name?'

'Sally Paine.'

'Well Mrs Paine, let's set sail while there's a fair wind.'

Together they walked the length of Beach Street and along the gravelly shore until they reached Sally's cottage. The first floor of the house was made of brick, the second white painted wood, and it stood defiantly on a stretch of elevated earth one hundred feet from the surf.

'Welcome Vicar,' Sally said as she ushered him through a small hallway and into a stone floored kitchen.

In the centre of the room was a table made of elm at which a large man was sitting. He wore a fisherman's jersey of Breton design and was sipping a mug of tea through his mutton chop whiskers.

Sally coughed several times.

'The new sky pilot of Deal,' she said.

'Sky pilot?' Pryce said.

'That's our name for Vicars here,' Sally said. 'On account of the fact that men such as you live higher up the mast than the rest of us, pointing the way.'

Pryce smiled.

The boatman put his mug on the table and stood up to his full height. Pryce was tall enough at six feet but this man was a giant, a good four inches taller. His chest bulged like a man-o-war in full sail. He grasped Pryce's hand firmly. 'Call me Jack.'

'I hear you're a boatman,' Pryce said, sitting on a wooden chair at the table.

'I make my living as a huv'ler on the Sands.'

'A huv'ler?'

'We rescue crews and cargos on the Goodwin Sands. Sometimes we get to claim salvage, sometimes we bring chains and anchors to incoming ships.'

'Ah, I see,' Pryce said.

'We live by bombing.'

'Bombing?'

'Buying provisions on land and then selling them at a profit to the ships at sea.'

Pryce nodded. 'Now then,' he said, 'I'm told you have a new boat.'

'That's my cat out the front there, the *Endeavour*.'

Jack pointed through the window to a clinker-built boat tilting to its left on the beach, forty feet long and fourteen feet wide, with a small cuddy or forepeak for shelter. It had two masts, a foremast at the bow and a mizzen positioned well aft. The boat was lying with its bluff stem pointing down the shingle towards the breakers. It was made of elm which had only recently been varnished.

'Brand new, it is,' Jack said. 'I would be much obliged if you'd bless it. No one sets to sea in a new boat in these waters without God's hand upon it.'

Pryce nodded and opened his black bag and fetched a silver-topped bottle from inside a black leather box padded with a royal red cushion. He beckoned to Jack and Sally before walking back through the cottage towards the front door. He gathered his cape around his lean frame and walked across the crunching gravel stones towards the *Endeavour*.

Sprinkling the sacred water over the bows and gunwales of the boat he began his incantation, speaking an ancient benediction over the newly built craft. With the bottle in his left hand, he made the sign of the Cross with his other.

'It's done,' Pryce said.

'Thank you,' the boatman replied, as he grasped the Vicar's hand. Pryce smiled.

'If ever I can repay you with my services,' Jack said, 'please let me know.'

'Maybe you can show me the Downs and the Sands sometime.'

'Have you been to sea?' Jack asked.

'Oh yes, many times. I was brought up just up the coast at Broadstairs. My father was a boat builder. My wife's father is too, at

Saint Malo. We are both people of the sea.'

'Well, in that case why don't you come out with me and my boys one day? It's not dull around here. We have the lot in these parts - storms, wrecks, coves, spies and smugglers.'

'Smugglers?'

'Yes, Vicar, this town is full of men who have turned their hands to the free trade – several hundred at least.'

Pryce raised his eyebrows. 'I'm going to have my work cut out.'

'Aye,' Jack replied. 'Deal is a good place. But don't be deceived, Vicar. This side of the Downs some do more harm than good.' The boatman paused looking out to sea. 'The other side of the Channel, there is a great evil whose grim shadow will soon reach our shores.'

Pryce nodded.

'Maybe Providence has brought us together for a purpose this day,' he said.

'Perhaps, Vicar,' the boatman smiled, 'Perhaps.'

CHAPTER 3

Doctor Vacher looked furtively at his surroundings before clambering over the wall that enclosed a small Breton chapel and its graves. He dropped to the ground in front of a tall, weathered crucifix carved in stone. He stopped for a moment, put on his silver rimmed spectacles and peered at the crucified man. 'You've had your day,' he said.

Masson, following the physician like a shadow, tugged on his master's coat. 'Why do you hate him so?'

The doctor turned, his eyes burning. He removed his tricorn hat. 'It is because of this,' he snarled, pointing to his bald scalp.

'How did it happen?'

'When I was a boy I had an affliction that tormented me. A priest said that if I prayed, God would take it away and restore my hair, like Samson's.'

'And did he?'

'Of course he didn't.'

'I'm sorry.'

'That was my liberation from the superstition of religion. From that day to this I have hated the God to whom these statues pay homage.'

'But did not the priest mean well?' Masson protested.

'It is the priests I hate most of all,' the doctor said.

'All of them?' Masson asked.

'All of them.'

'I can understand you hating the refractory priests,' Masson said. 'They oppose the Revolution. But surely you do not hate the constitutional priests who have signed up to support us in the cause of liberty?'

'Quite the opposite, Masson. In a strange way, I respect the refractory priests. At least they have the courage of their convictions, even if their convictions are wholly contrary to reason. But the constitutional clergy I detest. They are cowards, all of them.' Vacher turned towards the granite chapel. 'I think we may be about to meet one of them right now.'

The two men stood a moment among statues of the apostles in the porch of the church. The doctor knocked three times loudly, then twice softly, on the heavy oak door. There was the sound of an iron bolt being drawn and a handle being turned. Old hinges whined in protest. Then, before them stood a priest, dressed from his neck to his feet in a black cassock buttoned all the way down the front.

The doctor looked into the priest's eyes.

The priest in turn looked down his pale nose at the doctor's bag. He stretched out a thin hand and pointed at it, shaking his head slowly from left to right.

The doctor handed over his case to Masson. 'Take this,' he said. 'Return to the horses and wait for me there.'

Masson took the bag.

When the sound of his feet had disappeared, the doctor looked up at the priest. 'I suppose you also want this,' he said. The doctor reached inside the left hand pocket of his waistcoat and took out a silver skeleton key. He placed it carefully on the palm of his right hand which he stretched out towards the cleric.

The priest took the key and lifted it to the same height as his eyes. It was no longer than his thumb and no thicker than his little finger. The shank – a cylindrical shaft - was conventional, but the bow, that was different. It was an oval shape sitting on a horizontal bar, like the sun resting on a far horizon.

The priest fetched a monocle from a hidden pocket and peered through it at writing engraved along the shaft, just above the rectangular tooth of the key. 'You may go in. He's waiting for you,' he said.

The doctor stepped into the chapel, momentarily turning up his nose at the ornately decorated pews and pulpit, font and screen, on his right. He made his way to the back of the church to the door of a confessional. He opened the intricately carved portal a little wider to make room for his thick frame and sat down on a small, uneven bench. He turned right to look through the grating to see if anyone was there. There was not. He breathed a sigh of relief.

His respite lasted only a moment. There was a candle burning on his side of the booth. Its flame had been tall and vigorous after he had sat down but now it was straining against the wick, like a bed sheet pulling against a washing line in a fierce wind.

Then it went out.

The doctor removed his hat and looked to his right again. As he put on his spectacles he saw the shadow of a man moving into the other side of the confessional. He seemed to slide into the seat with an incorporeal ease.

'You have something to report?' the visitor said.

'Yes, master,' the doctor replied. 'I have information about the Marquis de la Rouërie.'

The shape shifted. 'That fox,' he said.

'He's been hiding out in the woods near Dinan,' the doctor whispered, 'and he's been using the tactics he learned fighting in the Carolinas. Many of our national guardsmen have been killed these last two weeks.'

The shadow stirred. 'Danton will not permit this,' he growled.

The doctor shuffled before speaking again. 'I have interviewed a British agent who was due to meet the Marquis.'

'Interviewed?' the shadow interrupted.

'Interrogated,' the doctor conceded.

'There's more than one use for those scalpels you carry in that bag of yours,' the shadow said.

'Indeed.'

'What have you learned?'

'Not a lot from the British agent. He was stubborn. But from my torture of several Breton rebels I now know that the Marquis is intending to meet with his leaders to plan a military campaign against our government.'

'Tell me more.'

'According to my sources, it will involve a march on Paris. One army – consisting of royalist rebels and British infantry – will attack from the west. Another, from Koblenz, will attack from the east.'

'How many men do they have?'

'There will be up to 10,000 rebels in Brittany – once the British have arrived – and over 10,000 in the army from Koblenz.'

'Who are their leaders?'

'The Marquis will lead the Breton force, the Comte d'Artois the army from Koblenz.'

The shadow spat like a cobra as the count's name was mentioned. 'When are they planning to strike?'

'It will be soon,' the doctor replied.

'It may be sooner than you think,' the shadow intoned. He paused for a moment. 'Within the next three weeks the world as we know it will be changed forever.'

'How?' asked the doctor.

'The King will die.'

The shadow drew himself to his full height as the physician gasped. 'The king will die but the true Sovereign – our Nation – will remain. And it will be stronger without a monarchy, strong enough to declare war on the perfidious English and all who threaten the new order in France.'

'How do you know this?'

'Two days ago I was at the tribune in Paris and I voted for the king's death. I told my brothers that we must be decisive and strong - as impassive as gods.'

'What was the outcome?'

'Death without appeal... the blade will fall on the 21st of this month.'

'What of the Marquis?' the doctor asked.

'You must assassinate him,' the shadow whispered. 'A body is useless without its head.'

'I will do it.' The doctor paused, rubbing his chin for a moment. 'All I need to do is wait until he calls me on some medical matter and then I will strike.'

'And when you do,' the shadow added, 'France will know what terror awaits those who want to drag us back to the old days before the revolution.'

The doctor leaned towards the grill. 'I will do this for you and for France.'

The shadow's head moved closer. 'If you prove faithful in this lesser task,' he whispered, 'there is one far greater that I will give you.'

'What task is that?'

'When it is time, the passkey will tell you. All you need to know is that your name will be remembered forever in the history of our great Revolution.'

The doctor gasped. 'I will not let you down,' he hissed. 'Now is the time to purge Brittany of its unquestioning loyalty to the king and the church. Now is the time to replace superstition with science and faith with reason!'

The doctor finished with a flourish of his hand but as he peered through the miniature lattices he saw that he had not been heard and that the shadow had silently left. He sat back and wiped his brow. He placed his spectacles in his pocket, donned his hat and exited the confessional booth, making his way towards the church door. As he opened it, he was met by the tall priest who had been waiting the other side, a black cape over his head to protect him from the biting January wind.

'You will need this,' the priest said, drawing the silver passkey from his pocket and proffering it to the doctor. 'And when it's time, you will be told where to find the lock that matches it.'

The doctor snatched the passkey and returned it to his waistcoat pocket.

As the priest returned to the chapel, the doctor walked through the graveyard, leaped over the stone wall before scurrying down a muddy track to the place where his accomplice was guarding their nickering horses.

'Are you all right, chief?' Masson asked as he handed over the surgical bag.

'I'm fine.'

'Did you meet with him?'

'Yes.'

The doctor took the faded reins of his horse, placed his foot in a stirrup, and lurched into the saddle. The horse bucked its head and sent a cloud of steam from both nostrils.

'Did he tell you his name?' Masson enquired.

'No.'

'He is but a shadow,' Masson said.

'The Shadow of Death,' the doctor added.

Masson shuddered.

'Let's get going,' the doctor said, goading the flanks of his horse. 'We've got a fox to catch.'

CHAPTER 4

Pryce lifted an oyster shell to his lips and tipped his head backwards as the door to the library opened.

'I heard you were working on your sermon and eating alone,' his wife said, her English betraying only a hint of a French accent. 'I thought I should investigate.'

'Eloise,' Pryce smiled. For a few moments he gazed at her. She was wearing a white chemise dress with a blue sash around her waist. The toes of her flat slippers were peeping out from underneath the bottom of the dress. Her chestnut hair fell about her shoulders in the French style.

Pryce walked towards his wife and she reached out to him and drew him to her chest, kissing him on his lips.

'How did your visiting go?'

'I got through it,' Pryce replied.

'I'm so proud of you.'

Pryce pulled himself away and turned to a plate standing on a small mahogany table.

'Would you like some oysters?'

Before she could answer, they were interrupted by a persistent banging on the front door of the Rectory.

'My goodness me,' Eloise replied. 'Whom can that be?'

They heard the housekeeper rushing into the hallway towards the entrance.

Pryce put his food down and stood to his feet, wiping his hands as he did so. 'Duty calls,' he sighed.

'Duty can wait,' Eloise said, taking the collars of his double breasted coat and pulling him towards her. 'You look so handsome, my darling.'

Holding him tightly she kissed Pryce, forcing her tongue into his mouth.

'Darling!' he whispered, stepping back. 'Not here. Not with others in the house.'

'Scandal in the library?' she said playfully, releasing him.

Pryce laughed before straightening his cravat and adjusting his dark-coloured breeches. 'Later,' he said.

Pryce turned towards the door as it opened suddenly.

'I'm sorry, but he insisted on seeing you,' the housekeeper said as she stood in the doorway. 'A young lad, sleeps rough under the boats. Parents are dead.'

In front of Pryce was a diminutive boy, cap in hand, a look of urgency on his face.

'What is it lad?'

'They've killed him!' he stammered. 'Sliced his head right from his neck.'

'Who's killed who?'

'The Frenchies.'

'My wife is French.'

'I'm sorry, ma'am. But they've killed your king.'

Eloise stood to her feet, put her hands over her mouth, and suppressed a gasp.

Pryce put his arm around her waist. 'Sit down,' he said to her.

Eloise fell back into her chair.

'Tell us what you know, boy,' Pryce said turning to the housekeeper. 'Mrs. Kemp, get him something to eat.'

The woman soon returned with bread and cheese and a tankard. The boy took it in his hands and started to nibble at the cheese like a church mouse.

'Now tell us what you know,' Pryce said as the lad took a gulp of water.

'I was down at the naval yard. I overheard a midshipman talking to a marine. He had been in Calais yesterday and heard that two days ago the king was taken from the tower prison in front of the whole of Paris to the guillotine.'

Eloise groaned.

'They strapped him face down and then the blade fell. Apparently the crowds cheered as his head was lifted up by a young soldier. Barbaric, that's the word the midshipman used, barbaric.'

'Tell me, boy,' he continued. 'Did the navy officer say any more?'

'He said that people would be coming to Deal. That there would be many more houses, jobs too.'

'Why?' Eloise whimpered.

'Because war is coming, and when wars are declared, the town of Deal prospers.'

Pryce turned to the housekeeper. 'Take the boy to the kitchen and let him get cleaned up. Give him a bag of food for his supper.'

'Thank you, Vicar,' the boy said as the housekeeper ushered him towards the door. Looking at Mrs Pryce the boy stopped. 'I'm sorry, ma'am. I really am.'

As the boy and housekeeper left the room, Pryce turned back to Eloise. 'When did you last hear from your parents?'

'Not for some time.'

'Do you know where they are?'

Eloise sighed. 'The last I knew, father was hiding in the woods with the Chouan army.'

'Is there any news of Jean Marie?' Pryce asked.

'I heard she was at our country residence at Sévignac.'

Pryce frowned. 'If there is one thing I know about Michael-Alain Picot,' he said, 'he'll find a way to keep your mother safe.'

'He will try,' Eloise said, 'but you should not underestimate the persistence of those opposing them.'

As Pryce stood to leave the library, he reached down and took his wife's hand and kissed it. When he opened his eyes again, he saw the sparkle of a tear. 'I will do all that I can to help them,' Pryce said. 'All is not lost.'

CHAPTER 5

Doctor Vacher peered through his spectacles and carefully decanted a teaspoonful of white powder from a small globe bottle into an envelope.

'What's that?' Masson asked.

'It's medicine to take to the Marquis.'

'Why would we want to help that fool?'

'This medicine will not help him.'

'Why?'

The doctor sealed the envelope, rubbed his hands vigorously, and looked through his lenses into Masson's inquisitive eyes. 'It's arsenic.'

Masson gasped.

The doctor continued. 'Consider our good fortune. I have been waiting here for the Marquis to contact me, have I not?'

Masson nodded.

'This time of the year the Marquis often suffers from a fever. He was bound to have to send for me at some point and now his men have summoned me.'

Vacher placed the envelope in the inside pocket of his jacket and then stood. He donned his black cape and hat. 'We must hurry,' he said, grasping his black leather bag. 'The message from the Marquis' men was sent to my Paris residence before being forwarded here. It's at least three days old.'

'Three days!' Masson exclaimed.

Masson stood to his feet and put on his heavy, black coat. 'Bring money in case we need to bribe anyone.'

'And brandy in case we need to get someone drunk,' Masson added.

The two men hurried down the stairs into the hallway of the Hotel Pelikan and darted through the front door, their heads bowed. They mounted their horses and trotted down the gravel road.

'This is going to be easy,' the doctor confided. 'The Marquis thinks I am still his friend and he and his accomplices assume I am a Chouan sympathizer.'

Masson laughed. 'Those fools at the chateau won't know the difference between medicine and poison. You can put it in a glass of water right in front of them.'

The doctor wrapped his black scarf about his reddening cheeks and kicked the flanks of his horse. The two men broke into a canter and then into a gallop, their black capes flowing in the cold wind behind their cambered backs, riding like horsemen from hell.

A league later, they slowed to a trot. A gate stood several yards in front of them.

'It's not guarded,' Masson whispered as he slipped from his weather-beaten saddle and quietly opened the gate. 'There should be sentries,' he said as he climbed back onto his horse.

Moments later the two visitors reached the weather beaten front doors of the chateau and dismounted, tying their steeds to a wooden post outside.

The doctor knocked loudly. He had to pound a third time before there was an answer. A heavy set man appeared and stared at Vacher. 'What do you want?' he asked.

'I am Doctor Vacher, the Marquis' personal physician, and this is my assistant.'

The doctor raised his surgical bag.

'Ah, doctor,' the man sighed. 'You're too late.'

'What do you mean?'

'You'd better come in,' he said.

The men walked into a capacious hall shrouded with tobacco smoke that hung in the air like Havana fog. Soldiers in grey uniforms were everywhere. Some were sleeping, their heads drooping on their chests or resting on the shoulder of a slumbering comrade. They still wore their boots and their dirty bayonets and swords were lying on the ground next to them. Others were sitting, staring blankly at a fire that struggled to remain alight in a great hearth. The few muskets they had were strewn carelessly on the floor or propped against the walls.

'Let me introduce myself,' the man said, as he led the two agents into a private study, in the centre of which stood an ornate desk covered in a welter of papers.

'My name is Saint-Pierre,' he said. 'I was the Marquis' private secretary.'

'Was?'

'Yes, our leader passed away yesterday morning.'

'What?' the doctor exclaimed.

'It's true. The Marquis is dead. He was buried last evening in the gardens, along with his papers.'

'How did this happen?' the doctor asked.

'He was struck down by a fever so we brought him from the woods here to the chateau. He was very weak.'

The man paused and bowed his head. 'It was after the King was executed. We withheld the information from him because we knew the news might kill him. Unfortunately, one of the men left the Paris newspaper lying on this very desk and... he read of what had happened.'

'What did he do?' the doctor asked.

'The blood left his face and he collapsed. He died a few hours later in his bed.'

'A sad end,' the doctor demurred.

'Indeed.'

'What will come of the rebel army?' Masson asked.

'No one outside this chateau knows of the Marquis' death. We are going to say that he is still alive. The cause must go on. We must dethrone the king killers and restore the ancient regime in France.'

'Yes!' Vacher and Masson replied in almost liturgical unison.

'And you must not tell anyone the Marquis has died,' Saint-Pierre urged.

'I cannot and nor can my assistant. A physician is bound to honour the confidentiality of their client. We will be silent.'

'Good,' the secretary nodded. 'We have new plans to make this night and more Republican soldiers to hunt and dispatch in the morning.'

Saint-Pierre showed the two men to the door and closed it firmly behind them.

'Say nothing,' the doctor whispered after the two men had walked a few yards.

They climbed onto their horses and trotted to the gate. They cantered beyond the grounds of the chateau until they were a good distance along the road.

'Stop here,' the doctor shouted.

'What's wrong?' Masson replied.

'Do you have that brandy?'

'Are we going to toast the Marquis' death?'

'No, I have a plan.'

Masson handed over the bottle.

'Listen,' the doctor said. 'I am going to the gardener's cottage. He will have dug the Marquis' grave. I'll get him drunk and he'll tell me where the body is.'

'Why do we need the body?'

'To prove that the Marquis is dead and retrieve the papers.'

'What do you want me to do?' Masson asked.

'I want you to ride to the gendarmerie in Dinan and assemble a squad of national guardsmen. Bring them here at dawn. We must strike while our enemies are exhausted and demoralised.'

Masson smiled.

'And one more thing,' the doctor added.

'Yes, chief?'

'Bring the great chain.'

'Why?' Masson asked.

'You'll see.'

CHAPTER 6

The doctor dismounted and walked his mare quietly to a cottage at the bottom of a track next to a walled garden. He tied his horse and approached the ivy covered door. There were lamps lit in a downstairs room.

He took out the brandy bottle, opened it and poured some into his throat and a little onto his coat.

He knocked three times and waited.

The next moment a man with grey hair appeared. He was smoking a small clay pipe. His hands were rough and his fingernails were lined with earth.

'Fancy a drink?' the doctor said, slurring his voice. 'The lads at the chateau thought you might like… might like… to toast… to celebrate our great leader… to pay last respects… and so forth.' The doctor slewed like a wild horse and stretched the bottle towards the gardener.

'Looks and smells like you've been paying your respects for a while,' the man replied. 'You'd better come in. I don't mind raising one more glass to the Marquis.'

They drank through what was left of the night. Vacher proposed toast after toast. The gardener drank his fill and slumped in the chair by the fire.

'I would like to see the place where my master is buried,' Vacher said solemnly.

'That cannot be,' the man answered. 'I am the only one that knows.'

'I need to pray at his graveside.'

The man thought for a moment as a blood red dawn crept over

the hills. 'You seem like a good man. I will take you to the orchard and see the place. We can pray together.'

The gardener lifted a smudged glass to his bristled chin.

'Let's do it,' the doctor stammered, knocking his chair over as he rose to his feet.

'He loved this place, he did,' the gardener said when they arrived several minutes later. 'I would often find him reading a book… yes, a little book… under a tree in the summer.'

'Where did you bury him?'

'Over here,' the gardener said, stumbling towards an uncultivated space between the trees and the wall.

The doctor could see that there were signs the earth had been disturbed and the grass replaced. A spade was standing next to the wall.

'Dig him up,' the doctor barked.

'You must be mad.'

'I am perfectly sane. Dig him up.'

'Not on your life,' the gardener spat.

Vacher drew and cocked his pistol.

'You will dig the body up right now or you will end up in this grave yourself.'

The gardener, hearing the flint lock, submitted. 'All right, all right,' he said.

He took the spade and started prodding the topsoil.

'Dig properly!' the doctor hissed.

Soon, the gardener had unearthed the Marquis' body. The corpse was wrapped in a white shawl. A bottle was clearly resting in its hands.

The doctor spotted a small cart nearby. 'Put the Marquis' body on that.'

The gardener snorted like an angry horse before grabbing the Marquis' feet and pulling the body to the cart.

'Quietly,' the doctor snapped.

The gardener loaded the makeshift funereal and pulled it as

Vacher kept his pistol trained upon him.

They reached the unguarded gate and walked down the avenue until they were at the place where Masson and he had parted the night before.

'Kneel before your master and pray.' Vacher said as he aimed the pistol.

'Are you going to kill me?'

'Lights out,' the doctor said, as he raised the pistol by the barrel and brought the butt crashing down upon the gardener's skull. The man fell limply into a roadside hedge. 'You'll have a headache in the morning but at least you'll live – for the time being anyway,' the doctor whispered.

He covered the gardener with foliage before lifting the Marquis' shrouded body and concealing it beneath the lower branches of a leafy bush. He pulled the cart to a dyke on the opposite side of the road and then wheeled it into the water, watching as it sank. Then he hid behind a tree and waited, cradling the bottle containing the Marquis' papers.

It wasn't long before he began to hear the sound of horses' hooves on the gravel of the avenue. It was coming from the direction of Dinan. A few seconds later he saw Masson, his red, white and blue cockade dancing majestically on top of his black tricorn hat as he rode his stallion. Behind him was a column of fifty armed guardsmen. Their blue coats, white lapels and red collars seemed almost luminous in the early morning light. Several of their yellow metal buttons glinted in the yawning sun.

When they were just yards away the doctor stepped out and waved to them to stop.

To a man they slowed to an orderly halt.

'My God, you look terrifying. The Marquis' men will be no match for you,' the doctor said.

The guardsmen dismounted, tied their horses to whatever boughs and branches they could find and then formed into ten ranks along the avenue, five men abreast. The front rank was composed of five officers, each bearing a sword. Behind them, every soldier stood with their infantry musket.

The doctor stood in front of the soldiers and spoke. 'Gentlemen, before you is the lair of the Marquis de la Rouërie. Most of his fellow Chouan leaders are in the chateau. Try to capture them alive. Many of them will still be sleeping.'

'What about the Marquis, sir?' a young lieutenant asked.

The doctor walked to the bush at the side of the road and hauled a shrouded corpse in front of them. 'Give me a bayonet,' the doctor said.

A guardsman marched forward.

The doctor took the blade and slashed at the linen, separating the sheet from the body. 'Help me,' he said to the guardsman.

The two men lifted the corpse so that it was standing awkwardly in front of the soldiers. There was a gasp from some of the men.

'Gentlemen, let me introduce you to your former enemy, the Marquis de la Rouërie - now very much deceased.'

The doctor pressed a finger to his lips to stop them cheering. 'It's time to march,' he whispered.

The officers in the front row turned to the next man behind them and issued an order which was then passed to the back. The doctor watched as every man in unison took a lead ball from the leather cartridge box on their belts and in swift movements involving flints, cartridges and powder loaded their muskets. When every soldier had finished, the officers turned again and the soldiers fixed their bayonets.

'Remember,' the doctor said. 'Surprise is vital. Remove your water cans from your belts. We don't want the rebels to hear you coming.' The soldiers instantly obeyed.

'The rear rank will stay here in reserve and guard the body,' he said.

Then he paused and removed his hat, holding it in his left arm. 'When you have rounded up the ring leaders, I want them put in one long chain. We will parade them in every town and village on the way to the *Tour le Bat* prison in Rennes and we will make a public demonstration of what happens to those who would take up arms to restore the monarchy in France.'

The doctor nodded to a captain on the front row, indicating that he could now take command.

The captain turned towards his soldiers, raised his sabre, and signalled to them to advance slowly. The men began to move, their backs arched, their eyes squinting, muskets at the ready.

The doctor turned to Masson and handed him the bottle with the papers. 'You have done well, my friend. I want you to stay here and take charge of the detachment guarding the body. When I give you the order, bring the cart with the chain, along with the body and these men.'

'Yes sir.'

'In an hour we will have dealt this foolish rebellion a mortal blow.'

Twenty minutes later, the force of men reached the chateau. Vacher hurried towards the rear rank of the blue coats. They passed furtively through the gates and began to fan out into two long lines in front of the ornate building.

The guardsmen were soon at the downstairs window shutters. They smashed at them with their hatchets, splintering the wood.

Quickly soldiers entered - all except five men, who stayed outside the building with their muskets trained at the front door.

And then the firing started.

Inside the chateau men began to scream as shots woke them from sleep.

The doctor smiled.

Four rebels jumped from an upstairs window. Before they reached the ground they were cut down by a fusillade of musket shot.

Two were wounded. They tried to get to their feet. Staggering like drunkards they were bayonetted. Long blades sliced through arms and legs.

The Guardsmen stood back as a young rebel tried to run. They mocked as he staggered and fell. Getting up again he walked towards the gate as if he had forgotten the war.

'Where are you going?' Vacher mocked as he walked alongside.

'Back to my mother,' the man panted.

Vacher aimed his pistol and fired. The ball smashed through his neck. The doctor laughed as a fountain of claret red blood sprang from the penetrated artery. The man - his throat and mouth instantly flooded with blood - gargled. 'Mother!' he cried.

The attack on the chateau was over in minutes. Long strands of gun smoke came from the upper windows.

A Guardsman dragged a rebel through the front door and threw him down the steps. 'We have taken seven alive as you asked. The rest are dead.' The Guardsman said proudly.

'And our casualties?' Vacher asked.

'Not a single shot was fired against us,' the soldier answered.

The doctor smiled as Masson arrived with the cart carrying the heavy chain.

'The Shadow will be pleased with this,' he said, turning to Masson.

'Line up the prisoners and let me see who we have captured,' the doctor shouted to the Guards. 'Tie them to the chain and make sure each one sees the Marquis' body.'

Each prisoner was placed in an iron manacle and attached to the chain.

Vacher walked along the line. 'What a glorious assembly of traitors. Welcome back to the Republic my dear friends. Madame Debussy - Count Francois - Henri d'Ardennes - Jean Paul Monet - Louis Hollande - Charles de Lyon.'

Vacher stopped as he looked at the last man.

'My, my. What have we here?'

'I know a dog when I smell one,' the man spat.

Vacher raised his hand and slapped the man on the side of his face.

'From this day on you will respect me, Michel Alain Picot...'

CHAPTER 7

As the carriage moved along the road from Deal to Walmer, Pryce looked out of the window at the sea pounding the shingle on the shore.

'What are you thinking?' Eloise asked.

'He's still out there somewhere,' Pryce said, gazing out at the ocean.

Eloise shifted closer. 'It has been two years,' she said. 'I don't think his body will ever be found.'

'Not until the sea gives up its dead.'

'It's terrible,' she said, a tear forming in one of her blue eyes.

'What's terrible is that I don't feel the tragedy of it. In fact, I don't seem to feel anything anymore.'

'Anything?' Eloise asked.

'Only rage,' Pryce replied.

'Do you not feel love?'

'I know in my mind that I love you and that I love God, but it's as if that part of me that feels love has been tied to a great boulder and hurled into the deepest ocean.'

Eloise sighed.

'Don't worry about us, Eloise,' Pryce said. 'Our love is strong. Many waters cannot quench it.'

'Neither can the floods drown it,' she added.

Pryce smiled at her as the horses slowed.

'Walmer Castle,' the coachman cried.

Pryce and his wife gazed out of the righthand window as the coach and horses turned from the road.

'The castle is heavy with cannons,' Eloise said.

They were now approaching the grey stone castle through an avenue of Holme Oak trees. They could both see the jet black cannons protruding from the four round bastions of the looming edifice ahead.

'There are eight cannons mounted on the upper battlements in the two lunettes, four in each,' Pryce said, 'and see there, a further ten guns beneath them.'

'My countrymen would be foolish to try and invade these shores,' Eloise declared.

'I'm afraid they would,' Pryce said. 'The castle walls are round and very thick. They are made of Kentish ragstone. Cannon balls fired from the sea would simply bounce straight off them.'

The carriage crossed a small bridge above the dry moat. The surface of the bridge was punctuated with iron studs to stop the horses from slipping. The heavy oak doors of the gatehouse - which were now opening in front of the carriage - were studded with the same metal bolts.

The horses came to a halt in a cramped stable beyond the doors of the gatehouse. Several footmen helped Pryce and his wife from the carriage and then escorted them down an uncovered alleyway towards the gunners' quarters.

As Pryce walked he slid his hand along the cold wet surface of the castle walls. 'See this?' he said to Eloise as he pointed to a patch of cream-coloured stone and traced a finger over the gallatting. 'This softer stone is from your country, from Caen to be precise. It was some of the stone left over when St Augustine's Abbey was built in Canterbury.'

'Is there no end to your plundering?' Eloise smiled, as she took hold of Pryce's arm.

The two of them walked underneath wooden apartments occupied by the castle gunners and into a square room warmed by a freshly stoked fire. Their hats, coats and scarves were taken before they walked up a flight of stone stairs to a room on the first floor at the west end of the castle.

'Lady Hester's drawing room,' a footman said.

The small room - shaped like the quarter of a cake - was filled with people.

As soon as they entered, a slightly built man with wispy hair and tired eyes stood to his feet and stretched out his hand as he strode confidently towards them. 'Let me introduce myself,' he said, 'my name is William Pitt and since last year I have had the privilege of being the Lord Warden of the Cinque Ports and living here when I am not in Downing Street.'

'Don't be so pompous, dear cousin,' a voice interrupted. 'You know you hate titles.'

Pryce looked to see who had spoken. He saw a remarkably tall woman walk towards them, no more than eighteen years old, swaggering in her long and elegant gown.

'You may be the Prime Minister, sweet cousin,' she said, 'but that does not give you an excuse for pontificating about your credentials.'

'Quite so, my dear, quite so,' Pitt chuckled. 'I am most dreadfully sorry for my tiresome self-promotion. Let me introduce my favourite cousin, Lady Hester Stanhope.'

Pryce watched as Hester and Eloise curtseyed, Eloise with flawless decorum and Hester with more than a hint of frivolity.

Pryce took Hester's gloved hand and raised it to his lips.

'I am the Reverend Thomas Pryce.'

'Ah yes,' Lady Hester said, 'our recuperating Vicar.'

Pryce turned to Eloise. 'Let me present my wife.'

'Your beautiful French wife,' Lady Hester added with a coy smile.

'I am indeed French,' Eloise said proudly.

'And you speak perfect English,' Pitt replied.

'And my husband speaks perfect French – just as in all things he is perfect.'

'That is so sweet,' Hester squealed, jumping giddily and clapping as she did. 'You must be the most handsome and romantic clergy couple in England.'

Pryce frowned. 'We were childhood sweethearts,' he said. 'We met in Brittany.'

'Brittany, you say,' Pitt interjected. 'Tell me, Mrs Pryce, what is your family background?'

'My father is called Michel Alain Picot de Limoelan, after the chateau of Limoelan which he bought as our family home. His family can be traced back to the days of Duchess Anne of Brittany in the fifteenth century. One of his ancestors was secretary to King Louis XV. My father is a ship builder, just as my husband's was.'

'So that's how you two met?'

'Indeed, sir,' Eloise replied. 'Our families spent every summer together, mostly in Brittany. Thomas and I were the closest of friends. Later we fell in love and when we were eighteen we married just before Thomas gained a scholarship to Christ Church, Oxford, where he was also awarded his doctorate.'

'In what subject, pray?' Pitt enquired.

'Nothing terribly interesting,' Pryce replied, 'just a rather oblique study of Ancient Egyptian civilization.'

'Capital,' Pitt cried.

'And you have children?' Hester intruded.

'Cousin!' Pitt blurted before turning to Eloise. 'I apologize for Lady Hester's intrusions.'

'That is all right,' Eloise said. Then she turned and looked into Pryce's eyes and smiled. 'We have no children – not yet anyway.'

'It is a dangerous world for children,' Pitt said gravely. 'I am not a married man but if I were, I would be loath to launch a child into such stormy seas.'

'Well, I'm not married either,' Hester said, 'which is why I am ideally suited for helping you to host these dinners, and also why I must break this quartet up and escort everyone to the dining room.' Lady Hester clapped her gloved hands and a servant banged a small gong in the doorway.

'Dinner is served!' she shouted.

CHAPTER 8

One by one the diners – numbering eight in all – made their way down a long corridor that stretched from the west to the east end of the castle.

Halfway, Lady Hester tugged Pryce's arm just as they were passing through a rotunda illuminated by a hanging lantern. 'My cousin had this corridor built,' she said. 'Isn't he a clever Lord Warden?'

'He is,' Pryce said as they proceeded to an ante room at the end of the hallway.

Pryce gazed into the white panelled dining room adjacent to it. A mahogany dinner table, with room for three guests either side and two hosts either end, stood in the centre of the room. Every place was set with glittering cutlery and cut glasses. Candles blazed in silver candlesticks beneath an orange lamp hanging from the ceiling. A fire was burning in a hearth on Pryce's left as he looked down the room, while the freshening winter wind pushed insistently against the windows on his right. There were framed pictures covering almost every space of the walls. Most of them were of distinguished noblemen, including previous Lord Wardens. The only exception was an oil painting above the fireplace depicting men of war at anchor in the Downs.

Lady Hester ushered everyone to their chairs and asked them to remain standing.

Pitt went to the far end of the dining room and stood just in front of an alcove where the steward was preparing the first course.

'For what we are about to receive,' Pitt said, 'may the Lord make us truly thankful.'

'Amen,' the guests replied.

'Please be seated,' Hester said. 'We are eating 'a la Russe' tonight, as is our custom here.'

'A la Russe?' Pryce enquired.

'It is an innovation of my cousin,' Lady Hester said. 'The servants prepare each course in that little alcove behind his chair.'

'I had it built especially,' Pitt said.

'Instead of having the courses, apart from dessert, on the table from the start, my adventurous cousin prefers the Russian way.'

'I have my foibles,' Pitt smiled.

'And one of them,' Lady Hester quipped, 'is to give a long and rambling lecture about the castle's history before the soup is served.'

'It is,' Pitt chuckled.

'And while you do, we not only have to suffer the tedium of your history lesson but also the broth getting cold.'

Hester paused for a moment, looking down the table at her cousin. 'With that in mind,' she intoned, 'I am going to provide an abbreviated version instead.'

Pitt chortled.

'All right cousin, you may stand in for me tonight,' Pitt said with an air of contrived weariness.

In a perfect imitation of Pitt's voice and mannerisms, punctuated by giggles from both her and the Prime Minister, Hester proceeded to tell how the castle had been built by the corpulent King Henry VIII, when France and Spain were threatening to invade, how it first came under siege in the time of the English Civil War, and how in 1708 it became the official residence of the Lord Warden of the Cinque Ports.

Hester used the five fingers of her right hand as she recited the names of the ports – Hastings, Romney, Hythe, Dover and Sandwich.

She stretched out a long arm and pointed with her white gloved hand to a sleek black cannon visible through the window of the dining room. 'It forever faces towards France,' she said.

She concluded by saying that if it was spring or summer they could all have gone out onto the terrace and used telescopes to look for invading ships on the Downs.

By the time she had finished, Pitt was laughing.

'Hester the Jester,' Pitt said breathlessly, 'that's what I call her.'

'You love me, cousin,' Hester laughed.

'I do,' he replied. 'I truly do.'

'Before we start dinner,' Hester said, 'I'd like everyone at the table to introduce themselves. Husbands, you are not allowed to introduce your wives. Wives, you are certainly not allowed to introduce your husbands.'

Hester turned to her left. 'You start.'

The first person in the circle introduced himself. 'My name is William Wickham and I am superintendent of aliens, based in Whitechapel, London.'

'You're going to have to explain what that is,' Hester interrupted.

'The government passed the Alien Act a few weeks ago. This grants powers to magistrates all over the country to arrest and deport unwelcome aliens in our midst.'

'What kind of aliens?' Pryce asked.

'As you will have heard,' Wickham continued, 'there has been a huge introduction of émigrés from France since the early days of the Revolution. Most of these are our guests and friends. But some of them are spies, masquerading as fugitives, and they are plotting great mischief against our king and our government.'

'We have granted legal powers to men like Wickham,' Pitt interjected, 'so that he can keep and interrogate suspected French agents.'

'Thank you, Prime Minister,' Wickham continued. 'My job is to root out these spies.'

'And to play the French at their own game,' Pitt chuckled.

'Indeed,' Wickham replied without the faintest hint of a smile.

'Thank you, Mr. Wickham,' Hester said. 'Next please.'

An elegant lady on Wickham's right began to speak. 'My name is Eleanor Wickham. I am originally from Switzerland. My father is a leading banker in Geneva and so my husband and I often travel back and forth from there.'

'Next,' shouted Hester.

'My name is Father Henry Essex Edgeworth. Until recently I was an English priest working in Paris and the personal chaplain to King Louis XVI.'

There was a gasp.

'You were present at his execution?' Hester enquired.

'I was, Lady Hester. I was the only person who travelled in the tumbrel with him, the only one who climbed the scaffold by his side.'

'What did he say?' Eloise stammered.

'He stood before the crowd, under the shadow of the guillotine, and declared that he was innocent, that he forgave those who had occasioned his death, and that he prayed the blood they were about to shed would never be visited on his beloved France.'

'I fear that prayer may not be answered,' Wickham said gravely.

'I fear the same,' the priest replied.

'How did you get out of Paris and back to England?' Eloise asked.

'Just before the King walked across the stage to the guillotine, he turned to the military escort and said words that I will never forget: "Gentlemen, I commend to you this good man; take care that after my death no insult or injury be offered to him – I charge you to prevent it. And I charge you to protect him".'

Pryce put his hand on Eloise's arm.

'Animals!'

The expletive had come from a man sitting on Pitt's right.

'Animals!' he repeated.

It was clear that the man was distinguished. He was wearing a red coat with blue and gold collars, cuffs and lining. He sported silver epaulettes on his shoulders and a medallion with a white star around his neck. His eyes were brown and misty. His hair was fair and full of curls. He wore a white cravat and a light blue sash and his waist coat was studded with silver buttons.

'I apologize, ladies and gentlemen,' he said, in a thick French accent.

'That's perfectly alright, Count,' Pitt said. 'I think this is the moment to tell my guests who you are.'

'My name is the Count of Artois and I am one of your émigrés.'

'You're a great deal more than that,' Pitt exclaimed. 'Tell them who you really are.'

The man hesitated, looked straight into the eyes of everyone around the table, and then spoke. 'My name is Charles, and I am the younger brother of the late King, Louis XVI.'

There was a sharp intake of breath from several at the table.

Eloise rose to her feet, knelt beside him and took hold of his hand and kissed it.

'My lady,' the Count said. 'There is no need. We are all of us at the same level, eating tonight from the same table, guests of the honourable Prime Minister.'

'But sire...'

'No, my lady, you must be seated and we must converse as equals.'

Eloise returned to her seat.

'Thank you, Father Henry,' the Count said, turning to the priest on his left. 'You gave my brother comfort in his final moments.'

The priest did not answer. He bowed his head and then produced a breviary from the folds of his cassock, holding it out towards the Count. 'I want you to have this,' the priest said.

'What is it?'

'It is my prayer book – the prayer book that your brother held in his hands in the tumbrel on the way to his death, the book from which we read and recited the Psalms that seemed most pertinent.'

'I am deeply moved, my friend. Thank you,' the Count replied.

Pitt nodded his head and a footman ushered two maidservants from a wooden door which led into the servery beyond. They were laden with silver receptacles which they placed on a table behind the Prime Minister. As soup was poured into bowls, Pitt spoke up.

'The Count has been in England several months now. Originally he was to lead an army towards Paris from Koblenz, while the Marquis de la Rouërie...'

Pitt never got any further.

'You know of him?' Eloise exclaimed.

'Know of whom, my dear?'

'The Marquis… I mean the Marquis de la Rouërie, leader of the Chouan army in Brittany.'

'Yes,' Pitt replied.

'It was a tragic blow when he died,' the Count sighed.

'Died? The Marquis has died?' Eloise raised her hands to her mouth.

'I am afraid so. He was taken by a fever just at the moment when his army was preparing to march from the west on Paris. His death was catastrophic.'

'What happened to the others, to his leaders?' Eloise asked.

'I'm afraid they were captured and taken in irons to the prison in Rennes.'

'Do you know who was arrested, their names?' Eloise asked.

'Yes.'

'Was my father among them?'

'What is your father's name?'

'Michael-Alain Picot.'

The Count paused. 'I'm so sorry,' he said.

Pryce touched Eloise's hand.

'And his wife, Jean Marie Picot,' Pryce asked, 'what has become of her?'

'She was not among those arrested,' said the Count. 'I am guessing she is in hiding somewhere in Brittany, as are several others.'

'Oh sweet Jesus, have mercy,' Eloise cried. 'What will befall my father?'

'I'm afraid all the prisoners will be taken to Paris and put on trial in a Revolutionary Court. Some may be released…' the Count paused, 'but I fear for your father. From what I know, he was one of the Marquis' most trusted leaders.'

Eloise daubed one of her eyes with the side of her white gloved hand.

The count looked down at the table.

'His chances, Madame, are not good.'

CHAPTER 9

'What can we do?' Pryce asked once Mrs Wickham had led Eloise from the dining room.

'Not much,' the Count replied. 'There are French agents everywhere in Brittany, hunting down our scattered army. It is not easy to infiltrate that region without detection at the moment.'

'We can't just sit around while others suffer so,' Pryce blurted. 'Our inaction will be the seedbed for evil to grow and flourish.'

'I agree,' Father Henry replied, fetching a scroll of paper tied in a blue ribbon from another pocket in his cassock.

'Here,' he said, placing it in the centre of the table. 'I offer this.'

'What is it?' Pryce asked.

'It is a letter from a member of the tribunal in Paris giving me unhindered movement in France.'

'How did you come by that?' Wickham asked.

'It's a long story but after the King had told the guards to protect me, an officer who had been deeply moved by the King's death took me to the home of a member of the National Convention. I cannot divulge his name but what I can say is that he had voted against the execution of the king. He had no hesitation in issuing a special pass to me. It's worth a handsome price.'

'I'll say,' Wickham exclaimed.

As the conversation continued, and the growing horrors of the Revolution were bemoaned, Pryce kept silent and stared at the scroll in the centre of the table. Pitt sat opposite and studied Pryce carefully.

'Where did you get the scar on the back of your right hand?' Pitt asked, changing the course of the conversation for no reason.

Pryce looked up and instantly covered his hand.

'At Christ Church, Oxford.'

'How?'

'I had a passion for sword fencing,' Pryce answered reluctantly.

'Were you any good?' Pitt continued.

'I was College champion for two years.'

'You are a priest and a fighter, then?' Pitt asked.

'I stopped fighting when I was ordained,' Pryce answered.

'Do you ever feel there is a time when it is just for a priest to fight?' Wickham interrupted.

'It is not something I have thought about,' Pryce said.

'When the enemy is at your door and about to kill your wife and children, is that not a time to fight?' Wickham asked.

Pryce did not answer.

'Did you ever meet my old friend Dean Jackson?' Pitt butted in.

'I was one of his students and I am proud I can call him my friend.' Pryce said. 'He has been a great support to me. He encouraged my fencing and pistol shooting and he served the best claret in college.'

Pitt turned to Wickham. 'Then we all share the same friend. Wickham and I have spent many a night drinking his claret.'

'Indeed,' Wickham said. 'It is good to know that you are friends with the Dean. He is a fine man.'

'And all these fine men that surround me should follow to the drawing room,' Lady Hester said, bringing an end to the conversation.

The party left the dining room and followed Pitt along the passageway. Pryce brought up the rear of the group, turning over the conversation in his mind. It was then that he noticed Lady Hester close behind him. With great stealth, she pulled him by the arm into a dimly lit library.

'Quietly,' Hester said, as she pressed her tall thin frame against Pryce's body, her head almost at the same height as his. She put her finger to his lips, her piercing blue eyes dilated with excitement, the rouge on her alabaster cheeks bursting with colour.

Hester waited a moment before stepping away and then reached her long arm for the door which she closed quickly, deftly and quietly.

'What do you want?' Pryce asked.

'You're going to try and help them, aren't you?' Hester whispered with almost uncontainable excitement.

'What are you talking about?'

'I could see it in your eyes all the way through dinner,' Hester blurted. 'I think you are a projector, sir.'

'What am I projecting?'

'It's obvious - a rescue for your wife's parents.'

'I'm just a Vicar,' Pryce protested. 'Vicars don't go on secret missions.'

'Ordinary Vicars don't,' Hester agreed. 'But I have this feeling you are more than ordinary. You fight with swords and shoot pistols. Apart from anything else, you're far too handsome to be a clergyman.'

'Your eyes deceive you.' Pryce exclaimed. 'And in any event, I am a married man.'

'I can see that,' Hester pouted. 'I'm very jealous, I don't mind confessing.'

'Well, in the interests of good manners I need to...'

'Not just yet,' Hester replied quietly. 'I have something for you.'

Hester moved closer to Pryce, pressing him against a bookcase. 'Here,' she said, raising a jewel encrusted reticule. 'I have a few things to help you with your mission.'

'For pity's sake,' Pryce whispered. 'I have not said anything about a so-called mission.'

'No, Mister Pryce, you haven't, not with words anyway, but your obvious love and devotion for your French wife tells me otherwise.' Hester paused before opening her ornate handbag and resting her hand on Pryce's sleeve. 'Frankly, my darling, I think it's the most gallant and glorious thing I've ever seen.'

Pryce sighed. 'All right, Lady Hester, I confess. I love my wife's parents as if they are my own. There is no way I can remain in Deal while they are suffering in France.'

'Then let me help you,' Hester said. 'And for goodness sake, stop calling me Lady Hester and call me Hetty.'

Hester opened her bag.

'You will need this for a start,' she said, producing the scroll that Father Henry had placed on the table at dinner. 'I said that I knew someone who could use it.'

Pryce took the paper in his hands, unrolled and read it. 'It is worth its weight in gold,' he said, placing it in his pocket.

'And here,' Hester replied, producing three gleaming pieces of metal from a purse. 'The French are desperate for gold right now.'

'Are you sure?' Pryce said.

'I'm sure,' Hester replied. 'You are relieving me of the unremitting tedium of my daily routine and you simply cannot put a price on that. Use them wisely, Mister Pryce. They will get you out of some tight corners, I fancy.'

Hester fumbled one more time in her bag. 'Please do not make a noise when you see my final little gift,' she said.

Hester drew an over-and-under, four barrelled pistol, six inches long, made of silver, and festooned with elaborate floral engravings.'

'What is this?' Pryce asked.

'It's a rather pretty pistol which delivers a rather mighty punch,' Hester said as she traced two gloved fingers slowly over one of the barrels.

'Where on earth did you get that?'

'My half-mad cousin, Thomas Pitt – also known as Lord Camelford – had two of these made at Clarke's the gunsmith in Cheapside. One was for him and one for me. I'd like you to borrow mine.'

'I can't,' Pryce said.

'Yes you can,' she replied firmly. 'I know you're a Vicar and that you're supposed to abhor violence but you're about to embark on an enterprise of unimaginable peril and you need to be armed.'

'Those who live by the sword perish by the sword,' Pryce said, as he showed Hester the scar on his hand.

'But what if you need a weapon in self-defence, or to defend those whom you love? What if you need it to save a life that cannot and must not be destroyed?'

'Then I will trust in God.'

'That is pious but hardly practical,' Hester scolded. 'Do you not remember what Oliver Cromwell said? "Trust in God and keep your powder dry".'

Pryce bowed his head in resignation. 'Very well,' he said.

'You'll need these as well,' Hester squealed as she drew a small bag from her purse.

'What's this?' Pryce asked.

'Powder flask, balls, flints and a cleaning rod – all small enough to conceal in the pockets of a coat or jacket.'

Pryce took the silver pistol and placed it in an inside pocket of his waist length jacket, just over his heart. He placed the small bag in the breast pocket.

'See!' Hester whispered. 'You'd never know they were there!'

'We really should go to the others,' Pryce insisted.

'I agree,' Hester replied. 'Please just take this,' she said, handing him a small card. 'This has my address in London. Call on me.'

Pryce took the card as they left the library and walked together to the west end of the castle. Pitt was already on to his second glass of port wine and the Count was smoking a cheroot. The men were engaged in vigorous conversation with Eloise.

'Ah, Vicar,' Pitt exclaimed. 'Your wife has been extolling the art of rational conversation.'

'At that she truly excels,' Pryce smiled.

'Are you acquainted with Elizabeth Carter of Deal, my dear?' Pitt asked Eloise.

'I am, sir. She and I are members of Mrs Montague's Blue Stockings society in London.'

'Capital!' Pitt exclaimed, taking a deep gulp of port wine.

An hour later, Eloise was leaning on Pryce's shoulder, as their carriage sped along the sea's edge back to Deal.

'I am sorry I had to leave the dinner table tonight, Thomas,' she said.

'Your tears were entirely justified.'

'Perhaps they thought my reaction was a little extreme, especially for Englishmen,' she sighed.

'For some Englishmen,' Pryce said.

'The situation is so utterly hopeless,' Eloise said.

Pryce turned and looked into his wife's eyes. 'Not entirely,' he said.

'What do you mean?' Eloise asked, pulling on his arm. 'Was something decided while I was out of the room?'

'Maybe.'

'What, Thomas?'

'I decided that I am going to try to rescue your parents.'

Eloise gasped. 'You can't. It is too dangerous.'

Pryce slowly drew the silver, spring loaded pistol from his pocket. He turned it in the half light provided by the moon, examining its four numbered barrels. 'Lady Hester gave me this and some gold. And Father Henry has given me the use of his warrant.'

'No, Thomas!'

'I've thought about it. I speak fluent French. I know Brittany better than any Englishman and I have the perfect means of getting to and from the French coast.'

'And what is that?'

'Jack and his men, who have offered to transport me any time across the Channel.'

Eloise looked for a moment out of the carriage to the ocean.

'I believe it can be done,' Pryce said.

'But I don't want you to,' Eloise said, turning back, a tear in her eye.

'I have to,' Pryce said, clasping her arm.

'I cannot lose you, husband.'

'You won't.'
'But I'm frightened, so frightened.'
'Don't be.'
'I cannot help it.'
'Why, my love?'
'Because I've been meaning to tell you...'
'Tell me what?'
'I am... I am with child.'

CHAPTER 10

'We are here,' the doctor said as his carriage arrived at the Tower Prison in the northeast quarter of Paris.

The prison was an imposing structure with lofty turrets, more like a castle from a fairy tale than a jail. It was originally built in the twelfth century as a fortified monastery for the Templar Knights, who stored and hid their treasures in its secret chambers. After the demise of the knights, the King took over the monastery, using it for the same purpose – as a safe place to store his riches. The impregnability of the edifice impressed the monarch to use it as a secure location to incarcerate debtors and criminals. After the attack on the Tuileries just over six months before, in August 1792, the purpose of the tower had been changed yet again. This time a king had been imprisoned there, and it had been from the main tower that King Louis XVI had been taken to his execution.

After entering through ornamental gates, the doctor stepped down from his carriage and marched towards what was once the mansion of the Grand Prior of the Knights Templar. He then proceeded to a large stone guardhouse, followed closely at his heels by Masson.

'The Chouan prisoners from Rennes,' the doctor announced, as he handed over a document with all twenty seven prisoner's names to a portly Republican official. 'They are due for trial in seven days before the Revolutionary Tribunal,' he added.

The doctor watched the man as he scanned the scroll, scrutinized the signature, and twitched his bushy moustache. He stamped the paper and rose to his feet. 'Where are the prisoners?'

'They are in four carts guarded by one hundred mounted

guardsmen,' the doctor replied.

'That's a lot for an escort.'

'We needed that many in case anyone decided to try to rescue them,' the doctor said. 'We have taken them through every village, town and city on the way from Rennes to Paris as a demonstration of what happens to those who try to strike against the new order.'

'They will be cold and hungry,' the official said.

'They are,' the doctor replied. 'But do not feed them or grant them blankets until I say. I will be interrogating some of them immediately. The military escort, on the other hand, may be given everything they need.'

'Yes, sir,' the official said, as he presented the prisoner admission document. The doctor scrawled his signature and then watched as a young lieutenant exited and called a squad of prison guards to attention.

A moment later the first group of prisoners approached the guardhouse. They were exhausted and shivering, shuffling more than walking. All of them were gazing up at the massive square stone building in the centre of the yard.

It was five stories high with barred windows. On each top corner there was a circular tower with a conical red tiled roof at its summit. This was the main part of the prison known as the Great Tower. Alongside this was a smaller, rectangular three-storied building known prosaically as the Little Tower, with circular towers on its two outer corners. The vast edifice cast its deathly shadow over every one of the prisoners, whose backs seemed to the doctor to be cambering under the weight of its awful reputation.

'We must lose no time,' the doctor said to Masson.

As the first prisoners were escorted into their cells, Masson turned to his superior. 'Who shall we interrogate first, chief?'

'Let's start with Monsieur Picot.'

'Why him?'

'I have been eager to question Picot since we captured him two weeks ago. I know he was one of the Marquis' two treasurers. I know he'll talk if we persuade him to. And if he's stubborn, I have an Ace up my sleeve.'

'What's that?'

'You'll see.'

Guided by two guards, the doctor walked up the stone steps of the main tower to a cell on the second floor. A guard drew back the grill, peered through and shouted, 'Picot, you are to come with us immediately.'

The cell was unlocked and Picot was dragged out by the guards. He had been wearing the same white dress shirt since he had been arrested and it was now stained with dirt and stank of sweat. His dark brown corduroy culottes were faded and his beige stockings were torn. The metal buckle on one of his black shoes had been torn off. His dark hair hung loosely and untied, more like that of a Breton peasant than a provincial nobleman.

The doctor watched Picot stumble clumsily forward, his feet and hands still bound by chains. 'This should not be too difficult,' he whispered to Masson.

The men made their way to a larger cell which Masson had seconded as an interrogation room. The doctor's leather case was there and some of his surgical implements were lying on a handkerchief on a side table.

'Good work,' the doctor muttered.

The guards made Picot sit down and forced his chained hands between his thighs underneath the table.

'You are Michel Alain Picot of Limoelan?' the doctor asked.

'You know I am,' Picot replied.

'Answer yes,' Masson said, slapping the prisoner with one of his gloves.

'Yes,' Picot replied slowly, as he recovered his poise. 'I am Michel Alain Picot of Limoelan.'

'Do you know why you have been brought here?' the doctor asked.

'Yes.'

'Why?'

'You believe I have betrayed my country.'

'And have you?'

'I love my country.'

'So why did you conspire to overthrow the government?'

'I love my country.'

'Do you deny that you were part of the Chouan resistance in Brittany?'

'I affirm that I love my country.'

The doctor turned to Masson and nodded.

Masson slapped Picot harder, so hard in fact that the smack echoed around the cell like a pistol shot.

The doctor could see that one side of Picot's stubble-covered face was now throbbing from the blow.

He smiled.

'Come, now, Monsieur Picot, we know that you were close to the Marquis de la Rouërie and that you were acting as his treasurer.'

'How do you know?'

'We know because that drunken gardener, Perrin, buried some papers with the Marquis' body, in a bottle no less. Why they didn't burn them is a mystery to me, but there you have it. The average intelligence of the Chouan is not much greater than a mosquito's.'

'That may be so,' Picot replied, 'but a mosquito can keep you awake all night with the sound of his humming and the threat of his bite.'

'Enough!' the doctor bellowed. 'You will not play games with me, Monsieur Picot. The papers buried with the Marquis contained your financial accounts. They clearly and conclusively implicate you.'

Picot raised his eyebrows for a moment. 'You are lying,' he said.

'I am not, Monsieur. Maybe you think that all your accounts were destroyed by Therese Limoelien in the fireplace at the chateau. Well, she did dispose of many papers and she will face the consequences for that. But we still have some of yours from the grave.'

'Prove it.'

'Very well.'

The doctor turned to Masson who brought what looked like a brown post bag from a table behind Picot's chair. He opened it, felt his way into one of the compartments of the case, and withdrew several sheets.

The doctor took one, squinted at it through his silver rimmed spectacles, and then spread it on the table in front of his prisoner.

Picot looked impassively at the document.

'You see,' the doctor said, 'the evidence is before you and you stand condemned.'

'There is no signature on those papers,' Picot replied. 'They could have been written by anyone.'

'So, you say, Picot, but I believe they are written by you and that you are nothing more than a traitor and a common criminal.'

The doctor watched as the veins protruded on Picot's neck.

Picot erupted with rage. 'You are the traitor and the common criminal! It is you and your kind who are destroying France. I was prepared to support the reforms that your government proposed. I thought some of them were fair because many of the aristocrats had been greedy and unjust. But when you forced the clergy to sign the Civil Constitution and then began to terrorize your enemies, I realized that you were no better than the regime that you were trying to replace.'

'Now, now, Monsieur, you protest too much,' the doctor said mockingly.

'I do not, sir. And the evidence that you were worse than the ancient regime you despise is simple. In the lands that I oversee in and around the parish of Sévignac, where noble men and women have nearly always treated the people of the land fairly, the average Breton is paying three times more in tax and is at least twice as poor and twice as hungry now you and your kind are in power.'

'Silence!' the doctor shouted as he brought his fist crashing down upon the table, causing even the two guards to flinch. 'We are not here to discuss politics. We are here to confirm your guilt. And you are guilty, Monsieur Picot, and you will be tried and condemned.'

'Except that the documents you possess cannot be used to implicate me because they do not have my signature.'

The doctor sat back in his chair.

'What about your wife, Monsieur?' he asked.

'What about her?'

Picot sounded surprised.

'She is on the run in Brittany,' the doctor said, 'and we have agents pursuing her. We will find her. She can't hide forever. And if you cooperate I promise we will be merciful. And if you do not...'

The doctor did not finish his sentence but took out a cleaver from his collection of surgical instruments and ran its radiant blade several times slowly through the flame of a candle on the table.

Picot gasped. 'You wouldn't.'

'Oh, I would.'

'He most certainly would,' Masson added.

Picot's brow furrowed. 'What do you want from me?'

'In return for just one piece of information, I will give my word that your wife will not suffer any unnecessary pain and that her misery will be nothing in comparison with what you have endured.'

'What information?'

'I want you to tell me the whereabouts of your brother, the Abbé de Clorivière.'

The doctor spat as he mentioned the Abbé's name.

'What is your interest in my brother?' Picot asked.

'I know about the sermon,' the doctor replied.

'What sermon?'

'The one he preached to two thousand peasants in the parish church at Sévignac just a month ago.'

'I don't know what you're talking about.'

'Oh, but you do. You know as well as I that the church was waiting for the arrival of a constitutional priest. Your brother, the Abbé, seized the empty pulpit and preached a sermon denouncing the revolutionary leaders as idolaters, worshipping a new divinity called

'Nature' rather than God.'

'Sounds like a good sermon.'

'Enough!' the doctor snorted. 'If you give him up to me I will be merciful both to you and your wife.'

The doctor leaned forward and looked into Picot's bloodshot eyes. 'I believe that you aided your brother's escape from Brittany and that you gave him one of your horses, as well as some forged papers, and that he came here to Paris. Tell me where he is and I will show mercy.'

Picot leaned forward. 'Never,' he said.

The doctor sat up straight. 'Then you leave me no choice,' he said.

The doctor reached into the inside breast pocket of his dark blue jacket. He withdrew a letter and stood up to read it by the light of the candle which he held in his other hand.

'This letter is from one of your daughters,' the doctor said.

'What?' Picot stuttered.

'It was sent to you from your own home and addressed to the Chateau de la Fosse Hingants just before you were discovered and arrested there with your nieces. We intercepted it before it reached you. I'm afraid it is quite – how shall I say? – damning...'

The doctor watched as Picot's eyes filled with tears.

The doctor carefully adjusted the glasses on his nose and started to read from the hand-written letter.

'*My dearest Papa,*

I am so sorry to have to write to you so soon after you left for Uncle's chateau.

But circumstances have made it necessary.

You see, I have learned that all the servants where you are staying know of our friend, the Marquis' death.

These things must be kept secret, Papa.

Please speak to the servants, especially to Saint-Jean, who has been talking about it to the chambermaids.

You must intervene.

Only this will repair the evil which this gossip may cause.

My dearest Papa, see what a house of indiscretion the home in which you're staying has become.

Please take great care.

I love you.'

As the doctor finished reading, Picot broke. 'All right, all right,' he sobbed. 'Just don't hurt my daughter.'

'Tell us where the Abbé is,' the doctor whispered.

'I don't know much,' Picot coughed.

'Tell us what you do know,' Masson said.

'I gave him one of my horses and a forged passport and papers with a change of identity.'

'Where did you get these papers?'

'The Marquis acquired many passports and commissions on his visit to the Count of Artois in Koblenz last year. I got it from him.'

'And what name does the Abbé now have?'

'The Abbé de Ribery.'

'And where is he hiding in Paris?'

'In the basement of some mansion, but I was not told where.'

'Come now, Monsieur Picot, you must know something.'

'All I know is that he had started up a new order called The Sacred Heart of Jesus and that he had gathered a group of men around him.'

As Picot finished, silence fell.

After several moments, the doctor nodded to Masson and the guards were ordered to take Picot back to his cell.

'Please don't hurt my children,' Picot stuttered as he left the room.

The doctor did not answer.

As soon as the door shut, Masson spoke. 'You are sly, keeping that letter back. Which daughter wrote it?'

'I have no idea.'

'Was it not signed?'

'Unfortunately not,' the doctor said, before adding, 'it seems not signing documents is something of a family trait.'

Masson smiled, before asking, 'What of the Abbé?'

'Dispatch two agents to look for him,' the doctor replied, 'and tell them what Picot has divulged.'

Masson nodded. 'What about Madame Picot?'

'I have agent Sicard already looking for her. It won't be long before he picks up her scent. He will track her down. She can't run forever.' The doctor beckoned to his accomplice to sit down and the two men rested for a moment at the table.

'Who shall we interview next?' Masson asked.

'Perrin, the gardener,' the doctor said.

'This should be fun,' Masson replied, getting to his feet.

'Bring some brandy,' the doctor said. 'A few glasses of that and he'll be singing like a caged canary.'

CHAPTER 11

Pryce fumbled with a set of unfamiliar and jangling keys as he unlocked the doors of St Leonard's Church and then the vestry inside. He put on his cassock, surplus, belt and stole and then walked into the Norman nave, pausing beneath the gallery constructed by the Pilots of Deal. It had a large painting in the centre depicting a fully rigged Man-of-War carrying the red ensign and fighting the rising waves. Dated 1705, it commemorated the appalling storm of 1704 that caused thirteen warships of the Royal Navy to sink in the Goodwin Sands. It was said that 1200 lives were lost in that one fateful night.

Pryce looked up to the trussed rafter roof of the church and uttered a quiet prayer.

Preserve us from the dangers of the sea and from the violence of our enemies.

Nearing the altar, Pryce bowed before the crucifix and then started to prepare the altar. He brought out a silver paten for the host and a silver chalice for the wine. As he placed the chalice on the altar he noticed an inscription on it: '1714 given by ye parishioners in exchange for a lesser to ye parish church of Deal, Kent.'

Pryce smiled.

As the golden light of the winter sun poured through the windows, people began to enter the church and quietly seat themselves in the boxed pews. A dozen pilots of Deal, wearing chimney pot hats and proud, ruddy faces, climbed the stairs to the gallery.

As Pryce scanned their faces, Sally Paine entered.

'May I have a word with you after divine service, Sally?'

'Yes, vicar,' Sally nodded.

Pryce led his flock through the order for Holy Communion, giving a short homily from the Gospel reading, interceding for King George the Third and the Prime Minister, William Pitt, and, having mentioned that St Leonard was the patron saint of prisoners, he made special supplication for those held captive against their will.

After presiding at Holy Communion, he took the silver paten and chalice to be washed in the greatest treasure of the church - a Norman piscina resting on an octagonal shaft made of stone, carved with chevron mouldings, standing in an alcove. It was as old as the church itself and stood next to three ancient stone sedilia in the chancel.

A few minutes later, Pryce was standing at the church porch shaking the hands of his parishioners.

'You have a fine preaching voice, Mister Pryce,' an old woman remarked as she pressed a penny into his hand.

Pryce smiled.

'George Whitefield preached here and his voice attracted two thousand people, setting Deal ablaze with a holy flame,' he said, before adding, 'he spoke as with God's voice, which is my desire one day too.'

Pryce took a deep breath of the cold air and then turned back into the church. Sally was waiting for him under the Pilot's Gallery.

'That was a beautiful service and a very fine sermon, my lord,' she said.

Pryce ignored the compliment.

'Sally, I need to speak to Jack urgently and I need to ask him a favour.'

'He will be very glad to help in any way he can. He has not stopped talking about you since you came to the cottage. I'll send him up here after Matins, if you like.'

'That would be most kind.'

After Sally left, a much larger throng assembled for the second service. Among them, Pryce saw his wife Eloise speaking warmly to those around her before sitting on the front pew. Her eyes looked red and her face was pale.

Pryce was about to begin the service when a boy burst noisily into the church. He dashed cap in hand towards the sanctuary, closely pursued by two wardens frantically waving their wooden staves.

Pryce leaned towards his grubby face, his ear close to the boy's mouth.

'It's war, Vicar. The French have declared war on us. The news is out.'

Pryce raised his eyebrows.

'So, it begins,' he murmured.

He thanked the boy and addressed the wardens.

'Announce the news and ring the bells,' he said.

After the hubbub had died down, Matins began. As Pryce read from the Book of Common Prayer, he made reference to the perils that war brings to family and friends and prayed for protection upon all loved ones.

O Lord, our Heavenly Father, Almighty and everlasting God, who hast safely brought us to the beginning of this day; defend us in the same with thy mighty power; and grant that this day we fall into no sin, neither run into any kind of danger; but that in all our doings may be ordered by thy governance, to do always that is righteous in thy sight; through Jesus Christ our Lord, Amen.

As Pryce proceeded to the Ministry of the Word he discarded his homily and began to speak.

'The times are grave,' he said. 'Deal once again stands poised at the very tip of the nation's sword as the storm clouds gather over France. As we seek together to do our duty in protecting those whom we love and defending our cherished way of life, we must not allow the darkness to consume us or the ways of the enemy to lead us into compromise. As Jesus said, "Blessed are the peacemakers, for they shall be called the sons of God".'

As Pryce continued, he talked briefly and discretely about his marriage to Eloise. He held it up before his people as an example of the bonds of peace that God can tie. 'She is French and I am

Welsh,' he said, 'a combination that could have only been imagined in heaven.'

The congregation laughed and Eloise blushed.

'And furthermore, she is from a Catholic family while I am of course a Protestant.'

Pryce paused before concluding.

'These are days when our nation will call us to stand as one to resist the darkness. We must be found to be a united not a divided house.'

As Pryce continued with the liturgy he asked God to defend the people of Great Britain in all the assaults of their enemies.

Before he gave the Blessing, he broke from the liturgy.

'The first priest of this maritime parish was a man who came to be known as Saint Richard of Chichester and he composed a prayer which I have been saying every day since I was ordained. In these uncertain times, let us hold fast to the one thing that is certain - the unending love of Christ - and pray together the words of Saint Richard,

Most Merciful Redeemer, Friend and Brother,
May we know you more clearly,
Love you more dearly,
And follow you more nearly,
Day by day, Amen.'

The sonorous Amen echoed through every ancient nook and cranny in the church.

Pryce stood. He pronounced the Peace and the Benediction. After the last straggler had left, he closed the door of the church and retired to the vestry where Eloise was waiting for him.

She embraced him and whispered into his ear in French, 'that was inspiring.'

Pryce removed his vestments before putting on his coat.

'I have asked Sally to send Jack here so that we can discuss my plans. I have to get to your parents as soon as possible. There's not a moment to lose.'

'But darling,' Eloise protested, 'is it necessary for you to go now?'

'Yes,' Pryce answered. 'The declaration of war has placed your parents in more jeopardy and made any delay on my part unthinkable.'

Eloise did not have time to reply. There was a knock at the vestry door. It was Jack holding a boatman's hat in his hands. 'Good afternoon, Vicar, Mrs Pryce,' he said. 'Sally told me you wanted a word.'

'I do. Thank you for coming so promptly, Jack.'

Pryce took Jack and Eloise into the sanctuary and then locked the church door. He checked throughout the building to ensure that they were alone before sitting down. 'Come,' Pryce said.

The boatman drew near and sat a few feet away on the pew behind.

'You said that I should ask you if I ever needed your help, Jack,' Pryce said. 'Well I do, urgently.'

'I am at your service.'

'I have to get to France very quickly.'

Pryce held nothing back. He told Jack that his wife was the daughter of provincial nobility in Brittany and that both her parents were in desperate trouble. He spoke of Michel Alain's arrest and his probable deportation to Paris, and of Jean Marie's escape from the national guardsmen and her concealment somewhere in the Breton countryside. 'So you see, I need your help.'

'What's your plan?' Jack asked.

'I have some papers given to me by an English Catholic priest which mean I can travel in France, provided I disguise myself as him.'

'I can help you with that, my love,' Eloise said, 'I will remove six of the buttons from the front of your cassock.'

'What for, ma'am?' Jack asked.

'Protestant priests have thirty nine buttons, symbolizing the thirty nine articles of religion. Catholic priests have thirty three, the number of years Christ lived on the earth as a man.'

'I'll also need you to sew several secret pockets for Lady Hester's gifts,' Pryce said.

'Do you need me to transport you to Calais?' Jack asked.

'I'd like you to get me across the Channel to Calais and then I'll take the coach to Paris. Once in Paris I can try and find out where Michel Alain is. Then I will need to head to the West Country to find Jean Marie.'

'When do you need to leave?'

'When is the earliest?'

'Tonight,' Jack said.

'So soon?' Eloise gasped.

'The tides and the weather are in our favour,' Jack said. 'My men and I can cross the Channel in under five hours on a night like this.'

'That would be perfect.'

'What about the way back?' Jack asked.

'I will need picking up from the coast of Brittany. And I will not be on my own. I will have others.'

Jack rubbed his chin.

'Sailing from here to Calais is easy,' he said. 'Fetching you from Brittany is a much bigger challenge.'

'Can you do it?' Pryce asked.

'All things are possible,' Jack replied. 'Isn't that what that good book of yours says?'

'Indeed, Jack, indeed.'

'When will you need to return?'

'In about ten days,' Pryce answered.

'Where will you want us to wait for you?' Jack asked.

'There is a chateau on the coast near Saint Malo. It has a concealed path from the top of the cliff down to a private inlet. I'll have my wife draw up a map this afternoon for you. The place belongs to her uncle.'

Jack stroked his bushy moustache. 'My men and I will use the island of Jersey as our base while we are waiting for you. I have traded with a man there by the name of Captain Philippe d'Auvergne. He works with a trustworthy gentleman called Henry who runs the Hotel Pelikan in Saint-Savant. If you make contact with Henry, he will alert the good captain of the time of your departure and we will be ready.'

'I have one more favour, Jack.'

'Name it.'

'Your men and your friends must be sworn to absolute secrecy. No one can ever know about this. As far as the good people of Deal are concerned, I am – and must remain – the Rector of St Leonard's and nothing more.'

Jack smiled. 'My men are like my boat,' he said. 'They do not leak.'

Pryce chuckled. 'I'm glad to hear that,' he said.

'You aim to be at my cottage before midnight and I'll have everything ready,' Jack said.

'Well, then, let's leave,' Pryce said. 'The sands of time are running fast.'

CHAPTER 12

'It's time, Picot,' a voice shouted through the iron bars of his cell door.

Michel Alain Picot wiped his eyes and stumbled to attention. Neither of these actions was straightforward. Picot's hands and feet had been in chains since the day he had been arrested at the Chateau de Fosse Hingant by Doctor Vacher and his men. Bruises and blisters had formed where the iron had constantly grated against his skin, causing Picot to groan every time he moved.

'Come on, come on,' a guard shouted as he marched into the room. 'We can't keep the court waiting. It's judgment day.'

Picot stood between the two guards who grabbed his arms and lifted him out of the cell into the corridor outside. There were already several prisoners standing in front of him outside his cell. He recognized Therese Limoelien who had burned the Marquis' papers just before she was captured. Beyond her he could see Monsieur Petit the wig maker and beyond him Perrin the gardener.

As doors were opened behind him and other prisoners joined the line, Picot whispered to Therese. 'Have courage, my dear friend.'

'Courage,' she whispered back.

'Long live the King and the good priests!' he added under his breath.

'Long live the King and the good priests!' she replied quietly.

A blue-coated guardsman with a stony face issued an order and Picot started to shuffle forwards, imitating the ungainly motions of those in front of him. Within a few minutes he was in the courtyard of the prison, being pushed by two stocky guards onto the back of a cart which soon started to roll out of the gates, underneath the shadow of Notre Dame Cathedral.

Picot sat silently next to Therese as the carts jolted and bumped down the cobbled streets, crowded with onlookers made curious by the sight of so many prisoners. A group of drunkards shouted, 'off with their heads,' as the carts rolled by an oyster seller's table.

When the carts came to a halt at the Palais de Justice, Picot – having been the last to get onto the cart – was the first to be pulled off. He waited at the head of a new line before being ordered by a sergeant of the National Guard to follow in an orderly way to the *Chambre de la Liberté.*

When Picot arrived outside the courtroom it was quiet. As he and the other prisoners began to enter, the crowd, which was packed tightly in the gallery, gasped and then shouted. Some were crying.

Picot was ordered to sit on the second of three benches reserved for the prisoners. Either side of him sat his three nieces – his sister Jeanne-Rose's young daughters - who leaned against him and each other in a desperate attempt to relieve their terror.

As they huddled close to him, Picot sighed. 'Be brave, my friends,' he said.

'But Uncle Michel, what will they do?'

'Whatever they do we will stay together. We are family and we will support each other. Now be strong. We don't want these Republicans to think that we Picots are from feeble stock now, do we?'

'We will be strong, Uncle,' the nieces said.

The attorneys entered first. Picot pointed to one of them. 'Monsieur Du Coudroy,' he whispered to his nieces. 'He's a friend of the family. I've paid him to represent us.'

After the attorneys, the jurors entered.

'Citizens, stand!' the court bailiff shouted.

Picot rose to his feet and watched as five magistrates entered the front of the court through a door at the side, on the same raised level. They were dressed almost entirely in black – black gowns, black waist coats, and black feathered hats. Only their tricolour ribbons stood out.

'That's the president of the court, Jacques-Bernard-Marie Montané,' Picot said softly to his nieces.

Behind the magistrates another man entered and as he did there were gasps in the crowd above Picot's head.

Picot shuddered. 'Fouquier Tinville, Public Prosecutor for the National Assembly,' he whispered.

Tinville had a full head of jet black hair which had been swept back above his high and frowning forehead. His nose was long and arched, his eyebrows trim and dark, his eyes black and lifeless. Even his cravat, folded underneath his wing collars, was black.

In an impassive voice, the Prosecutor began to speak and the room grew deathly still. 'I, Antoine-Quentin Fouquier, Public Prosecutor of the Revolutionary Tribunal, authorized by the National Assembly to arrest, try and judge citizens denounced, do hereby declare that the following persons have been, by virtue of arrest warrants issued by the Public Prosecutor, charged with conspiring against the Republic and plotting violence against its leaders and the people of France.'

Fouquier then read the names of all twenty seven prisoners and the court proceedings began.

One by one the witnesses against the accused were brought forward in session. Then those charged were summoned before the Prosecutor and questioned. Their attorneys made short pleas in each case.

After each plea, a written charge was presented to the nine jurors, outlining the accusation – soliciting the support of France's enemies and provoking civil war within France, with the purpose of annihilating liberty and restoring the despotic rule of the monarchy. By the time Picot's turn arrived, it was obvious that Fouquier was only interested in the appearance of legality.

'Are you Michel Alain Picot de Limoelan?' the Prosecutor asked coldly.

'I am.'

'And were you a friend of the late Marquis de la Rouërie?'

Picot did not answer.

'And did you or did you not act as the treasurer for the Chouan army led by the Marquis? Answer yes or no.'

Picot remained silent.

'I have here a letter from one of your children which implicates you as a member of the *Chouannerie*.'

Fouquier read it out without the faintest trace of pity.

Picot bowed his head.

'This letter was intercepted before it arrived at the Chateau de la Fosse Hingants where you were residing with your brother, Monsieur Marc Desillé, who fled from the scene, leaving his three daughters who are seated with you here in this court. This letter was addressed to you. Do you still refuse to admit that you were aiding the Marquis de la Rouërie in his rebellion?'

Picot said nothing.

'Come now, Monsieur Picot. You must understand that your silence will be interpreted as complicity. Your continuing refusal to answer my questions will be regarded by the jurors as a confession of guilt.'

Picot looked at the Prosecutor's twitching brows and widening eyes.

'Even though you are odious, I forgive you,' he said.

Picot was ordered by the Prosecutor's fawning clerk to sit down. His lawyer, Du Coudray, filed a plea and another paper was presented to the jurors.

By lunchtime the session was nearly over. The cases had been briefly made, the witnesses quickly questioned and the accused summarily judged. What should have taken a month had taken a morning.

Montane summarized the questions the jurors needed to answer before the court was adjourned and Picot and his fellow prisoners were taken downstairs to a spacious chamber beneath the courthouse.

Within an hour, twelve of the prisoners were called back to the court.

They were found not guilty and released.

Two other prisoners, including Francois Perrin the gardener, were recalled and sentenced to deportation.

As the remaining prisoners were brought back into the court by the gendarmes, President Montané gathered his papers and prepared to read the sentence.

There was growing tension in the crowd.

Picot's three young nieces pressed close to him again.

Therese held her head high.

Montané placed his hat upon his head and read out the names of all thirteen of the condemned one by one and then pronounced judgment upon them all.

His voice was flat, without the faintest trace of emotion.

'The court sentences you to death, at the holy guillotine in the Place de la Révolution.'

The crowd erupted, some cheering and clapping, others screaming into their handkerchiefs.

Most of the prisoners bowed, shed a tear and resigned themselves to their fate.

'Silence!' Montané shouted.

As the crowd calmed down, he concluded the sentence. 'All the property and possessions belonging to the condemned will be sequestered for the Republic.'

Therese held her head high and stared at the Prosecutor, the magistrates and the jurors, sneering at them.

Picot bent down and kissed the heads of his three nieces who were trying hard not to cry. 'I have often held your hands in this life,' he said to them, 'while playing in the fields of Brittany. I will hold your hands in the life to come,' he added, 'as we play together in the fields of heaven.'

'Oh please, Uncle, let it be so.'

'Stay strong, little angels,' Picot said. 'Our suffering is for a moment and death is just the gate to everlasting life.'

'We will be strong, won't we sisters?' one of them said.

'We will,' they reassured each other. 'God will help us and Uncle Michel will be with us.'

CHAPTER 13

Pryce listened to the sound of the waves breaking on the shingle and looked at his hands. They were shaking.

'Are you going to be all right?' Eloise whispered into Pryce's ear. 'You haven't been to sea in so long.'

'I will have to be,' Pryce said. 'If I'm going to find your father and your mother, there is no other way. Besides, the sea was at one time my happiest place. I'm sure it can become so again.'

'I love you so much for doing this,' Eloise replied. 'You are so brave.'

Pryce gave his wife one more gentle, lingering kiss before he knocked on the door of Jack and Sally's cottage.

Sally opened it, dressed in an apron, which was dotted like snowflakes from flour. 'Vicar, Mrs Pryce, do come in.'

Pryce waited for Eloise to enter before walking into the kitchen.

'Here,' Sally said, grasping Eloise's hand, 'I'll look after Mrs Pryce while you get on your way, Vicar. Jack is waiting for you outside.'

Pryce adjusted his cape and checked that his pistol and his gold were secured before he held his wife one more time, taking a deep breath to allow the scent of her chestnut hair to linger in his nostrils. 'Till we meet again,' he said.

'Soon,' she replied.

Pryce walked through the kitchen to the back door and opened it. An icy wind hit his face. Pryce pulled the scarf from around his shoulders and wrapped it over his mouth and chin, protecting him from the freckles of snow that were darting to and fro in the gusts. 'Good evening, Vicar,' a familiar voice boomed.

Jack had walked up the beach, his thick pumps crunching in the shingle.

'It's a cold night to be sailing,' Pryce said, shivering.

'Aye, it is.'

As the huge boatman spoke, Pryce looked beyond him to the men working on the *Endeavour*.

'Lads, stop working and say hello to the Vicar,' Jack said.

One by one the men trudged up the beach and gave Pryce their hand, each one removing their black, oil skinned hats and nodding.

'Twelve of us in all,' Jack said, 'just like the disciples, eh Vicar?'

Pryce tried to smile.

'Right men,' Jack barked, 'time to get going.'

The boatmen rushed to the lugger and jumped quickly in, ready for the launch.

Jack took Pryce's bag and stretched out a hand to pull him on board.

'Here, you can sit in the stern next to me,' Jack said. 'If you get really cold, you can shelter up front in the forepeak. There's some brandy in the cuddy.'

Pryce sat down next to Jack who was now standing with his hand on the tiller, tilting the rudder upwards to protect it from being damaged in the launch. He looked at the men now waiting in position for Jack's orders. Their tanned faces were marked by the gaze of experienced seafarers.

'Haul the mizzen sail!' Jack shouted.

Two of his men immediately sprang to action, pulling the ropes attached to the standing lug and the storm jib.

'Release the trigger!' he exclaimed.

A man whose face was as gnarly as old leather stood to his feet in the stern and pulled a lever. A long chain, which had up until now held the boat fast to the inclining plane, was now taken up through the ruffles in the bottom. The lugger began to move noisily along smooth square wooden blocks down the steep beach towards the surf. As it picked up speed across the skids, Pryce looked behind him at the long beach with its tiny houses made of brick and wood, surrounded by boats and sheds, and littered with capstans and tackle. He could just make out the silhouette of his wife in the warmly lit window of Jack's cottage, waving at him.

The boat was now rushing headlong down the skids towards the breakers. As it entered the sea and pushed through the surf, two men just in front of the caboose hauled the square dipping lug sail, pulling in unison on the halyards. The two red sails of the foremast and mizzen were then pulled taut and the *Endeavour* began to rush towards the ocean.

Once the boatmen took to their oars, the combination of their rowing and the winter wind in the full sails resulted in an immediate acceleration.

Pryce smiled with undisguised admiration as the *Endeavour* broke past the surf.

Within a matter of minutes, the wind haddied down and the waters became calm.

Jack tapped him on the shoulder and handed Pryce a telescope. As he squinted through it, he could make out the shapes of brigs, schooners, privateers, merchant ships, galleys, and even men-of-war anchored nearby.

'We are in the Downs,' Pryce said, as he lowered the telescope and turned to Jack.

'We are,' the skipper replied.

'There are a lot of ships anchored here tonight,' Pryce said.

'Aye, Vicar,' Jack replied. 'This is the best place for safe anchorage.'

'Why's that?'

'It runs from north to south, and is protected from westerly gales by the town and from easterly winds by the Goodwin Sands. It's a natural breakwater.'

As he said this, Jack pointed to a frigate bearing the Dutch flag sailing out in a northerly direction. 'Ships from all over the world pass through the Downs on their way to and from London, especially when there's a good south westerly.'

Pryce looked again through his telescope and watched as a Customs sloop tried to chase a thirty foot galley punt, whose oarsmen were rowing with rapidity.

Pryce had started to relax when the seascape suddenly changed. No longer were they in the calm waters of the Downs. Pryce could now hear the sound of pounding breakers and make out what looked like tall sandbanks in the light of the moon, which hung like an enormous lantern in the starry sky.

'The Goodwin Sands,' Jack said.

Pryce had heard of the Sands while growing up in Broadstairs, but he had never sailed near them. You had to be a Deal boatman to navigate your way through them. These men had a reputation for courage and skill that travelled far beyond the coast of Kent.

'What is this place?' Pryce asked.

'What we are about to enter, Vicar, is a swathe of great and treacherous sandbanks stretching eight miles long and four miles wide.'

'Why are they so infamous?'

'At low water, like tonight, the sandbanks are clearly visible. They can be as high as fifteen feet. At high water they sink beneath the surface and many a ship, carried by wild currents, becomes stuck on the edges of the Sands, their anchor fluke driven right through the bottom, holding them fast to the sandbank below.'

'Do they ever break free?'

'Just occasionally they are lucky and escape to fight another day, but most often their backs break in the trough of the great rollers and they fall slowly off into the ocean, which is between fifteen and thirty fathoms deep, usually with all hands lost.'

'Can't people use maps here?'

'Maps are useless,' Jack replied. 'The Sands shift all the time. They are never in exactly the same shape or place. There are all kinds of new spits, jaws and promontories every day and the swatches of water within the sandbanks themselves can change overnight from being a few feet to nine or ten fathoms.'

Pryce felt the hairs bristle on the back of his neck as the wind sloughed through mast and sail.

'Thousands must have perished here.'

'If you look carefully,' Jack replied, 'you can see the stumps and ribs of wrecked vessels, like gravestones in a watery cemetery. Many a vessel is buried deep in the Sands – often with their treasures still on board.'

'You must be glad to hear the roll of deep water underneath when you leave,' Pryce said.

'I am,' Jack replied. 'There's not a week goes by without some poor soul hearing the ominous grate of his keel on the sand below. It's not for nothing that these Sands are known as the Great Ship Swallower.'

'Are we going through them?' Pryce asked.

'Aye, we are. There are two or three swatches of water known only to us boatmen. While everything else changes, these channels through the Sands remain constant and even when their water is shallow, boats like ours are best equipped to traverse them.'

Just as Jack said this, an oarsman near the forepeak shouted out in alarm. 'Skipper, there's a sloop in trouble, five hundred yards, north east of us!'

Jack passed the telescope to Pryce who pointed it in the direction the boatman had indicated. As Pryce focused, he observed a hapless brig, with its sails still set, that had run aground on the edge of the Sands. It was being lifted up and down by the rough and tumble of the billows and it had become trapped like a frightened sea bird, its sails flapping wildly.

'Look!' Jack shouted.

As the lugger drew closer, there was a loud crash from the brig as one of its masts broke and fell over the side. As Pryce peered through the telescope, he saw that there were men on board and all of them were now trying desperately to escape drowning by clustering together in the rigging of the mainsail.

Pryce wiped his eyes for a moment and then looked through the telescope again.

But now he could no longer see the brig or its crew.

'Where have they gone?' Pryce asked.

'I'm afraid we're too late to help,' Jack answered.

'What do you mean?'

'Things happen very quickly out here,' Jack answered. 'That brig has disappeared. Pulled by the off-tide, it's rolled over the edge into the depths of the ocean. No chance of a rescue.'

Pryce prayed, his voice drowned by the shrill and eerie keening of the wind.

'Hard a starboard!' cried a man at the front of the boat. Then he added, 'Port, sir, quick - hard-a-port!'

As Jack pulled on the tiller, the lugger rushed past a tall black object, shaped like a large shark's fin, which was jutting out of the water.

'Part of the keel of a sunken vessel,' Jack cried. 'Many boatmen - even sometimes Deal boatmen - are lost to protruding wrecks like these.'

As the boat drew closer to the Sands, Pryce saw and heard a long line of breakers. They were rising up in foaming cataracts from ten to twenty feet high, thundering forwards towards the sandbanks at tremendous speed, only for their momentum to be abruptly halted by the stubborn sand beneath. Their power was colossal.

'We're near the main swatch,' Jack shouted above the sound of the waves.

'Steady men,' Jack added. 'Prepare to row through the Sands.'

Several of the men tied up the sails before the crew started to row at a slower and more deliberate pace, their tempo dictated by the skipper.

Once in the Sands, the boat went north easterly through the chief swatch - a quarter and of a mile wide. It was about five fathoms deep at low water, or so Jack said.

In the moonlight, Pryce could see the undulating and rippled sandbanks on both sides of the channel, some low and others high, all of them uninhabited except by resting seabirds and sprawling, wide-eyed seals.

After another hour or so of quiet rowing, Jack shouted, 'Trinity Bay!'

The boatmen upped their oars and crossed themselves.

'What's "Trinity Bay"?' Pryce asked.

'It's a large oasis at the heart of the Sands known only to us,' Jack replied. 'When the water is low the ground is hard and you can walk for miles across a spit of the yellow-brown sand here.'

'Is it safe?' Pryce asked.

'As long as you avoid the swirls of green sea water you come across from time to time. If you tread on the softer sand beneath their surface you will sink like a stone.'

'Are we disembarking here?'

'No, Vicar, I'm just giving the men a brief rest.'

'Look, look there!' Jack shouted. 'Starboard, two hundred yards, in the sandbank - it looks like the Osta Junis!'

The men immediately turned their heads and began to chatter like excited cormorants.

'What's the Osta Junis?' Pryce asked.

'It was a ship we went to ten years ago in the summer of '83,' he replied. 'Stuck here in the Sands it was – a ship of the Dutch East India Company, heavy with gold - a great prize for huv'lers like us.'

'Did you claim salvage rights?' Pryce asked.

'It was wartime so when my men and I returned to the shore with the ship's treasure on board it was all immediately impounded by the Customs men at Deal. They said it was prize to the Crown and so it all went straight into the Bank of England.'

'Didn't you get any of it?'

'All I got was the ship's cat. From time to time my men remind me about it. They saw me walking up the beach to my cottage with the poor creature under my arm, its green eyes staring at Sally from underneath its matted hair.'

The boatmen roared with laughter.

'Come on, get going,' Jack cajoled.

The boatmen took to their oars again and began to row. In under an hour they were out of the swatch and into open waters once again, heading east towards the coast of France.

Several hours later, Jack placed his hand on Pryce's shoulder and told him it was time to get ready. They were nearing a secret inlet five miles away from Calais.

Jack issued some orders and the men pulled up their oars. They clapped on a press of sail to drive the boat into the beach. They prepared a bow painter and stern rope and within the twinkling of an eye the *Endeavour* flew towards the land, like an arrow released from a bow.

Pryce watched in fascination as the boat got her nose down and her stern and rudder high into the air.

'We call this "taking a shooter"', Jack shouted. 'It feels like sitting on top of a huge seahorse.'

'Aye, that's why we are called the riders of the sea,' one of the boatmen shouted.

At the last moment before reaching the shore, Jack skilfully put the helm down and the boat arrived broadside on the beach, lying parallel to the shore, about twenty feet from the water's edge.

'Here,' Jack whispered, 'we'll leave you on this beach. There's a small path yonder to a track that leads to the main road. Head north for five miles on that and you'll come to the port. Make your way to the coach house there and you can find a ride to Paris.'

'Thank you Jack, to you and your men,' Pryce replied. 'Will you be able to put out to sea again from here?'

Jack nodded as he handed Pryce his bag. 'Remember,' Jack whispered, 'you need to make your way to the Hotel Pelikan at Saint Savant and tell Henry the owner to alert us when and where you want us to pick you up. We'll come to you from Jersey and we'll bring help.'

'I'll remember,' Pryce said.

'See you in ten days, Vicar,' Jack said. 'Godspeed.'

'Godspeed to you and your men,' Pryce replied, as he jumped from the boat and began to walk alone towards the track.

CHAPTER 14

Pryce woke with a start on the stage coach which ran between Piccadilly and Paris. He had arrived at Calais shortly before 4.00am, ensuring that his disguise and his papers were in order before making his way to the coach house.

'My name is Father Henry Essex Edgeworth,' he had said. 'I need to get to Paris.'

'You're in luck Father,' a coachman had replied. 'One of our passengers fell sick in the night after the crossing from Dover. He must have eaten a bad oyster or something because it was a fine night for a sail. Anyway, you can have his place.'

Pryce had paid the man and waited with other travellers in the coach house till dawn. When the carriage had arrived, Pryce had baulked at the ugliness of it. It had four wheels, two large at the back and two smaller ones at the front. Instead of just one compartment for the passengers, there were three bound to each other underneath a tent-like roof where boxes destined for the Paris markets were stored.

Just in front of the first compartment was the seat where the driver perched like a ship's captain. Everyone else sat in the three leather padded compartments behind it. As forms of public conveyance went, Pryce had never seen anything more ungainly. Even though it moved at a speed of seven miles an hour, drawn by six powerful Norman horses, it was to him a cumbersome machine.

By the time it had left Calais and was on its way to Paris, Pryce was already queasy. The smell of the heavy curtains of leather, coated with oil, had not helped, nor had the constant jolts of the spring-less chassis. All around him he was aware of objects shifting – hats, band boxes and swords in the netted compartments above him and snuffboxes, bottles and cosmetics in the pockets lining the inside of the coach. The boxes in the roof of the vehicle seemed to flinch at every bump in the road, giving the impression that the ceiling might at any moment give way, releasing an avalanche of seafood and linen on his head.

'Let me offer you a drink, Father.'

The voice came from the gentleman on Pryce's right. He was dressed in a black short breasted coat and wore cream knee length breaches and white stockings. There was a tricolour ribbon pinned to the front of his white shirt. He spoke in English but with a French accent.

'That's very kind of you, monsieur,' Pryce said, taking a tin cup and sipping the refreshingly cool water poured from a military water bottle.

'My name is Citizen Dessin.'

'Father Henry,' Pryce said.

'And what brings you to France, Father?'

'I'm here on an ecclesiastical matter.'

'And what matter is that?'

'I'm making a pastoral visit to some of my Catholic brothers.'

Pryce paused for a moment and then turned to Dessin. 'And what is your business, monsieur?'

'I am a Customs officer in Calais.'

'Ah, you're a lucky man.'

'Why?'

'It is a great thing to work where you can taste the salt of the sea on your lips.'

'I go where the Republic sends me,' Dessin said.

'And I go where God sends me,' Pryce replied, 'and today he has called me to Paris.'

'So you have been to Paris before?'

'Yes. Have you been to London?'

Dessin shifted uncomfortably in his seat.

'I see you have, monsieur,' Pryce said. 'And what, pray, was your business there?'

Dessin scowled and turned to the gentleman on his right.

When, after what seemed like an eternity, the carriage eventually began to make its way through the suburbs of Paris, Pryce covered his ears. The noise of the crowded streets increased with every turn of the carriage wheels.

There were peddlers and traders on every congested boulevard. Some were advertising for brooms and others for larding pins. One street vendor was offering small windmills carved out of wood. Another was hawking loudly for kindling for fires. As far as Pryce's eye could see, the streets were filled with people trying to make a living.

On one occasion a woman toted a large wooden platter full of pastries at the carriage window opposite him. Pryce was about to buy one when a man appeared at the window next to him with a kettle strapped to his back.

'Coffee, Citizen?' he asked.

'Yes, please,' Pryce said wearily, as he reached into his cassock pocket for a coin.

A moment later he was drinking a strong roast while watching a woman selling baked apples flirting with a man sporting scores of rabbit skins on his shoulders, and old hats upon his head.

Pryce smiled.

As the carriage stopped at the Rue Notre Dame des Victoires, the coachman informed the passengers that they had now arrived.

Pryce stepped out, brushing down his cassock and wiping his lips.

An organ grinder offered to entertain him for five sous but he waved his hand.

'Godspeed, Father,' the coachman shouted.

'Godspeed to you,' Pryce replied in French.

Pryce turned towards the bustling centre of the city. It was now well into the afternoon as Pryce walked towards the crowded market places of Les Halles. He approached a boot cleaner sitting on some steps. Just as he was about to ask him for a shoe shine, there was a sudden alteration in the crowd. The sounds of traders shouting out their deals were exchanged for another noise – the low-level hubbub of a rumour beginning to spread. The noise intensified until it reached a fever pitch of shouting. Pryce could only make out snatches but he heard a cheese seller mention the 'Place de la Revolution,' and a chimney sweep talk about the 'Chouans!'

'Do you know what's going on?' Pryce asked.

'I have my suspicions,' the shoe cleaner replied. 'Sounds to me,' he added, 'the barbers of Paris are about to use the national razor.'

'To the guillotine!' an oyster seller shouted.

As the word was repeated, Pryce watched with curiosity as the direction of the crowd shifted like a shoal of fish suddenly changing from a settled mass into a thousand darting but united shapes. The strains of the hurdy gurdies and warbling singers were now replaced in a moment by the growing sound of thousands of clogs running faster and faster on the stony streets.

'Who's being executed?' he asked the shoe cleaner.

'Royalists who have been on trial at the Revolutionary Tribunal, I fancy.'

'Do you happen to know the names of any of them?'

'No, Father, I'm sorry. All I know is that there were twenty seven of them accused. I don't know how many of those will be executed. But this will most likely be the first time more than one or two have been beheaded so there has been a lot of talk about it.'

Pryce paused and reached into his pocket. 'I was going to ask you to shine my shoes but I need to join the crowd and find out what's going on.' Pryce gave him a coin. 'That's for the information.'

'Thank you, Father,' the shoe cleaner replied.

Pryce was about to run after the crowd when the man spoke. 'For another coin I'll tell you something else – a matter of some urgency.' Pryce eyed the man suspiciously for a moment and then reluctantly placed a coin in the man's blackened hand.

'You're being followed,' the shoe shiner said.

Pryce swung round and as he did he caught the eye of the man who had sat next to him and questioned him on the diligence. He saw Pryce turn but had not reacted in time. Embarrassed by his exposure, Dessin turned and scuttled off like a startled crab.

'Thank you,' Pryce said.

'You're welcome,' he replied. 'Some of us still respect the good priests.'

Pryce blessed him and then started to run with the crowd. Being tall, he quickly picked up a swift pace. Towards the head of the crowd, Pryce could see a man with dirty white stockings and a long grey coat. He was a spoon seller covered in clanking metal. Pryce began to sprint until he caught up with the man. As soon as Pryce reached him, he realized that there was an even faster crowd ahead of the man – a group made up of gutter leapers, policemen, orphans, water carriers, soldiers and sailors.

Just then the crowd wheeled again, this time to the right, and as it did Pryce and his companions poured straight into the Place de la Révolution, drawn with the rest of the runners to its centre where a guillotine stood menacingly upon a wooden stage. Pryce shuddered as he pushed as close to the platform as he could. There were carts strategically placed throughout the throng, including several nearby, where men offered a better view for a small fee.

Pryce frowned.

Another opportunistic citizen had four coloured balloons tied to his shoulders and was shouting, 'Balloon Rides from the Tuileries Gardens, this Sunday, get your tickets here. Limited supply!'

The atmosphere was more like a carnival than an execution.

Soon the square was filled – all except for a wide pathway from the Rue Royale that had been cordoned off with rope and whose every yard was protected on both sides by line infantrymen in dark blue uniforms, their muskets shouldered, their bayonets attached.

As Pryce looked up he could see that almost every window, roof and balcony of the surrounding buildings was now filled with people waiting for the spectacle. Many of them were peering through lorgnettes, as if they were enjoying a matinee at the opera.

Then as suddenly as the crowd had begun to move when the news had come, it now became completely still as a fresh rumour began to spread.

'They're here.'

As silence descended upon the square, Pryce heard the sound of drummer boys. Two slow strikes, two fast strikes, one slow strike – over and over again. The rhythm was constant.

Every head turned to the mouth of the Rue Royale.

The prisoners appeared, accompanied by a heavy escort of soldiers. Two carts, their wheels moving at the same slow pace as the beat of the drums. As the tumbrels drew nearer to the platform, Pryce could see their occupants. All of them had bare heads and clipped hair. The flesh on their necks was visible. Many of them were talking to each other. A few of the men were laughing.

It was only when the second cart stopped that Pryce saw him. It was unmistakable. There was his father-in-law. His clothes were torn and filthy. His dishevelled hair had been clumsily cut. His face looked drained and as leaden as the sky.

'Michel, what have they done to you?' he whispered.

Pryce put his hand over his dry lips.

The first victim said goodbye to the prisoners nearest to him and shook their hands. He cast an agonized glance back at them before he climbed the steps of the scaffold.

A young man on the front row tried to start a cheer for the master of ceremonies – a black clad butcher turned executioner called Samson. But he soon piped down when no one chose to follow his lead.

Pryce watched appalled as the prisoner was forced roughly down upon a plank, his head thrust into the block of the guillotine. Samson released the blade and it fell with a resounding thud upon the wood, severing the man's head from his neck, sending a wash of blood onto the stage.

Three other men followed and then three women, all from the same tumbrel. Their heads dropped into the basket and their mutilated bodies were cast into cheap coffins on carts destined for the Madeleine cemetery.

As the second tumbrel was opened, a man stepped out and climbed the platform. He was determined to say something to the crowds but was silenced by Samson's assistants and quickly strapped to the plank and dispatched.

Next was a woman whose beauty was immediately striking. She had red hair and pale skin. Pryce recognized her from his days at the Chateau de Limoelean. It was Therese Limoelin, a friend of the Picots.

As she approached the guillotine she would not allow anyone to touch her. She stood before it fearlessly and made the sign of the cross. She lay upon the plank of her own accord, shouting a loud 'leave me alone!' to a man who tried to assist her.

The next moment the bloody blade fell again.

Pryce felt nauseous as Samson's assistants pulled her body so inconsiderately from the guillotine that her dress became caught on a corner of the wooden base and ripped off, revealing her white legs. Pryce looked away.

When he looked up again her body had been thrown from the stage into a coffin and all eyes were now on the second tumbrel.

Out stepped three young girls, all clinging to each other, all crying. To his horror, Pryce realized who they were.

'Oh Lord, no!' he gasped.

One of Eloise's nieces turned back to the only person left in the cart and screamed, 'Uncle Michel, save us!'

At this, some around Pryce murmured. 'This is not right. They are too young. They should not be here.'

'They are royalists and traitors,' screamed a man from the crowd. The girl at the front turned to her sisters and said, 'hush now, let me show you.'

Imitating exactly the movements of the woman who had just gone before, she climbed the stage with dignity, never flinching for a second. She slapped Samson's men as they tried to manhandle her and shouted, 'leave me alone!' at which some among the crowd began a short-lived and subdued clap.

The child died without a trace of fear.

Her two sisters, their mouths open at the courage she had shown, went to their deaths with equal composure.

It was now Picot's turn. He descended from the cart and walked towards the stage. As he did, he seemed to look at a man on the front row a few feet ahead of Pryce. The spectator was wearing a black habit and his head was hidden beneath a hood. As Picot stared at the man, he raised the rosary that he had shared with his three nieces. He blew a tender kiss at it and wept. The hooded man bowed his head and Pryce could see him raise his hand to make the sign of the Cross.

Pryce reached into the folds of his cassock to the secret pocket that Eloise had stitched and felt for the shape of the four barrelled pistol. He took it out and held it in his right hand, sliding the safety mechanism back with his left so that it was now ready to fire.

He pushed past the people in front of him, ignoring their insults, and stood behind the man in the hood.

He began to raise the pistol but just as he was about to fire at the executioner, the hooded man turned round and grasped hold of Pryce's hand.

'No,' he said. 'You will not kill him from this range and this will cause a bloodbath.'

As the priest disarmed him, Pryce looked into his eyes.

The man removed part of the hood from his face and as he did, Pryce recoiled. 'Abbé!' he whispered. 'What are you doing here?'

'I'm here to stand with my brother at the moment of his death.'

With that the Abbé turned back towards the stage.

The blade fell upon Michel Alain's neck and the Abbé bowed his head.

He then turned back to Pryce.

'Quick, Thomas. We must leave!' he whispered.

CHAPTER 15

As the carriage pulled away from the darkened alley behind the Palais de Justice, the doctor walked to the front door of an old lodge. He looked round to check that he was alone and then knocked three times loudly and twice softly. The door opened and a man dressed as a valet ushered the doctor into the house.

'The master has summoned me here,' he said.

After the door had closed, the man spoke. 'The passkey, if you please.'

The doctor drew a chain from around his neck and cupped the silver key in his hand before handing it over. The man scrutinized it carefully. 'Thank you, sir. Please come this way.'

The doctor followed the man into a marble hallway with two staircases at the end, one on the left and the other on the right, leading up to a landing. He was escorted down a long and dimly lit corridor to a closed door at the end. His guide took an iron key from his pocket and unlocked the door. He stood aside and beckoned the doctor to enter. 'Stand in the middle of the room, please sir, on the pyramid.'

As soon as the doctor walked in, the heavy door slammed behind him and he could hear the clunking of the key turning in the lock. The doctor placed his glasses on his nose. He was in a huge room with a ceiling that extended to the roof. There were four candles on ornate brass stands in the corners of the room. They afforded enough light for the doctor to see where he was going as the sound of his shoes echoed in the cavernous chamber.

As he moved towards the centre of the room, he became aware of something glowing on the floor. He stepped slowly towards the low light and saw that it was a perfectly carved Egyptian pyramid, about three feet by three feet, in the middle of a golden circle. It was visible in the phosphorescent light pouring out of every detail etched into the marble floor.

Vacher stood in the centre of the pyramid as he had been ordered. Instantly he became aware of another light, this time emanating from above him, more incandescent than the one on which he was standing. As the doctor looked up he could make out a great eye staring at him. The lines of both the eye and its pupil seemed to be on fire and a bright shaft of light shot down from the retina and enveloped him. He lowered his gaze and then squinted at the darkness of the room in front of him. As he did he became aware of dark shapes moving from both sides of the room towards him. They were each carrying a candle and they were wearing long capes with pointed hoods.

'Is that you, master?' the doctor asked.

There was no reply.

He shuffled nervously.

The shapes began to move again, forming a circle all around him. The doctor wiped his eyes and as he did he became aware that someone was standing right in front of him, just inches from his face.

'*Illuminatio!*' the caped man shouted.

Immediately the darkness lifted as lights came on in every part of the room.

The doctor wiped his eyes.

The man in front of him was dressed in a black cape edged in gold. His hood was over his head and he was wearing the mask of a ram, two horns reaching upwards from a jaundiced skull. Behind him there were two tall pillars made of sandstone standing either side of what looked like an altar, above which hung a painting of a six pointed star.

'You have done well,' the voice spoke, and instantly the doctor recognized it as the Shadow's.

'Thank you, master.'

'You have passed the test of fidelity and now it's time for you to receive your reward.'

The Shadow turned. 'Come with me,' he whispered.

The doctor followed him to the steps between the pillars. Then the Shadow turned and bid him stop. The other caped men, numbering eleven in total, gathered behind the doctor.

'It is time for you to join the brotherhood,' the Shadow said.

'What brotherhood?' the doctor asked.

'We are the last remaining band of the *Illuminati*, dedicated to creating a more enlightened France.'

'I thought the *Illuminati* had been disbanded,' the doctor said.

'They were,' the Shadow replied, 'all but us, and we are known by a different name.'

'What name are you known by?'

'We are the Amunites, those who bow to the god Amun, whose name means the Hidden One.'

The doctor shivered. 'Why am I here?' he asked.

'Every person in this room has passed the test of fidelity,' the Shadow replied.

'Do you mean they are agents?'

'Yes, they are agents of death to the enemies of France and agents of life to France's friends.'

The doctor smiled. 'Is this my reward?' he asked.

'Part of it,' the Shadow answered.

'What do you want me to do?'

'You are here to be initiated into the order of the Amunite priesthood, a privilege given only to the few.'

The Shadow paused. 'Do you accept?'

'I accept.'

Instinctively, the doctor knelt.

'Get up,' the Shadow said. 'Those who kneel are slaves.'

The Shadow turned and faced the huge painting of the star. As the doctor followed his gaze, he saw that the picture was moving upwards. As the star disappeared, a large dais appeared surmounted by a throne. In front of it stood a gold leafed table covered in jewels, gold coins, a sword, a crown and a sceptre. Candles were flickering.

'Look,' the Shadow said.

The doctor was already looking, dazzled by the glinting gold and the shimmering jewels.

'If you are to become a follower of Amun, then look upon these riches.'

The doctor obliged.

'If this crown and sceptre, these monuments of degradation and imbecility, tempt you; if your heart is with them, if you would help kings and queens to oppress their subjects, then we will place you as near to this throne as you desire. But our sanctuary will forever be closed to you and we will abandon you to your folly.'

The Shadow paused then turned back to the doctor. 'If you are willing to devote yourself to making men happy and free, you are welcome here.'

The Shadow raised his cloaked arms, like a rook spreading and shaking its wings.

'Decide!' the assembled priests declared in unison.

'I have decided,' the doctor said immediately. 'I choose the brotherhood.'

The Shadow turned and signalled in the direction of the throne. A breeze blew across the table and the candles were extinguished. The screen with the six pointed star was lowered and the throne and its riches disappeared.

The Shadow walked slowly to his left, to a book sitting on a small lectern. 'Behold, the *Code Scrutinateur*,' he said. 'This book contains a history of your faults, discovered and recorded by the insinuating brethren of our order.'

The doctor frowned.

"But I have done nothing wrong...' he answered.

'In these pages, all your gravest sins are preserved – your predilection for the women of the night in Paris, your embezzlement of hospital funds in Nantes, and above all... the murder of your father.'

The doctor gasped.

'Do you confess your faults before the brotherhood?'

'I, I... I confess them,' he trembled.

As he spoke those words, the hooded priests behind him drew near. They placed sacerdotal robes over his shoulders and a red Phrygian cap on his head.

'Wear this cap,' the Shadow said, 'it means more than the crown of kings.'

When the doctor looked up, everyone was facing the six pointed star. He followed their gaze and watched as the star disappeared and a new picture materialized. It was a picture of Jesus, after the fashion of the Renaissance masters.

'What's he doing here?' the doctor growled.

'This is not the Christ of the Institutional Church,' the Shadow said, 'this is the Messiah of the masses.'

'But...'

As the doctor looked more closely, he could see that the painter had depicted Jesus wearing knee breeches and long stockings, a torn white shirt with a tricolour ribbon pinned to his chest. This Jesus was being interrogated by priests dressed as Catholic bishops and clergy.

'This is the Sans-Culottes Christ, the one who came to spread the light of reason and to teach equality and liberty for all.'

The Shadow leaned forward towards the doctor's face. 'The true Jesus, the liberator of man, we respect. It is the church that we detest.'

The doctor relaxed.

'This Jesus,' the Shadow said, 'is not a god to be worshipped. That right we reserve for Amun.'

The doctor nodded. 'I can assent to that.'

'Good,' said the Shadow. 'In that case, follow me.'

The doctor walked behind his master to a door on the right side of the altar. The Shadow opened it and the two men entered.

The room was small. It had a table with a white cloth in the centre and a solitary candle blazing in a small brass holder.

'I promised you a greater task,' the Shadow said.

The doctor smiled.

The Shadow reached to the table and fetched a purple purse.

He opened it and withdrew a passkey, exactly the same shape as the silver one the doctor owned, only this one was made of gold - glittering gold.

'This is now yours. You won't need the other one anymore.'

The doctor removed the silver key from his neck and placed it on the table. He then took the golden passkey in his hands. 'Thank you, master.'

'That is not all,' the Shadow said, as he lifted the candle.

Along the right hand wall of the room there was a safety deposit box standing on a chest of drawers.

'Open it,' the Shadow whispered, 'your mission is inside.'

The doctor took his new key and marvelled as it slid effortlessly into the lock. He opened the lid. Inside there was a scroll with a seal, a ram's head imprinted on it.

'Break the seal,' the Shadow said, handing him a paper knife with a pearl handle.

He took the scroll in his trembling fingers and slid the knife through the paper. He opened the scroll and leaned forward towards the light coming from the table. As soon as he had read the first sentence, he put his hand to his mouth.

'Are you serious, master?'

'I am,' he replied, 'deadly serious.'

CHAPTER 16

'Abbé, I cannot believe it's you!' Pryce exclaimed, as the two men hurried down bustling boulevards and arcane alleyways, away from the Place de la Révolution towards the Marais district.

'I had to be there for my brother,' the Abbé said.

'It was a comfort for him, I'm sure,' Pryce sighed.

'He saw me, thank God, and heard my prayers.'

'I'm grateful you stopped me,' Pryce said. 'I'm not a killer.'

'You'd be amazed what we are capable of *in extremis*,' the Abbé replied.

As the two men increased their pace, Pryce whispered, 'we have to find Jean Marie Picot, and fast!'

'Has anyone been following you, Thomas?'

'Yes.'

'Do you know who?'

'A man called Dessin.'

The Abbé stopped and pulled Pryce into a doorway. 'Dessin... are you sure?'

'Yes, he was on the coach sitting next to me.'

'That was no accident,' the Abbé said. 'Dessin works with a French agent called Titus Morgues. The two of them monitor who travels between London and Paris. Dessin works in Calais. Morgues is based in London.'

'Dessin was suspicious of me, wasn't he?' Pryce said.

'He would most certainly have been,' the Abbé replied.

'I saw him following me into the market after I left the carriage this afternoon.'

'In that case, he is still after you. In all likelihood he has been trailing you since the Rue Royale. We need to make sure.'

The Abbé seized Pryce's arm and the two men dashed along the Rue St Antoine, their cassocks billowing. 'Turn right into St Louis' church ahead – the one with the octagonal dome,' the Abbé cried.

Several moments later the two men scaled some stone steps and opened the door to the church. It was dimly lit and unoccupied.

'Quick!' the Abbé whispered. 'Go and kneel. Pretend you're praying to Our Lady.'

Pryce ran and rested his weary knees on a hassock in the last row of pews. He looked up and stared at a painted statue of the Madonna who looked down on him with pity from underneath a white shawl. Pryce closed his eyes.

He began to pray as the door to the church opened.

Pryce heard it click shut again and stayed still, his hands clasped prayerfully as he leaned his elbows on the back of the pew in front of him.

He could just make out the sound of someone approaching behind him and a shadow spreading over him.

'Father Henry, we meet again...'

Pryce turned round.

It was Dessin.

But his face was frozen in shock.

The Abbé had just appeared with Pryce's pistol and the butt had come down with an echoing thud on Dessin's skull, accompanied by the words, 'Bless you.'

The man fell unconscious to the floor, the startled look fixed on his face.

'Blessing and bludgeoning are a strange combination, Abbé,' Pryce said.

'We Jesuits are a strange combination,' he replied. 'We're warriors and mystics – just like our founding father, Saint Ignatius.'

Looking down at the body, Pryce frowned. 'There must be times when that combination becomes a contradiction.'

'Sooner or later we all have to learn to live with our contradictions,' the Abbé said.

Pryce helped the Abbé carry Dessin into a confessional, sitting him upright in one of the booths. 'He can sleep it off in there,' the Abbé said.

As the two men hurried out of the church onto the street, the Abbé started to laugh. 'That man won't like waking up in the church of St Louis,' he said.

'Why's that?'

'It was built by Jesuits and it stands for everything Dessin detests.'

'You mean the Pope?'

'Not only the Pope. There are some very valuable royal relics kept there.'

'Like what?'

'Like the heart of King Louis XIII for one thing. He laid the first stone. In fact, the church is named after him.'

'I almost feel sorry for him,' Pryce mused.

'We're nearly there,' the Abbé remarked after several more minutes.

'Good, I'm beginning to feel weak.'

'You must be hungry.'

The Abbé slowed down and stopped at a man sitting on a stool. He was cooking some meat pasties on a patty pan by the side of the street. There was a warm glow from the coal beneath the grill and the smell of cooked pastry had already invaded Pryce's nostrils.

'Two please, my friend,' the Abbé said.

The vendor presented the pasties on napkins.

'Here,' the Abbé said giving the man an extra coin. 'That's for giving us the ones with proper meat.'

The man frowned and turned his face away.

'We've had enough of rats for one night,' the Abbé winked at Pryce.

'Thank you, Fathers,' the man stammered.

'And this,' the Abbé said, handing him another coin, 'this is for your sick son, Jean.'

'How… how… how did you know?' the man gasped.

'I hear things,' the Abbé replied as he and Pryce began to walk away.

'Do you mean you hear God's voice?' Pryce asked, after they were round a corner.

'Not in the way that a madman does.'

'Then how?'

The Abbé took a bite of gravy-stained crust, chewed it for a moment, before answering. 'I have learned to tell when it's him speaking.'

The two men passed down a side alley and then into a small, cobbled square with mansions on all four sides.

'Come this way.'

Pryce followed the Abbé through a gated pathway beside one of the mansions. They climbed down two flights of well worn steps and arrived at a door with ivy clinging tightly to its timber. The Abbé took a key from his pocket. 'Hold onto my belt,' he said.

The room inside was pitch black. As the door shut behind them, Pryce clung to his guide for a few yards until they stopped. The Abbé lit a candle.

'Over here.'

In the half-light, Pryce could see they were in a wine cellar. There were rows and rows of dusty bottles in racks on the cobwebbed walls, and scores of kegs and barrels stacked haphazardly on the floor. At the far end of the room, there was another door.

'Before we enter, I must ask something of you Thomas.'

'What?'

'You are about to be taken into my confidence in a way that I would not allow unless you were a loyal friend of the family. You must tell no one of what you are about to see and hear. Swear it, on Michel Alain's grave.'

'I swear.'

The Abbé scrutinized Pryce's face and then relaxed. 'I believe you,' he said.

The Abbé knocked on the door five times. It was opened by a giant of a man, armed with a pistol. 'Welcome to the Order of the Sacred Heart,' the Abbé said.

Pryce walked into a large, well lit, underground chamber. In front of him were men sitting at tables, poring over unfurled scrolls and maps. Two were dressed like Catholic clergymen but the remaining five were in jackets, shirts, cravats and culottes. Their swords were lying on the tables where they were working.

'Who are these people?'

'They are the people who will help us find Madame Picot,' the Abbé replied.

He sat Pryce down and poured him some wine. 'These men and women work for me,' he said. 'Most of them were on the faculty when I was the Dean of the Ecclesiastical College in Dinan, before I was expelled because of my outspoken criticism of the Revolution. They also supported the Marquis de la Rouerie, as did I.'

The Abbé turned to his men. 'Let me introduce Thomas Pryce, an old friend of the Picot family and of mine. Don't be fooled by his disguise. He is not a Catholic priest. He is in fact a Church of England minister and married to Michel Alain's daughter. He speaks our language perfectly.'

The men stopped what they were doing and stood to shake Pryce's hand, some offering condolences, before returning to their seats.

'They are working hard tonight,' the Abbé said. 'We know something big is being planned by the enemy – something more momentous and destructive than we have yet witnessed.'

'How do you know this?' Pryce asked.

The Abbé drank slowly from his cup. 'We have a man on the inside of Fouché's lodge.'

'Fouché?'

'He is one of the most dangerous men in France. He sat on the Tribunal which voted for the King's death. He now works for the Police Chief here in Paris and controls a number of extremely ruthless spy networks throughout the country.'

'You mentioned a 'lodge',' Pryce said.

'Yes, it used to be a Freemason's lodge.'

'Used to be?'

'Fouché used to be a Freemason. But when the ideas of the *illuminati* began to infiltrate the French lodges, he developed his own secret society, based on the worship of the ancient Egyptian god Amun and grounded in the teachings of the *Illuminati*. He is the chief priest and grand master.'

Pryce shivered. 'He sounds mad.'

'I wish it was as simple as that.'

'What do you mean?'

'Fouché is far from insane. He is extremely intelligent and cunning.'

'What is he devising?'

'That we do not know. All we know from our man in the Lodge is that there was great excitement after they inducted a new Amunite priest last week. Apparently the novitiate was given a momentous mission. Everyone was talking about it though no one knew what it was, except of course for Fouché and the man himself.'

'Do we know who this agent is?'

'His name is Dr Vacher. He is the person responsible for Michel Alain's death.'

'We must stop him,' Pryce cried, 'whatever he is intending to do, and we must bring him to justice. He has done terrible things to our family.'

'I know, my friend,' the Abbé replied, putting his hand on Pryce's shoulder. 'Leave that to us. We will find him. Even if he leaves France, we will find him.'

'But how – you are so few?'

'We may be few in number but we are part of a much larger correspondence.'

'Correspondence?'

'A network of agents,' the Abbé explained. 'Thomas, we have friends in high places in London and Geneva - friends who control agents throughout Britain, France and Switzerland. We will find Vacher and we will either capture him or kill him, be assured.'

'Kill him?'

'Yes, if necessary, we will indeed kill him.'

'You would be prepared to do that?'

'Yes.'

'I'm not sure God can condone killing,' Pryce said.

'Extreme times necessitate extreme measures.'

'But Saint Augustine condemned the passion for inflicting harm, the cruel thirst for vengeance, and the fever of revolt?'

'He certainly did,' the Abbé replied, 'but my men and I are not operating out of a cruel passion or fever. We believe this is a just fight and we are, to quote Saint Augustine once again, warring peacefully.'

Pryce smiled. 'That sounds like a contradiction,' he said.

'I told you earlier,' the Abbé replied, 'we have to learn to live with our contradictions and, if necessary, to die with them too.'

Pryce took a sip from his wine.

'How are we going to find Jean Marie?' he asked.

The Abbé turned around and called to one of his men. 'Charles, come over here.'

'Pleased to make your acquaintance,' the man said to Pryce as he reached out his hand.

'I want you to help us find Madame Picot,' the Abbé said. 'She is in hiding somewhere, we think in Brittany.'

'Brittany is a huge place,' the man replied, 'almost a country within a country. Do you know where exactly?'

'Not yet.'

'Are you intending to locate her yourself?'

'My friend here and I will both look for her.'

'Which route do you want to use?' the man asked.

'The secure route to Saint-Malo,' the Abbé replied.

'I'll prepare our best horses immediately. I'll also alert the safe houses so they have fresh horses ready on the way.'

The man walked back to a table, drew out a map, and began to talk with two colleagues animatedly.

'We need a disguise,' the Abbé said to Pryce. 'Your apparel and your papers have aroused too much suspicion already. You will need a new identity.'

'What do you suggest?'

'I suggest it's time you became an Abbé in the Order of the Sacred

Heart of Jesus,' the Abbé replied, 'that's if you're prepared to pretend to be a Jesuit for the duration of our mission.'

'If it's just for a week that will not be too onerous,' Pryce smiled.

The Abbé reached inside his robe. 'And here,' he said, returning Pryce's pistol under the table. 'Keep this somewhere safe.'

'Do you think I'll have to use it?' Pryce asked.

The Abbé grasped hold of his sleeve.

'What did our Lord say? 'Be as wise as serpents as well as innocent as doves.'

'That's beginning to sound like a contradiction too,' Pryce replied.

CHAPTER 17

Jean Marie Picot took the knife from her son and slit the rabbit's throat, waiting as the blood drained and the twitching of its muscles subsided. In no time at all she had skinned, gutted and decapitated it. 'Here, prepare a spit,' she said.

Jean Marie looked at her son. He was now twenty-five years of age. In the light of the crackling fire, she could see the contours of her husband's jaw and forehead in Joseph Pierre's face. Her eyes welled with tears. 'Do you think father is still alive?' she asked.

'I don't know, mother. It's hard to say.'

'I don't think his prospects are good,' she said. 'If he was captured at Marc Desillé's house and taken in irons to Paris, then I fear for him. He will most likely be in the Tower Prison.'

'They may spare him, mother.'

'But if they could send the King to the guillotine, they will have no scruples about sending your father there too.'

'Hush mother,' Joseph replied, reaching out and gathering her under his arm. With his free hand he turned the rabbit. It was now perched on a wooden skewer between two small boulders and beginning to hiss above the eager reach of the flames.

'We must eat,' Jean Marie said, drawing herself away from her son's embrace as the pink meat began to turn black.

She took the stick from its makeshift platform and placed the remains of the animal on a cold stone to cool down. After no more than ten minutes, she began to cut pieces and pass them to her son. 'Here, just like I used to cook at home when you were little,' she laughed.

'I may have to exercise my imagination when it comes to the garnish and the vegetables,' Joseph replied.

The two sat side by side, wrapped in dirty cloaks, devouring the food and drinking river water from a metal canteen. After every last shred of meat had been gnawed from the bones, Jean Marie looked around at the ruins of the castle in which they were hiding. 'Do you remember when we used to come up here for picnics when you and Eloise were children?'

'I do mother. I have always loved this place. I'll never forget father teaching Eloise and I how to fence and shoot up here.'

Jean Marie laughed.

'Do you remember Eloise's first shot?' he asked.

Jean Marie had never forgotten. Eloise and Joseph had been seven at the time. Michel had brought them to the ruins to give them some target practice with the family pistol. He had torn a picture of a wicked murderer out of a book of fairy tales and fixed it in a frame.

'Now daughter, it's your turn first.'

He placed the framed picture on a rock and marched Eloise twenty paces from her prey. He had handed her the pistol and cocked it. 'Here, when you are ready, turn around, aim and pull the trigger.'

'She hit the wicked murderer straight between the eyes,' Joseph reminisced, 'and she shouted the word 'bastard', much to father's delight and my surprise.'

'Your father was truly amazed by her,' Jean Marie added.

'So was I. Turns out that she was by far the best shot in the family.'

'And when it came to swords,' Jean Marie added, 'she was not to be trifled with either.'

'She gave me a hiding several times with those old cavalry sabres father kept,' Joseph laughed.

'She is strong, that one,' Jean Marie mused.

'Just like you, mother.'

Joseph took a gulp of water from the bottle. 'This place is still magical,' he said. 'Father used to tell stories of Bertrand du Guesclin and his adventures here. I never knew if they were true.'

'A story doesn't have to be factual to be true,' Jean Marie replied.

Joseph smiled.

The two leant towards each other, Jean Marie resting her head upon her son's shoulder. 'We will need to leave soon,' she whispered.

'Let's wait until the fire goes out,' Joseph replied. 'Then we can leave here and make our way home. We should easily get there before daylight.'

Jean Marie closed her eyes as her son rubbed his head gently against hers.

She was happy not to be alone. When the soldiers had come to their house to arrest her, all the children except Joseph had been away with relatives. Joseph had been out in the fields and seen the approaching squad. By the time the National Guard had reached the chateau, the two of them had fled into a dense forest nearby. Now, after several weeks of hiding out in caves and gullies, they were heading back to the chateau to a secret chamber that only Jean Marie and her husband knew.

'If ever either one of us is in trouble,' Michel had said, 'then we must find a way to our secret place until we can be rescued.'

Those were the last words Michel had said to her before leaving for the Chateau de la Fosse Hingants, where he had been arrested. As Jean Marie remembered them, tears ran like quiet Breton streams down her face.

As the fire began to glow and then eventually died, Jean Marie shook her sleeping son, whose head had now become heavy on her shoulder. 'Come, Joseph, it's time to leave.'

Without a word, Joseph stood up and extinguished the last remaining sparks with the heels of his army boots.

Jean Marie gathered her cloak tightly around her and began to follow her son from the ruined castle and down into the valley below. They walked at the edges of fields and through woods and copses until they reached a familiar road, not far from the byway leading to the Chateau de Limoelan.

All of a sudden, Joseph froze. 'Hide!' he whispered.

They darted from the roadside and slid into a ditch. It was about four feet deep, with still water lining the bottom. Tall grass protruded from the bank nearest the road, affording the two fugitives some cover.

The two of them lay in a clump of reeds, their legs tucked under their thighs which were now soaking in the dirty and foul smelling water.

After several seconds, Jean Marie heard the sound that her son's more attentive ears had discerned.

There were feet running on the road.

'In here,' she heard a voice say.

Then more feet, running hard.

Lanterns.

A command.

'We know you're hiding in there. Come out, right now, or I'll order my men to fire a volley.'

Joseph turned and grabbed hold of his mother's arm. He put his finger over his lips to signal to her to be silent and then drew his knife.

Jean Marie shook her head. 'You cannot give yourself up for me,' she whispered.

As Joseph prepared to charge the soldiers, Jean Marie grasped him around his waist and whispered into his ear. 'Look!'

She pointed to the middle of the road where the blue-coated soldiers stood with their muskets raised, their officer shining a lantern into the ditch. Only the lantern was facing in the opposite direction. And so were the muskets. 'It's not us they're after,' Jean Marie whispered.

'This is your last chance. Come out now or my men will fire!'

The voice came from a young officer whose sabre was drawn.

A few moments later, three men emerged.

The men wore grey red woollen hats with the tricolour and grey vests of homespun cloth. Their breeches were baggy and they wore wooden sabots with blood red straps across the insteps.

One of the three men kissed the rosary that was round his neck. Another bowed his head and was clearly praying. The third placed his hand on a red patch over his chest.

105

Jean Marie recognized it immediately. It was shaped like a heart and had a cross on top. Underneath were stitched the words, 'For God and King' – exactly the same as those she had sewn onto a heavy grey coat belonging to her husband.

The soldiers kept their muskets trained on the men.

The officer stepped forward. 'Chouans!' he spat.

'Long live the King and the good priests!' one of the men shouted.

The two others repeated it.

But their cries were drowned out by the officer's order and the crack of the soldier's muskets.

As the smoke cleared, Jean Marie and her son saw the bodies of the captives lying motionless on the ground.

'Bring them,' the officer barked.

Six men from the detail seized the limp arms of the rebels and started to drag them away from the scene. As his men began to march away, the officer raised his lantern and looked into the ditch. He turned a full circle, scrutinizing the area. For a moment, Jean Marie thought that he had seen them. But then he swivelled round towards his departing troops and ran to catch them up.

'They've gone,' Joseph whispered. 'We must get to the chateau, and fast.'

Chapter 18

Jean Marie and Joseph stepped out of the gulley, wiping down their cloaks and shaking the water out of their shoes and stockings.

'This way,' Jean Marie said.

Within minutes they had passed a monastery and were walking in a fallow field full of yellow gorse and the stumps of gnarled trees. After passing a familiar charcoal burner they increased their pace. They were near their home now. As they drew nearer and nearer to the chateau, Jean Marie yearned to return to the time when she and her husband had cared for the land and its tenants. She longed for the days when they had gathered the farmers, foresters, gardeners and woodcutters, together with their families, for summer suppers in the woods around the chateau. The family would drink wine and the tenants would drink hard cider, and all of them would sing Breton songs. Often these feasts would extend until dawn when the nights were warm, and sleepy heads would wake to the sound of the birds and the sight of wild animals chewing at leftovers beneath the tables.

Those days, she knew, were gone forever.

The two of them hurried down a byway off the main road and followed its course towards the chateau. In the moonlight they could see the outline of the three-storied mansion with its mansard roofs, as well as the pavilions either side. They climbed a gentle slope towards the house, darting between clumps of pine trees on the green lawns, skirting the stream which ran from the chateau to the village and climbing some stone steps. Now they were just feet away from the light yellow stone of the house's façade and Jean Marie could smell the vines and the wreaths of moss on the walls.

As the two of them made their way to the front door, Joseph

suddenly stopped. 'Do you see that?' he whispered.

Jean Marie strained her eyes in the moonlight. As she squinted she could see the door had been boarded up and a notice pinned on one of the planks.

'This chateau is now the property of the Republic, by order of the National Tribunal.'

The seal of the Municipal Authority in Rennes was clearly visible below.

'This doesn't look good for father,' Joseph sighed.

Jean Marie's heart sank. 'They have murdered him,' she whispered.

'Not necessarily,' Joseph replied. 'They may have imprisoned or deported him.'

'My poor husband,' she sighed.

'Mother, we cannot make assumptions and we must make haste.'

'We need to get inside,' she said. 'Quick! Go round the back!'

Within moments they had gained access to the kitchens through a backdoor whose key was always left beneath a stone nearby.

'I need to get out of these clothes,' Jean Marie said. 'You get as much food as you can and meet me in the study in ten minutes,' she added.

Jean Marie hurried through the kitchen into a hallway. She bounded the stairs to the second floor and made her way to the master bedroom. She tore off her cloak and threw it in a large washing sack, then took off her muddy shoes and stockings. Quickly, she peeled off her torn gloves and the dirty casual jacket she had been wearing for months and then removed her floral over petticoat. With a few more swift movements she had divested herself of both her under petticoat and her corset, now looser on her leaner frame. Everything Jean Marie had been wearing was now in the sack and she was now ready to dress again. Opening her husband's mahogany wardrobe, she took a pair of his sabots and tried them on. Then she found some of his stockings, a pair of dark corduroy hunting breeches, and a white shirt. Donning a grey waistcoat and a short grey jacket, she then walked to the tall mirror in their closet. For a moment she stared at her reflection and looked at her husband's clothes. She could smell faint traces of his cologne. As Jean Marie looked into the mirror, she tied up her dark chestnut hair which had been loose and untidy around her shoulders for many days. With shaking hands, she washed the last vestiges of white powder from her face. When she was done she walked back into the bedroom. Jean Marie stared for a moment at her dressing table, which was covered in lace, silk flowers, feathers, powder, rouge, and caskets covered in mother of pearl and tortoise shell.

'I won't need these,' she muttered.

She turned away from the dresser and crouched down beneath the wardrobe, reached for a box concealed behind a set of slippers and pulled it out. Inside was the family pistol, with its silver barrel and its pearl butt, decorated with the family crest – two hatchets, symbol of the ancient sea raiders. Jean Marie tucked it into her belt and thrust the cartridges and powder inside her pockets.

As she left the room, she paused.

'I will always love you,' she whispered.

Hurrying down the stairs with the sack of dirty clothes, she darted into the study. Joseph was there with a large box of wine, cheese, olives and other food.

'My goodness, mother, you look terrifying!'

'Only to those who have caused our family such suffering,' she replied.

Jean Marie dropped the sack of dirty clothes and lit a candle.

She walked to a purple painted bureau standing at the end of the room. It was decorated with gilt bronze mounts. Even its brass hinges glinted in the candle light.

Jean Marie knelt down and fumbled for something.

'What are you doing mother?'

'You'll see.'

She found the trigger and released a spring mechanism. A concealed drawer shot out of the side of the bureau.

'I didn't know that was there!'

'You weren't supposed to, my son - not until now, anyway.'

Jean Marie held the light over the drawer. There, standing on a purple cushion, were two passkeys, designed in the exact same shape as the two hatchets on the Picot coat of arms.

'What are they for, mother?'

'Come with me and you'll see.'

Jean Marie led her son to the wardrobes behind the bureau. They were made of the same wood and fashioned in the same ornate way as the desk. She pressed down on the head of a tiny bronze figurine and immediately the central wardrobe opened up before them like a door.

'What's this?' Joseph cried.

Jean Marie took out one of the hatchet keys and placed it in the lock of a second door behind the first. She turned the mechanism and the door swung open.

'Fetch candles,' she said, 'and give them to me. You can carry the food and the dirty clothes.'

Joseph dashed back into the room. A moment later he was behind his mother and the two of them were walking slowly down a long, damp corridor.

'What is this place?' Joseph asked.

'It is a secret tunnel.'

'Where to?'

'To a place your father had constructed by trusted labourers.'

The two walked to the end of the corridor where there was another door.

'We're underground now,' Jean Marie said.

The door opened after the second passkey was turned and they walked into a dank chamber.

'We are under the Rosary chapel,' she said, shining the light of her candle around the room.

Joseph put the food and clothes down.

'Look,' Jean Marie said, 'there are beds and books and a stove and pantry.'

'It never even occurred to me that this was what those builders were doing all those years ago,' Joseph exclaimed.

'Your father had great foresight.'

'He did, mother, he did.'

Joseph paused and rubbed his chin. 'I am a little worried. If father was the only other person who knew of this place and he's now in prison, or in his grave, then who will come and rescue us?'

'I do not know,' Jean Marie sighed. 'But I do know your father, and I am certain of this. He will have found a way to tell someone where we are. So this will have to be our hiding place until help comes.'

CHAPTER 19

'Where are all the Picot children?' Pryce asked, as the four seated fast-coach sped out of the Parisian suburbs into the countryside.

'They are safe, my friend, have no fear,' the Abbé replied.

'I am concerned,' Pryce said, 'especially after what I saw at the Place de la Révolution. The murder of Michel's nieces was a slaughter of innocents.'

'Thomas, let me assure you, the Picot children will be fine,' the Abbé said.

'But where are they?'

'The three daughters are with their cousins in Versailles and will stay there until this darkness has dispersed. Nicholas is serving in the navy far away in warmer waters. Young Michel is studying in Switzerland and will be there another three years. Joseph Pierre is almost certainly looking after his mother.'

'Joseph is with Jean Marie?'

'That is what my sources indicate,' the Abbé replied, 'and it is good news. Joseph is an accomplished soldier. When the Revolution started, Joseph initially stayed as an officer in the army but after the death of his cousin Andre Desillé, an officer in the King's Regiment, he decided enough was enough and he offered his services to the émigré army in Koblenz.'

'I had wondered what happened to him in the last few years,' Pryce interjected. 'Do you have information about his recent whereabouts?'

'Joseph was with his mother when the National Guardsmen came to arrest her. They got away just in time and as far as I know they are in hiding in the woods somewhere around the town of Broons.'

'That will be tough for them.'

'Not as tough as you might think,' the Abbé replied.

'Whatever do you mean?'

'There is a lot about your wife's twin brother that you do not know.'

'Tell me,' Pryce said.

'Joseph has been acting as the aide de camp to the Marquis de la Rouërie.'

Pryce gasped. 'When did he join the Chouan army?' he asked.

'Last year,' the Abbé replied. 'He had been training in Koblenz with the royalist army when the Marquis de la Rouërie came to visit their commanding officer, the Comte d'Artois.'

'I have met him!' Pryce exclaimed. 'I spoke with him, as did Eloise, just a matter of days ago and he seemed like a fine man.'

'Joseph was one of the Count's officers, but when he met the Marquis he asked to be released. He wanted to be back in Brittany, closer to home, but he was also impressed by the Marquis because he was actually fighting. Joseph was eager to get in on the action so the Count let him go and the Marquis made him one of his senior officers.'

'So he has seen action?'

'Yes, often – so often, in fact, that the Republican army is terrified of him and his own men refer to him as the Knight of Limoelan.'

'He always loved stories about knights,' Pryce said with a smile. 'When he was a boy he used to pretend that he was the Eagle of Brittany.'

'Ah yes,' the Abbé replied, 'the celebrated Bertrand du Guesclin. We could do with men like him right now.'

'Joseph is such a man,' Pryce said.

'Indeed,' the Abbé replied, 'and he is a man of great faith too. I was his spiritual director when he was a boy. Jean Marie is in good hands.'

'Where do you think they are?' Pryce asked.

'Ah, now that is the question. I would conjecture that they are in Brittany, probably making their way towards the coast around Saint-Malo.'

'Do you think they will try to escape by sea?'

'Almost certainly,' the Abbé replied. 'That's what Marc Desillé did. He managed to evade the national guards by running from his chateau down the cliff face to the beach and boarding a bugalet for Jersey.'

'If Jean Marie and Joseph are working their way towards Saint-Malo, they are probably somewhere near the Chateau de Limoelan by now,' Pryce said.

'Precisely, and they may even try to enter the house to fetch some belongings.'

Pryce rubbed his chin. 'That is interesting,' he said.

'Why do you say that?'

'I have been thinking.'

'What?'

'I have been thinking about Michel's conduct just before his execution.'

'What about it?'

'It was as if he was trying to say something.'

The Abbé smiled.

'You noticed it too,' he said.

'What I noticed,' Pryce answered, 'was the way he paused at the bottom of the scaffold and turned to you. He raised his rosary in a very unusual manner, right above his head, and then looked as if he was sending a kiss to it.'

'And what do you think that means?' the Abbé asked.

'I think Michel was telling you where Jean Marie was hiding.'

Just at that moment the fast-coach hit a large rut, sending the two passengers and their luggage into the air.

'These roads haven't got any better,' Pryce exclaimed.

'They've become worse since the Republicans declared war on your country. The heavy boots of 300,000 soldiers have been digging up the gravel and causing havoc.'

'You need some of Macadam's invention,' Pryce smiled.

'Behold, I make the rough roads straight,' the Abbé exclaimed, and both men laughed.

After a moment, Pryce leaned forward. 'Listen, I think I know what Michel was trying to convey to you just before he died.'

'Go on.'

'Do you remember when he bought the Chateau de Limoelan, he had a chapel built on the grounds, a few hundred yards from the house.'

'Of course I do,' the Abbé replied. 'I used to take services there regularly.'

'And do you remember what the chapel was called?'

'The Rosary Chapel!' the Abbé exclaimed. 'That's what my brother was saying! Jean Marie is somewhere in the chapel. Well done, Thomas!'

'If that's where she's hiding, then we need to get there quickly. How long does this journey take?'

'In this fast-coach, it will take us about thirty hours, not including the stops at our safe houses for food and new horses.'

Pryce frowned. 'Let's hope we get there in time,' he said.

'There's another problem,' Pryce added after a pause.

'What's that?'

'We don't know where exactly in the chapel they are hiding. It could be anywhere, including in the grounds. Do you have any idea where they might be?'

'No I don't,' the Abbé said. 'But I have an idea how we might know.'

'How?' Pryce asked.

'We are going to make a brief stop outside Rennes.'

'Isn't that dangerous?'

'It is, but we need to get some information and I think there is a man who might just know.'

'Who's that?'

'His name is Petit and he is a wig maker.'

'Why would he know?'

'I don't know for sure, but what I do know is he shared a cell with Michel in Rennes prison. When the two of them were carted off to Paris, Petit was released. If Michel gave a message to pass on to us it will be with Petit.'

'Let's hope and pray so,' Pryce said.

As the coach hurtled down country roads, between phalanxes of poplar trees and pines, Pryce watched as the darkness grew thick and the landscape more and more invisible. It was gloomy and stuffy in the carriage and Pryce was starting to yawn. Remembering the hour, he began to pray silently. As the coach rumbled on its way, Pryce fell into a deep sleep. As he did, a great and icy wind began to batter at the carriage.

'What's that?' the Abbé cried.

The four horses started to bellow frantically at the front of the coach and the driver shouted to them to calm themselves. The temperature suddenly dropped. The open window was edged in frost. From all around them the wind howled like mad dogs.

Pryce gripped the upholstery of his seat. 'Start praying!' he shouted to the Abbé. 'There is evil upon us!'

As Pryce looked at his friend, the back of the coach seemed to disintegrate completely so that the Abbé was now exposed to the cold and violent wind.

'What's happening?' the Abbé shouted above the howling.

Pryce made the sign of the Cross and began to pray out loud. 'Lighten our darkness, we beseech thee, O Lord; and by thy great mercy defend us from all perils and dangers of this night; for the love of thy only Son, our Saviour, Jesus Christ, Amen.'

No sooner had Pryce finished than he began to make out a shape in the gloom behind the coach.

It was a horseman.

As the rider drew closer Pryce could see that the horse was black like a raven and had a fountain of funereal feathers pouring from its fetlocks.

As Pryce squinted, he also saw that the rider was dressed in the garb of an executioner, with a hood over his head and two narrow slits for eyes. The nearer he came, the clearer Pryce saw him. He looked like the executioner at the Place de la Révolution only his eyes were not black but dark red, swirling like miniature whirlpools of blood. As the horse approached the coach it seemed as if he was galloping at a speed impossible for any earthly creature. Legs were moving furiously, with an unnatural energy. The hooves of the beast barely touched the ground.

When the ghostly rider reached the rear wheels of the carriage, he stretched out his arms. He opened his mouth and hissed like an angry snake and as he did, a blade appeared where his top front teeth should have been. It was shaped like the blade of the guillotine and its edges were covered in clotted blood and matted hair.

Pryce shuddered.

As the rider slid like a slippery shadow from the front of his horse into the back seat of the carriage, Pryce tried to speak but his chest tightened and his jaw locked in a paralysis of fear.

Just as he was about to give in, a roar began to ascend from deep within him – from a space between his spirit and his soul. It rose and rose until it passed through his throat and out of his mouth. 'I will not be afraid of the terror by night!'

The rider, who was sitting next to the Abbé now, had opened his hideous mouth and was about to bite at the Abbé's neck. When he heard Pryce he stopped still and turned, like a predator distracted by more promising prey.

The rider stared right into Pryce's eyes.

'I do not fear you, demon,' Pryce declared. 'You are the one who must yield here, to the name that is above all other names – the name of Christ the Holy One.'

As Pryce spoke the sacred name, the rider opened his mouth and hissed, spitting blood and torn flesh from the exposed blade hanging from his upper jaw.

'Almighty God,' Pryce shouted, 'give your angels charge over us!'

The shadow shrieked.

It shrank back and began to crouch within the coach, trying to find a place to hide.

The next moment, Pryce saw why.

From behind him a piercing light had appeared. As it illuminated the inside of the carriage, he could make out the form of a man standing. He was dressed in armour, as an ancient Knight, carrying a huge sword, whose glowing tip was now pointing towards the demon.

'Because He has set his love upon us, therefore He will deliver us,' Pryce shouted.

'And He will set us on high because we have known His name!' the Abbé added.

The black clad rider screamed and fled from the rear of the carriage, melting into his black steed and galloping off into the darkness.

The radiant Knight slowly disappeared.

The gale died down and the temperature rose.

And Pryce woke up.

'Are you all right, my friend?' the Abbé asked.

'Yes, I am,' Pryce replied, as he slowly came round.

'You were shouting all sorts of things while you were sleeping,' the Abbé said.

'I was having a nightmare,' Pryce replied.

'That is not altogether surprising, given what you've witnessed.'

'Nor given the great darkness we are facing,' Pryce responded.

'We are not fighting flesh and blood,' the Abbé said, 'but dark spiritual powers in high places.'

'But we must not fear,' Pryce said. 'The sacred name is more powerful than any other name.'

'There are angels,' the Abbé added. 'The hosts of heaven are encamped about us.'

Pryce sat back into his seat and looked out of the window of the carriage. As he gazed up at the full moon, he saw the outline of a great bird of prey flying above them.

'And the eagle of Brittany is watching over us,' Pryce said.

CHAPTER 20

Doctor Vacher smiled. He was outside the door of an apartment on the third floor of house number 315 on the Rue Saint-Honoré in Paris.

He knocked and waited.

He heard someone approaching the far side of the door.

'Dr Vacher, welcome. I am Citizen Fouché.'

The man in front of him was no more than five feet five inches tall. His pale face was thin and his skin looked as if it had been stretched too tightly over his hollow cheeks and pointed chin. His wispy hair was a light yellow colour and had been meticulously combed above his high forehead. His voice, when he had spoken at the door, was frail like his physique, but the look in his grey eyes was shrewd and sly. The doctor shivered as they seemed to look right into what once he would have called his soul.

Fouché ushered the doctor into a hallway and then on through a glazed door to the main living room. The walls of the salon were covered in portraits of great men of the Republic in oils, crayons, stump and bistre. There were terracotta busts of Danton and Marat on two tall, ornately decorated tables. Over the marble fireplace, where a strong fire was burning in the hearth, was a gigantic mirror framed in gold.

'Come this way, Doctor.'

The doctor followed his master into a study.

Fouché sat himself down behind a small wooden desk with nothing but a black inkwell on it.

'Take a seat,' he said.

The doctor sat on a chair that seemed at odds with the understated opulence of his surroundings. It was shabby and wooden, topped with torn cushions.

'This is my new toy,' Fouché smiled.

'What is?'

'You're sitting right in front of it.'

'But it's just a bureau!'

'Not any old bureau, Doctor. If you would care to stand and step to one side, I will show you.'

The doctor did as he was told.

Clad in the cleanest of dressing gowns, Fouché looked relaxed and at ease in his own home. And now he seemed actually to be enjoying himself.

'Watch this,' Fouché smiled.

In one swift movement, Fouché's bony right arm reached out and his small fist fell upon the inkwell. There was a loud crash, a billow of smoke and then the tattered chair in front of the desk fell over.

'Let's look at the damage,' Fouché said.

He walked round with a magnifying glass which he drew from his dressing gown pocket. He picked the chair up and examined a new hole in the ripped upholstery. 'There,' he said, pointing to the shape of a bullet in the back of the seat.

'What is this contraption?' the doctor exclaimed.

'It's a gun desk, one I had especially made.'

'I was sitting in front of a loaded gun,' the doctor exclaimed.

'Don't worry, Doctor, you weren't at risk of being shot by me, which is more than I can say for the traitors I've been interrogating.'

'What do you mean?'

'I took this to the Tower today and tried it out on two prisoners.'

'With what results?' Vacher asked.

'The first man took a bullet in the groin and the second one in the stomach. The first one will be saved by a surgeon if he talks but the second one died slowly this afternoon, but not before he had betrayed some confidences.'

Just then there was a knock on another door and the sound of excited voices behind it. Fouché's eyes lit up and the warmest of smiles appeared on his face. 'Enter!' he shouted.

Straight away the door flew open and four small children, dressed in perfectly tailored little suits and dresses – all adorned with tricolour ribbons – rushed into the room and threw themselves at Fouché. 'Papa!' they shouted. 'Come and play with us!'

Fouché bent low to each one and kissed their heads, grabbing hold of as many of the wildly flailing arms and hands as he could. 'In a little while I will, my children, in a little while.'

'But play now, papa, please play now!' they insisted.

'After I have spoken to our guest,' he laughed. 'I won't be long.'

'Oh all right, papa.'

Just then a woman entered the room. She was small and plump and had a complexion as wan as her husband's.

'My darling wife,' Fouché cried, as he walked towards her and kissed her.

'Excuse us,' she said to the doctor. 'I am Madame Bonne-Jeanne Fouché.'

The doctor took his hostess' hand. 'Enchanted,' he said.

Fouché stepped forward and took his wife's hand from the doctor's. 'Sweetheart,' he said, 'would you mind taking the children to the nursery for a while?'

'Not at all,' she replied.

With that, the tiny but vociferous flock was herded from the room and the study fell quiet again.

'Let us sit before the fire and talk,' Fouché said in a grave voice.

The two men walked back into the drawing room. Fouche pointed to an armchair and the doctor sat down. There was a bowl of fruit standing on the table next to him.

'Have a peach,' Fouché said, pointing to the bowl with a poker, before he applied it to the burning logs in the fireplace. 'They are succulent.'

The doctor took a ripe peach and a small china plate and started slowly and methodically to apply an ivory handled knife to its flesh. 'You cut with great precision, Doctor,' Fouché said.

'These days I have to.'

Fouché rested his hand on a bronze pig standing on the mantle shelf. 'One day I will have a farm and breed these beasts,' he said.

'You come from farming stock?' the doctor enquired.

'No, my father was a Breton sea captain. I was expected to follow suit but...' Fouché patted his lean and bony frame, 'my constitution wasn't up to it.'

'Did you want to be a farmer?'

'No, I wanted to be a priest.'

The doctor only just managed to catch the plate in his hands. 'You wanted to be a priest?'

'Yes, I spent twenty years at an oratory in Nantes. In the end I became a teacher, but for a long time it looked like I was going to be ordained.'

'Why didn't you?'

'I became disillusioned with the lives of many of the senior clergy, by their corruption and greed while the peasants were starving.'

'So you have rejected the faith?'

'I still have faith,' Fouché said, 'but I invest it in Public Reason and, of course, in the Hidden One.'

Fouché walked from the fireplace and sat down on an armchair opposite the doctor.

'Now then, Doctor, we have some business to attend to. Let's start with your mission.'

Fouché reached underneath his chair and fetched what looked like a walking cane and a brown leather post bag. He then looked back at the doctor. 'You are to travel by the diligence to Calais and then on to London, to Piccadilly. You will join the French delegation there under the name Marat. All your papers as well as your passport are prepared.'

Fouché took some documents from the post bag and placed them on the table next to him. 'When you arrive at Piccadilly, take a carriage to the Crown and Anchor Tavern in the Strand. There will be a room booked in the name of Monsieur Marat. Stay there until you are contacted.'

'Who's my contact?'

'He's one of our agents called Titus Morgues. He will come to your rooms and give the secret knock. He will be wearing a golden passkey like yours under his shirt. Ask to see that before you let him in.'

The doctor nodded.

'After that you must make your way at the appointed time to the country residence of the aristocrat, Lord Charles Stanhope. He is a cousin by marriage to William Pitt, the Prime Minister.'

Fouché stood up and approached the doctor with the cane. He removed a tiny cap from the top of the curved handle and pressed an invisible switch. Immediately a long blade shot out of the other end of the cane. The doctor could see that it was razor sharp.

'You will need this,' Fouché said, using the floor to push the blade back into the cane.

The doctor took the secret weapon and Fouché returned to his seat.

'Now,' he continued, 'there is another mission and that must be undertaken by your assistant, Masson. It involves two priests who are heading to Brittany to try and rescue Madame Jean Marie Picot.'

'Pah!' the doctor spat. 'Those damned refractory priests!'

'It's slightly more complicated than that,' Fouché replied. 'One of the priests is French. He is a Jesuit called the Abbé de Clorivieres. But the other is English and is called Edgeworth.'

'Where have I heard that name before?' the doctor asked.

'He was the English chaplain who was with the king at his execution, Father Henry Essex Edgeworth.'

'What is he doing back in France?'

'We do not know, but he has official travel papers signed by a member of the Tribunal – the Tribunal that voted for the King's death.'

'How can that be?' the doctor exclaimed.

'Not everyone voted in favour of the death sentence,' Fouché replied. 'One of the men, it turns out, had royalist sympathies and took seriously the king's request to look after Edgeworth – the last order the King gave.'

'That was foolish,' the doctor sighed.

'It was more than foolish. It was treacherous and the man will die for it. As for you, I want you to send Masson to Brittany to find these two priests.'

'Is he to operate alone?'

'No, I have seconded an agent by the name of Sicard to go with him. They are to head to the Militia in Rennes and speak with the chief there. One hundred soldiers will be released to them.'

'That is a large force.'

'It's needed,' Fouché replied. 'There are many rebels in the area and there's also the threat of a landing force from Jersey.'

'Where do you want the soldiers to be based?' the doctor asked.

'I want them to use the Chateau de Limoelan as their headquarters. That way, if Madame Picot tries to return there, she will be in for a rude shock.'

'Brilliant!' the doctor cried.

'Masson's orders are to bring Madame Picot and the Jesuit traitor back to Paris where they will be brought before the Revolutionary Tribunal.'

'What about the English priest?'

'Masson and Sicard are to make him disappear – permanently.'

'I'll tell them.'

'And also tell Masson to be careful,' Fouché said. 'These priests have already attacked one of my agents who tracked them from Calais to Paris. He is now nursing a terrible injury and some wounded pride.'

'I will,' the doctor said.

'And there's another thing,' Fouché added. 'Madame Picot is being guarded by her son Joseph. He is a former aide de camp of the Marquis de la Rouerie and a very dangerous man. He has killed many national guardsmen.'

'I know of him,' the doctor said. 'He was an officer in the King's army and a very able soldier.'

'Quite so,' Fouché said. 'But he cannot hide forever in the forests and his days are now numbered.'

Fouché stood in front of the doctor and reached out his hand.

The doctor stood and grasped it.

'Good luck, fellow Amunite. May the Eye of Ra watch over you,' he said.

'And may Reason be your guide,' the doctor answered.

'Go swiftly...'

The doctor walked from the drawing room through the study, past the pistol desk and out into the hallway leading to the entrance of the apartment. He tapped the tip of the cane on the floor as he went.

'Thank you, sir,' the doctor said as he retrieved his hat and coat.

'You are welcome,' Fouché replied.

As the doctor stepped out into the cold stairway, Fouché looked into his eyes. 'One final thing,' he said. 'If you ever divulge my identity, I will use that cane on you.'

'Of course, sir, I would never tell anyone.'

'And remember,' Fouché concluded, 'this meeting never happened.'

CHAPTER 21

———∽∼∽———

'We're lost without our horses,' Pryce sighed.

Pryce and the Abbé had reached Rennes the previous day and swapped their fast coach for horses at a safe house. They had spent the night in a cave on a rocky hill and then much of the next day riding on horseback along narrow country lanes and over Breton fields, avoiding the main roads. At sunset they were contemplating lighting a fire when an albino badger with pink eyes had come hurtling past them, followed by three howling bloodhounds. The horses had taken fright and bolted. Now Pryce and the Abbé were stranded in the heart of the forest.

'It's no good,' Pryce exclaimed. 'They've gone.'

Pryce started to gather some mushrooms in preparation for their supper. 'How will we get to Petit's house without the horses?'

'Let's wait a while,' the Abbé replied. 'The horses may return. It's been known.'

'But it's unlikely,' Pryce sighed.

'I have been in this situation twice before,' the Abbé said.

'And how did you get out of it?'

'The first time I was walking in the woods near Josselin and got lost. I simply prayed and the next thing I knew I heard this mysterious voice giving me directions. In no time at all I was back on track.'

'Our situation is a little different,' Pryce said.

'The second time I was riding from Dinan to the Chateau de Limoelan and I stopped to recite my breviary. I didn't have time to secure my horse before it ran away, leaving me in the middle of the forest.'

'What did you do?'

'I don't want to sound too pious about this but there was only one thing I could do and that was pray.'

'And did God answer?'

'It was strange. I was kneeling in the dirt with my eyes closed, imploring the Lord to return my horse, and I lost all sense of time. I don't know how long it was but when I opened my eyes, there he was.'

'Had it simply come back?'

'No, that was the funny thing. It was brought back to me by a complete stranger. When I mounted my unholy horse to continue my journey, I turned to say thank you to him but he had completely disappeared.'

'Sounds to me like an angel.'

'Indeed,' the Abbé said. 'Time to pray, I believe.'

The Abbé knelt on the grass and beckoned Pryce to come and join him. Pryce sank to his knees beside his friend and the two of them began to intercede, the Abbé holding his rosary, Pryce clasping his hands.

'You pray,' the Abbé exhorted.

'I don't remember there being a Collect for Lost Horses,' Pryce replied.

'Invent one.'

Pryce paused and then improvised. 'Almighty God, you have revealed through your Son in the parables that you have compassion on the lost. We beseech you to send your angels to find our horses and bring them back to us. As the lost sheep was restored to the shepherd, we pray that our lost horses will be restored to us, through Jesus Christ, our Lord, Amen.'

Pryce opened his left eye and conducted a quick scan to see if the horses had returned.

They had not.

He then closed his left eye and opened his right, to see if the Abbé was still praying.

He was.

Two hours later the light in the forest had descended to a murky grey – everywhere that is except the turf where they had prayed and where a small fire was now burning. Pryce turned from the flames and looked at his friend's ascetic face and melancholy eyes. 'You look so like my father-in-law,' Pryce said.

The Abbé smiled.

'Do you think he gave the wig maker information that will help us?' Pryce asked.

'I believe with all my heart he did. My brother was utterly devoted to Jean Marie. He would have moved heaven and earth to ensure that she was looked after. He was an adoring husband.'

'He was the best of men,' Pryce said.

'You loved him, didn't you?'

'Like I loved my father.'

'And he loved you like a son,' the Abbé said.

'When my own father was lost to the sea,' Pryce whispered, 'Michel Alain told me that he would stand in the gap. He said I was theirs now. "Adopted, like the sons of God", he said.'

'I am so sorry about what happened to your father,' the Abbé said. 'I can't imagine what it must have been like going through that.'

Pryce looked away and gazed once again at the dying flames.

'What happened exactly?'

Pryce was silent for a few moments. 'Mother and I were standing in the hall of our home in Broadstairs. Eloise and I were there for a week, taking rest from my parish duties in London. The Mayor and the Vicar arrived. My mother sensed immediately that something dreadful had happened.'

Pryce paused and looked from the fire to his friend. 'They said a freak wave – over sixty feet high - had hit my father's galley amidships and turned it right over. There was nothing those on board could have done. All hands lost, they said. All the bodies of the drowned men were retrieved except my father's.'

Pryce put his head in his hands. 'The mayor said that there was weeping on the streets. The Vicar said that there would be a big funeral and that the coffins would be carried through the York Gate from the sea to the church.'

Pryce's hands began to shake.

'What about your mother?'

'I ran to her and caught her, just in time. I held her head in my lap. My tears began to fall, slowly at first, then in a torrent. They splashed upon her face, causing her eyes to open with a look of surprise which turned to shock, then to confusion and finally to torment.'

Pryce pressed his lips to his pale fists.

'She shook her head from side to side, as if pleading with me to say, "They made a mistake; father is fine." But I could offer no such consolation. I knew he was gone. And I knew that there was nothing I could do – or ever do – to take that haunted look away.'

A piece of burning wood cracked, and then there was silence.

'I'm so sorry, Thomas, so desperately sorry.'

'Mother never recovered, you know? She died of a broken heart.'

Pryce paused.

'And all of a sudden I was an orphan.'

Pryce paused again.

'That day was the last time I shed tears.'

The Abbé stood, moved to Pryce, and sat next to him on the same stone, looking into the fire.

'Is that why you moved to a parish by the sea?' he asked.

'That was Dean Jackson's idea. He was my old Dean at Christ Church and he suggested that a mariner's church would be a better environment for my recuperation than the grimy streets of London.'

'Was he right?'

'I love the sea and I hate it,' Pryce answered. 'I hate it because it took my father, but I also love it because I feel closer to him there.'

'A contradiction, then,' the Abbé mused.

'Exactly.'

Pryce turned his shoulder and looked into his friend's eyes. 'You know, when I was crossing through the Goodwin Sands to come here, I thought I could hear my father call to me in the sound of the waves.'

Pryce turned back to the flames again. 'And I swore I heard my mother call my name in a seabird's cry.'

The Abbé presented a handkerchief.

'I don't need that, but thank you,' Pryce said.

'Are you sure?'

'I'm sure.'

'Do you not feel any grief over the death of your parents?'

'I feel nothing. That's the problem.'

'Really?'

'I'm as cold and hard as that menhir.' Pryce pointed to a rock twenty feet away. It was shaped like a huge finger, tapering towards the tip, and was lying on its side in thick and wild undergrowth.

'Did you feel nothing at the Place de la Révolution?'

'I felt the stirrings of rage, that's all.'

'Rage?'

'I wanted to do something, anything, to stop what I saw as a great injustice.'

'What specifically made you angry, Thomas?'

'Separation.'

'What do you mean?'

'I mean the enforced, cruel, unnatural separation of loved ones from each other. If I feel anything in my life, it's anger about that.'

'How strong do you feel it, Thomas?'

'Like this fire – more like glowing embers than a roaring flame.'

'What if the strong wind of the Spirit blew across these embers?'

'I do not know the answer to that question. The truth is I feel cold towards God. I feel cold towards my congregation. There are times when I even feel cold towards Eloise. It is as if two years ago I stared into the eyes of some great Medusa and my heart turned to stone.'

'That maybe true now,' the Abbé said, 'but you and I know that there is one who can turn a heart of stone into a heart of flesh. Perhaps this is just a season and perhaps this is what you need to survive.'

'Perhaps.'

The Abbé stood, placed his hand gently on Pryce's shoulder.

'You know why men like me are called by the name "Abbé"?'

'I have never considered it.'

'It comes from the Aramaic word that Jesus used when he prayed to God.'

Pryce looked quizzically at his friend.

'Abba, in the mother tongue of our Lord, meant "Papa".'

'So?'

'So those of us who are Abbés are called to represent the one called "Abba".'

'I don't see how that helps.'

Pryce raised his head and looked into the Abbé's eyes.

'Thomas, while your earthly father may have gone, there is always our Father in Heaven. He is, as King David said, a Father to the fatherless.'

A strong wind blew across the fire, causing the dying flames to rise for a moment and reach towards the sky.

'My true calling is not to fight against the Republican army but to tell you and others that even though our earthly fathers leave us and die, there is a Father who will never forsake us and who lives for evermore.'

The Abbé pressed down on Pryce's shoulder and for a moment he felt as if a warm and healing wind was spreading through the secret chambers of his heart.

'Thank you,' Pryce said.

'You're welcome,' the Abbé replied as he returned to his mossy tree stump to add fresh kindling to the fire.

Just as he sat down, both men heard it. It was the sound of an owl hooting, and very close. The Abbé put his finger to his lips and quickly doused the fire with a few handfuls of dirt. The two men froze. They heard the sound of rustling branches and snapping twigs about thirty feet away. Pryce could just make a figure before a larger shadow seemed to fall upon them under the blue light of the moon. Then the feet began to move again, less of them this time, loud at first and then softer as they moved away.

Silence returned.

There was the sound of an owl hooting once again, but this time far away.

Pryce and the Abbé kept still. They stayed motionless for what seemed like an eternity until the Abbé whispered.

'Thomas, did you hear that?'

'Hear what?'

'It was like someone shaking their head.'

'I thought it was you.'

'No, it wasn't.'

The Abbé lit a match.

'Be careful,' Pryce urged.

'I will.'

The Abbé ignited a small lantern and pointed it away from his body.

And then Pryce saw them.

There, tied by their reins to the sagging bough of a nearby tree, were the horses. They were all saddled up as they had been when they cantered off and the unopened bags were still strapped to their flanks.

'Oh my,' Pryce exclaimed. 'Angels have returned our horses.'

'Yes, indeed,' the Abbé replied, 'though I suspect they were clothed in grey, not white.'

CHAPTER 22

The doctor smelt London before he saw it. He had lost count of the hours he had spent trying to find a comfortable position in the diligence from Dover. The only times his rump had been relieved were the brief stops at the turnpikes and the longer breaks at the inns along the way. Now, although he was keen to stretch his legs, the increasing stench of sewage, horse's dung and butcher's offal had weakened his longing to alight.

As Vacher peered out of the window with a scented handkerchief over his nose, he marvelled at the houses, some of whose upper stories were jutting out into the road so far it seemed that they would meet in the middle, like leaning lovers. He gazed at glass-fronted shops, their windows crammed with merchandise – everything from linen and ornaments to brandy and tobacco.

Above it all loomed the unmistakable form of Saint Paul's Cathedral, its massive dome ruling over a skyline stained by coal smoke and soot-filled rain. Under its shadow, the doctor's face froze somewhere between wonder and scorn.

As the carriage drew nearer to Piccadilly, the streets became more and more frantic with the commotion of vendors trading, tinkers shouting, beggars pleading and prostitutes soliciting.

There was only one other person in the carriage, a portly English gentleman sitting on the other side of the vehicle, who was taking some snuff. As the carriage proceeded through the streets, he began to recite some verse between sneezes:

'Many a beau without a shilling,
Many a widow not unwilling;
Many a bargain if you strike it:
This is London! How d'ye like it?'

The doctor looked at servants running on their errands, squires swaggering along the streets, bankers bragging about the price of gold and footmen hailing new fangled carriages for the wealthy, and he decided, 'I don't like it. I don't like it all.'

The carriage came to a halt at the coach station in Piccadilly and the doctor hurried to a row of Hackney carriages nearby, their coachmen perched and ready.

'To the Crown and Anchor in the Strand,' the doctor said to the first one.

Within seconds, the doctor's rump was bouncing once again as the carriage rattled over ruts and bumps to the relentless clatter of wheels and hooves. He gazed enviously at passengers in more comfortable conveyances - the hooded gigs and buggies, and especially the sedan chairs, which were being carried along the sidewalks rather than the roads.

Everywhere he looked, the doctor could see coffee houses, inns and churches.

'We're approaching the Strand,' the driver called.

The last of the late afternoon light had now all but gone. Street lights – vast numbers of them - were coming on everywhere.

'Best lit city in Europe,' the driver shouted.

'And the least enlightened,' the doctor muttered.

As the coach neared its destination, the environment changed. The vulgar air had gone. There were establishments advertising finer goods – like Thomas Chippendale's furniture – and shops selling books and chic clothes. There were art exhibitions and theatres, taverns and up-market coffee shops everywhere.

'Berkeley Square, nearly there,' the coachman sang.

The next moment the cab slowed down and came to a halt. The doctor breathed a sigh of relief. He paid the driver and took his bag. As he turned round from the departing Hackney, he saw the tavern sign swinging above him in the wind. 'Crown and Anchor,' it read.

The Crown and Anchor was a far larger tavern than the doctor had imagined. It was nothing like the much smaller inns he had visited on his way to the great metropolis. It was four stories high and it stretched the length of an entire block, from Arundel Street to Milford Lane. The symmetry of the façade was simple yet impressive. There were seven windows on each floor, all of them impeccably aligned. The ground floor windows, unlike all the others, were arched and surrounded by rusticated stonework. The rest were square and set in pilasters.

The doctor walked through the main entrance facing Arundel Street and entered a spacious foyer which was illuminated by a huge lantern hanging overhead. He tapped the tip of his walking cane on the stone paved floor as he proceeded with his bag to a desk.

'Monsieur Marat, room 19, first floor,' said the concierge, handing him his key.

A porter took the bag and they walked past the dining room. As the doctor glanced through its doors he could see that it had chandeliers and carved cornices, panelled walls and floral festoons cascading down them. There was room, he estimated, for at least 500 guests to eat there.

The doctor followed the man up a carpeted stone staircase flanked by ornamental iron rails. They arrived at the first floor and the porter opened a door to one of the rooms. As a lamp was lit, it illuminated a well-appointed bedroom with a four-poster bed piled so high with feather mattresses that a short set of wooden steps had been placed next to it. Around the bed there stood a mahogany bureau and desk chair, a recently upholstered armchair, and off to the right a cupboard with a wash basin, next to one of the two tall and curtained windows.

'Thank you,' the doctor said, as he tipped the porter. 'This will do nicely.'

The man tapped his cap, the door closed and the doctor threw himself wearily into the armchair.

As shadows cast from the wax candles began to dance upon the walls, he remembered what Fouché had told him.

'You will use the Crown and Anchor as your base. It is an ideal location for acquiring intelligence. On the surface it appears to be a centre for the dissemination of knowledge. Its commodious halls host regular lectures and concerts. Coleridge has recited his poems there and Handel has conducted several of his compositions in the Great Assembly Room. But underneath the surface, the tavern is a snake pit - seething with secrecy and sedition.'

At this, Fouché's eyes had opened wide and half a smile had forced its way across the stretched skin on one side of his sallow jowls. 'A Masonic lodge meets there regularly,' he had added, 'and on one notorious occasion, just over twenty years ago, it admitted a French transvestite called the Knight of Eon as a member.'

The doctor had frowned at this.

'Most important of all, in the rooms of this vast tavern, groups regularly gather to plan the overthrow of the monarchy and the establishment of a British Republic, and sometimes quite openly parade their rebellion.'

'How?' the doctor had asked.

'Two years ago, over one thousand Englishmen filled the dining hall to the point of overflowing in order to celebrate the storming of the Bastille.'

The doctor had gasped.

'Yes, my friend,' Fouché had concluded, 'the Crown and Anchor is a place of occult rites and rebellious intrigue and its portals are regarded by conservatives as the gates of hell itself. It is the perfect place for a man of your... how shall I put it... your sentiments.'

The doctor smiled and walked towards the left hand window of his bedroom. Turning the handle, he walked outside onto an iron balcony and watched the people below.

A young girl was trying to sell oranges and apples to what looked like a group of laughing lawyers. A boy who could have been her brother was trying to sell nuts of all descriptions to them. Neither of them was having any joy.

Feeling the chill, the doctor closed the windows and unpacked his bag. He was about to draw the blade from his cane and practice his swordsmanship when he heard the sound of a sequence of familiar knocks - three loud, two soft.

The doctor opened the door. 'Do you have something for me?' he asked.

The man, who was taller and leaner than he, unbuttoned the

front of his shirt and showed a golden passkey hanging from a chain around his neck. It was exactly the same as the doctor's key, which he now also revealed.

'May the Eye of Ra watch over you,' the doctor said.

'And Reason be your guide,' the man replied.

'Enter,' the doctor whispered.

The doctor ushered the man into his chamber and bid him sit in the armchair. The doctor sat behind the bureau.

'I'm here as Monsieur Marat,' the doctor said, 'a member of the French delegation in London.'

'My name,' the stranger said, 'is Titus Morgues. I am responsible for the committee of surveillance - a network of French agents who are watching the movements and activities of former citizens of France who have emigrated here. Many of them are plotting to destroy the Republic and restore the monarchy in our beloved country. We are committed to preventing them.'

'Who are you watching right now?'

'Mainly former French aristocrats and bishops,' Morgues said.

'Give me some names.'

'Currently our agents are keeping an eye on the Count of Artois, the Duke and Duchess of Aguillon, the Count of Narbonne, and the Bishops of Angoulême, Saint-Pol-de-Léon, and Coutances.'

'What progress are you making?'

'You would think it would be easy enough to conduct our business without attention in a city of nearly one million people,' Morgues replied, 'but the task has been made a great deal harder in recent months.'

'Why?'

'First of all, because an Alien Office has been set up under William Wickham and there are magistrates everywhere checking on the real identity and purpose of every French citizen in this country.' Morgues paused and looked into the doctor's eyes.

'And secondly,' he said, 'William Pitt has managed to persuade the government to abolish *Habeas Corpus* for all foreigners in England.'

'What does that mean?'

'It means that any French citizen in Britain can be arrested and imprisoned without trial for a limitless period of time, if they are deemed to be suspicious.'

The doctor scowled. 'So much for the Englishman's respect for people's freedoms,' he said. 'What are my orders?' he asked.

'Your orders are to come with me to the dining room and have some dinner,' Morgues replied.

The doctor nodded.

An hour later, the two men were seated in the vast dining hall, close to a marble fireplace where a fire was roaring in the cast iron grate.

'Pah! Rosbif!' the doctor spat. 'Defoe was right, the English consume more flesh than half of Europe.'

'This is baked leg of beef in gravy,' Morgues replied, adding, 'one of Mister Collingwood's disgusting recipes. The chefs of this nation would perform a great mercy if they could just learn to cook some sauces.'

'This ale is no substitute for a good bottle of Bordeaux either,' the doctor replied, wincing as he sipped from his tankard. 'It tastes like horse piss.'

'I would recommend you avoid the coffee,' Morgues remarked. 'It is little more than tepid water.'

The doctor sighed. 'Tell me,' he said, 'how am I to proceed?'

Morgues leant forward. 'We have a man working at Saint James' Palace. He is an Irish rebel masquerading as an English royalist. He gives us vital information on the movements of the nation's principal leaders, including the Prime Minister and the King. He is also a visitor to the meetings of the secret societies which meet in this very building.'

'Do I get to meet him?'

'Sooner than you think,' Morgues replied, looking over the doctor's shoulder.

As the doctor turned, he saw a stocky man walking towards them dressed for dinner. He came to the table and sat down at one of the two free chairs.

'Let me introduce you,' Morgues said. 'Richard Moore, this is Monsieur Marat.'

'Very pleased to make your acquaintance,' Moore said, reaching out his hand.

'Likewise,' the doctor replied.

'What news?' Morgues asked.

'There's a meeting of the Friends of the People in an hour in the Great Assembly Room. The man you want will be there.'

'Friends of the People?' the doctor asked.

'Ostensibly they are a group committed to parliamentary reform,' Morgues replied, 'but in truth they are a secret society dedicated to changing the British constitution and establishing a Republic in this country.'

'Listen,' Moore said, 'this meeting is likely to be very well attended, and even though I have tickets for all of us, we should probably get to our seats.'

'I'm done with this pathetic excuse for a meal anyway,' the doctor said.

The three men left the dining hall and proceeded up two flights of stairs, until they arrived at the second-floor lobby, which was lit by a seven-foot lantern. The doctor led with his walking cane and pushed his way through a growing crowd of milling and expectant men to the entrance to the Great Assembly Room. He had heard about its size, that it was almost 3000 square feet and capable of hosting 2000 people. But when he saw it, it seemed unimaginably vast.

'Is this the largest hall in London?'

'One of them,' Moore replied.

The three men took their assigned seats.

'This is going to be packed,' Moore whispered. 'It's the first gathering of the Friends since the King's execution.'

'Yes, and the topic of the evening's debate is an interesting one,' said Morgues.

'What is it?' the doctor asked.

'The Assembling of a Convention for all England.'

As the room continued to fill, Morgues tugged at the doctor's arm. 'See him?' Morgues was pointing discretely to a man dressed as a Republican.

The doctor donned his spectacles and nodded.

'His name is Sennett. He is a British agent, sent by Wickham to infiltrate the societies.'

The doctor frowned.

As he did, the room fell quiet.

In the silence, the doctor could hear the sound of heavy boots coming from behind him. He looked round. The chamber was completely full and there were many people standing at the back, crammed into the hall outside, even lining the edges of the top of the staircase.

As the sound of the approaching boots grew louder, the doctor heard the first strains of a familiar song.

Ah! It'll be fine, it'll be fine, it'll be fine
Aristocrats to the lamppost
Ah! It'll be fine, it'll be fine, it'll be fine
The aristocrats, we'll hang them!

The doctor's mouth opened in surprise. He nudged Morgues. 'It's an English translation of Ça Ira, the song we sing in the Jacobin clubs.'

Morgues smiled and nodded.

If we don't hang them, we'll break them
If we don't break them, we'll burn them!

The sound of the singing – which had gripped almost everyone – was now accompanied with the beat of sticks and boots upon the floor.

We have no more nobles, nor priests
Ah! It'll be fine, it'll be fine, it'll be fine
Equality will reign everywhere
Ah! It'll be fine, it'll be fine, it'll be fine
Aristocrats to the lamppost
And their infernal clique shall go to hell

The doctor smiled. He nudged Morgues again. 'It will be fine,' he whispered, 'when there is a guillotine in Hyde Park and English crowds are singing the Marseillaise.'

And when we'll have hung them all
We'll shove a shovel up their ....

As the song reached its crescendo, the men in the entrance to the Assembly Room began to part and the singing came to an abrupt end. Into the hall marched seven men. But it wasn't the six who were following that interested the doctor. It was the man leading them – a man with an obvious, aristocratic bearing.

'Lord Charles Stanhope,' Morgues whispered.

And as he did, the doctor's right hand – which was still grasping the top of his cane – began to twitch.

CHAPTER 23

'Leave the horses here,' the Abbé said. 'We need to walk the rest of the way.'

Pryce and the Abbé were just outside the village where Petit the wigmaker lived. The sun had set several hours ago and the two men were now stealthily striding towards the wigmaker's shop. The Abbé led the way down a gravel covered road and Pryce followed close behind him, keeping a watchful eye out for Republican guards and local gendarmes, trying to make his footsteps as quiet as he could.

'It's round the corner,' the Abbé whispered.

Pryce's heart was beating faster. By now they were one hundred feet from the building. Even in the poor light afforded by the moon, Pryce could make out the words on the sign outside. 'PETIT: WIGMAKER.'

As they drew near, Pryce could see lights on in the house. It was occupied. He peered through a window that had only recently been cleaned, crouching just below the sill. The shop was still open. There were four men inside. One man, evidently a customer, was sitting back in what looked like a barber's chair. He was being shaved by a young man, in preparation for a wig fitting. Another young man, most probably an assistant like the barber, was trimming the hair on a wig that had been placed on an oval piece of wood. This was connected to the top of a five foot pole that had been thrust into a cross shaped base on the floor. The man was fastening tresses to the hair. A third assistant was by an open fire in the middle of the back wall on the far side of the shop. Pryce could see that he was no more than a boy. There were tools on a table next to him and he was heating an iron in the fire. No sooner had it begun to glow than he used it on a wig to make its hair curl.

Everywhere Pryce looked, there were wigs hanging on the walls. They were nothing like the ones he had seen in the days before the Revolution. None of them was excessively tall or intricately sculpted, like the ones worn by the aristocrats of the ancient regime. These wigs were modest in comparison – simple and yet elegantly made.

As he gazed with fascination at the man working at the wig on the stand, an older man with long white whiskers entered through a door in the far right corner of the room. He inspected the wig and nodded his approval. The assistant carried the wig over to the man reclining on the barber's chair who nodded.

The next moment the wig was on his head being carefully fitted and the man with the whiskers had gone back into the side room.

'Quick!' Pryce whispered to the Abbé.

He tugged gently on his friend's cape and the two men ducked and weaved their way from the front to the right hand side of the shop. There was a white painted door there. Pryce knocked softly. He heard someone dragging a wooden chair on a stone paved floor. And then there he was - the whiskered wig maker.

'What can I do for you?' he said.

'We'd like to ask you a few questions,' Pryce replied.

'I am about to close my shop. Can it wait?'

'No,' the Abbé replied. 'It is a matter of some urgency.'

'All right, but make it quick.'

The three men walked into the room – a humble kitchen - and sat at a table.

'This is a delicate matter,' the Abbé said. 'I am the younger brother of Michel Alain Picot de Limoelan and this man is a friend of the Picot family.'

'No,' the man exclaimed. 'Not you Picots again!'

'What do you mean?' Pryce asked.

'You Picots landed me in all kinds of trouble.'

'How?'

'I went to your Chateau at the end of January in order to fit a wig for Monsieur Picot. But no sooner had I arrived, I realized I'd walked into a rattrap. There were soldiers everywhere and the agents in charge assumed I was one of the Chouans like the rest of them. I was slapped in irons and the next thing I knew I was in the Tower in Paris. I thought I was done for. So you can understand why I'm not exactly overjoyed to make your acquaintance.'

'I'm sorry,' Pryce said. 'But listen. We have to ask you a vital question. We know that you shared a cell with Monsieur Picot in the prison at Rennes, before you were transported to Paris.'

'So what if I did?'

'Did he give anything to you while you were on your own together in the cell?'

The wigmaker gazed at the two priests, cautiously first and then nervously. 'How do I know you're not Republican agents trying to trick me? They're everywhere now. I don't even trust my horse.'

'We're not,' the Abbé said calmly.

'But how do I know? I don't want to end up in front of that Tribunal again. That Public Prosecutor was terrifying. His eyes were like a demon's!' The man crossed himself. 'No, I'm not saying anything,' he insisted. 'My mouth is going to remain shut.'

'Monsieur Petit,' the Abbé protested, 'lives could be saved if you help us.'

The man sat with folded arms and a defiant and petulant look on his face.

'How's business at the moment?' Pryce asked.

'What's that got to do with anything?' Petit replied.

'How many customers are you getting these days, now that you've been in prison and on trial?'

The man looked wistful. 'Not as many,' he said, 'nothing like as many.'

'So you're down on your luck and you're out of pocket.'

'I'm going to have to lay off some of my workers.'

'So this might come in handy, then.'

Pryce reached into his pocket and produced a small, gold bar that gleamed in the lamplight of the kitchen. The wigmaker's eyes grew wide. 'Is that… is that gold?'

'It is. If you tell us what we want, then I will leave this on the table and we will be on our way.'

'What's it worth?'

'It could keep you in business for a long time.'

The man hesitated for a moment.

'Come now,' Pryce said, 'if we were working for the Republic then the one thing we would not be offering you is gold.'

The man reached for the shiny bar. But he was too slow. Pryce anticipated the move and had closed his hand into a fist, gripping and hiding the priceless metal in the centre of his palm.

'I'll give you the gold if you give us the information,' Pryce said.

The man sat back in his chair. 'Very well,' he replied.

He stood up and walked over to a shelf and reached for a wicker bread basket. He brought it to the table and removed a half eaten loaf of bread and then a layer of white linen. As he did, both Pryce and the Abbé saw it – a piece of dirty, creased paper with hand writing on it. It was a letter.

The man made to pass it to Pryce. 'Here,' he said, drawing the letter back to his chest. 'You promised me the gold if I give you my letter. You look like priests, both of you. Keep your word.'

'And so we will,' Pryce replied.

Pryce took the miniature bullion from the palm of his hand and gave it to the wigmaker, who snatched it greedily and held it up towards the light of the lantern hanging from the ceiling.

'Looks real enough to me,' he said.

'It is,' Pryce replied. 'Hand over the paper, Monsieur Petit.'

'I've read it,' the wigmaker said. 'If you ask me, it's just the pious ramblings of a man who knows that he's not long for this world. It won't tell you anything.'

'We'll see,' Pryce said.

He smoothed out the folded paper and began to read out loud the words scribbled in ink.

My beloved family,

If you are reading this, the chances are I have been condemned.

In that case, I have some final words of counsel for you.

Take heed of what I write.

Do not seek what you long for in the tents of the wicked, but search for it in the House of the Lord.

Look up to our Lady and take hold of her hand.

Let her Rosary be your guide and let the Cross be the key to salvation.

I pray with all of my heart that you will find the Rock on which the church is built and the treasure hidden in the secret place.

Everything depends on it.

For where your heart is, there your treasure is also.

So God bless you.

I love you forever.

'That's beautiful but it doesn't help us,' the Abbé said.

He took the letter from Pryce and held it close to his face, inspecting every letter of every word.

'It's definitely my brother's handwriting,' he added.

The Abbé took a candle from the kitchen table and held the letter at various angles beneath the searching light of its flickering flame. 'There don't appear to be any words written in invisible ink,' he said. 'He didn't have anything like that in the prison cell,' the wigmaker said. 'He just had paper and an ink pen and a couple of old books he'd asked for, including a breviary which he read morning and evening.'

Pryce took the letter and stood to his feet. 'You have been very kind, Monsieur Petit, and we are both very grateful to you. It's time for us to go.'

The Abbé looked surprised but then rose from the table. He blessed the wigmaker, who seemed grateful, and then followed Pryce out of the kitchen into the night.

'What are you doing?' the Abbé whispered. 'We needed more information. We know nothing more than we knew before. That letter hasn't helped us in the slightest.'

'You're wrong, my friend,' Pryce replied.

'What do you mean?'

'That letter tells us everything we need to know.'

'Please explain.'

'It's written in code.'

'Are you serious? It's just a valedictory letter.'

'No, my friend, it's more than that.'

The two men returned to their horses and mounted them. They galloped to the woods before dismounting at a cave. They lit a fire and huddled together eating stale biscuits and drinking the remains of a flask of wine.

'Tell me what you saw in the letter,' the Abbé said.

Pryce took the paper from his pocket. 'It was the mention of the Rock,' Pryce said.

Lifting the letter close to his eyes, he read.

'*I pray with all of my heart that you will find the Rock on which the church is built and the treasure hidden in the secret place.*'

'But those are just phrases taken out of the Scriptures,' the Abbé cried.

'Yes, but they are more. Do you recall Jean Marie's maiden name, the name she had before Picot?'

'Remind me.'

'She was called Jean Marie La Roche.'

'Jean Marie the Rock!' the Abbé cried.

'And notice what your brother added, 'the Rock on which the church is built.' As a Catholic you would think of Saint Peter, the rock. But here, perhaps, my Protestant eyes were an advantage to me. I saw it as a reference to a church building, to the Rosary Chapel.'

'My God,' the Abbé said. 'My brother was referring to a place beneath the Rosary chapel – a chamber in which Jean Marie Rock, his greatest treasure, is to be found.'

'Precisely,' Pryce replied, 'and there's more. He's telling us how to access that chamber.'

'The statue of Our Lady!' the Abbé cried.

'Indeed,' Pryce said. 'The answer lies in the hands of the Mother of our Lord.'

'As it always does,' the Abbé said.

'I have to concede that in this instance the key to salvation is in her hands.'

'You mean the key that will rescue Jean Marie?'

'And Joseph Pierre, if they are both still there,' Pryce added.

Pryce put the letter back into his pocket.

'You are a very resourceful man for a Church of England Vicar,' the Abbé laughed.

Pryce smiled at the Abbé.

'I was very fortunate that my grandfather left money in a trust for me to go to Christ Church Oxford. If it hadn't have been for that, I doubt whether I would have ever had the resources I have today.'

'Speaking of resources,' the Abbé said, pulling Pryce's sleeve. 'Where on earth did you get that gold from?'

Pryce smiled and tapped his nose. 'I received it from an English angel in a castle far away beside the sea.'

CHAPTER 24

Jean Marie woke from a disturbed sleep in the chamber beneath the Rosary Chapel. She groped in the darkness for a match at her bedside table and struck it. Locating the candle in the brief flare of light, she ignited the wick, lifted the candle and looked to her right where her son Joseph was sleeping in a bed adjacent to hers. He was snoring loudly.

'You could sleep on the back of a horse in a thunderstorm, my son,' she whispered.

She took the eiderdown from her bed and draped it over Joseph. Then she slipped into her shoes and tiptoed across the stone floor as quietly as she could, holding her candle as she went. She took her son's pocket watch which he had left on a plain, rustic dresser and checked the time. It read three o'clock.

She put on her clothes and thrust the family pistol in her belt. She then opened the door of an old cupboard that was doubling up as a wardrobe. There was barely any food left - just some dry, crusty bread, the remains of a block of cheese, some stale biscuits and some wine.

Jean Marie put her husband's short grey jacket over her shoulders and walked softly to the entrance of the chamber with her candle in hand. She pulled the keys from a pocket in her breeches and turned one of them in the lock. With strong hands she pushed the door gently and left with barely a sound.

Once in the subterranean corridor, Jean Marie was greeted by the smell of wet stone and damp wood. The wooden pipes built to connect the house's water supply to the chamber had deteriorated so badly that they were now useless.

They needed food and water and they needed it now.

Jean Marie reached the second door that led into the study. She was about to put the key in the lock when an instinct gripped her. Her husband had been prudent and placed an observer's platform behind a portrait of her father which hung on one of the walls of the bureau. She climbed up onto the small wooden stage in the secret passage behind the painting. Using a tiny sliding mechanism, she was able to remove the eyes in the painting and place her own in the spaces left. Now she was looking through her father's eyes.

As she scrutinized the study, she saw nothing untoward at first. It was clearly the afternoon and the sun was pouring through the windows. Everything looked exactly the same as before. There was no one in the room and the furniture seemed to have been untouched. It was only as she stared beyond the room that she began to notice something in the grounds of the chateau. Through the windows on the opposite side of the study she could sense movement on the lawn.

She could make out uniforms – dark blue jackets with red fringed epaulettes, white breeches and stockings with black shoes – and black bearskin hats with plumes in red, white and blue.

Black bearskins!

That meant Grenadiers!

Jean Marie was startled.

Why were they here?

There had to be a good reason. Her father had been an army officer and so she knew that these were no ordinary soldiers. Originally established as a regiment of grenade throwers, they had developed into a crack regiment of elite assault troops. Their height, accentuated by their tall fur hats with their glinting silver plates, made them front line and first rate troops.

As Jean Marie watched, she could see that some of the soldiers were practicing a bayonet drill with a dummy made out of a sack and some straw. They were thrusting their muskets into the hessian with choreographed precision.

Others were engaged in shooting practice, firing their muskets at large round melons perched on a garden wall, hooting with delight whenever one was hit, its red and green flesh flying into the air in wet fragments.

Just then, Jean Marie turned round.

'Mother,' Joseph whispered. 'What are you doing?'

'I was trying to fetch some food and water,' she said. 'But the house has been occupied by a company of Grenadiers.'

'Grenadiers! Are you sure?'

Jean Marie stepped down from the platform and watched her son as he leapt up as deftly as a wolf.

After several moments, he descended from the staging, his face sombre and his voice grave. 'Troops like this should not be here in Brittany. They should be fighting the British, the Dutch or the Austrians. Why are they based at our chateau?'

'I imagine it's because Danton has had his fill of the Chouan army and they're now scared.'

'Scared of what, mother?'

'They're scared of a royalist army from Jersey joining up with the Chouan's in Brittany.'

Joseph smiled. 'You may be right, mother.'

'How many troops do you think are stationed here?' Jean Marie asked.

'I counted about seventy out the front so I am guessing there are over a hundred in the house and grounds.'

'They could do awful damage to the resistance,' Jean Marie sighed.

'Indeed, mother. Fighting the National Guardsmen is one thing. They are easy picking. Fighting Grenadiers is altogether a different proposition. They are courageous and skillful soldiers.'

'We must warn our friends. They are in grave danger,' Jean Marie whispered.

'Graver than you think,' Joseph replied. 'Did you see them?' he added.

'See what?'

'The three cannons standing in the shade of the pine trees, just beyond the stream?'

'They have artillery?'

151

'Yes, mama, and if that is used against our friends it will cause a massacre.'

Jean Marie held her son by the arms. 'Joseph, you need to help me get some food and water and then you need to get the message to...'

She was about to continue but she froze. There was the sound of voices the other side of the painting. Jean Marie climbed back on to the stage. She slid open the eye slits. There were three men in the study. Two were behind the desk, one sitting and the other standing. They were dressed as citizens. In front of them was a captain of the Grenadiers, his officer's sabre hanging from his belt.

'What are my orders, Citizen Masson?' the captain asked the seated man.

'Your orders are to keep your men in the greatest state of readiness,' he replied. 'Citizen Danton wants you here to quell the Chouan resistance and prevent a royalist army invading from Jersey.'

'Is there anything else, Citizen Masson?' the officer asked.

'Yes, I want you to hunt down and arrest Madame Picot. This used to be her home and she may try to return. If she does, she will be in for a great surprise.'

Jean Marie trembled as the man mentioned her name.

'Why is she important?' the officer asked.

'Citizen Danton is eager to finish the job that Doctor Vacher began when he arrested the Chouan suspects at the Chateau de la Fosse Hingants.'

Jean Marie reached down to her waist and tightly grasped the butt of her pistol.

'Half of them were executed,' the soldier said.

'Yes, but there were some who managed to escape the holy guillotine,' Masson replied, standing to his feet and pushing past his assistant to the window.

Staring out at the men under his command he smiled before turning back to the captain. 'Madame Picot's head must roll at the Place de la Revolution,' he said, 'just as her husband's did.'

Jean Marie thrust her hand over her mouth and whispering her husband's name as she fainted. 'Michel!'

A moment later, she was in her son's arms. He had broken her fall and was wiping the tears from her eyes and her face. 'Your father has been executed,' she stammered quietly.

'Those animals will pay!' he said.

'Michel!' Jean Marie whispered again. 'My poor, Michel, what did they do to you?'

Joseph quickly stepped up to the platform and listened to the conversation taking place in the study. He stood there for several minutes before crouching next to Jean Marie and holding her again. 'Mother, I know the man in father's study. He is called Masson. He was responsible for papa's arrest, along with that dog Vacher.'

'Then he must pay,' Jean Marie whispered, fury lining her face.

She rose to her feet and hurriedly climbed the platform behind the painting.

Taking the pistol from her belt she cocked it and made to push its barrel through one of the eye holes.

'No, mama,' Joseph whispered, taking her arm and forcing the weapon from her hand. 'That is not the way. And in any case you will not get a clear shot.'

Jean Marie looked furiously at her son as he reset the cocking mechanism of the pistol and tucked it into the back of his breeches. She was about to speak angrily to him when she was aware of more voices.

'What is it, mother?' Joseph asked as she peered through the eyeholes of the picture.

Jean Marie beckoned with her left hand for him to be quiet. In the study, the officer had now been replaced by another man – an older man with grey whiskers. He had a red bonnet in his hand and was standing before Masson who was still seated at the bureau.

'And what are you doing here?' Masson asked. 'I thought after the trial we had seen the last of you.'

'I thought you should know,' the man said. 'Last night I was visited by two men who looked like priests, one of whom was the brother of Michel Alain Picot.'

Masson stood abruptly to his feet. 'You're sure?'

'Yes, I am very sure.'

'What did they want?'

'They wanted a letter that Mister Picot wrote to his family while he was with me at Rennes prison.'

'Why did you not tell us of the letter before?'

'I considered it unimportant. I read it, you know. It was just a string of religious words about how he wanted them all to look to Our Lady and seek salvation in the house of the Lord.'

'How do you know there wasn't a message in sympathetic ink?' Masson asked.

'Because they studied it and they couldn't find anything. They looked quite disappointed.'

'So why are you telling us this?'

'I don't want to get into any further trouble,' the man said. 'I'm just a wigmaker and business is very slow at the moment.'

Masson reached into his waist coat pocket and drew out a silver coin. 'You have done the right thing,' he said, handing it to him.

'Thank you, sir,' the wigmaker said as he bowed and left the study.

'This is good news,' Masson said to the man beside him. 'It means that the Abbé de la Cloriviere and the English priest are looking for Madame Picot. With a bit of fortune, we will catch all three of them.'

The two men left the room.

Jean Marie stepped down from the wooden platform.

'Your uncle and an English priest are looking for us,' she said to Joseph.

'The Abbé is a resourceful and clever man,' Joseph answered. 'He will find us.'

Jean Marie took hold of Joseph's shirt collars and peered into his eyes.

'I will not rest,' she hissed, 'until Masson is dead.'

CHAPTER 25

Pryce was the first to see the checkpoint half a mile ahead. 'Quick!' he whispered to the Abbé.

The two priests turned their horses into the woods and hid amongst a clump of trees.

'What is it, Thomas?'

'There are soldiers.'

'Are you sure?'

'Yes, absolutely. They aren't National Guardsmen either. They look like infantry of the line.'

'What are they doing here?'

'I don't know, but we have to get past them if we want to get to the chapel.'

'We need a miracle,' the Abbé said in a whisper.

The two men rode away from the blue coated sentinels - along the edge of the road, in and out of bushes, trees and ditches, away from the chateau.

'Here, we should be safe in this grotto,' Pryce said.

Pryce knew the lie of the land like the back of his hand. He had spent every summer as a child at the Chateau de Limoelan. He and Eloise had played in the woods and the fields where she had taught him how to shoot and fence. As an only child, Pryce had loved these hazy summers in the grounds and the estate of the moss-wreathed mansion. His parents were the Picots' closest friends and it seemed like nothing would ever spoil those idyllic days. But something had. The shadow of death had fallen on the Pryce's family, with the drowning of his father and the subsequent collapse and death of his mother.

Pryce looked at the Abbé who had dismounted and was kneeling in the soil, holding his Rosary lightly in one hand and clutching his breviary tightly in the other. No sooner had the Abbé finished praying than both men heard the sound of a cart being drawn slowly along the road towards the chateau. They peered through some branches. Two men were sitting on a driver's seat behind the tallest and stoutest pack horses Pryce had ever seen. Behind them was a covered cart.

Pryce did not hesitate. He summoned to the Abbé and the two men, who had both now dismounted, walked out in front of the vehicle.

'Whoa!' one of the men shouted, pulling on the reins of the horses, which stopped just shy of the two priests.

'What's the matter?'

'We need to borrow your cart and horses,' Pryce said, seasoning his French with some Breton salt.

The first man, whose lips were almost completely covered by a black moustache that draped over them like a curtain, uttered a deep belly laugh.

'I don't think so,' he said.

'We're stonemasons on a specially commissioned job,' the other insisted.

'What job is that?' Pryce enquired.

'We're heading to the Rosary Chapel to strip it of all its gold, silver, statues, bells, crosses and anything else of value.'

Pryce ruefully suspected they were telling the truth. The Revolution had dealt a bloody blow to the Catholic Church throughout France. Much of its land had been confiscated, its priests forced to swear fidelity to the new order, and its historic faith replaced by the veneration of the goddess of Reason. This simmering, satanic cauldron had come to an inevitable boil just eight months ago, on September 2nd '92, when a salivating mob had seized and slaughtered three bishops and two hundred priests in Paris.

'And you approve of this task?' the Abbé asked.

The two men looked at each other surprised. 'Are you... are you...

the Abbé de la Clorivière?' the man with the moustache asked.

'I am.'

The two men removed their red bonnets and bowed. 'Abbé,' they said reverently.

'Do you know him?' Pryce asked.

'We heard him preach the finest sermon ever heard in these parts.'

'It's true,' the other man said stoically, 'he preached to two thousand of us in the parish church here in Sévignac and warned of the things to come.'

'Including stripping churches of their sacred furniture?' Pryce enquired.

The stonemasons glanced at each other before the man with the thick black whiskers spoke. 'Look, we'd like to help, but we'll get into trouble if the job doesn't get done.'

'And we'll lose the pay,' the other man said, 'and we have families to feed.'

'Let me make you a proposition,' Pryce said. 'If you give us your clothes, your papers and your cart, we will do the job for you – properly, mind – and we'll return the cart, fully laden, to this grotto here at sundown tonight and you can return our clothes and our horses to us.'

'I don't know,' the two men said. 'Pretending to be two priests is dangerous. As much as we respect the Abbé here you're asking too much.'

'But I haven't finished my proposition,' Pryce said.

He reached into the secret pocket of his cassock and pulled out the remaining two bars of gold and held them in the palms of both hands.

The two men jolted and their horses snorted.

'If you agree to our terms,' Pryce said, 'these will be yours tonight.'

'Agreed,' the two men said without hesitation.

The stonemasons led the horses and cart into the grotto. The four exchanged their clothes and papers, Pryce secreting his pistol underneath his shirt.

'Remember,' Pryce exhorted, 'sundown here this evening with our clothes and papers.'

'No offence, fathers,' one of the men said, 'but dressing as priests is not something we'd choose to prolong any longer than we have to.'

'No offence taken,' the Abbé replied.

'Godspeed,' Pryce cried, slapping one of the horses on its rump.

As soon as the two stonemasons had cantered out of the grotto, Pryce clambered onto the driver's seat and took the reins of the horses. 'Let's go,' he said to the Abbé, who had donned the red cap with its tricolor cockade.

As the cart rolled down the lane towards the checkpoint, the Abbé whispered to Pryce. 'Let me do the talking.'

Pryce nodded. His heart was beating faster now and he could feel a bead of sweat beginning to moisten the rim of his bonnet.

'Halt!' one of the sentinels shouted.

'Your papers,' he added, as soon as the wheels of the cart had rumbled to a halt.

The Abbé handed over his papers to the soldier and then Pryce's.

'What is your business at the chateau?'

'We are stonemasons from Dinan,' the Abbé replied. 'We have been sent to strip the Rosary chapel of all its religious effigies and ornaments.'

The Abbé handed over a sealed document, signed by a Citizen Masson.

Seeing the signature, the soldier waved to two guards behind him. 'Open the gate,' he said, 'and let them through.'

As soon as they were in the grounds, Pryce could see that the chateau and its grounds were filled with soldiers in blue coats and bearskin hats.

'Grenadiers,' the Abbé whispered.

Pryce directed the horses on a smaller pathway towards the Rosary chapel, which was tucked away behind a neat row of poplar trees and had been left unguarded.

He stopped the cart in front of the chapel and got out with the Abbé. They hurried through the door and into the empty nave of the chapel.

'Please read the letter again,' the Abbé said.

Pryce drew the crumpled paper from his breeches and began to read.

'Do not seek what you long for in the tents of the wicked, but search for it in the House of the Lord.'

'That's here, the Chapel,' the Abbé cried.

'Look up to our Lady and take hold of her hand.'

The Abbé climbed into the pulpit of the church and reached up towards the statue of the Blessed Virgin fixed on a stone ledge above. He took hold of the only outstretched hand of the finely carved figure and pulled it. Immediately there was the sound of an object moving on some runners, coming from the direction of the high altar. As the two men looked towards the source of the noise, they saw that the front of the altar had completely disappeared and that there were steps leading down towards a door beneath the sanctuary.

'Let her Rosary be your guide and let the Cross be the key to salvation.'

The Abbé seized the Rosary from the statue. It came away easily in his hands. As he stepped down from the pulpit, he showed Pryce the Cross hanging from the end of the beads. It was a key. As the two men hurried to the altar, Pryce was now breathless as he read.

'I pray with all of my heart that you will find the Rock on which the church is built and the treasure hidden in the secret place.'

The two men climbed underneath the altar and made their way down some stone steps towards a door. The Abbé put the key in the lock and it turned. As the door opened, they could hear the sound of whispering in the darkness beyond them.

'I'm here with the Abbé to rescue you, Jean Marie!' Pryce cried.

'Come quickly,' the Abbé added.

There was more whispering. Then they heard the sound of a woman weeping. As they peered into the chamber ahead of them, they saw the shadow of first one figure, then two. Pryce squinted. As he did, he saw her. Jean Marie, in her husband's clothes, was walking towards them. Her son Joseph was right beside her, holding a cocked pistol in front of him.

'It's all right,' Pryce whispered, his voice faltering. 'Eloise sends her love and says she cannot wait to see you in Deal.'

'Oh my Lord,' Jean Marie cried. 'It's you, Thomas, it's truly you.'

She ran the short distance to the edge of the chamber and threw herself into Pryce's arms.

'Mother,' he whispered.

Joseph, who had holstered his pistol, was now embracing his uncle, the Abbé.

'Uncle, is it truly you?' Joseph cried. 'I have missed you so.'

Pryce pulled himself from Jean Marie's arms and gave her a canteen of water. She gulped some and then passed it to her son.

'Look,' Pryce said to them, 'we are masquerading as stone masons and we have to strip the chapel and put everything in a cart outside. You are going to have to wait while we work. We will fill the cart in such a way that you can hide behind and underneath the cargo. Then we will be on our way and can head to the coast.'

'Thomas,' Joseph said, 'I think I should tell you something before we leave.'

'What is it?'

'I overheard a conversation between Masson and his accomplice in the study.'

'You never told me that?' Jean Marie said to her son.

'Mother, you were too upset.' Joseph put his arms around her and kissed her head.

'What is it?' Pryce asked.

'Masson was saying something about an operation that he'd heard about from his boss, Doctor Vacher, when they were sharing a few bottles of wine in Paris. I only overheard snatches because they were whispering some of the time but I distinctly heard them say that it involved a mission to London.'

Pryce shuddered. 'Did he say anything about it?'

'Not much,' Joseph replied. 'I got the distinct impression from Masson's manner that Vacher shouldn't have told him anything at all and that it was only because he had drunk too much and being boastful that he was talking about it at all.'

'Was there nothing?'

'Only one thing and this is what I think you need to hear.'

'And what is that?'

'The last thing Masson said to his assistant was something about a mission called, 'Roi de Pique,' 'the King of Spades.''

'What does that mean?'

'I didn't understand it myself until Masson said something about striking right at the heart of the British monarchy.'

Pryce shuddered. 'And what did you understand by that?' he asked.

'I understood it to mean that Vacher is in London to do unspeakable malice to your King.'

CHAPTER 26

'We haven't a moment to lose,' Pryce said.

'Jean Marie and Joseph,' the Abbé urged. 'Return to your hiding place until we are ready to conceal you on the cart.'

'Make haste,' Pryce urged.

Jean Marie and Joseph scurried through the aperture in the altar while Pryce and the Abbé set to work.

'We need to arrange the furniture very carefully on the tumbrel,' Pryce said once the two fugitives were out of sight.

The men began with two large oak chests. They emptied these of vestments, hassocks and prayer books before loading them onto the cart. They then proceeded to strip the altar of its silver crucifix and cloths, agreeing to set the altar cloths on top of the chests and the silver cross above them once their friends were on board.

'If we are stopped by the Grenadiers,' Pryce said, 'this crucifix will form a suitable distraction.'

Next the men divested the chapel of its silver chalices, patens, flagons and candlesticks, as well as a sun monstrance, thurible and an ornate, silver-covered prayer book. These they placed outside the doors of the chapel.

Pryce then climbed the small pulpit and removed the effigy of the Virgin from the wall. 'I apologise for this,' he said to the Abbé, who crossed himself vigorously as Mary made her undignified descent from the wall.

Within an hour everything had been loaded onto the cart, including crosiers and curtains, screens and pendants, cinctures and stoles, cassocks and albs. Only the pews and the stained glass windows remained. The chapel was now laid bare. Even the pulpit, lectern, stone seats and font were dragged on board and placed strategically.

Pryce, his brow now glistening with sweat, turned to the Abbé as they stood and gazed at the tumbrel. 'I have arranged things so that this unassuming vehicle can be an ark for our loved ones.'

'Magnificent,' the Abbé said.

Pryce returned to the portal in the altar and called to Jean Marie and Joseph who appeared in the twinkling of an eye.

'Swiftly,' Pryce said. 'The men who own this cart and these horses will be waiting for us in one hour.'

Pryce escorted Jean Marie to the heavily-burdened cart and guided her through an invisible corridor between the ecclesiastical furnishings to her hiding place. Spying his surroundings to check for Grenadiers, he did the same for Joseph.

'Are you ready?' the Abbé called as he clambered on to the driver's seat.

'Ready,' the two replied from behind.

Pryce flicked the reins and off the horses strolled, shaking their heads in disapproval at the heavy yoke they now were bearing.

'Keep a look out, brother,' Pryce said.

The horses snorted and snickered as the cart moved yard by yard towards the entrance to the gardens of the chateau. The light was dying now and the skies were turning grey, threatening rain and even snow. Most of the Grenadiers had taken refuge from the cold in the spacious rooms in the chateau. Only a handful remained outside but they seemed preoccupied with lighting fires and guarding cannons, unperturbed by the rolling tumbrel exiting the grounds before their very eyes.

'We're going to make it,' the Abbé said as the cart passed through the unmanned gates and out onto the gravel road beyond.

'I'm not so sure,' Pryce sighed.

One hundred yards ahead he saw a troop of cavalry bearing down upon the chateau grounds, their silver breastplates clearly visible even in the gloom.

'Curassiers!' the Abbé cried.

'Keep still and quiet in the back,' Pryce cried as the sound of trotting hooves drew ever closer.

'Halt!' an officer shouted, his sabre drawn.

Pryce pulled on the reins and the horses stopped.

'Papers please,' the officer said.

Pryce handed the official documents to the man who had now sheathed his sword and was studying the orders and the signature in the half light.

'What are you conveying?'

'Just the furnishings from the chapel at the chateau,' the Abbé said. 'We have been ordered to requisition them for the Republic and take them to the Municipal headquarters in Rennes.'

The officer rose in his saddle to peer at the objects in the tumbrel.

'It's just superstitious clutter,' Pryce said.

'We'll see about that,' the officer snapped. 'You,' he said, pointing to the two cavalrymen either side of him. 'Check the cart for anything of value.'

The men dismounted and headed to the rear. One climbed aboard while the other drew his sword and passed it through the gaps in the side of the tumbrel.

'Here!' the first man cried. He pulled the covers from the two oak chests and raised the silver crucifix.

The second man stopped thrusting his sabre into the nooks and crannies of the cart and took the ornament and lifted it to his officer.

'This will fetch a pretty sum,' the man said.

The officer kicked the flanks of his steed and drew alongside the drivers' seat. 'What's in those chests?'

'Nothing of any interest,' Pryce replied.

'Open them!'

The two cavalrymen roughly swept the vestments from the tops of both the boxes. They pulled on the lids but could not budge them.

'They're locked,' one of the men said.

'Give me the keys,' the officer barked.

'We don't have them,' Pryce replied.

'I don't believe you.'

'We don't have them,' the Abbé repeated.

The officer drew closer and raised the point of his sabre to Pryce's throat. 'If you don't hand them over, you'll bleed out right here where you sit.'

Pryce froze.

The Abbé thrust his hand into his pocket and withdrew a set of iron keys. 'Here,' he said. 'We found these in the church. They may be what you're looking for.'

The officer withdrew the tip of his sword from Pryce's neck and snatched at the ring.

'Use these,' he said.

One of the men turned a key.

'What have we here?' he cried.

'What is it?' the officer asked.

The soldier lifted out a haul of silver artefacts. 'Treasure!'

They emptied both the chests of every precious item, using a curtain as a makeshift sack. Within a minute candlestick and cross, every flagon and chalice, every paten and pendant had been removed.

'On your way,' the officer said.

Pryce urged the horses into action and the cart began to roll again. Little by little it made its ponderous advance away from the cantering cavalry who were now heading through the gates and towards the chateau.

'It worked,' Pryce said.

'They fell for it!' the Abbé cried, clasping Pryce's hands.

A short while later they arrived at the grotto in the woods. They exchanged the cart and horses, with all remaining contents, for their own horses and their clothes and bid farewell to the two stonemasons, whose relief at receiving their promised gold and being reunited with their belongings was palpable.

'That was ingenious,' Jean Marie whispered.

'Thank you mother,' Pryce said. 'I thought it wiser to fill the chests with silver rather than you and Joseph. Silver and gold are a fine smokescreen behind which to conceal what is of infinitely greater value.'

'But to simply hide us underneath a curtain at the front of the cart,' Joseph said, 'well, that was bold indeed.'

'The avarice of man is quite predictable,' Pryce said.

'And murder is quite despicable,' the Abbé sighed.

'Indeed,' Pryce agreed. 'We must make haste. We have a king to save.'

CHAPTER 27

'The man we are about to meet is an Englishman whose name is known throughout the whole of France,' Morgues said, as the coach hurtled through the Kent countryside. 'He is even referred to as the British Jacobin!'

Vacher turned towards his companion. 'Tell me more,' he said.

'I have not met him before,' Morgues continued, 'but we both saw him in the Crown and Anchor and we heard his eloquent defence of the Revolutionary cause. No Frenchman could have made the case more passionately.'

'Nor more physically,' the doctor said. 'Did you see the way he waved his arms when he spoke of the end of the British monarchy?'

'I couldn't miss it,' Morgues laughed. 'He was like a human windmill.'

'Do you think he will help us in our mission?'

'I believe he can be persuaded.'

The doctor tightened his thick woollen scarf about his neck. It was an unusually cold February and there were patches of snow on the ground.

The coach sped along the road until the driver called out, 'Chevening House, ten minutes away.' No sooner had he spoken than the coach began to climb up towards a high ridge. The road on the top, which ran beside a forest of silver beech trees, allowed a stunning view of the chalky, undulating hills of the North Downs of Kent.

'Look through the keyhole, that avenue of trees over there!' Morgues said, nudging his companion.

The doctor and his friend peered out of the windows and saw an arcade of trees standing tall and proud like soldiers on guard. The two arched, arboreal ranks led down a hill to the front of Chevening House.

'Stanhope's residence,' Morgues said.

'The estate is enormous!' the doctor gasped.

'It's well over three thousand acres.'

'It's a contradiction, if you ask me,' the doctor said.

'Don't be fooled, my friend,' Morgues replied.

'What do you mean?'

'Well, have you noticed anything odd about our transport?'

'It's commodious, fast too.'

'Yes it is, but let me ask you a question. You know the British. Where's the family crest on the sides of the coach?'

'There isn't one.'

'Doesn't it strike you as strange, my friend, that Stanhope did not send his own coach and horses?'

'Now you mention it. Why is that?'

'Stanhope is not the contradiction you think. He's done away with many of the trappings of his class, including the family's coach and horses, much to the annoyance of both his children and what's left of his staff.'

'He's certainly unusual!'

'Yes, he is. And look at that!'

Morgues pointed to the great wrought-iron gates that were now about to be opened. 'Do you see?'

The doctor squinted. 'It says Democracy Hall!'

'It used to have the family coat of arms but Stanhope had those removed and replaced with a new name for his country residence.'

'I like him already!' the doctor said.

The coach was barely through the gates when Morgues nudged his companion. 'Look there!' Morgues was pointing out of the windows at a lake where black swans were pushing against the cold wind. There were some small docks along one side with a strange looking vessel tied to them. It was about forty feet long and had two masts with sails folded around them, one at the bow and one at the stern. Just behind the bow mast there was a funnel and behind that a large wheel amidships on both sides. Each wheel had nine oars protruding outwards from the hub. Several were under the water line.

'That's one of Stanhope's inventions.'

'What is it?'

'It's a ship that runs on steam and uses a screw propeller for propulsion.'

'You mean it doesn't rely on wind?'

'No, the sails are only required if the engine breaks down.'

'Did Stanhope create this?'

'He designed it, in discussions with an American Republican living here in England - a man by the name of Robert Fulton.'

'I have heard of him. Does it actually work?'

'Oh yes.'

The coach ran past the lake through a field where wild geese waddled lazily beneath the yew trees, and then alongside several gardens protected by red bricked walls and a maze marked by box hedges.

The two guests arrived in front of the house and alighted from their carriage.

'Splendid! Splendid!' a man shouted.

The man shouting was a tall, bald gentleman and he was fast approaching them across the gravel, his arms flaying.

'Welcome to Democracy Hall!' he cried.

'Forgive me,' the doctor stuttered, 'I took you for the butler.'

'No, no, no,' the man chided, 'we Republicans have no time for such outmoded and oppressive ways. My name is Citizen Charles Stanhope. Welcome, fellow Citizens.'

The doctor proffered his hand.

'Now then,' Stanhope said, taking it in his. 'It's freezing cold out here. I have a fire burning in the study.'

Just then, a lean and lithe young woman with long limbs and bright blue eyes appeared at the door.

'Who are these gentlemen, father?'

'They are friends of mine from across the Channel, daughter, and they are friends of the Republican cause.'

'Pleased to meet you, I'm sure,' the young woman said, stretching out her gloved hand. 'Let me introduce myself, my name is Lady Hester Stanhope.'

'Enchanted,' the doctor replied, kissing her fingers. 'I am Citizen Marat and this is my colleague, Citizen Morgues.'

'What brings you both to Chevening?'

'We are here about your father's business,' the doctor replied.

'How intriguing.'

'Now, now, daughter,' Stanhope interrupted. 'Enough of this - go and feed the turkeys on the common.'

'Later, father, when it's not so chilly. You wouldn't want your favourite child to catch her death of cold.'

'All right, all right, just try and keep out of mischief, there's a good girl.'

Hester swivelled back towards the house and strode inside, humming loudly the melody of the Marseillaise as she went.

Once inside the entrance, the doctor removed his great coat and carefully placed his cane beneath it on a chair. He gazed at the wooden staircase in front of him and then at the ceiling where there was a looming lantern hanging from a whorl of muskets, all tightly packed together. There were weapons cross-hatched all over the walls - daggers, swords, bayonets, axes. The chamber looked more like an armoury than a foyer.

'Come this way, Citizens,' Stanhope urged.

Within a few moments the two guests were sitting in the study behind closed doors, enjoying the welcome warmth of a fierce fire crackling in an iron hearth.

'I expect you'd like a drink,' Stanhope said, pouring a rich red Burgundy from a crystal decanter. 'Here you are Citizens,' he said, passing a glass to both.

'Thank you,' the doctor said, as he studiously allowed the bouquet from the wine to scent his palate. 'This is a fine vintage, Citizen.'

'I received several cases from Citizen Fouché,' Stanhope said.

'He is reputed to have a fine cellar,' the doctor said.

After a few moments, Stanhope put his glass down and looked at the fire, resting both his feet upon the grate. From the doctor's armchair he could see that his host's forehead was unusually high and his nose was shaped like the beak of an eagle. He had the appearance of a deep thinker but from the look of melancholy in his piercing blue eyes it seemed that his thoughts were rarely happy.

It was the doctor who broke the silence.

'We saw your steamship, Citizen. Is it a working model?'

'Oh yes,' Stanhope replied. 'I'm an inventor.'

'Really?'

'Yes, look at this.'

He reached over to his desk and pulled what looked like a large, thin, rectangular box to his chest. 'This is my adding machine.'

'What's that?'

'It's a machine I designed for adding, subtracting, dividing and multiplying large numbers. Look at these twelve dials. They all have different functions. This dial here has HM next to it. That stands for hundred million. If I use this small stylus and insert it in the hole in the periphery of the dial, like so, I can add and multiply unthinkably large numbers, and indeed sums of money.'

'That's extraordinary,' the doctor exclaimed.

'See here,' Stanhope replied, pointing to a metal plaque on the side of the box. It read, *Viscount Mahon and James Bullock, 1780*.

'Viscount Mahon is one of my titles, and Mister Bullock was the extremely able manufacturer of my invention.'

'What of your steamship?' the doctor asked.

Stanhope snarled. 'I offered it to the Admiralty just a month or so ago but they aren't interested in new inventions.'

'Why not?'

'Too busy protecting their existing contracts. I have no time for them. They are Luddites, all of them.'

Stanhope replaced the calculator on the table and then turned to his guests. 'Now then, what can I do for you, Citizens?'

The doctor took a deep breath. 'We are here because everyone in France knows of your commitment to our Revolutionary cause and your support for the eternal virtues of liberty and equality.'

Stanhope nodded.

'In France we appreciate the way you have written so powerfully and persuasively against those like Edmund Burke who hate what we stand for.'

'His views are odious and contemptible,' Stanhope said with a sweep of his hand.

'Quite so, Citizen, quite so, and my companion and I were at the Crown and Anchor tavern in the Strand just days ago when you stood and eloquently proposed an end to the monarchy and the beginnings of a Republic in Great Britain.'

'Thank you,' Stanhope said.

'And it is really that which we want to ask you about.'

'What do you want to know?'

'We want to know how far you are prepared to go in order to see these aspirations fulfilled.'

The doctor paused. A brilliant spark spat from the whirling fire with a loud smack and landed on the rug. Stanhope let it burn until its last glowing light had died out in a tiny black crater in the fabric.

'I have already spoken in the House of Lords against the views and the policies of my cousin, the Prime Minister, William Pitt, and I have made public my Republican sympathies,' Stanhope said. 'All of which is to say,' he whispered, 'that I would be prepared to do anything to see the death of the monarchy and the birth of liberty and equality in this country.'

'Anything?'

'Almost anything,' Stanhope reiterated, before adding, 'some of your countrymen's more recent methods have been too extreme for me. I am not in favour of butchering priests, nor do I support the mass execution of prisoners at the guillotine, especially when many of those beheaded are themselves sans culottes.'

'Sometimes, Citizen,' the doctor replied, 'a noble end necessitates ignoble means.'

'That is well said, but I still have my misgivings, even though I saw with my own eyes how the Bourbon aristocracy in your country was capable of an equal if not greater cruelty before the Revolution.'

The doctor smiled. 'That is also well said.' He took another sip of his wine then leaned towards his host. 'You say that you want to bring an end to the monarchy.'

'I do,' Stanhope replied, leaning forward until the two men were only inches away from each other.

'And it is said that you rejoiced publicly when King Louis was executed in Paris a month ago, even though it made you immensely unpopular.'

'I did.'

The doctor paused, with his brow furrowed and his eyes aflame. 'Would you be willing to help us bring an abrupt and dramatic end to the reign of King George?'

Stanhope's eyes opened wide. He sat back deep into his chair and stared for a moment into the fire. Turning back to his guests, he asked, 'what have you in mind?'

'There is a meeting of a group of inventors in a week's time at Saint James' Palace, is there not?'

'How did you know that?'

'My companion, Citizen Morgues, has acquired the intelligence. He is, let me say, extremely efficient.'

'He most certainly is. There is indeed an audience with the King. My secretary Reverend Jeremiah Joyce and I have been invited to present petitions to His Majesty for funding. Even though the King is in most cases an irrelevance, he has been a most generous patron to men of science in the past and for that he should be thanked.'

'And are you planning to attend?'

'I wasn't going to, given my very public denunciations of the monarchy.'

'I think you should accept the invitation.'

'Why?'

'Citizen Morgues and I would like to go with you, disguised as your secretaries, and in place of Joyce.'

'For what purpose?'

The doctor leaned even closer to his host and whispered. 'Our purpose is a noble one. We intend to abduct your King, take him to the Tower Prison in France and force him to abdicate and to renounce the monarchy.'

'How on earth do you propose to achieve that?'

'We have a contact at Saint James' Palace.'

'Can we trust him?'

'You can,' the doctor said. 'He's Irish.'

'Irish, you say?'

'Yes, though he's assumed an English alias so he can work against your government without suspicion.'

'What's his role?'

'He has already secured safe passage for us back to France on a schooner moored in the Thames. It will set sail as soon as my colleague and I arrive on board with the King. The sailors are all Irish sympathizers who make their living as wool traders.'

'Free traders more like,' Stanhope interrupted.

'I cannot either confirm or deny that,' the doctor smiled. He took a sip from his glass. 'Will you help us?'

'Before I answer, I need to have one reassurance.'

'Name it.'

'Although I support the Republican cause and want to see an end to the monarchy, I have also grown weary and indeed sick of the bloodlust of some of your compatriots. Citizen Marat, I do not wish King George any personal harm. Will you assure me that his life will be spared and he will be treated with decency?'

The doctor looked straight at Stanhope. 'I can absolutely assure you of this,' he said without flinching.

Stanhope closed his eyes.

'Will you help us?' the doctor asked.

'I am probably the only man in England who can, or indeed who would.'

He rose to his feet and walked over to a mahogany desk. He fetched a medal from one of the top drawers.

'You see this?' he said, stretching out his hand, with the medallion in his palm.

'I do,' the doctor replied.

'I had it especially made. It has my motto inscribed upon it. Can you read it?'

'Yes I can.'

'What does it say?'

'It says "a Minority of One".'

'Well, that's exactly what I am, and that's precisely why you can count on my support.'

CHAPTER 28

Pryce held tightly onto the Abbé's chest as the two of them rode on the same horse, avoiding the roads. He glanced to his right and observed Joseph just ten yards away urgently kicking the sweaty flanks of his horse, causing Jean Marie to clasp to her son as the stallion snorted loudly and accelerated to a gallop.

'Catch them up!' Pryce shouted into the Abbé's ear. 'Catch them up!'

Without hesitating, the Abbé struck their horse with his silver stirrups and the two priests were soon alongside their friends again.

Pryce looked at Jean Marie's chestnut hair flowing behind her as she rested her head on her son's shoulder, her brown eyes fierce and focused on the path ahead.

'She is truly my wife's mother!' he said to the Abbé.

'Slow down!' Jean Marie shouted after several minutes.

The riders pulled on the reins and the two horses relaxed into a trot.

'We must go through these woods,' Jean Marie said. 'I know where we can get two more horses.'

'Where, mother?' Joseph asked.

'Do you remember Marie, my maid?' she replied.

'Yes, I do. She was the kindest and most cheerful of all your servants.'

'Well she was also the wife of a farmer, Jean-Jacques, who lives about a mile beyond this forest.'

'Was?' Pryce interjected.

'It's a very sad tale, I'm afraid,' Jean Marie said, 'she bore a son called Philippe and then was with child again almost straight away. There were, how shall we say, complications.'

176

'What complications?' Joseph asked. 'I don't remember this.'

'We kept it all from you, my son. You were young at the time.'

'What happened?' he asked.

'When Marie went into labour it was clear that something was wrong. I was at the farmhouse with my own physician to help her but there was nothing that could be done. Marie started to bleed and we couldn't stop it. Within an hour, both she and her baby daughter had gone. Jean-Jacques was beside himself.'

'Dear Lord, I had no idea,' Joseph cried.

'It was the most tragic spectacle,' Jean Marie sighed. 'I am sure that it was only because he had to look after his son that Jean-Jacques didn't take his own life. He was completely devoted to her. She was a radiant lady. The lights went out when she died.'

The four fugitives kept quiet for several minutes as their horses walked between the trees, the silence only broken by the sound of snapping twigs and the occasional 'korr kok' of a startled pheasant.

'Will Jean-Jacques help us?' Pryce asked.

'He will,' Jean Marie replied.

As the path between the trees began to narrow, Pryce and the Abbé lagged behind their friends.

'We may only have these horses,' Pryce whispered into the Abbé's ear, 'but they are considerably faster than those two old nags the stonemasons leant us!'

'Truly,' the Abbé replied.

As the two horses and their four riders reached the edge of the forest, Jean Marie put her finger to her lips and urged all to be quiet.

Pryce slid off the side of his beast before helping the Abbé.

Jean Marie tied the bridle of her horse to a sturdy branch and then took the second horse and tethered it to a neighbouring tree. 'This way,' she whispered.

Pryce followed her as she passed through bracken and branches, sometimes walking tall and sometimes crouching. They climbed over a wooden style and crossed a small field until they arrived at a copse on top of a hill. As they moved through the undergrowth, a murder of jet black crows sprung from the tree tops and launched into the sky, cawing and circling above.

'Damn them,' Jean Marie snarled, before kneeling on one knee behind a tree and waiting until the cacophonous sound of the birds had abated.

A few yards further and they were at the periphery of their woodland cover.

'There,' she said, pointing down a grassy slope to a farmhouse surrounded by stables and outhouses. 'There's Jean-Jacques' farm!'

The old house was about three hundred yards away from where Pryce was hiding. As he spied the grounds, he could see movement in the stony courtyard outside the front door of the house. As his keen eyes squinted in the dying light of the late afternoon sun, he saw them.

'Soldiers,' he whispered, 'there are two soldiers in the courtyard, with muskets.'

Joseph, who was crouching next to him, had already observed them.

'National Guardsmen,' he murmured.

'What are they doing here?' Pryce asked.

Before anyone had time to speak, one of the soldiers stepped aside and Pryce saw a man and a boy kneeling on the cobbled ground.

'You're under arrest!' one of the soldiers shouted to the man.

'No!' the boy screamed. 'Leave papa alone!'

'Silence!' the soldier snapped, bringing his hand down across the boy's ear. 'Your father is a traitor.'

'He's going to prison and then he's going to get his head shaved!' the other barked.

At this the boy howled.

Pryce began to tremble.

As one of the soldiers started to bind the farmer's hands behind his back, the other pushed the boy towards the house and then slammed him into the front door.

'Go and snivel to your mother!' the soldier sneered.

'I don't have a mother. I won't have anyone if you take papa!' the boy yelled.

'Well then, you'll be an orphan, won't you?'

Pryce's scarred right hand began to reach towards a sharp edged rock at the tip of his right shoe. He was shaking now. Without turning to his companions, he set his face towards the farmhouse and started running, the stone in his hand.

'Thomas, stop!' Joseph cried.

Down he sped, down towards the farm, running faster than he had ever run, his face staring wildly ahead, his nostrils furling like an angry horse, his eyes livid with a sudden and unquenchable conflagration.

As Pryce reached the courtyard, a yell began to rise from the pit of his stomach. It was louder than any sound Pryce had made before, more furious than any noise he'd ever heard from the lips of a man or a woman in his life.

It was wordless, primal, terrifying.

The guardsman who had been trying to subdue the farmer let the rope fall to the ground and reached for his musket.

Pryce was now just a few feet from the soldier who had struck the boy. He roared at the soldier and he brought the stone down on the startled man's face, gouging the man's right eye, causing him to yelp. The soldier dropped his musket and fell to his knees, his tricorn hat falling to the floor, the white feathers of his cockade already splattered with blood.

'You will not separate this boy from his father,' Pryce yelled.

There was a crack as the rock hit the soldier's head.

Pryce turned to face the other guardsman but as he did he heard another crack, followed immediately by another. He stared ahead at the soldier in front of him, whose weapon was raised. There was smoke all around Pryce's head. He lowered his eyes, looking for traces of blood on his body and clothes. But there was none, no wound, no pain.

He raised his head again. The guardsman looked surprised, embarrassed even. His musket fell to the ground, the bayonet clanking on the stone. He lowered his head to his chest, looking at something. There were smudges of blood beginning to seep from the white waistcoat underneath his blue jacket.

Pryce shuddered.

He looked to his right and there was the boy, the other soldier's musket at his shoulder, smoke lingering at the end of its barrel.

As the soldier fell to his knees, mortally wounded, the boy turned back to the guardsman who was lying unconscious at his feet. He crouched down to the man and spat on his hair which was now clotted with dark red blood. 'Go snivelling to your mother!' he shouted, as he plunged the bayonet into the man's spine, twisting it full circle, skewering him like a pig.

Pryce stared at the soldier at his feet. He fell to his knees and made the sign of the Cross upon the soldier's fractured, matted brow.

'Thank you,' a deep voice said, as a strong hand gathered Pryce under his arms and lifted him to his unsteady feet. 'Thank you,' the farmer repeated, trying to shake Pryce's scarred hand.

'If it wasn't for you,' the boy cried, holding onto Pryce around his waist, his head nestled into his stomach, his tears soaking the robes.

Just then, the others rushed into the yard.

'My God, Thomas,' Joseph said, 'you've killed them!'

'I killed them,' the boy stammered through pouting lips. 'I killed them,' he repeated.

'You're a brave one,' Joseph said, extricating the boy from Pryce, patting him on the head.

'This will take a little clearing up,' Jean Marie sighed.

At the sound of her voice, the farmer looked up. 'Oh my dear sweet Lord,' he cried, 'it's you, Madame Picot, my lady!'

'Jean-Jacques,' she said, reaching out to hold him. 'It's been too long!'

'Far too long,' the man replied, 'and now we meet like this. I'm so sorry.'

'You have nothing to apologize for,' Jean Marie said, 'it is my son-in-law who has been a little headstrong.'

'I'm grateful to him, my lady, grateful beyond words.'

'You must leave,' Jean Marie urged. 'You can't stay here now. It won't take long before more soldiers will be back and when they are there will be no escape.'

'But this is the house that Marie and I built, this is our home,' the farmer said.

'We have all had to say farewell to homes and to loved ones in these dreadful days,' Jean Marie said.

'I know,' the farmer replied, 'I heard what happened to your husband. And I learned just yesterday that the government had seized your home.'

Jean Marie looked away for a moment. 'It has been hard,' she said, 'I do not deny it. But duty calls, Jean-Jacques, and when she does we must not complain.'

'What shall we do?' he asked.

'Why don't you and your boy come with me?' Joseph interjected. 'I can find somewhere for you to live and some work for you both to do, that's if you are agreeable.'

'What kind of work?' the farmer asked.

'Well,' Joseph replied, 'let's put it this way. You have been accused of being a rebel. You would now be arrested and executed as a rebel. So you might as well become a rebel.'

The farmer smiled. 'What about Philippe?'

'He has revealed some, let's say, special qualities today. I can find something a little safer for him to do until he is old enough to display them again.'

'I don't think we have much choice, do we?'

'We always have a choice, monsieur.'

'Well, then, I choose to go with you.'

The farmer turned to his boy. 'Fancy killing a few more bluecoats, my son?'

'Yes, papa, many more, until they are all dead and buried and we can be free again.'

The boy took hold of Pryce's right hand and held it in both of his, prizing away the bloody rock that had been in its unyielding grasp.

'I know what you did may seem wrong to you,' the boy said, 'but

I think God is pleased when children are prevented from becoming orphans.'

The boy turned away and began to help his father and Joseph carry the dead soldiers to a nearby cart, ready for burial.

The Abbé, who had left with them, walked back into the yard after several minutes, leading two saddled horses by their bridles. He had a broad grin on his face. 'The Lord gives and the Lord takes away,' he said.

'Where did you find those two horses?' Pryce asked.

'They belonged to our dead friends. I'm confiscating them.'

'Confiscating, borrowing, requisitioning - these are just words.'

'Well, let's just add it to the ever growing list of things we need to bring before the good Lord next time we confess our sins.'

'I hope he's got lots of time,' Pryce sighed.

CHAPTER 29

'You saw them with Stanhope?' Wickham asked his cloaked visitor.

'With my own eyes,' the man replied.

William Wickham closed the door of his small office in Whitechapel and ushered the man in. The chamber was cold and poorly lit. There was barely room for another person to sit down in front of the desk, which was covered in meticulously arranged papers and carefully stacked registers.

'I apologize for these cramped conditions,' Wickham sighed as he squeezed round the back of his desk and sat down, groaning as he did. 'Infernal knee,' he said, rubbing his leg vigorously with his mitten clad hands. 'I fell from a tree in my student days at Christ Church and it's proven to be quite out of the reach of medicine.'

'I'm sorry to hear that,' the man said.

'Not to worry,' Wickham replied. 'I'm sure the good Lord wants to teach me something through it.'

Wickham finished massaging his knee and leaned forward across the space in the centre of his desk. 'Now then, Mister Clarke, tell me what you observed?'

'Well, governor, it's like this. I was informed by one of your agents, a Mister Sennett, that there were two Frenchies at the Crown and Anchor Tavern. He had seen them at a public meeting where Lord Stanhope had been holding forth. He suspected that they'd ask for a meeting with Stanhope at some point after that.'

'And did they?'

'Most certainly they did, governor. So I was ready in the entrance hall of the Crown and Anchor, having paid a driver to let me pose as his colleague. When they approached us we told them we could get them to Chevening House quicker than any other man or beast.'

'I hope you have kept the receipt for all that,' Wickham said, squinting at his guest.

Clarke passed him a piece of paper. 'Here,' he said, 'signed, just like you asked.'

Wickham took the paper, scrutinized it, before nodding his approval and placing it in a file on his desk marked 'expenses'.

'Continue,' Wickham said.

'Well, it's like this, I took the two men to Chevening House and they were met by Lord Stanhope. He seemed very pleased to see them, very pleased indeed. If you ask me, governor, it's not right that a peer of the realm is gallivanting with Frenchies.'

'I didn't ask you, Mister Clarke,' Wickham retorted. 'Your job is to observe. Mine is to interpret. So let's keep to our proper places, shall we?'

'Sorry, governor, anyway the Frenchies stayed two hours with Lord Stanhope. Talking, they were, in his study. Lord knows what about, but I'm sure they were up to no good.'

'Mister Clarke!' Wickham snapped. 'Observations, not interpretations, if you please.'

'Apologies, governor, can't help myself.'

'Did you hear any of their conversation in the carriage?' Wickham asked.

'My French isn't perfect but I did hear one of them say something about their mission and he asked if Stanhope could be persuaded to help.'

'What did the other one say?'

'Something like, "leave the talking to me".'

Wickham frowned. 'Is that all?'

'That's all, guv.'

Wickham reached down behind the bureau. He opened an iron safe and fetched a banknote from the top drawer. He locked the safe again and placed the key in his waistcoat pocket. Taking a quill pen, he dipped it in an ink well and made an entry in one of his registers.

'Sign here, please,' Wickham said.

Clarke stood to his feet and obliged.

'You have done well, Mister Clarke. I will be requiring your services again.'

'If it's for King and country, governor, you can rely on me.'

Just then there was a knock on the door. Wickham rose to his feet. 'Enter,' he barked.

A man of average height in his early forties strode into the office. He had light brown hair, black pupils, pale complexion and a pronounced nose. He was wearing a dark jacket over a white waistcoat and his short neck was covered by a silk white cravat.

'Sir Evan Nepean,' Wickham said, 'may I introduce you to Mister William Clarke, before he leaves.'

'My Lord,' Clarke said, proffering his hand.

'I'm a baronet, not a Lord, Mister Clarke, but thank you for the elevation. What is your business?'

'I work for Mister Wickham here.'

'Oh yes, what as, pray?'

'I run a network of watchers here in London, sir.'

'Ah, yes,' the baronet nodded, 'I have heard of the good work done by you and your men. Capital, capital, Mister Clarke, the Home Office is grateful to you.'

'Thank you, sir,' Clarke said as he tried to pass the baronet in the confined space between his chair and the open door.

Having let Clarke through, Nepean closed the door behind him and sat down.

'I do apologize for the lack of space, Sir Evan,' Wickham pined. 'I do hope you'll be able to find me a larger room in the Home Office before long, not to mention an increase in my expenses.'

'I'm working on it, old chap. Just give me time. An undersecretary only has so much power, you know?'

Wickham sighed.

'And in any case,' Nepean added, 'there are more pressing matters of state that are occupying my attention at the moment.'

'Quite so, sir, quite so,' Wickham replied, 'and that brings me to the matter in hand.'

Wickham paused and took a file from the top of a welter of

papers stacked on top of the safe underneath the dirty windows behind him. He opened it methodically and drew out a piece of paper. 'This,' he said, 'is a copy of the speech given by Lord Charles Stanhope at a recent public meeting of the Friends of the People, held at the Crown and Anchor Tavern, infiltrated by Mister Sennett, one of my best agents.'

The undersecretary took the paper in his hand and read it quickly. 'It's the same old nonsense, reformist guff about annual parliaments and universal suffrage.'

'No, sir,' Wickham said, 'I believe it's more than that. I believe that what you call the language of reformation is really the rhetoric of revolution.'

'What are you saying, Wickham?'

'I'm saying that I believe there is evidence that Stanhope's talk of ending the monarchy is more than just a rhetorical statement.'

'What is it, then?'

'It's code for doing mischief to our leaders.'

The undersecretary sat up with a start. 'What kind of mischief?'

'I'm not certain yet but I do know this: he recently welcomed two agents from France at Chevening. Sennett has been tracking them and Clarke, whom you've just met, drove them to and from the house. He's a key asset. He understands and speaks French.'

'Stanhope's a fool,' the undersecretary snorted. 'He's hot air, that's all, like one of those balloon contraptions. He's an embarrassment to the Prime Minister. I don't know what the poor man did to deserve such a brother-in-law.'

'He may be all of those things but he also has the influence to open doors for those whose hearts are intent on an evil greater than any we have ever seen.'

'What kind of evil, pray?'

'It is my suspicion that these two agents are here to assassinate the king.'

'But that's preposterous!'

'Is it, sir?'

'Yes, it is.'

'Well, then let me try to convince you otherwise.'

Wickham reached into his jacket pocket and produced a tiny leather bound note book, which he opened carefully. 'I have more than enough reasons for believing the king's life is in imminent danger.'

'Let's have them then.'

'The first is to do with our times in general. The sudden downturn in the economy has meant a rise in food prices, especially bread. And the costs of the war aren't helping either.'

'So?'

'Six months ago, the King's carriage was stopped and attacked by an angry mob crying 'no war' and 'no king'. The king was on the way back from opening Parliament.'

'I didn't know of this,' the undersecretary said as a frown appeared like a dark cloud upon his face.

'What you may also not know is that the two men who agitated the crowd and attempted to attack the king were in fact French agents. They were here under the names Colla and Godoni. They managed to get away in the chaos but we arrested them a week ago at Ostend.'

'Have you extracted any information from them?'

'Not yet, but they are being questioned even now. They will talk eventually.'

'This is interesting but it is hardly conclusive,' the undersecretary said.

'Then there's the incident at Christmas,' Wickham said.

'What incident?'

'The King was at the Theatre Royal when a man shot a pistol at him from the pit. It missed and the king reported that it was just a squib. But it was close. It has been kept secret, but everyone will hear soon enough.'

'Why do you say that?'

'Mister Sheridan, the theatre manager, composed an extra verse to 'God Save the King.' He did it in the interval on that very night and had the audience sing it. I'm told it was greeted with rapturous applause and is set to become an official part of the anthem.'

Wickham turned the pages of his little book and began to read. 'From every latent foe, from the assassin's blow, God save the king… Something along those lines, anyway.'

'Good Lord,' the undersecretary exclaimed.

'Since that time there was a further attempt on the king's life a few weeks ago, when the king was inspecting the 1st Foot Guards in Hyde Park. A Navy clerk standing very near him took a bullet in his shoulder. It wasn't a serious wound but we are sure that the bullet was intended for the king, not the clerk.'

The undersecretary looked up at the ceiling for a moment and grimaced. 'And you think that there's a new and more sinister plot?' he asked.

'I do,' Wickham replied, 'and I don't think it's without cause that a week ago the king said to Lord Eldon, our Attorney General, that it is not improbable that he will be the last king of England.'

'Why so?'

'Since France declared war on us, the threat to the king's life has, in my opinion, become a matter of immediate and urgent concern.'

'We are aware of the growing unrest and indeed seditious talk in London and some of our other cities,' the undersecretary conceded.

'I take it you know of the London Corresponding Society,' Wickham replied.

'Yes, indeed, they're a large and growing group of troublemakers who want to see the monarchy abolished and a national convention here in England.'

'Quite so,' Wickham interjected, 'but I think they may be more than that. One of my agents has infiltrated their meetings. He told me yesterday that the heads of the Society have ordered thousands of nine inch daggers and they intend to use them to assassinate the king, the prime minister, and other leaders of our nation.'

The undersecretary's mouth opened wide, his face aghast.

'I'm anxious, sir, I really am,' Wickham sighed.

'Then we must increase the number of watchers in the streets and agents in the coffee shops and taverns. And we must also detain and interrogate any French émigré about whom we are even remotely suspicious, especially now that *Habeas Corpus* has been suspended for troublesome aliens.'

'That may be more difficult than you think,' Wickham interrupted.

'Why?'

'We have limited resources and the task is huge. You know that in the last ten weeks of last year over 4000 French émigrés entered our shores. These registers on my desk are full of their names and the names of many others who came over before then.'

'Well, that's what the Alien Act is supposed to address,' the undersecretary retorted. 'And that's why we appointed so many magistrates throughout the land to enforce it. They need to start sending these foreigners back.'

'I appreciate that, sir,' Wickham said, 'but the rule of law must be respected.'

'Damn the rule of law,' the undersecretary shouted. 'Deporting a suspicious Frenchman is no worse than drowning a fish. It needs to be done, for the sake of the king.'

'Sir, you know that my sense of patriotic duty is as strong as any man's, but we need to focus on those who are genuinely guilty and not punish the majority who are running from a great and terrifying darkness. Dark times should not be countered by sordid measures.'

'Well then, man, what do you suggest?'

'I suggest we set Mister Sennett onto the two French agents that visited Stanhope and we alert the city watchers to look out for any other suspicious aliens. Given our lack of manpower, there is not much more we can do - besides pray to the Almighty.'

Nepean took a deep breath before replying. 'I know you are right, Wickham,' he said, 'we need more recruits, and able ones too. Perhaps it's time for you and me to start talking with the Home and Foreign Secretaries about setting up a correspondence, a network of spies, here and abroad.'

'I think it is,' Wickham agreed. He paused for a moment before looking into undersecretary's eyes. 'It's time for His Majesty's Secret Service,' he said. 'And it is His Majesty, more than anyone, who needs it.'

CHAPTER 30

'We need to speak to Monsieur Henry and quickly,' Jean Marie said as she tugged on the sleeve of a waiter who had appeared at the back door of the hotel.

Pryce watched as the man scuttled back into the mansion house, carrying the pot whose hot and oily contents he had just emptied into a drain in the backyard.

'Tell him it's urgent,' Jean Marie shouted after him.

A few minutes later a man whom Pryce guessed was just shy of fifty years opened the back door. He was dressed in beige knee-length breeches, white stockings, and faded black shoes. He wore a creased shirt and an olive green waistcoat, both of which were visible beneath a white cotton apron. He was cleaning his hands with a cloth as he spoke.

'My name is Henry. Welcome to the Hotel Pelikan. What can I do for you?'

'It's good of you to see us, Monsieur Henry. I am Jean Marie Picot and this is my son, Joseph.'

At the mention of their names, the man threw his cloth down and hurriedly removed his apron. 'Madame Picot,' he said, bowing his head gravely, 'my deepest condolences.'

Jean Marie proffered her hand and he took it gently before kissing it. 'Thank you,' she said quietly.

Henry paused before continuing. 'And you must be the celebrated Knight of Limoelan,' he said, turning to Joseph.

'At your service,' Joseph replied, before adding, 'this is my uncle, the Abbé de Clorivière.'

'Abbé!' Henry exclaimed in a muted voice, shaking the priest's hand vigorously. 'It is a great pleasure to meet you. I was there when you preached that sermon in Sevignac! What a great storm that caused.'

The Abbé blushed.

Joseph then pointed to the farmer and his son. 'These two friends we have 'acquired' along the way.'

'Ah!' the innkeeper said, shaking their hands with a knowing smile.

'And this,' Jean Marie said, taking hold of Pryce's right hand, 'this is my son-in-law, Thomas Pryce. He is from England and married to my daughter, Eloise.'

'How do you do?' the innkeeper said in broken English, stretching out his hand to Pryce.

'There is no need to speak in English,' Jean Marie interjected. 'He speaks perfect French.'

'I am pleased to make your acquaintance,' Pryce said in an impeccable Breton accent.

'You have been expecting us?' Jean Marie asked.

'I have.'

'And what are your instructions?'

'I am ordered to send a message to Captain Philippe d'Auvergne on the island of Jersey with the date and time of your pick-up from the beach beneath the cliffs of your chateau by the sea.'

'What is the earliest you can get word to him?'

'I have carrier pigeons that fly between here and Jersey regularly. He will know by tomorrow.'

'Good,' Jean Marie said. 'Please tell him that we will meet him on the beach in three days, on Tuesday morning at daybreak.'

'Very well,' the innkeeper replied. 'But there's something you need to know. There is a company of Grenadiers based in your chateau.'

Jean Marie sighed. 'I know,' she said.

'But do you know that they are soldiers who have seen action?'

'No!' Joseph exclaimed.

'I'm afraid these are not snotty nosed, inexperienced recruits,' the innkeeper said. 'These soldiers have been in battle and part of the reason they're here is to regroup and recover.'

'Where did they fight?' Joseph asked.

'I'm told it was the beginning of the month, in and around two villages in the Prussian Province of the Rhine. One of them was Maastricht.'

'What happened?'

'They took a ferocious beating by the Austrian army. They were part of two battalions of the third and fourth Grenadiers in an army of nine thousand.'

'How many men did they lose?'

'I was told two thousand of our soldiers were killed or wounded. Three hundred were captured, along with two colours and seven guns.'

'No wonder they were guarding those cannons up at the chateau,' Joseph sneered.

'These men are licking their wounds,' the innkeeper said. 'They were demoralized by two regiments of Austrian cavalry and fell back west. The Austrians only lost fifty men dead or wounded in the battle.'

'That was a massacre!' Joseph declared.

'Yes, but that doesn't mean they've lost the will to fight. They want to restore their pride. They want revenge. And as far as they are concerned, a royalist French army is as good an enemy for them as any.'

'They only have one company,' Joseph replied. 'They can't do much damage with 100 plus men, even if they are Grenadiers.'

'But that's the problem,' the innkeeper said.

'What do you mean?'

'Well, we don't know if it's just one company. Our intelligence hasn't yet revealed any more than that but the truth is, where you have a company of line infantry, there's usually a company of light infantry nearby.'

'What's the difference?' Pryce asked.

'Line infantry march towards the enemy in line formation. Light infantry are more agile and tend to fight as skirmishers. The two kinds of soldier usually fight together. It's the French way, Mister Pryce.'

'Do we know who's leading them?' Joseph asked.

193

'They are currently under the command of two French agents called Masson and Sicard, who are in turn working for Danton.'

'Have you met these agents?' Joseph enquired.

'Sicard I don't know, but Masson has stayed in this hotel before, with his boss Vacher. Evil men. They even tortured a British agent in an upstairs room. Made a terrible mess, they did. There was blood everywhere, even on the walls. Poor man must have suffered terribly.'

'Where are these agents right now?'

'We haven't seen Vacher here in Saint-Savant for some weeks and Masson hasn't been back since he requisitioned your mansion. I think he's sleeping more comfortably there than he could in one of my humble rooms.'

'Pah, that dog,' Jean Marie spat. 'I cannot bear the thought of him in one of our beds.'

'There, there, mother,' Joseph said. 'Soon enough he will be sleeping permanently.'

'Given all that you have told us,' Joseph said to the innkeeper, 'you had better ask Captain d'Auvergne to bring at least one company of Jersey Grenadiers with him, two if he's got them at his disposal.'

'And there's one more thing,' Pryce said to the innkeeper. 'Please inform Captain d'Auvergne that I have to get back to London as fast as it's humanly possible.'

'I can do that,' the innkeeper replied.

'It's imperative that you stress the urgency of the situation, that there isn't a moment to lose. Tell him… just say the words 'lese-majesty' and he will understand.'

'Very well,' the innkeeper said, 'I will prepare a coded message and release the pigeons immediately. In the meantime, I suggest that you and the Abbé change into clothes which will attract less attention. Madame Picot we have fresh garments that will fit you too.'

Jean Marie nodded gratefully.

'The three of us do not need to change,' Joseph interrupted, pointing to the farmer and his boy. 'We will be leaving immediately.'

'Joseph!' Jean Marie pined, grasping hold of her son.

'Mother, these two need to sign up,' Joseph said. 'And I need to get back to work.'

'But when will I see you next?'

'Soon enough, mother, soon enough.'

'My child,' Jean Marie sighed, holding him tightly. 'I am so grateful for your company over these days. You are a son to make any mother proud.'

'Now I want to make father proud,' Joseph replied.

With that, he turned away towards his tethered horse. 'Come,' he said to the farmer and his boy. 'It's time to leave.'

As the three of them pulled themselves up into their saddles, Joseph smiled. 'Godspeed,' he said.

'Godspeed,' Pryce replied before adding, 'I know I'm not one to talk right now, brother, but please try and keep out of trouble.'

'I'll do my best,' Joseph replied. 'But as you now know all too well, Thomas, the darkness only triumphs when the children of light are idle.'

Joseph made the sign of the cross on his chest and then steered his horse towards the arched gateway that led to the road.

'Come,' the innkeeper said, leading them to the warmth of the kitchen beyond the back door. 'You need to get indoors. The Grenadiers often march through this village and it wouldn't do for you to be seen by them. Even with fresh clothes you will arouse suspicion.'

'Thank you, Monsieur Henry,' Jean Marie replied. 'Do you have anywhere we can stay in your hotel?'

'I have rooms that you can use over the next few days. Madame, you can have the best room in the hotel.'

Then Henry turned to the two priests. 'If you two gentlemen don't mind sharing …'

'The Abbé and I have enjoyed some most unusual bedrooms since we became reacquainted,' Pryce mused.

'Indeed,' the Abbé added, 'everything from caves to stables.'

'Well,' Pryce concluded, 'if it was good enough for our Lord, it's certainly good enough for us.'

CHAPTER 31

The doctor poured a generous glass of port for his accomplice Titus Morgues and then moved to the corner of his room in the Crown and Anchor Tavern. He picked up his walking cane by its shiny silver handle and grasped the long black rod with his free hand. With a swift movement which betrayed frequent practice he drew the razor sharp blade from its hiding place and lifted it so that it glinted like one of his scalpels in the lamplight.

'My God,' Morgues whispered, 'I've never seen a weapon like that before.'

'Nor had I, until I met the Shadow. Our master had it especially designed by a Swiss sword maker in Paris. He has a fondness for secret weapons.'

'Do you intend to use it when we have our audience with the king?'

Before answering, the doctor walked to the door of his room. He pressed one side of his head against its wooden panels before quickly and quietly opening it. There was no one there. He then strode to the windows, ensuring they were locked and that both balconies were unoccupied. Finally, he looked under the bed and inside the wash cupboard before sitting down in his armchair, nodding his head.

'It's safe to talk,' he said.

'By the looks of your cane,' Morgues whispered, 'our mission is more drastic than I thought.'

'Forgive me, Morgues, but the Shadow ordered me not to divulge the details until after our visit to Lord Stanhope. It was important that you believed the deception too.'

'So what you said to Stanhope is untrue?'

'More like a half-truth. We are going to see the king but we aren't going to abduct him. That is far too clumsy. No, once we have an audience with him, you are going to hold him, force him to the floor, and then I am going to decapitate him.'

'Mother of God,' Morgues exclaimed. 'That will bring the monarchy to its knees.'

'Quite literally. A shadow will fall across this nation. England will be a headless creature, groping about in the dark. Then, while it is wavering, our fleet will strike a decisive blow against the Royal Navy, giving us control of the Channel.'

'That's brilliant!'

'Of course, it is the Shadow's idea.'

Morgues took a sip of his port. 'What's our exit plan?'

'That's our task for tonight,' the doctor replied. 'We are heading out to an inn here in the city in order to meet our Irish friend from St. James' Palace. He is going to help us devise a proper escape route.'

'What do you have in mind?' Morgues asked.

'We have already arranged for a schooner to take us from the Thames to the coast and then back across the channel to France.'

'There really is a compliment of Irish sailors, then?'

'There really is,' the doctor replied.

'Then what's still to be done?'

'We need to devise a safe route from the audience chamber at St James' Palace to the Thames, where our vessel of escape will be ready and waiting for us. That will need careful thought.'

'When are we heading out to meet our Irish friend?'

'Right now, so finish your drink.'

'If we're heading to an inn, I hope we're not having some of that disgusting English ale,' Morgues quipped.

The doctor laughed. 'I have good news for you, my friend. This is an inn owned by Frenchmen. They have an excellent cellar of wine and a proper chef, who knows how to create an outstanding sauce and how not to destroy vegetables. Furthermore, we can choose our food rather than suffer a set menu.'

'Magnificent!' Morgues cried. 'If you plan our escape as

meticulously as you plan our dining, then I shall be more than content.'

'Come, then,' the doctor smiled.

The two men donned their black greatcoats, scarves and hats and descended via the stone staircase to the ground floor of the tavern. Passing underneath the immense lantern in the foyer, they proceeded through the front doors into the cold night. A short brisk walk and they were at the coach stand outside St Clement's Church in the Strand. Within moments they had climbed into the shabby interior of one of the thousand plus hackney cabs on London's streets.

'The Sabonière tavern in Leicester Square,' the doctor shouted.

'Sixpence every 'alf mile,' the driver called back. The heavy coated coachman flicked his long whip and his two horses lifted their drooping heads, shook their scanty tails and began reluctantly to pull the carriage underneath the burning streetlights of the city, rattling their harnesses as they went.

'La Sabonière?' Morgues asked once the sound of the wheels on the stone streets had made it safe to talk. 'What is this place?'

'The Shadow told me that there are two taverns in London that only take foreign guests. The first is the German Inn in Suffolk Street. The Saboniere is the other - a French tavern in Leicester Square, or Leicester Fields as it used to be called.'

'It will be a blessed relief to taste our own food and wine,' Morgues sighed.

'Indeed.'

'I hope we will also be permitted to wear our own shoes rather than those filthy slippers they give us in English inns?'

'We will, my friend, and they will also give us napkins when we dine so that we don't have to wipe our fingers on the table cloths, as these English barbarians do.'

'I'm looking forward to this,' Morgues laughed. 'I've had enough of beef steaks, plum puddings, stilton cheese - not to mention two pronged forks.'

'Me also,' the doctor said.

'What about our Irish accomplice? Will they allow him in at the Sabonière?'

'We will meet him in the foyer and take him into the dining hall with us. They will not question it.'

As the coach made its way from the Strand, the doctor began to shift on his straw-filled canvas seat, every so often peering over his shoulder through an aperture in the back of the carriage.

'What's the matter?' Morgues asked.

'Don't look round,' the doctor replied. 'We're being followed.'

'Are you sure?'

'When we boarded this coach I noticed that there was already one ready to go. It was occupied and when we departed, it departed too. It has been right behind us all the way along the Strand.'

'You truly have eyes in the back of your head,' Morgues said.

'Listen, my friend, if you are going to excel as an agent you must always observe your surroundings whenever you board a vehicle. Take three or four seconds to see whether there are any conveyances which might follow in your wake.'

'What are we going to do about them?'

'We need to set a trap.'

The doctor took his cane and prodded the driver, indicating to him to slow down.

The driver swore vociferously but obliged.

When the horses had slowed from a trot to a walk, the doctor leaned up and forward.

'Turn down that side street,' he said.

The driver steered the carriage off the cobbled road into a gravel covered street where new houses were being built.

'Perfect,' the doctor whispered to Morgues. 'This street is dark, quiet and unoccupied and it leads back to the main road of the Strand.'

'What are you going to do?'

'Driver,' the doctor hissed, 'stop over there and set us down. Go back to the Strand and pick us up there in thirty minutes. I'll pay you for time.'

'Very well, sir,' the driver replied, pulling on the reins of his two horses.

The large green wheels of the carriage drew to a halt. Its blood red axletree now fell silent. There was not a sound to be heard anywhere on the street.

The doctor and his colleague alighted, marching swiftly into the front garden of a half constructed mansion, before climbing furtively through a rectangular sash window frame into its shadowy halls.

'Keep very quiet,' the doctor whispered, as they hid behind a tall pile of yellow bricks.

'Don't move,' the doctor added.

They heard the sound of one of the horses neighing as the driver whipped her and their hackney cab pulled away from the front of the house.

The doctor squinted as he forced his eyes to acclimatize to the chiaroscuro of the downstairs rooms. On his right there were stacks of slates intended for the roof. On his left a large iron cauldron used for molten lead was perched on top of a metal trivet. Around it was a brick fire pit covered in charcoal stains underneath the cauldron. Coals still glowed in the pit as steam rose from the urn.

The doctor looked up through the joists and planks of the uncovered floor above, through the spacious opening beyond where the roof truss stood exposed to the night. He could see that the moon was full and the stars were bright.

As the doctor protected his nose against the lingering odour from the cauldron, his ears began to twitch like those of a hunting dog. He could hear the sound of a coach approaching on the unfinished street outside. The wheels drew to a halt. A horse shook its head wildly and puffed its nostrils loudly. There was the crunch of footsteps outside. And then the doctor saw the silhouette of a lean man in a top hat and long dark coat standing in the empty frame of the front door.

As the man walked into the centre of the room, he lit a match and raised it.

The flame flickered for a matter of seconds before being snuffed out by a gust of wind blowing through the hollow halls of the house.

'Sennett,' the doctor whispered to his accomplice.

The doctor lowered himself behind the bricks but the man was moving slowly towards them, trying to light another match as he walked. The doctor looked at Morgues and drew his hand like a dagger across his own throat.

'Now!' the doctor whispered.

The two men sprang like foxhounds towards their prey, startling the man and causing him to fumble and then drop his ignited match.

'Hold him!' the doctor barked.

Morgues took the man, who had been caught off guard, and held him from behind in a locked embrace.

'Force him to his knees,' the doctor hissed.

The man's legs buckled as Morgues' greater strength prevailed. The interloper's hat fell to the stony ground and rolled for a moment on the floor.

The doctor took his walking stick as the man began to cry out.

'What do you want with me?'

'I want you dead,' the doctor said.

As he drew the blade from the cane, the man's cool air deserted him.

'No!' he screamed.

Morgues pushed the man down so that one side of his terrified face was in the detritus of the building site. With another hand he pulled the collar of the man's coat, forcing several buttons to break.

As a scream arose from the man's throat, the doctor brought the sword swiftly down. It flashed like lightning towards the nape of his neck, slicing through flesh and bone as if they were silk. For a moment the doctor saw a thin red line appear and then heard the thud of the head as it fell upon the stone. The two assassins stepped back as the arteries in the man's neck sent spurts of blood over the yellow bricks.

'You scum!' a voice shouted.

A second man had appeared at the frame of the door. He had a patch over his left eye. 'I'll bloody kill you.'

The man charged towards the doctor and barged him like a battering ram, forcing the blade out of the doctor's hand as the two men crashed into a pile of timber.

The man was on top of the doctor and had his fingers around his throat, applying a pressure intensified by rage. The doctor tried to call for help but he could not speak. He felt his consciousness begin to ebb. As he struggled for breath, he punched at his assailant with his right hand while with his left he tried to prize the man's fingers from his neck. Suddenly, the man loosed his grip. And then the doctor saw why. Morgues had brought a thick plank of wood down upon the man's skull, causing him to stand, step back and then topple uncontrollably towards the cauldron.

'Quick!' the doctor shouted.

As the man teetered at the fire pit, Morgues tripped him up so that he fell upon his back - face up towards the dark, grim receptacle.

'Now!' the doctor cried.

Morgues ran to the other side of the pit and seized a piece of timber, ramming it into the lip of the vessel, tipping it away from his body. The man on the floor understood what was happening but he was too late and too disoriented to react. He opened his mouth to scream but there was no sound. The molten lead poured over his lips and then his throat, stripping the flesh until his sallow jawbone appeared. As the liquid lead began to congeal in his larynx and lungs, the man began to asphyxiate.

'Quick, finish him!' Morgues shouted.

The doctor walked over to the sword cane. He picked it up, placed the tip of the blade methodically at the point of the man's heart, before making a fatal incision. The victim's tensed and struggling limbs relaxed as one of his feet twitched momentarily before his body became fixed in death. Morgues dropped to his knees and retched.

'Good work, Morgues,' the doctor said, as he helped his friend.

'What shall we do with the bodies?' Morgues gasped.

'We won't have time to clean up the mess and dispose of the remains,' the doctor replied.

'We will be discovered.'

'I have a plan.'

'What is it?'

'I have brought something to throw our pursuers off the scent.'

The doctor put on his spectacles and drew a gilded white card from the inside pocket of his jacket. 'This is an invitation to members of the French delegation with the Prime Minister, William Pitt, on Friday in the House of Commons.'

'That's day we have our audience with the King,' Morgues said.

'Precisely, and it will form a perfect distraction.'

'What is the meeting about?'

'Members of the delegation have asked for an audience to discuss the suspension of habeas corpus for French citizens in this country. In my capacity as Monsieur Marat, I could be there if I so chose.'

The doctor paused and tore a corner off the invitation. 'This should be enough to divert them,' he said.

The doctor knelt beside the corpse at his feet and placed the fragment of the card in the palm of the dead man's hand and then forced the hand into the shape of a fist, with a tiny part of the card showing through the second and third index fingers.

'When rigor mortis sets in this will be a most effective dissemblance,' the doctor smiled.

'They will think we're going to assassinate the Prime Minister,' Morgues quipped.

'Indeed they will.'

The two men brushed themselves down and walked outside. The driver-less coach stood motionless in front of them. One of the horses shook her shaggy mane from side to side as a stray dog howled in a neighbouring street. The two men walked past the coach towards the end of the road, the doctor drew the sword once again. Its blade was slaked with the blood of the two British agents. The doctor wiped it from the tip to the hilt with a handkerchief which he then threw, crumpled and blooded, into the front yard of another half-built mansion. As he returned the blade to its hiding place, the doctor saw their coach and horses standing underneath a street light just ahead. Their driver had his hands thrust deep inside his trouser pockets and his feet were shuffling, as in an impromptu dance, to keep warm.

'As rehearsals go,' the doctor said, 'that wasn't bad.'

'When the play is finally performed,' Morgues added, 'the curtain will come down on the British monarchy.'

'In the meantime,' the doctor smiled, 'it's time for a decent meal and a glass of wine at the Sabonière.'

CHAPTER 32

'You will forgive me, Monsieur Henry,' Jean Marie sighed, 'but I cannot enjoy this beautiful food. I have taken a vow concerning that dog Masson and I will not eat until he is dead and buried.'

'I understand, Madame,' Henry said as he placed a bowl of piping stew before Pryce and the Abbé.

'Are you sure?' Pryce asked.

'Absolutely certain,' Jean Marie replied.

'Then you will forgive us, I trust, if we enjoy our food.'

'Of course I will, Thomas.'

Pryce took his spoon and savoured a gulp of the seafood broth which Henry had set down. 'This is exceptional,' Pryce gasped as he looked up from his seat into the puffed and rubicund cheeks of the innkeeper, who was hovering for a compliment.

'The clams, muscles and scallops were caught off Saint Malo,' Henry panted. 'I chose them at the market there just this morning.'

'And is this lobster?' Pryce asked.

'It is, caught in one of my own traps.'

'Monsieur, you are too generous,' Jean Marie said, 'especially in such austere times.'

'In Paris,' the Abbé said, 'people are desperate for a loaf of bread right now. They are queuing up outside the shops for many hours and are often disappointed.'

'Ah, but this is Brittany,' the innkeeper said, resting his hands on his pendulous stomach. 'And here we have learned to work the land as well as the sea and to scratch one another's backs.'

'Well, I must congratulate you, Monsieur Henry,' Pryce said. 'This fruit wine is glorious and the butter on this bread, it is divine.'

The innkeeper smiled. 'I'm glad you're happy, my friends.' The man bowed his head and navigated his path through the six-seat tables of the small dining room back towards the kitchen, bidding a genial good evening to the other guests who were now delighting in the dishes he had created.

Pryce took another sip from his wine and sat back, staring for a moment at the candle burning brightly on the red, white and blue tablecloth. 'No offence, Abbé,' he said, 'but I'm glad to be out of those priestly garments and into these more - how shall I put it - practical clothes.'

'None taken, dear friend,' the Abbé replied. 'If we are to proceed to our seaside mansion on horseback, and then by sea to Jersey, we would be better served by these outfits than the clerical costumes we were wearing.'

The Abbé patted his chest as he did, rubbing the fabric of his waistcoat and short jacket, before adjusting his collars and cravat. He then leaned towards Pryce and whispered. 'I take it you have transferred Lady Hester's gift to the garments you are now wearing.'

Pryce pressed his hand hard against his heart and as he did the outline of the pistol momentarily and unmistakably surfaced.

At that moment the innkeeper reappeared with a wooden board covered in cheese and fruit preserves. A young maid with a sallow smile followed hard after him, bringing a bottle of apple brandy, freshly opened.

'Bon appétit,' the innkeeper said as he placed the cheeseboard in front of the two men.

'Cheers,' they replied, raising their glasses and admiring the copper and golden hues of the brandy against the light of a hanging lantern.

As the innkeeper turned to leave, he stopped dead in his tracks. He turned quickly back to the table and started to brush invisible crumbs from the tablecloth into the bottom of his creased apron. As he did, he bent low and looked Pryce in the eyes. 'Masson, Sicard, they're here,' he whispered.

Pryce shuddered.

Jean Marie took hold of the handle of the curved cheese knife and grasped it so tightly that the skin on her knuckles began to turn red and white.

Pryce placed his hand gently on hers.

'Peace, mother,' he said under his breath.

As the innkeeper left the table, the two men looked around the room. They were dressed almost entirely in black and were carrying hats with strident tricolor cockades.

As they scanned the chamber, their eyes fixed upon Pryce's table. It was the only one with unoccupied seats, three to be precise. 'These seats are free, Citizens?' the taller man enquired as he and his accomplice drew near.

Pryce nodded.

The two men handed their hats to the young maid.

Fumbling, the maid dropped both hats.

'Imbecile!' the taller man snapped, causing the whole room to fall silent and the trembling maid to start snivelling, her eyes misting.

'Is that any way to treat the colours of the Republic?' the shorter man hissed.

'Sorry, Citizen, I am most terribly sorry,' she said tremulously.

The girl swept the hats into her lap, leapt to her feat like a frightened doe, before scampering into the safety of the kitchen.

'Forgive us, Citizens,' the taller man said, turning back to the table. 'My name is Citizen Masson and this is my colleague, Citizen Sicard.'

Pryce waited for a moment for Jean Marie to respond first. But she was silent, staring at the two men.

'Let me introduce to you my mother, Madame Pericot,' Pryce said, exhibiting his flawless Breton dialect.

'And I am her brother, Citizen Corbieres,' the Abbé said.

'My name is Citizen Pericot,' Pryce added.

'And where are you all from?' Masson asked.

'My mother lives with her brother on a farm not far from here, just outside Dinan,' Pryce replied.

'And you, Citizen?'

'I live with my mother.'

'And what brings you here this evening?' Sicard enquired.

'We are here to celebrate my mother's birthday,' Pryce replied.

'Ah, felicitations,' Masson said, revealing an uneven set of yellowing teeth.

He tapped his glass with a spoon and stood to his feet, the legs of his wooden chair dragging noisily on the stone floor. A hush fell once again upon the room. 'Citizens of the Republic,' Masson declared, gesturing towards Jean Marie, 'it is Citizen Pericot's birthday today. We should congratulate her.'

The diners rose to their feet, raised their glasses and pronounced their congratulations before sitting back down and returning to their conversations. As the echoing hubbub of the room was restored, Masson turned to Jean Marie. 'Madame, you seem not to be in the mood for celebrating.'

'She has a pain in her neck,' the Abbé interjected.

'But even with such a discomfort, Madame can speak for herself, unless of course it is so severe she cannot speak, in which case she must be too incapacitated to be capable of dining here at all.'

Jean Marie was about to reply when Henry returned with two bowls which he placed, without finesse, in front of the men. Gone was the gourmet fruit-de-la-mere. In its place there was a steaming brew of brown liquid with little islands formed out of re-boiled potatoes.

'No bread, Citizen?' Sicard wheezed.

'I'm afraid bread is in very short supply and my ration for the evening has been exhausted,' Henry replied.

The terrified maid stepped out from behind Henry's corpulent frame and poured cider into the men's glasses.

'Not even cidre bouche for us?' Sicard asked.

'I'm sorry, very sorry, but I was told to bring you the table cider.'

Henry, who had kept within easy range of the table, sprang back into view. He removed the two glasses of cider. 'If our local apples are not to your Parisian tastes, I will bring you some water,' he sneered.

'No, no, Citizen,' Masson retorted, laying his hand across the innkeeper's outstretched arms. 'The cider is quite sufficient. We were merely asking your maid why she brought us table cider when our friends here were given fruit wine and apple brandy.'

'It is because it is Madame's birthday, as every one of my guests now knows,' the innkeeper sniped. 'Now unless by some extraordinary circumstance it is yours as well, perhaps you will allow me to attend to my guests.'

Masson sighed and shook his head before turning to the uninviting soup in front of him. 'This is disgusting,' he gasped.

'It tastes like dishwater,' Sicard moaned.

'Looks like it too,' Masson added.

'I'm most terribly sorry about that,' Pryce interjected. 'Our seafood broth was the finest I have ever tasted.'

Masson set his spoon down and stared into Pryce's eyes. 'I am beginning to wonder,' he said, 'whether it is simply a birthday that has elicited this preferential service.'

'What do you mean?' Pryce asked.

'I mean that something is not right here. I have a nose for these things.'

'There is nothing sinister going on, I can assure you,' the Abbé interrupted.

'Before you say anything else,' Masson said, 'let me tell you who you are dealing with. My colleague and I are working with the police in Dinan and the city authorities in Rennes, obeying the orders of our masters in Paris.'

'I am very happy for you,' the Abbé said. 'But what has that got to do with us?'

'I wonder whether it is merely coincidence that we are looking for three people at the moment and we are sitting with three people here at this table.'

'It is a mere coincidence,' the Abbé said diffidently.

'But is it?' Masson replied. 'You see, we are looking for a woman of provincial nobility, and her brother-in-law - a Jesuit Abbé - and a younger Englishman masquerading as a Catholic priest called Edgeworth.'

'Well that's settled it, then,' the Abbé said.

'What do you mean?'

'Well, we are Bretons, not Britains.'

Masson ignored the comment and stared right into Pryce's eyes, his pupils widening as he tilted his head first one way, then another. 'You will permit me to ask you some questions?' Masson asked.

'If you must,' Pryce replied.

'If you really have a farm near Dinan, then you will be familiar with the town's history.'

'Of course,' Pryce replied, adding, 'it is a beautiful medieval town, one that I know well.'

'If that is so,' Masson continued, 'then answer me this. What is the name of the town's most famous Knight?'

'Bertrand du Guesclin,' Pryce replied.

'And what was he known as?'

'The Eagle of Brittany,' Pryce said.

'In what year did he die?'

'He had a sorry end for such a brave man, dying from dysentery. I believe it was around the year 1380.'

'And my final question,' Masson asked, 'where is Bertrand du Guesclin buried?'

'He was buried in the church at Monterrand,' Pryce said, 'but whether his remains are still there I do not know.'

'And why is that?'

'The church was destroyed by the government a few months ago, as everyone around these parts knows.'

Masson scowled and returned to his dishwater broth, which he sipped gingerly. He took a large gulp of cider straight away, swilling it around his mouth before gargling and then swallowing it, his nose upturned in distaste.

'You sound like a Breton, you eat like a Breton and you dress like a Breton,' Masson said quietly, 'but I suspect you are not from these parts.'

With that, Jean Marie snapped. 'Enough!' she shouted, slamming her fist upon the table, causing Masson's glass of cider to topple and spill all over the cloth. Every diner in the room froze and looked towards Jean Marie, who was now standing, her eyes flaring. 'Your manners are inexcusable,' she said to Masson. 'I am here for my birthday dinner. I already had pain before you two came to the table but now I find myself afflicted beyond description.'

She turned to Pryce and the Abbé. 'Come, my son. Come, brother. I do not find the company of these men congenial.'

Pryce stood. 'Thank you for ruining my dear mother's birthday,' he snapped.

Masson and Sicard rose to their feet.

Jean Marie and the Abbé were allowed to pass. When Pryce tried to negotiate his passage, Masson grabbed him by the arm, digging his long and unkempt fingernails into his flesh. 'You think you have had the last word, monsieur,' Masson spat, 'but I assure you - this is not the last you have heard from us.'

Pryce turned and pulled away. As he walked past the kitchen and followed his friends up the wooden staircase towards their bedrooms, he flicked a bead of sweat from his forehead.

As the three fugitives slipped into the Abbé's bedroom, they closed the door firmly and held one another for a moment before lighting a lamp and sitting on the bed. A moment later there was a soft tapping on the door.

'You cannot stay,' Henry gasped, as he entered the room. 'They are onto you.'

'Are you sure?' Pryce asked.

'I'm certain. Those two weasels left the moment you went upstairs. They didn't take another sip of their soup. I caught them just in time to give them their bill and also a list of costs for the room repairs after Masson's last visit.'

'What do you suggest we do?' the Abbé asked.

'Make your way right now to your second home, Madame,' the innkeeper replied.

'Is everything prepared for dawn?' Pryce asked.

'Yes,' the innkeeper replied. 'Captain Auvergne and his men will be on the beach below your house at sunrise.'

'He'd better bring soldiers,' the Abbé replied.

'He'll need them,' the innkeeper panted.

'Why is that?' Jean Marie asked.

'The Grenadiers have been joined by a company of light infantry.'

'They can muster as many men as they want but it will be of no use if they do not know where to find us,' Jean Marie said.

'Not unless someone talks,' the innkeeper said.

CHAPTER 33

'Look there!' the doctor whispered.

'What is it?'

'Just there,' he pointed, as their coach proceeded through Charing Cross.

'It is an equestrian statue,' Morgues said. 'What is so special about that?'

'It is King Charles the First,' the doctor smiled, 'whose head was cut off one hundred and fifty years ago by the axe blade of Oliver Cromwell.'

'The English are bizarre,' Morgues mused. 'They celebrate those they decapitate.'

The doctor laughed. 'They will have cause to do that again, my friend.'

A moment later the carriage had made its way down Leicester Street and into Leicester Square.

'My God, what is that?' Morgues blurted after the two men had alighted.

In front of them, on one side of Leicester House, was a gigantic half-painted picture, the length and height of the mansion itself. On the canvas the doctor could make out men-of-war sailing towards a harbour with a full press of sail and their colours fluttering in the breeze. They were traversing a lake surrounded by mountains whose summits wore the billowing clouds like white wigs. On the right hand side of the canvas there was a wooden staircase running up to the timbered roof. This gave access to two floors with raised galleries on which spectators could stand and marvel at the painted panorama of the fleet.

'What is this, driver?' the doctor asked before the man pulled away.

'It is one of Mister Barker's panoramas, sir,' the coachman replied. 'It will be ready in the summer.'

'What does it show?'

The driver paused and looked at the two men, a glint in his eyes. 'It shows the royal navy off Spithead,' he said.

'What's the point of that?' Masson muttered.

'The point is to remind our enemies that Brittania rules the waves,' the driver quipped as he raised his whip and goaded his mares into action.

The doctor ignored the remark and he scurried to the entrance of the French tavern where the Irishman was waiting. The three of them were shown to a table.

An hour later and the doctor was lowering his napkin with a contented sigh. The skeletons of two fish lay side by side on his plate, their wide-eyed heads meticulously severed from their spines. 'Let's retire to a side room so we can talk privately,' the doctor said.

The three men found a small, well lit chamber with three armchairs and a lit fire.

'Thank you for meeting with us, Mister Moore,' the doctor said, closing the door.

'It's not a problem.'

'Do you have something for us?' the doctor enquired.

The Irishman drew a folded, faded parchment from his jacket and laid it across the table. 'This is a map of the first floor of Saint James' Palace,' he whispered.

The doctor's eyes widened.

'It is not entirely up to date,' he added. 'It is nearly seventy years old and there have been some alterations in the reigns of the three Georges.'

'But it is still accurate enough?' the doctor asked.

'Very much so,' the Irishman replied.

'Please, Mister Moore, share your thoughts with us,' the doctor whispered.

'You will need to act this Friday,' the Irishman said. 'The King is coming from Buckingham House to Saint James' Palace for an audience with Lord Stanhope and the other inventors, at two o' clock to be precise. It is his last appointment of the day.'

'Will he be guarded?'

'There is talk of security being increased, but the costs for that haven't yet been agreed between the Royal Household and the Government, so there will be the standard complement of one royal equerry and the yeoman of the guard, the man who guards the king's chambers.'

'Is that all?'

'It is.'

The doctor smiled.

'Here,' the Irishman said, pointing to the entrance of the palace. 'You will enter through the gatehouse, along with Lord Stanhope. You will all be asked to present your invitations and your proof of identity. I take it you have those?'

'Stanhope has the invitations, we have our counterfeited identity papers,' the doctor replied.

'Good, that's good,' the Irishman said. 'In that case, you will be ushered through the gates and into the main courtyard, the Colour Court, with the Chapel Royal on your right. You will then proceed to the far end of the court and pass beneath a stone arch up a staircase to the King's chambers on the first floor.'

'Where are they?' Morgues squinted, scrutinizing the map.

'Here,' the Irishman said, indicating a set of three rooms leading one to the next at the end of a long gallery. 'The first is the guard's chamber where the yeomen control access to and from the king's quarters.'

'Will they be armed?' the doctor enquired.

'Yes,' the Irishman replied, 'there is an armoury beyond the guard's room.'

'We will need to take great care not to arouse suspicion as we pass,' the doctor mused.

'From the Guard's Chamber,' the Irishman continued, 'you will be escorted into the third of the king's rooms, the Presence Chamber, also known as the Tapestry Room. Beyond that is the Privy Chamber.'

'Where will the audience be held?' the doctor asked.

'Here, in the Tapestry Room,' the Irishman replied, pointing to a chamber adjacent to two courts, Paradise Court to the left and Engine Court to the right.

'On my signal,' the doctor said, 'we will immobilize the equerry and force the king from the Tapestry Room into the Privy Chamber beyond.' The doctor paused. 'There we will strike,' he added.

He paused again. 'If we are efficient,' he concluded, 'we should take a matter of seconds to do something whose effects will be felt for centuries.'

'Ha!' the Irishman cried. 'The whole world will be shaken.'

The three men sipped from glinting glasses filled with golden dessert wine and sat back in their chairs.

It was the Irishman who broke the silence first. 'Forgive me for asking, but what is Lord Stanhope's role in all of this?'

'He has only one task and that is to secure our access to the Presence Chamber,' the doctor replied.

'Does he know what you're planning to do?'

'No,' the doctor replied.

'What does he know?'

'We have told him that we intend to abduct the king and take him to Paris to the Tower Prison.'

'What if he suspects that you are planning something darker?'

'That is why we must remove the king from the audience chamber.'

'Are you not sure of Stanhope's compliance?'

'I am sure that he wants an end to the monarchy in England but I am not so sure that he would approve of our methods.'

'Would he try to intervene when we apply the coup de grace?'

'He might.'

'Then he must not leave the Presence Chamber,' the Irishman insisted.

'He will not,' the doctor replied.

'So how do we escape from the Privy Chamber once we've struck the fatal blow?' Morgues asked.

'You cannot return the way we came,' the Irishman said. 'You will run straight into the armed yeomen?'

'So what is our way out?' the doctor asked.

'You will lock yourselves inside the Privy Chamber as soon as you enter it with the king, preventing anyone from following.'

'You have a key?'

'I will 'borrow' one,' the Irishman replied. 'Then you will head left through a small unoccupied drawing room, through the King's Bed Chamber and into the Stole Room.'

'What in heaven's name is that?' Morgues asked.

'It is where the royal chamber pot is located - a room guarded by the Groom of the Stole, a man whose unenviable duty is to watch over the king while he defecates and then empty and clean the pewter receptacle.'

'Let's hope he hasn't just been before he attends the audience,' Morgues sighed.

'I think we will have more testing challenges than that,' the doctor interjected.

'From there you will proceed through the old kitchen and down some stairs into an empty wine vault beneath. There is a tunnel from the vault beneath Paradise Court to the remains of an ancient hall belonging to the Leper's Hospital, situated beneath the Chapel Royal.'

'What is this hospital?' Morgues asked.

'Saint James' hasn't always been a palace,' the Irishman replied. 'There was a hospital there in the twelfth century, dedicated to Saint James the Less. It housed fourteen virgin sisters who had leprosy. They committed themselves to a life of prayer and purity as the disease took its toll. They were true women of God, intent on living chastely and honestly in divine service.'

The doctor sneered.

'Citizen Marat does not share your Catholic sensibilities,' Morgues smiled.

'No matter,' the Irishman replied, 'we share many others.'

'Quite so,' the doctor nodded. 'So how do we get from there to your countrymen on the Thames?'

'The underground tunnel leads beneath the gatehouse under Pall Mall and out through a concealed drain at one end of the lake in St James' Park. From there you will run through Horse Guards Parade and Whitehall, past Scotland Yard to Whitehall Stairs.'

'What are the Whitehall Stairs?' Morgues asked.

'They are one of the watermen's stairs built as safe plying places to pick up and set down passengers on the River Thames. The Thames is a tidal river and so boats use causeways at low tide and the watermen's stairs at high tide.'

'And how will the tide be on Friday evening?' the doctor enquired.

'It will be high tide, so you can use Whitehall Stairs to board the sloop. Then you will set sail for France, proceeding up the Seine into Paris, no doubt to be given a hero's welcome.'

'No doubt,' the doctor smiled.

'How long will it take us to run from the palace to the Thames?' Morgues asked.

'About fifteen minutes, if you meet with no obstacles,' the Irishman replied.

'This might just work,' Morgues gasped.

'It will work,' the Irishman insisted, as the three men simultaneously quaffed some more sweet wine.

'Tell me,' the doctor said. 'What is the king's present mental state? We know he has been suffering for some time with a form of madness. Will he be coherent?'

'He has been much more lucid of late,' the Irishman replied, 'although he still has a tendency to go out into the gardens and dig up the flower beds for no reason, hence his nickname in the Palace, 'the King of Spades."

'He can be trusted not to do anything, let's say, unexpected?' the doctor asked.

'I believe he can,' the Irishman replied. 'He has been holding audiences, drawing rooms, levees and Privy Council meetings for some months now. Everyone is giving good reports of his condition.'

'And how many will there be in the audience?' the doctor asked.

'There will be approximately twenty in all, including the King, his equerry and myself.'

'How have you managed to gain access to this meeting?' Morgues asked.

'I am one of the royal secretaries, employed to take notes in meetings like these.'

'And it is your turn to do this on Friday?'

'It is.'

'If I wasn't a man of reason, I'd almost say that this feels like providence,' Morgues exclaimed.

'Maybe it is,' the Irishman replied.

'Maybe it is the product of careful planning and fine timing,' the doctor said.

'Whatever the reasons,' the Irishman continued, 'we three will see each other again soon, although next time I will be wearing the royal livery.'

'That's in four days,' Morgues gasped.

'Four days until this royal madness ends,' the doctor said, raising his glittering glass to the light of the iridescent lamp above. 'Four days until the shadow of death falls upon the palace of Saint James.'

CHAPTER 34

Pryce tried to keep his eyes open and his reins tight as his horse chased hard after the two mares in front.

'It's just beyond that forest,' Jean Marie shouted, as she pointed to a wood half a mile ahead of them.

Pryce, Jean Marie and the Abbé had been cantering most of the night, heading to the coast north east of Saint Malo.

'Let's relieve the horses of their burdens,' Jean Marie said as they slowed to the trot.

The three fugitives dismounted.

Pryce caressed the nodding nose of his dappled mare, soothing her with the promise of an impending drink to slake her thirst, and his.

'Come,' Jean Marie said. 'We can lead the horses from here.'

Pryce followed his mother-in-law across the field. It was blanketed in a thick mist which seemed to hang in the clock-calm wind. As he heard the Abbé and Jean Marie murmuring the words of the Angelus as they walked, he remembered the Daily Office and began to whisper his own liturgy.

'We have followed too much the devices and desires of our own hearts,' he said under his breath, 'we have offended against thy holy laws.' Pryce sighed. 'We have left undone those things which we ought to have done and we have done those things that we ought not to have done. And there is no health in us.' Pryce paused. 'There is no health in me,' he said, exhaling a cloud of air like incense. He gathered himself and continued. 'But thou O Lord have mercy upon us miserable offenders and spare thou them who confess their faults, restore thou those who are penitent.'

He felt a hand on his shoulder. It was the Abbé. As Pryce finished his prayer, the Abbé whispered into his ear.

'Dominus noster Jesus Christus te absolvat...'

Pryce was taken aback for a moment. Then he smiled. 'Thank you,' he said.

As they made their way through the far side of the wood, Jean Marie cried out. 'We're here!'

The three pushed their way down an overgrown path through a row of hedges into a fallow field. It was then that Pryce saw the manor house through the mist. There were no signs of life. It was empty.

'Thank God,' the Abbé said.

'You have never been here, have you Thomas?' Jean Marie asked.

'No, mother,' Pryce replied.

'Michel had it built as a second home. Many of the shipbuilders in Saint Malo did the same thing, although our *moulinière* is unusual because it overlooks the sea. Most of Michel's friends had had their fill of staring at the ocean. But not our Michel.'

As Pryce drew near to the house, he stopped and gazed up at its impressive facade. The mansion had been constructed in a simple H shape, with two wings built either side of a central section where the entrance was situated. The roof was large and steep and covered in slate stones, which Jean Marie confided had been quarried locally, as had the cut granite stone of the house's walls. The tall surmounted chimneys were made of terracotta and seemed almost to be lost from view as they jutted upwards into the grey sky. As Pryce lowered his gaze, he noticed a thick belt of stone around the middle of the entire house, highlighting the division between the two storeys, as well as stone bands running perpendicular to the tall windows.

At ground level, in front of the house, there was a dove-cote and a short tree-lined allee, either side of which there were high walls separating the cultivated gardens from the wild landscape beyond. It was a house with minimal adornments and an austere, almost military feel. And yet, as Pryce himself confessed to his two companions, its lines were undeniably elegant.

'It is providential that those dogs that sequestered our chateau have not found and requisitioned this place too,' Jean Marie said.

The two men nodded.

'We must go inside and find supplies,' Jean Marie added. 'But first we must take the horses to the stables.'

A few minutes later the three tired mares were drinking greedily from buckets of water and munching noisily from a trough of freshly laid straw.

'Come,' Jean Marie said, making her way from the stables back to the entrance of the house. Jean Marie opened the white front doors with a key she had retrieved from its hiding place in the stables. There was a stone staircase immediately in front of them which led to the first floor. Below that, privateer's weapons festooned every available space on the ground floor walls. Everywhere he looked Pryce could see the knives, swords, pistols and muskets that had once been used in the pirate raids by Breton corsairs. The only exception was an ornately framed oil painting of the family crest - two crossed hatchets gilded in gold against a sea blue background. She walked to a wall beside a door to Pryce's left, leading to the drawing room.

'Here,' she said, as she reached for two boarding axes. 'Help me get these down.'

Pryce seized hold of the two handles, taking care with the steel blades and the spikes of each axe. 'What are these for?'

'They are to cut down the rigging and the stays of an enemy ship's sails,' Jean Marie replied.

'Ah,' Pryce mused. 'A ship would not find it easy to manoeuvre after that.'

'Quite so,' Jean Marie agreed. 'Now, take them down for me.'

Pryce removed the poleaxes from the walls.

'Let's eat and drink,' she said. 'We can talk in the kitchen.'

An hour later they sat around the wooden table.

'We're going to need more than those blades if we land in trouble,' the Abbé said.

'We have muskets in the armoury,' Jean Marie replied as she led the way back to the entrance hall, 'and even a blunderbuss.'

For a moment they laughed.

Pryce then followed Jean Marie through the drawing room into the study, and then through a secret door in the panelled wall into a chamber filled with hunting gear and an assortment of muskets and other weapons.

'This might come in useful,' Pryce said as they foraged through the ordnance.

'What is it?' the Abbé said, as he greedily filled his pockets with cartridges and shouldered two muskets, one on each arm.

'It's a marine telescope,' Pryce answered, removing the brass dust shutter to the eye piece and pointing the smooth mahogany barrel out of the armoury through the window of the bureau beyond. 'And it appears to be in perfect working order.'

'Thomas, why don't you head up to the top floor and keep watch through the fanlights in the gables?' Jean Marie said, as she thrust a pistol into the front of her belt. 'You could look out for our friends from Jersey.'

'And Masson and Sicard,' the Abbé added.

Pryce nodded. He walked back through the study and the drawing room and into the entrance hall. Twenty heartbeats later and he had made his way to a glass aperture at the front gable, level with the bottom of the slate roof. He removed the brass shutter once again, noticing the gleaming brightwork as he did, and extended the two draw telescope from fifteen to forty - five inches in length, peering out towards the ocean. There was not a hint of discolouration and the optics afforded a clear magnification of twenty to thirty times.

'Thank you father,' Pryce sighed.

Pryce gazed beyond the cliff edge to the mist-draped sea. The sun was just starting to rise and he could make out a bugalet emerging from a rolling bank of fog, the sails on its fore and aft mast braced around to catch the breeze as the small galley was skilfully brought with her bow towards what there was of the wind.

Pryce smiled.

He lowered the telescope for a moment and wiped his eye before lifting it once again.

It was then that Pryce saw them. Three brigs were emerging

majestically from the sea fog. They were bearing the English colours at the tops of their two masts, their sails bent fast to the yards and stays.

Pryce lowered the telescope and rubbed his eyes.

Raising it again, he shook his head as the bows of all three ships pierced the sea mist, their fore and aft brigsails towering above those of the bugalot, dwarfing the Breton vessel which was now tacking urgently.

Pryce studied the three gun sloops and whispered, 'Bravo, Captain d'Auvergne!'

As the brigs drew closer Pryce observed the sixteen guns on each and counted up to one hundred men in their respective compliments. Anchors were now being dropped and square rigged sheets gathered in and secured. There was much commotion upon the decks, with boats being lowered into the water. Armed soldiers appeared from below decks like scurrying ants and then scampered down rope ladders draped over the gunwales on the larboard side of the brigs. These soldiers were dressed in bright red uniforms and were shouldering their muskets. Pryce counted over twenty boats of all sizes, with red coated soldiers in each. They were making ready to row the half mile or so from the ships to the shore.

Pryce distended the telescope as he stood to his feet and ran to the top of the stairs. As he arrived, he paused for a second, his head turning quizzically towards the gable facing from the rear of the manor house. A look of concern spread over his face like a scudding raincloud. Quick as a flash, he darted to the window at the rear of the mansion and fully extended his telescope.

He saw them immediately.

Marching in column formation, about two hundred foot soldiers dressed in blue uniforms were moving towards the house which stood between them and the three enemy brigs at anchor within half a mile from the shore. They were far away but Pryce could still see the soldiers at the front of the column, marching in close order, touching each others' elbows.

The men in the front ranks were wearing the headwear of light infantrymen while those in the ranks behind were in bearskins.

'Grenadiers!' Pryce exclaimed.

Just as he uttered the word, the front three ranks started to hurry forwards. They were running in pairs towards the mansion. Some of them already had their muskets trained on the windows at the back of the house.

'Light infantry!'

As the agile infantrymen began to draw to within a mile of the house, the Grenadiers behind them deployed from column formation into lines in open order, their commanding officer marching on their right flank, his sword drawn.

The Grenadiers were now in battle formation with their bayonets at the ready, their muskets loaded.

Some of the skirmishers, clearly acting as rangers and scouts, were already sniffing like foxhounds at the edge of the grounds.

Pryce shuddered as he stood quickly to his feet. This was no *grande bande* - no formless mob of badly led revolutionary soldiers. These soldiers had been well drilled and trained. They had seen action. They were professionals.

Pryce lifted the telescope one more time and raised it above the line of Grenadiers to a group of men and horses walking at the very rear. Three cannons were each being drawn by a team of horses, led at the reins by artillerymen. And behind them, Pryce could just make out the corpulent form of the innkeeper Henry, his face and shirt covered in blood, led in irons by two black coated men.

'God help us!' Pryce cried.

CHAPTER 35

———∾∾———

'I'm afraid it's more like a charnel house than a building site in there, guv,' Clarke said as he and William Wickham were set down from their cab in Church Lane, just off the Strand.

Wickham alighted and strode swiftly through the gate and down the muddy path towards the entrance of the half-constructed mansion.

Clarke told the coachman to stay put.

The sky was leaden and the clouds were heavy. Tiny drops of rain were beginning to freckle Wickham's gaunt face. As he stepped through the unfinished doorway into the fusty chamber, he lifted his handkerchief to his nose. The fetor of death was unmistakable. 'Get these men out of here immediately,' he snapped.

Clarke motioned to the builders who were standing along one side of the room, some gawping at the pile of yellow bricks sprinkled with blood, and others at the fire pit. Fascinated by the sight of the slaughter, they were clearly not in a mood to leave so Clarke chivvied them on with a wave of his hand and a 'C'mon lads', shepherding them out of the chamber of death.

'This is an abattoir,' Wickham sighed.

Clarke returned to the crime scene and turned to his master, removing his hat. 'I'm sorry they've trampled all over the place in their dirty boots, guv,' he said, 'but I was only alerted after the builders arrived.'

'Those ragabashes have been around this scene like a riot of hunting hounds,' Wickham snapped, before calming himself and turning to Clarke. 'Were none of your watchers alert to this last night?'

'I'm afraid not, guv. It was a couple of Bow Street Runners from the night time foot patrol who told me just before dawn. I got 'ere as quick as I could.'

Wickham frowned and walked towards the bricks, tracing the pattern of the blood spatter with the silver tip of his dark brown cane. He then lowered it and knelt beside the body, which was face down in the dust. 'This is some blood-letting,' he sighed.

Wickham removed a monocle from his waistcoat pocket and leaned forward, scrutinising the corpse and the coagulated blood on the surrounding floor. 'He was forced to the ground, probably to his knees,' Wickham said. 'See here,' he added, pointing to the bloodied stump where the man's head had been. 'His collar has been pushed downwards towards his chest. One of his shirt buttons has broken.'

Wickham stood slowly to his feet, his face stern. 'This was more like an execution than a murder.'

He paced around the corpse. The ground in front of the neck was as red as spilled claret. 'It appears there were two assailants. One pinioned Sennett. The other applied the coup de grace.'

Wickham paused, looking at the man's severed glottis and then at the wash of blood upon the bricks. 'His blade was as sharp as a scalpel,' he added.

Wickham gently took the man's clotted scalp in his hands and turned the head so that his face was now in plain view to both of them. The victim's mouth was agape, his eyes dilated.

'Blimey,' Clarke exclaimed. 'Poor bloke didn't deserve that!'

'No one deserves this,' Wickham said as he studied the man's physiognomy.

'Is it Sennett?' Clarke asked.

'It is,' Wickham whispered, lowering the lids of the man's eyes with a slow and reverent sweep of his hand. 'May he rest in peace.'

'You'd better take a deep breath before looking at this next one, guv,' Clarke said.

Wickham paused at the edge of the fire pit. 'This is even more savage,' Wickham gasped.

He crouched in the ash and examined the corpse. The man was lying on his back. His face - what was left of it - seemed to be looking up through the roofless expanse above at a racing nimbus in the grey sky. His hair, forehead, eyes and nose were still perfectly preserved, frozen in a rigour of terror. But the rest of his features were grotesquely disfigured. The flesh was gone from his jaw and neck, and the inside of his throat was visible, severely inflamed and ulcerated.

As Wickham looked more closely, he could see that lead had solidified in the man's windpipe. 'La Corriveau would have been proud of this one,' he gasped.

'La Corriveau?'

'Marie-Josephte Corriveau murdered one of her husbands by pouring molten lead into their ears.'

'What a 'orrible way to go, guv,' Clarke shuddered.

'Indeed. Do we know who this is?' Wickham asked.

'It's one of my watchers, guv, man called Bolton. He was working with Sennett.'

'What were they doing?'

'Sennett kept 'imself to 'imself, guv,' Clarke answered. 'My guess is 'e was trailing some John Bells.'

'That's my conjecture, too,' Wickham said before adding, 'though these John Bells were no ordinary French spies. These were more assassins than lurchers.'

'Yes, guv,' Clarke nodded.

Wickham placed the monocle in his right eye socket once again and studied Bolton's body and the footprints in the dappled fire pit. 'Again we can see that there were at least two men at work in this brutal mutilation. One must have forced the man to the floor and the other tipped the urn or, more probably pushed it.'

Wickham turned back to the cadaver and continued his inspection, taking hold of the man's hands and scrutinising his fingernails. 'Hello,' he said. 'What's this?'

Wickham forced the fingers of the man's right hand apart and removed the torn fragment. Peering through his monocle, he studied both sides.

'What is it, guv?'

228

'It's a piece of card.'

Wickham stood up and passed it to Clarke.

'Looks like part of an invitation, guv.'

'Indeed it is. It's an invitation to a member of the French delegation here in London.'

'What to?'

'It's for an audience with the Prime Minister.'

'Stone me, guv. Do you think the frogs are planning to kill Mister Pitt?'

'Perhaps.'

Wickham was about to speak again when he heard the sound of footsteps approaching the entrance.

Clarke swivelled round and peered through the frame of the door. 'Come in, come in,' he said to a caped man who stopped dead in his tracks, shocked by the gory spectacle which now held his attention.

'Who's this?' Wickham enquired.

'This is the coachman who brought two men 'ere last night. I had him tracked down by a parish constable from the local station.'

Wickham studied the man. He had possessed a rubour in his cheeks when he entered but the sight of the slaughter had drained that quickly away.

'What is your name?' Wickham asked.

'Steadman,' the man stuttered. 'Alfie Steadman.'

'What were you doing here last night?'

'I set two men down here, sir. That's my hackney cab out there.'

The man pointed through the door frame to the street outside, clearly glad to be facing away for a moment from the corpses.

'In your own time, describe what happened here last evening,' Wickham said.

'I picked up two passengers at St Clement Danes at about eight o clock. They wanted me to drop them off at Leicester Square at that French place, the Sabonière Inn. But we didn't go straight there. They made me pull off the Strand here onto Church Lane.'

'Why?'

'I don't know, sir. It seemed queer at the time. There's nothing down here, just half built houses.'

'Did you leave them here?'

'Yes, sir, but they asked me to wait for them around the corner, just off the Strand.'

'Describe them to me, please.'

'One of them was clearly in charge. He was a stocky fellow, with a completely bald head, a sharp little nose and silver spectacles. Gave me the creeps, he did.'

'And the other man, did you get a good look at him?'

'He was about the same height - a more jovial feller.'

'Were they English?'

'No, sir, I'd say they were Frenchies, both of them.'

'Why?'

'I heard them speaking to each other in French and when they spoke to me they had an accent - you know the kind.'

'Thank you, Mister Steadman,' Wickham said.

Wickham rubbed his cold hands together. 'Do you have any idea why these two men might have wanted you to bring them here?' he asked.

'I'm not sure, but it seems to me they thought they were being followed.'

Wickham reached into his pocket and drew out a shilling. He handed it to the man.

'Thank you, sir,' the coachman replied.

'Sign this receipt, please,' Wickham said.

The man scratched his name on a piece of paper and then departed quickly.

When he had left, Wickham turned to his companion. 'If they got on at St Clement Danes,' he said, 'then they may have been the two men you followed from the Crown and Anchor Tavern to Chevening.'

'That makes sense, guv,' Clarke said. 'The descriptions certainly match.'

'And if they were prepared to go to these lengths, then they are on a mission of the utmost secrecy.'

'They're up to some great mischief, no mistake,' Clarke concurred.

'I think it's time I made a visit to the Home Office,' Wickham said.

CHAPTER 36

Pryce and the Abbé took a torch from the granite wall of the tunnel.

'Let me light them,' Jean Marie said.

Pryce and the Abbé presented their torches to Jean Marie's ignited flambeau. Fanned by the draft, the bound rags roared into flame immediately.

'Michel found this secret tunnel when we built the house,' Jean Marie said as she led the way. 'It ran from underneath some hedgerows in the grounds of the house right down to a cave in a secret inlet beyond the cliffs. It must have been used by pirates and smugglers in times past. My Michel was elated when he discovered it.'

As the three of them marched quickly over the shingle-covered rock, the carefully mined passageway began to descend towards a deeper darkness.

Pryce lowered his head as the damp ceiling and the walls encroached.

'Be careful, Thomas,' Jean Marie urged. 'This was not designed for men as tall as you.'

Pryce arched his back and held his torch out, taking care over his footing while keeping the flames away from the Abbé's coat in front of him.

'Tell me, Thomas,' Jean Marie called back. 'You said that soldiers are coming. How many did you see?'

'I estimate there were two companies, making a division of two hundred men.'

'What they were doing?' Jean Marie asked.

'There were light infantry at the front. They dispersed and fanned out in pairs. The men behind moved from column to line formation.

They were Grenadiers, most probably the ones you and Joseph saw.'

'Sounds like they're following the Règlement,' Jean Marie sighed.

'What's that?'

'The rules for military marching, formations and combat,' Jean Marie replied. 'They were only formalized a couple of years ago. It shows these are well trained men, doing things by the book.'

'Dear Lord,' the Abbé shouted. 'Our rescuers won't stand a chance. Masson and his men have the advantage of height, cover, numbers and experience.'

'There's worse,' Pryce added. 'They have cannons with them.'

Jean Marie gasped. 'Our only consolation,' she said, 'is that our enemies will not be able to get down onto the beach. This tunnel is the only means of access.'

'But how will our friends save us if they are pinned down?' the Abbé asked.

'I don't know,' Jean Marie said.

As they manoeuvred through the winding tunnel, a sudden draft of briny air caused the flames of their torches to roar in protest.

'It's just around this corner now,' Jean Marie whispered.

As they walked round a tight bend, the natural light of the sky beyond began to infiltrate the tunnel. Pryce wiped sea fret from his lips. He could hear the sound of the breakers now.

As they negotiated a final corner they found themselves in a rocky vestibule walking on a small stretch of sand, dotted with sea-wrack. Pushed to the three sides of the cave were caskets, cases, scuttle-butts, lanterns, ropes, nets and piles of old poldavy used for sails.

Pryce stopped in the cave and thrust the handle of his flambeau into the sand. 'What is this place?' he asked, picking up a rusty cutlass.

'It is a hideout for privateers,' the Abbé replied.

Pryce dropped the cutlass and withdrew the telescope from his belt. He took it from its brown leather case and extended it. Moving cautiously to the lip of the cave, he knelt and put the glass to his eye. The cave was in a secret bay and faced out towards the sea at an angle of about 45 degrees. A sandy beach stretched from the edge of the sea back to the foot of the cliffs in front of the mansion to Pryce's right. The entire inlet was surrounded by high rocks above, bracketing the inlet completely. No one would be able to climb down to the beach or the sea without using the concealed tunnel.

As he turned his perspective glass towards the ocean Pryce noticed that the tall rocks which ran from the cliffs to his right extended both sides of the bay and reached round towards each other about three hundred yards off shore. This created a natural channel of no more than fifty feet in width through which only flat bottomed boats could navigate their way into the bay from the ocean beyond.

And that was exactly what was now happening. Pryce could see small landing craft beginning to move away from the three brigs towards the fairway that ran between the rocks towards him. There were gigs, jolly boats, skiffs, pinnaces and longboats, bristling with oars on both sides, all of them filled with the unmistakable colours and outlines of Jersey infantry.

'They're here!' Pryce muttered.

Pryce lowered the telescope and wiped the end with his handkerchief. He raised it again, this time craning his head out of the entrance of the cave and observing the cliff top to his right. It stood roughly one hundred feet above a scattering of rocks covered in bright green algae on the sand below.

As he continued to peer through the glass, Pryce became aware of movement on the cliff top. Blue-coated soldiers were running hither and thither in pairs. 'Light infantry!' Pryce whispered.

'What are they up to?' Jean Marie asked.

'They are spreading out on the tops of the rocks. Some of them are looking through telescopes at the boats and calling back to their officers.'

'They're scouts,' Jean Marie said.

'Others are looking for places to climb down from the cliffs,' Pryce continued.

'Rangers,' Jean Marie interjected.

'And the rest are taking up firing positions.'

'Marksmen,' Jean Marie sighed.

'The Grenadiers are now lining up behind cover on the cliff top, training their muskets on the beach,' Pryce added.

'Any sign of the cannons?' Jean Marie asked.

Pryce squinted through the glass. 'Yes, they are being detached from their limbers and positioned facing the fairway into the bay. They are being primed and the gun layers are aiming them. If they open up, I fear they will create carnage.'

'We must warn our friends,' Jean Marie cried.

'We cannot,' Pryce said. 'It will betray our position.'

'God have mercy,' the Abbé exclaimed.

Pryce crept back inside the cave. Under cover once again, he trained the telescope towards the advancing boats on his left. A clinker-built jolly boat with a broad stern and a shivering sail was now making its way through the channel. It was coming in before the wind which had freshened noticeably. Its double banks of oarsmen were rowing in unison, under the direction of a pilot who was standing in the bow. Behind him twelve redcoats wearing bearskins were sitting with their muskets and bayonets pointing up at the gloomy sky.

As Pryce watched, he was suddenly startled by the sound of the cannonade opening up on his right. All three guns had spoken simultaneously, releasing a deathly volley upon the unsuspecting rescue party. Two plumes of water arose either side of the leading jolly boat, just missing their target. But the third struck home, the cannon ball eviscerating the pilot and mutilating the bowmen. There was a sudden shower of blood and then the keening of a dying man as wood and bones splintered simultaneously. Men and arms spilt into the clearer water of the channel, which was now turning red.

The two boats behind kept moving forward, ignoring the cries of drowning men, desperate to get out of the fairway and onto the beach. The cannons fired. Once again there was a direct hit. The second boat miraculously escaped but the third boat was not so lucky. Its bluff bow caved in before the ball exploded amidships, killing everyone on board, leaving nothing but a wash of timber and limbs in the water.

'Come on!' Pryce said as the second boat kept its course towards the shore.

'Come on!' the Abbé repeated.

Pryce lowered his telescope and watched as the boat beached and the soldiers spilled out. There was a baker's dozen, twelve infantrymen and a sergeant.

'Jersey Grenadiers,' the Abbé said.

As the boat and its oarsmen hastily departed, the soldiers ran onto the beach. Even though were exposed they looked resplendent. Their woollen redcoats were cut away in the front, revealing a white waistcoat covering a white shirt topped by a black stock. Their white breeches reached down to their black, calf-length gaiters. The silver buckles on their black shoes shone brightly even they were flecked with drops of rain.

Pryce directed his telescope towards them. He could see the metal plates on the front of their bearskins and just make out the words beneath the royal crest.

NIC ASPERA TERRENT. 'Difficulties do not dismay us.'

The sergeant barked an order and the twelve men reached into the black cartouche box hanging from their buff leather belts. Even while shots were beginning to rain down from the rocks, they unhurriedly removed a white cartridge, bit off the top, took the lead ball in their mouths, poured powder into the flintlock and then the barrel, took the ramming rod from their musket, forced the paper-cased ball into place, and raised their weapons to fire.

The sergeant pointed his spontoon at the guns and then issued an order. The muskets fired in unison, sending a cloud of white smoke into the air.

Pryce was about to look up towards the cliff when he heard the sound of muskets, scores of them, opening up from the cliff top and from the rocks to the left and right of the Jersey Grenadiers. Clutches of French marksmen had found vantage points closer to the Jersey militia and were now firing at will towards the doomed invaders on the beach.

Eight of the men were hit within several seconds. Six died

instantly, their white waist coats and shirts turning as red as their tunics. Another man was hit in the neck and started caterwauling as he stumbled back towards the sea, wading wildly for a moment in the surf, before teetering and falling in the water face down. The eighth man took a bullet in his thigh which severed an artery, drenching his white breeches right down to his half-splatterdashes.

Within moments a second volley opened up on them. A bullet passed straight through the sergeant's bearskin and into his skull. He fell back into the sand, a look of surprise on his rugged face.

The four surviving soldiers now began to panic. They looked back towards the sea and started to run, desperate to get out of range of the muskets. Two were struck down by the marksmen who were positioned above and behind Pryce on the rocks. They fell forwards into the sea as lead balls tore the backs of their tunics, ripping the cloth from their flesh.

The remaining two waded knee deep, then up to their waists, then neck high until they were out of range of the muskets. One of them began to lose his footing as he sought to remain upright. Unable to swim he started to grasp and tug at his companion who was trying to pull him by his yellow collars so that his head was above the waves. But this just seemed to intensify the man's alarm and his arms began to wave madly. The second man now began to panic too and within moments they had both pulled each other underwater. A few heart beats later a solitary hand broke the surface reaching for something invisible before it disappeared.

As the two men drowned, the French soldiers on the cliff top began to raise their bearskins and release a faronnade of insults upon the corpses in the bay.

Pryce could just make out the words 'goose shit' before he turned away from the chaos outside.

No sooner had he walked back inside the cave than the Abbé took up a position at the entrance. He held a loaded musket in his hands and aimed it towards the cliffs.

'What are you doing?' Pryce snapped.

'I can't stay here while our friends are being slaughtered,' the Abbé retorted.

'And you think killing is the answer?'

'Saint Ignatius always taught us,' the Abbé replied, squinting at Pryce, 'that sometimes you have to make the better of two good decisions. Your decision not to kill is a good one and I respect it. But I believe my decision to help our rescuers is a better one.'

'And you think this is the way of love, Abbé?' Pryce asked.

'Thomas, love is only love when it is an action.'

'Well in that case, you shoot, I'll pray,' Pryce sighed.

Pryce walked back into the bowels of the cave just as the Abbé fired his musket, adding 'bless you.'

Pryce knelt upon the damp sand and bowed his head.

He was about to pray but was immediately interrupted by a commotion behind him. He turned and hurried back into the vestibule of the cave to find Jean Marie tending to a man who had fallen into her arms. His wet head was in her lap and he was uttering a long, dolorous groan.

'What happened?' Pryce asked.

'There's been another disastrous landing,' she replied.

Pryce stood over the man. He was a Jersey Grenadier just like the men who'd been slaughtered on the beach. He had silver epaulettes and silver buttons, clear indications that he was an officer. And yet he looked so young, no more than twenty years old.

As he gazed on the man, Pryce noticed that the silver gorget around his neck had been dented. And then he saw why. 'Dear God,' he cried.

A bullet had hit the metal armour piece and deflected up through the young man's chin, through the roof of his mouth and into his head.

The young captain was struggling for breath now and his lungs were rasping. 'It's freezing in here,' the young man stuttered. 'Do you have a blanket?'

Pryce removed his coat and draped it over him.

'Thank you, sir,' he gasped.

The young man's eyes began to mist and a tear fell down his face. He looked up for a moment into Jean Marie's eyes.

'Mother, is that you?' he whispered.

Jean Marie smiled. 'Your mother is here,' she said, bending forward gently and kissing his pale forehead.

With that the officer closed his eyes and died, his head resting in Jean Marie's chest as she stroked his hair and sang softly to him.

Pryce turned away.

He watched the Abbé load his musket, aim and fire.

'Bless you,' the Abbé cried again.

Pryce crept up behind his friend. He looked back at the young Grenadier officer still cradled in Jean Marie's arms and then turned again towards the beach, where a platoon of Jersey Grenadiers was now valiantly trying to silence the guns with a volley of Brown Besses from the centre and fusils from their flanks.

But theirs was a forlorn hope.

The cannons kept firing, as did the snipers and the French Grenadiers.

The redcoats took a terrible beating, falling like ninepins in the blood-soaked sand.

And as they did, anger began to rise in the pit of Pryce's stomach.

CHAPTER 37

'This is simply no good,' Pryce snapped as he watched the slaughter on the beach. 'Enough is enough.'

The Abbé turned towards him. 'What shall we do?' he asked.

'Collect the best muskets and plenty of ammunition and come with me.'

The Abbé selected four muskets from the weapons they had brought down from the house and four cartridge boxes. The two men shouldered the arms.

'I'm coming too,' Jean Marie cried, as she wedged her two boarding axes in the belt at her back.

Pryce retrieved his coat and then took his torch from the floor of the cave. 'Follow me,' he said. He led the way up through the secret tunnel, marching as fast as possible through the narrow throat of the passageway back up through the concealed entrance. He could just see past the house to the blue-coated artillery men loading the cannons which fired almost immediately, white smoke billowing from their barrels.

'We have to silence them,' Pryce cried. He hurried to the postern and led the way through the trees round the front of the house to a tall, thick hedgerow within site and range of the cannons.

'We can use this for cover,' Pryce whispered. 'I'll keep loading the muskets. You fire them.'

'Aha,' the Abbé smiled.

'Surprise is essential,' Pryce said. 'We must kill the artillerymen before we are discovered. Then we can return to the house and back to the cave.'

'Here,' the Abbé said, passing a musket to Jean Marie. 'It's time to administer some divine justice.'

Pryce knelt behind his mother-in-law and looked down along the barrel of her gun as she aimed at the officer in charge of the three pieces of artillery.

'I'll take the captain,' she whispered to the Abbé.

'Wait for the cannons to fire,' the Abbé replied. 'Their noise will cover ours.'

Two heartbeats later and the three guns fired again. Immediately the two snipers discharged their muskets. Both hit their targets. The Abbé's musket ball travelled two hundred feet and hit one of the gun loaders in the centre of his back, causing him to stumble forwards and plunge from the cliff onto the rocks below.

'Bless you,' the Abbé whispered.

Jean Marie's aim was even truer. Her shot went straight into the back of the captain's head, propelling him forward, his limbs limp, his hair matted with blood.

'Here,' Pryce said softly, as he took their two muskets and passed the loaded ones forward.

The artillerymen were now confused, gabbling loudly. Their officer was dead and they had witnessed one man plummet from the cliff onto the boulders beneath. The illusion of invincibility had deserted them and their faces looked haggard and afraid.

'Wait until they fire again. You take the sergeant,' the Abbé whispered.

The sergeant shouted fiercely at the stunned gunners and they immediately snapped out of their momentary timidity and loaded up again. The gun aimers lit the fuses and another barrage broke upon the bloody bay below. As the cannons bellowed on the cliffs, the muskets in the hedgerow cracked.

'Bless you,' the Abbé muttered.

Two gunners fell, including the sergeant.

The artillerymen had now lost both their officer and their sergeant and they were looking at each other, demoralized and dismayed.

Pryce had loaded two muskets and now exchanged them for the used ones. His fellow marksmen took aim as a blue-coated captain of the Grenadiers took charge of the gun teams, barking furiously at his men. The gunners began to load up again. This time, however, they performed their tasks with less celerity, glancing about them nervously.

'You take the right hand gun, I'll take the left,' the Abbé whispered.

When the moment came, the sound of the muskets was once again masked by the cannon fire.

'Bless you,' the Abbé said as his target toppled over the cliff. Jean Marie's victim slumped over one of the cannons.

The remaining gunners were now in disarray. But one of them, inspecting the wound in the man draped over his gun, turned towards the hedgerow where Pryce and his friends were hiding. He lifted up his arm and pointed towards the curling wisps of white smoke rising above the bushes, shouting angrily and gesticulating to the Grenadier Captain.

'They know we are here,' the Abbé exclaimed.

'Shoot anyway,' Jean Marie snapped.

Pryce handed the two loaded weapons forward.

The muskets fired again.

Two men fell. One dead, the other wounded.

The three artillery teams were immobilized. But the hidden snipers had also been discovered.

'We'll never make it back to the house,' Pryce said as he spied a platoon of Grenadiers peeling away from the cliff top and form up in three ranks, their bayonets fixed. They were facing directly towards them, ready to charge.

'Reload, Thomas!' Jean Marie shouted.

'There's no point, mother. We're hopelessly outnumbered.'

'I'd rather die here than at the guillotine.'

'Me too,' the Abbé said.

Pryce was about to reply when he heard a sound behind him.

'Thank God!' he cried.

Jean Marie and the Abbé turned around.

'God be praised!' the Abbé exclaimed.

Crouching behind them was an impeccably turned out officer, at the head of a line of redcoats who were pouring out from the

241

mansion, their bayonets fixed and their muskets ready to fire.

'Captain Philippe d'Auvergne at your service,' the handsome officer said, bowing.

'Are we glad to see you,' Pryce gasped.

'May we be of any assistance?' the Captain asked.

'You may,' Jean Marie replied. 'You can help us see off some unwelcome visitors to our home.'

'Very happy to oblige, Madame,' the Captain said, touching the edge of his tricorn hat. 'Although I don't think we are the only ones who've come to your aid.'

Captain D'Auvergne pointed through the hedge towards the French Grenadiers. They had stopped in their tracks, a look of surprise on their powder stained faces.

'Joseph!' Jean Marie shouted.

Pryce squinted through the leaves of the hedge. Suddenly, left field, a spate of grey-jacketed soldiers fell violently upon the Grenadiers, both those approaching the hedgerows and those at the top of the cliffs. Leading them was Joseph, firing a pistol at the Grenadier captain's head and transfixing another man with his sword.

'Our Royalist allies,' Captain d'Auvergne laughed.

He turned to his men. 'Prepare to charge!' he barked. 'And leave the commanding officer to me. He's mine.'

The men stood to attention. The captain drew his sword, raised it, and shouted, 'Long live the King and the good priests!' The soldiers shouted back antiphonally.

'We can leave this to the professionals now,' Pryce said, as Captain D'Auvergne and his men ran headlong into the enemy ranks.

A fierce fight ensued, with the bluecoats on the broken right flank staggering as they tried desperately to hold the line. As more and more grey-coated soldiers hurled themselves with a roar against the flank, Captain D'Auvergne and his redcoats attacked the now disorganized centre. Some of the light infantry, seeing that they were outnumbered by Captain D'Auvergne's recoats, tried to escape by clambering over the rocks either side of the bay towards the ocean. One by one they lost their footing and fell onto the jutting crags below, or into the ocean where the cross-grained tides in front of the fairway pulled them under. There was nowhere for any of the bluecoats to go but backwards. But falling back meant retreating to the edge of the cliffs.

'No prisoners!' Captain D'Auvergne shouted.

His men, their bloodlust fortified by the sight of the pitiless destruction of their friends upon the beach, shouted with approval and ran like frenzied predators towards the cowering ranks in front of them. They rammed the terrified Grenadiers with their muskets, standards and spontoons. Many of the bluecoats dropped their weapons and were trying to surrender. But the thirst for revenge would not be so quickly slaked.

Pryce watched with horror as the remnant started to run out of space.

'No, for pity's sake, no!' some men at the back cried as one by one they were pushed to the brink of the cliff.

One more charge from the redcoats and the hapless rear guard began to teeter and fall down upon the sharp rocks, screaming in terror before their bones smashed like shattering glass upon the granite below.

'They deserve it,' Jean Marie mocked. 'They are swine.'

'Gadarene swine,' the Abbé quipped.

Pryce turned away from the slaughter, fell to his knees, leaned forward and vomited on the snuff-colored earth as the sound of the screams began to subside. As he wiped his mouth, he opened his eyes. He was looking at two pairs of silver buckled, black shoes, polished to perfection. Slowly he lifted his gaze, up from the black breeches to the black coats and then to the faces of the men standing above him. It was Masson and Sicard, and they were both holding a cocked pistol in each hand.

'Oh no,' Pryce sighed.

'What is it, Thomas?' Jean Marie said as she turned.

'French agents,' he gasped.

Hearing those words, the Abbé swiveled round.

'Vade retro, Satanas!' he shouted as he wielded his musket like an axe.

But he was too slow.

The two agents fired.

Sicard missed and cursed.

But Masson's aim was true. His bullet struck the Abbé in the throat, leaving a stain of black powder and a first smear of blood on the priest's white cravat.

The Abbé fell, puling like a sick child.

'No!' Pryce shouted as he bent down to hold his friend.

'Get up!' Masson snapped, 'or you will suffer the same fate.'

Pryce paused. He gently wiped a thin line of blood that was coursing down the Abbé's chin from the corner of a mouth gasping a desperate prayer. Then Pryce slowly rose to his feet, his face fixed in fury.

The two agents grabbed their prisoners, swivelled them round and held them from behind with one arm while using their other hand to position the muzzle of their remaining loaded pistols at their captives' throats.

Clumsily they began to back away from the hedge towards the house, their hostages locked in an unholy embrace.

Pryce groaned as he looked at the Abbé, whose body was now limp, his face already as pale as a cast, his lifeblood spilling onto the green grass.

'You won't get away,' Pryce growled.

'There will be no parley for you,' Jean Marie spat.

'We will escape,' Masson replied calmly. 'Your friends are distracted by their butchery.'

As Pryce peered past the hedgerows he could see a crowd of grey coated soldiers watching something. It was Captain d'Auvergne, fighting a duel with an exhausted captain who was desperately lunging until his sword broke, leaving only the quillons and the cross-guard in his hand.

Pryce heard him cry for mercy as he was forced backwards towards the entrance of the mansion.

The crowd around the doomed officer pressed in.

Pryce saw a sword fall and then the man's head lifted up on the end of a sergeant's spontoon.

Meanwhile, Pryce and Jean Marie were manhandled to the front door of the mansion. Within seconds they would be inside, their fate concealed from their rescuers.

Pryce was about to speak, but he was interrupted.

'Stop where you are!' a woman's voice snapped.

'Dear Jesus,' Pryce whispered.

He turned awkwardly with his captors. There standing in front of the portals, was Eloise. She was wearing a black cape around her shoulders and a tricorn hat upon her head. Her eyes blazed like a wild, forest fire. Her face was as cold as the rocks. Within the folds of her cape, Pryce could see that she was holding cocked pistols in both hands. He shuddered.

'Release them!' she said.

'You are joking of course,' Masson sneered.

'I will give you one more chance,' Eloise said calmly. 'Release them.'

'Whore!' Sicard laughed.

'That was a mistake,' Pryce whispered.

Eloise scowled. 'Bastards,' she shouted.

In one fluidic movement she raised, aimed and fired her pistols. One of them struck Sicard in the chest. The other hit Masson in his mouth, splintering several teeth. Both men sank to their knees whimpering. And as they did Jean Marie withdrew the two boarding axes from behind her back. She raised them high and brought them down sideways, her arms moving like pistons. Both men's torsos lurched forwards and slumped to the ground.

Jean Marie turned and ran back towards her brother-in-law, holding him in her arms.

Pryce stumbled.

The world was spinning on its axis.

He was falling.

'Thomas,' Eloise cried as she dropped her pistols and held him.

'Is that really you?' Pryce gasped, staggering in the blood soaked gravel.

'It is,' she said.

'What are you doing here?' Pryce spluttered.

'You cannot keep a daughter of the Picots from a fight like this,' she said. 'And besides, there isn't a better shot than me within a mile of this place.'

'I see you have not lost any of your humility,' Pryce murmured.

Eloise pulled him closer, gathering his arms underneath her cape, drawing him eagerly towards her body, pressing urgently at his back.

For a moment Pryce forgot the suffering of the last days.

Then he pulled himself away.

'The Abbé,' he whispered.

The two of them ran to where Jean Marie was nursing the dying priest. Joseph was kneeling beside him, his face drawn, his lips quivering.

The Abbé's eyes looked heavy now. He was struggling to breathe, but seeing Pryce he beckoned slowly with every remaining trace of strength.

Pryce knelt down.

'Get… back to London… save… your king,' the Abbé stammered.

'I will,' Pryce replied.

'And bury me at sea,' the Abbé whispered. 'You do it, Thomas… Promise me… you do it.'

'I promise,' Pryce said.

As the rain began to fall more heavily now, the Abbé stretched his arms out. He lay cruciform beneath the sky, his mouth open, his eyes staring into the clouds, his family gathered round him in a pitiful pieta.

As his gaze began to slip away, the Abbé sighed.

'Pater in manus tuas …'

And then he was gone.

CHAPTER 38

Pryce removed his hat as he watched the corpse of the Abbé being carried on a stretcher to the side of the frigate, which now lay at anchor a mile from the shore. Eloise clung to Pryce's arm, as Joseph and Jean Marie walked hand in hand towards the gunwales of the ship where they stood beside the corpse of the Abbé, their faces pale and grave.

The rain was falling harder on the deck now, pattering noisily like the sound of distant muskets.

The Abbé's body lay at the feet of a guard of Jersey Grenadiers who were all dressed in full ceremonial uniform. They were standing at ease with their Brown Bess muskets, their bearskins dampened by the rain.

Pryce took a handkerchief and wiped the brine from his lips.

Everything was ready now. The ship's carpenter and sail maker had prepared the corpse for burial by sewing it up in a heavy piece of canvas, fastening several iron shackles to the feet, before finally stitching up the dead man's nose.

The heavy silence that had fallen was suddenly ended by the bosun's shout. 'All hands, bury the dead!'

Four sailors with huge arms raised the body onto the sliding board.

As soon as it was in place, Captain Philippe d'Auvergne marched towards Pryce and stood to attention in front of him. The Captain was a good four inches shorter than Pryce but what he lacked in physical stature he more than made up for in his handsome features. His face looked rosy for such a bleak wintery day and his grey eyes appeared as animated as they had during the fight at the cliff tops.

'All ready and correct,' the Captain said, before turning towards the burial detail.

Pryce followed the Captain to the entry port on the starboard gangway and then stopped.

'Attention!' a Grenadier sergeant barked.

The eight men in the guard detail shouldered their muskets in flawless unison.

'Before I say the words of the committal,' Pryce said, 'Joseph Pierre Picot will share a brief reminiscence.'

Joseph stepped forward.

'The Abbé de Clorivière was my uncle and my spiritual director,' he said. 'Everything I have ever learned about the spiritual life I learned from him.'

Joseph looked at his dead uncle's body.

'One time I asked him what happens when we die.'

Joseph struggled as he recorded the conversation.

'He said, "According to Saint Hervé, the soul passes the stars and the moon on its journey to heaven, and from a great height looks down upon the countryside and bids it adieu. It then turns its gaze upwards to a far greater place and beholds the gates of Paradise and the saints pouring out to greet it. It is welcomed into the glorious palace of the Trinity and a crown is placed upon its head as heaven's melodies play."

"Will we meet again the ones we loved?" I asked.

"To be sure," the Abbé replied. "You will be greeted by your father, your mother, your friends and your ancestors, in front of a great army of archangels and angels. It will be bliss beyond description - bliss so deep and far and wide that it will cause you to forget all the dreadful pain and torment of this earth-bound life".'

Joseph paused again and looked up at the only flag that had been raised, a single black pennant which was fluttering frantically at the main mast, as if struggling for release. A solitary storm petrel flew above it and some of the men gasped.

Joseph lowered his gaze. 'The Abbé told me that when the soul is high above the earth it knows that the body it has left behind is like a lost vessel on the sea but wherever it turns its eyes in heaven it is overwhelmed by a thousand felicities.'

Joseph cleared his throat. 'The Abbé is in that place,' he said, 'and he has earned his rest and reward within the sacred heart of Jesus.'

He looked down at the corpse. His voice was softer now. 'The earth is emptier without him.'

Joseph nodded to Pryce.

Pryce stood to his full height and began to speak.

'For the sailors among you, I know that burial at sea is regarded as a fearful thing, but for the Abbé it was his last request. He and his brother Michel Alain loved the sea and to them it was their true home. While all our other comrades who have died in arms this day will receive their burial on Jersey, it was the Abbé's wish that his body would be committed to the waves. In his heart there were no grim superstitions about such an end, and he would wish that there would be no such misgivings in your hearts either. Respect his wishes as I say the prayer of committal now.'

Pryce paused and then continued. 'We are gathered here to pray that the soul of the Abbé de Clorivieres will bid farewell to the sorrowful burdens of this earth and enjoy an everlasting happiness without any equal.'

Pryce bowed his head, as did every man and woman aboard.

'And so we now commit our comrade to the deep, looking for the resurrection of the body (when the sea shall give up her dead) and the life of the world to come, through our Lord Jesus Christ: who at his coming shall change our vile body, that it might be like his glorious body, according to the mighty working, whereby he is able to subdue all things to himself. Amen.'

'Amen,' the congregated mariners replied.

The exclamation of that single word created an immediate reaction. The ceremony was over as quickly as it had begun. The body had fallen with a loud splash into the sea. Now it was time to get back to work. So off the men went, down below and up above and all around, in every direction, returning to familiar ropes and sails, masts and decks.

Pryce placed his hat gently back on his head and walked to Eloise, whose eyes were red. He was about to comfort her when the Captain hurriedly intervened. 'Your men are waiting for you,' he said, 'and there's not a moment to lose.'

'What men?'

'Come this way,' the Captain urged.

Pryce followed him to the leeward side of the frigate and looked down. There, resting by the ship, was the *Endeavour*, with Jack and all his fellow boatmen at the ready, sitting with their oars up.

'We need to leave now,' the Captain insisted. 'If we take the *Endeavour* we'll get to Jersey in no time.'

Pryce helped Eloise over the side of the ship. With great dexterity, she made her way down towards the lugger, like a spider hurrying effortlessly over gossamer.

'Good morning, gentlemen,' she said as Jack helped her into the *Endeavour*.

'Good morning, ma'am,' the men replied.

'You have clearly never seen a Breton woman working on a bugalet,' she said in English, as she saw their open mouths and wide eyes.

Pryce smiled. 'I've missed her,' he said to the Captain.

'She is both beautiful and formidable,' the Captain replied with a twinkle in his eye. He leaned closer to Pryce. 'It is a good thing she is already married otherwise I would have subjected her to my irresistible charms.'

'I am not sure that your charms have been altogether dormant,' Pryce replied.

The Captain laughed. 'I cannot help myself,' he chuckled. 'But my loyalty to you is not in question, nor is my respect for your sacred union.'

Pryce sighed. 'I am heartened to hear that.' He clambered over the side and down the Jacob's Ladder towards the *Endeavour*, jumping into the stern, taking Jack's outstretched hand to steady himself.

'Not quite as tidy as me,' Eloise quipped in English, with a smile.

'Not quite, my love,' Pryce replied as some of the men murmured their approval.

'I will show both of you how it's done,' the Captain declared from above.

The Captain took hold of a halyard and leaped over the side of the frigate, swinging out towards the ocean and then back into the ship's side, before grasping another rope hanging next to the ladder and sliding down it and landing in the forepeak of the boat.

'Huzzah,' he shouted as he raised his hat.

'Huzzah,' Jack's men responded.

'Today we bid farewell to a dear friend,' the Captain shouted in a thick accent as he made his way through the men from the bow to the stern, 'but we also say hello to a great adventure.'

The Captain, arriving at the tiller of the lugger, stood beside Pryce for a moment, grinned and then promptly sat down in the space next to Eloise.

'I think that's my seat, Captain,' Pryce said with a frown.

'My apologies,' the Captain replied, making to offer up his seat, but not before he had kissed Eloise's hand. 'Honour alone compels me to leave you, Madame,' he said. 'Forgive me for my impertinence.'

'You're forgiven, Captain,' Eloise replied decorously, removing her hand and patting the seat next to her as she looked at Pryce.

Pryce reclaimed the space next to his wife. He looked up as the Captain was now quickly distracted by the sight of Jean Marie slowly and with as much elegance as she could muster lowering herself from the frigate to the *Endeavour*.

'May I be of assistance, Madame?' he asked.

'You may,' Jean Marie replied.

The Captain took her hand and helped her into the boat. 'Let me escort you to the bow,' he said. 'The accommodation is, how we shall we say, a little basic, but there is shelter and, I'm told, plenty of brandy.'

'You are too kind, Captain,' Jean Marie replied, winking at Pryce and Eloise.

Pryce watched with amusement as the Captain led Jean Marie

through the Deal boatmen to the forepeak in the bow of the lugger.

'Here,' the Captain said, 'I will guard you from these rough men of Kent.'

The Captain glared playfully at the boatmen, who smiled back, before turning around and returning to assist Jean Marie. He rummaged around in the forepeak and found a flask of brandy. 'Here you are, Madame,' he said. 'This will keep you warm on our journey. It will take us four or five hours to reach Jersey so inform me if you finish it and I'll find you some more.'

'My dear Captain,' Jean Marie exclaimed, 'I will be pickled like a fish if you do!'

'Ah, Madame,' the Captain replied, 'then you will be the most perfect addition to the fruits of the sea being prepared for my table tonight!'

Jean Marie laughed and drew herself into the forepeak, covering her lap with an old canvas, pulling a blue knitted fisherman's jumper around her neck like a scarf. No sooner had she relaxed than Jack was barking an order to his men. The Deal boatmen immediately lowered their oars and began to row, their oars descending and ascending with impressive unity.

The lightweight *Endeavour* pulled quickly away from the large and heavy frigate.

'Godspeed,' a voice shouted from above.

It was Joseph, standing in his grey uniform, waving his hat above his head.

'Come to England,' Eloise shouted.

'Please come,' Jean Marie echoed.

'Maybe one day,' Joseph replied, 'but for now France needs me.'

'Until we meet again, then,' Eloise exclaimed, adding, 'Godspeed, brother.'

The two sails of the *Endeavour*, fore and aft, were swiftly hoisted and within what seemed like a few heartbeats Pryce could barely see Joseph's silhouette.

Captain d'Auvergne shifted from his seat near Jean Marie and stood next to the mast amidships, holding on to the wooden beam, staring ahead at the ocean waves into which the lugger was now accelerating.

Eloise leaned her head on Pryce's shoulder.

'How have you been, my love?' he asked her in French.

'A little sick at times, but nothing terrible.'

Pryce placed his hand on Eloise's stomach.

'And how's our little one?'

'Growing to be thoughtful and quick-witted like his father, or forceful and fearful like his mother.'

Pryce smiled. 'I'm glad.'

For a moment, Pryce nestled his nose into Eloise's hair, enjoying again the familiar scent, burying himself deep in her beauty as the boat lifted and lurched in the open sea.

'And you,' Eloise said. 'How are you, my love? You seem a little different, distant even.'

Pryce frowned. 'I have seen things that would turn the most jovial man to melancholy.'

'What have you seen, darling?'

'I have seen the shadow of death.'

Eloise held his hand.

'I have seen men die in the most inhuman ways. I have seen families torn apart. I have seen slaughter, torture, murder and death - even the death of children.'

'My poor darling,' Eloise whispered.

'And I'm afraid to say I saw your father die.'

Eloise squeezed Pryce's hand.

'He died with great dignity and courage.'

Pryce could feel Eloise shudder.

'The Abbé was present to comfort him.'

Eloise's grip was now so firm that Pryce winced.

'He sent a coded message to the Abbé as he climbed the scaffold, indicating where your mother was hiding.'

Pryce turned and looked into her eyes. 'It was the bravest thing I ever saw. You would have been very proud of him.'

Eloise looked up and turned towards the bows where the Captain was sharing a canteen of brandy with her mother.

'My mother owes you her life.'

'It was my duty,' Pryce said.

'But I know it will have cost you.'

'The only cost was compromise.'

'Listen,' Eloise said. 'I know we are different in this, that I am a Breton and don't see any contradiction between fighting and faith, but you could not have stood by and done nothing. If people do nothing then those monsters in Paris will eradicate every last footprint of goodness.'

Pryce smiled. 'You sound like the Abbé.'

'We are family,' she replied, moving closer. 'Whatever you have done, whatever you have seen, do not let it weaken you. Let it make you stronger - stronger for justice.'

'That's my fear,' Pryce said.

'What do you mean?'

'That I'm turning into a machine, as cold and ruthless as the guillotine.'

'Do you still not feel anything?'

'All I feel is anger.'

'Did you not grieve at my uncle's death?'

Pryce looked down. 'I could not.'

'What about when you saw my father die?'

'I felt rage.'

'Did you not shed tears?'

Pryce said nothing.

'Darling, I'm so sorry.'

Pryce looked away from his wife and those around him and stared out at the ocean. He was about to yield to a long awaited sleep when he felt a hand on his shoulder. It was the Captain.

'If I can break up this happy reunion for a moment,' he said in unpolished English, 'we need to agree what to do next.'

'Do you have a plan?' Pryce asked.

'The plan is for you to save the king's life,' the Captain whispered, 'and for that to happen we must get you back to London as quickly as possible.'

'That's easier said than done,' Pryce replied. 'Even with Jack and his boatmen I doubt whether I could get back in time to prevent disaster.'

'There is another way,' the Captain said.

'What other way is there?' Eloise asked.

'I will show you tomorrow, at first light.'

'You're being very elusive, Captain,' Eloise said. 'This is my beloved husband you're talking about.'

'I do have a plan,' the Captain said softly, 'and that plan is for you to rest tonight at my humble home on the beautiful and loyal island of Jersey. There you will dine at my table.'

'That is most kind, Captain,' Eloise said.

The Captain smiled and tapped his nose. 'Then, in the morning, I have found a way of getting your husband back to London in no time at all, provided the wind is favourable and also, provided your husband is not afraid of heights.'

CHAPTER 39

William Wickham knocked on the undersecretary's door in Whitehall and waited.

'Enter!' a voice shouted.

Wickham limped into Evan Nepean's capacious and opulent office.

'Is that knee of yours giving you some jip again, Wickham?' Nepean asked, looking up.

'I'm afraid so, sir,' Wickham replied.

'Care for a whiskey to take the edge off it?'

'Don't mind if I do.'

Nepean strode over to a sideboard and poured some golden liquid from a crystal decanter. 'It's nearly midday and the sun is over the yardarm,' Nepean said as he handed the tumbler to Wickham.

Wickham paused and turned the glass. 'This looks good,' he said.

'It's from the Bushmills Distillery Company in Ireland,' Nepean replied. 'Finest whiskey I've ever tasted.'

'Your very good health,' Wickham said as he took a large gulp. 'Ah, that feels better,' he sighed.

'Warms the cockles, doesn't it?' Nepean said.

'It certainly does,' Wickham replied.

'Right, Wickham. You're not here to discuss Irish whiskey, I'm sure. What can I do for you?'

'We have a problem,' Wickham said gravely.

'Fire away,' Nepean replied.

'I was present at a half-built property on Church Street, just off the Strand, first thing this morning. Two men were murdered there last night. One of them was beheaded. The other was killed with molten lead.'

'Good Lord!' Nepean cried.

'It is my opinion that they were killed by two French assassins, one of whom has been lodging at the Crown and Anchor Tavern.'

'Not that nest of vipers!' Nepean cried.

'I'm afraid so.'

'Have you arrested them?'

'I went straight there after inspecting the crime scene,' Wickham said. 'But the man who had occupied the room has paid and left.'

'What was his name?'

'He was called Marat.'

'What's he doing in London?'

'The person I spoke to said that he was here as part of the French delegation. For a shilling he also divulged that he'd been visited by another Frenchman.'

'Did you get a description?'

'The man in the room was short, had a beaky nose and was completely bald. He wore silver rimmed spectacles and had a somewhat sinister demeanour.'

'What about the other man?'

'He was said to be tall and portly, more congenial and less aloof.'

'How do you know they are the murderers?'

'The description of them tallies exactly with the one given by the coachman who set two Frenchmen down at the half-built house on Church Street.'

'Who were the victims, then?'

'One was one of our best agents, Sennett. The other was one of Clarke's city watchers.'

'Damn!' Nepean shouted. He stood and turned towards the window. 'We cannot afford to lose such good men,' he said. 'We are already spread too thinly.'

He turned back towards Wickham. 'What are they up to?' he asked.

'I believe they are in league with Lord Stanhope and planning some great mischief.'

'Not Stanhope again,' Nepean snarled. 'Have you questioned him?'

'Yes, sir, I went straight from the Strand to his London residence.

He denies ever seeing them even though we suspect he hosted them at his estate in Kent just a few days ago.'

'Of course he denies it,' Nepean said.

'I cannot force a peer of the realm to give me information,' Wickham replied. 'There is insufficient evidence but I suspect he is involved in some nefarious project, although he may not know the full extent of what is planned.'

'So what is this wretched Trinity up to?'

'It is possible they are planning to assassinate the Prime Minister the day after tomorrow.'

'God's teeth, you can't be serious!' Nepean exclaimed.

'I'm deadly serious, as I suspect they are.'

'What proof do you have?' Nepean enquired.

'The first is the most compelling.'

'Spit it out, sir. Spit it out.'

'I found a torn fragment of an invitation card in one of the dead man's hands. It was to an audience with William Pitt on Friday in the Commons.'

'I didn't know of such a meeting,' Nepean blurted.

'It's secret,' Wickham replied. 'Members of the French delegation have asked the Prime Minister to reconsider the removal of certain rights for French émigrés in Britain, especially *habeas corpus*.'

'And you think these two men are planning to be there to kill Mister Pitt?'

'I said I think it's possible.'

'Well then you must be there in person with some of your agents,' Nepean said.

'I fear I am in the same boat as you,' Wickham responded.

'Explain.'

'I have very few agents at present,' Wickham sighed, 'and I too am stretched to my limits. We simply don't have the manpower or the finances to cope with anything above and beyond our current operations.'

'You mean you need more money.'

'I need more money and I need more men,' Wickham replied.

'I don't have enough agents to infiltrate all the secret and seditious societies in our own capital, let alone those in other cities, including Paris.'

'Money is in short supply for all of us right now,' Nepean said. 'We are facing an unexpected crisis on that score, as you well know.'

'But this is the Prime Minister's life,' Wickham insisted. 'That surely takes precedence over all other costs and concerns.'

'I would agree, if we had incontrovertible proof.'

'Is the torn invitation not evidence?'

'How do you know it's not a decoy?'

'I don't, but the other evidence points towards it being of possible significance.'

'What other evidence?'

'You know as well as I do, sir, that there's no love lost between Lord Stanhope and the Prime Minister.'

'I know that Stanhope is the Prime Minister's brother-in-law and they don't get on.'

'I think it is more serious than that,' Wickham said. 'Lord Stanhope has become an embarrassment to the Prime Minister, using his seat in the House of Lords to oppose the government's stand on the French Revolution and the war with France. He's a leading member of the seditious 'Friends of the People' and we know he is active in communicating with the Jacobin Clubs in Paris.'

Nepean sighed and walked over to the dresser and poured some whiskey. He sat down and tipped the entire contents of the tumbler down his throat. 'This is utterly damnable!' he cried.

'It certainly is,' Wickham agreed. 'That's why we need to be prepared. I suggest you requisition a handful of armed foot guards from the barracks in Hyde Park. I can brief them and be there with them at the ready on Friday when the French officials meet with the Prime Minister.'

'Can't we do more?' Nepean asked.

'I have spoken to Mister Clarke, my chief watcher, and he has circulated descriptions of the two French agents to all his watchers and to the Bow Street runners. I'm sending them into coffee houses and taverns throughout the city. That's the best I can do presently.'

'And what if they see the two suspects?'

'I have instructed them to take great care. Clearly at least one of them is armed with a lethal weapon.'

'What kind of weapon?'

'They have a razor sharp blade, possibly some kind of special sword,' Wickham replied.

Nepean leaned back and crossed his arms. 'It can't be too hard to trace an entirely bald Frenchman carrying a sword,' he said.

'It's harder than you think,' Wickham interjected. 'And even if the runners or the watchers do locate him, the murders last night will not endear them to the notion of some kind of confrontation. The word is already out that these men have a predilection for decapitation.'

'It seems that these men have already outwitted us then,' Nepean sighed.

'Until you give me more men and more money there is little I can do above and beyond what I've already indicated,' Wickham insisted.

'Don't use this predicament as leverage, Wickham,' Nepean barked. 'It's not appropriate.'

'But it is, sir. If you truly want me to fulfill my duties then I need more support to conduct my operations, both covert and overt, at home and abroad.'

Wickham paused before delivering his coup de grace.

'Otherwise,' he concluded, 'it won't just be King Louis' head that will roll.'

'All right, all right,' Nepean said, 'you've made your point. But you must see it from my perspective. The Home Office cannot just accommodate everyone.'

'With all due respect, sir,' Wickham replied, 'the Home Office was set up ten years ago to safeguard the rights and liberties of the British people, including our leaders. You use the word 'appropriate'. Surely this is the most appropriate location from which to oversee the work of His Majesty's Secret Service.'

Nepean smiled. 'You're going to be like a dog with a bone on this one, aren't you, Wickham?'

'I'm afraid so, sir.'

'Then I'll have a word with Lord Dundas and petition him on your behalf.'

'Thank you, sir,' Wickham said.

But Wickham wasn't finished. 'We cannot underestimate the challenge ahead of us,' he said. 'Between the machinery of government and the use of the military there is a monumental gap that needs filling when it comes to maintaining public safety and order. We have our watchers and then there's Fielding's Runners, of course. The Police Act has helped too. But we need more than this if we are to guarantee civil law and order.'

'I am working on it, Wickham,' Nepean grunted.

Wickham continued. 'If we want to defend the constitution in these perilous times, then Old Harry Dundas has to put homeland security at the top of the agenda. The year of '92 has changed everything. There's a desperate need to keep an eye on the foreign undesirables now infiltrating our country. We must find the spies in our midst.'

'I can't deny that,' Nepean said.

'In addition, it would be greatly to our advantage if we could arrest, interrogate and turn some of these foreign agents so that they will work for us in France. There is, after all, no spy as good as a double one.'

'That's true,' Nepean averred.

'And we have precious few British agents who can read French, let alone who are fluent in it, although I'm working night and day to identify, recruit and train promising new candidates.'

'It is, I admit, a problem,' Nepean said. 'I do not speak French, nor does Lord Dundas.'

'We need men of calibre - men of the calibre of my colleague William Huskisson and our top agent Richard Etches. Men who can help me create a domestic security registry. Men who speak foreign languages flawlessly and who can slip in and out of French cities and institutions like shadows.'

Nepean sighed. 'Where are we going to find such men?' he asked.

'If you will permit me,' Wickham replied, 'I have an idea.'

'What is it?'

'I have spoken with our former Dean at Christ Church.'

'You've been speaking with Dean Jackson behind my back?'

'Forgive me, sir, but it was a conversation that grew naturally after dinner in Oxford. It was not premeditated.'

'Well then, what did he say?'

'He said that he had a list of names - young men that have been through Christ Church and whom he regards as having great potential either as administrators or as agents in His Majesty's Secret Service.'

'And do you have that list?'

'I do.'

Wickham withdrew a piece of paper from his pocket and handed it over to the undersecretary.

As he read, his eyes widened. 'I know some of these,' he said softly. 'They are indeed men of calibre.'

'Dean Jackson says they would be docile to our invitation if we mentioned his name and confided that he had recommended them.'

'And you think they could form a new department to confront the enemy within our own shores?'

'And further afield, if permitted.'

Nepean sighed. 'By further afield I take it you mean abroad, especially in France.'

'I do.'

'That may be a problem.'

'Why is that, sir?'

'The use of agents abroad comes under the authority of Lord Grenville in his capacity as Foreign Secretary.'

'I appreciate that,' Wickham said, 'but if we are to combat the great threat posed by secret agents and assassins then we need to have some sort of coordination between the Foreign Office and the Home Office, otherwise there may be a great catastrophe.'

'That may be so but I doubt whether Lord Grenville would agree to this level of coordination,' Nepean retorted.

'He's a Christ Church man,' Wickham insisted. 'The beloved Dean can be asked to prevail upon him if necessary.'

Nepean sighed and turned towards the window, gazing down on the streets below. 'You realize how un-English this all sounds, Wickham,' he said. 'In seeking so strenuously to protect our civil liberties you run the risk of eroding them.'

'That is certainly an argument, sir,' Wickham responded, 'but these are very dark days and what is put in place in times of war may not be needed in the same way and for the same purpose in times of peace.'

'Maybe you are right, Wickham,' Nepean conceded. 'But I fear that the development of a network of agents within our own country will cause us to undermine some of our most cherished values.'

'I am not proposing a radical transformation of our mores,' Wickham replied. 'All I'm proposing is an end to this ad hoc way of protecting our liberties. I am also simply suggesting that we develop the skeletal system of watchers you had the foresight to put in place a decade ago.'

Nepean smiled. 'All right, Wickham. Tell me what you want.'

'Get me out of that miserable hole in Whitechapel and set me up in a new department directly answerable to you. You have the ear of your friend, the Prime Minister. If you sell it, he will buy it.'

'I suppose that brings us to money,' Nepean sighed.

'Dean Jackson has agreed to provide a start-up fund from his own considerable estate,' Wickham said, 'provided that you persuade the Treasury to play their part.'

'Very well,' Neapean said. 'I'll see what I can do.'

Wickham stood and shook the undersecretary's hand. 'If I had the men right now,' Wickham said, 'I'd not only be watching over the Prime Minister. I'd have a network of agents all over London, guarding not only our Parliamentary leaders but also the royal family.'

The undersecretary withdrew his hand and frowned. 'You said when we last met that you thought the king's life was in danger.'

'I still stand by that,' Wickham said.

'So you believe it's not just the Prime Minister whose life is threatened?'

'I cannot speak with absolute certainty,' Wickham replied, 'but what I do know is this. We have a king who rides on a horse unescorted from Buckingham House to St James' Palace every week. Our leaders are far too vulnerable. It's just a matter of time.'

'So what are you going to do about it?' Nepean asked.

'I'm going to do my best with the little I have.'

'And what does that mean?'

Wickham finished the dregs of his whiskey. 'It means,' he said as he limped to the door, 'that I'm going to move heaven and earth to catch a very bald man with a very long razor.'

CHAPTER 40

As Pryce negotiated a path between the strutting peacocks, he began to make out the outline of a stone tower through the trees.

'The Prince's Tower,' the Captain said, 'the finest edifice on Jersey.'

Pryce could see it plainly now. A tower with turrets had been built on top of a huge mound of earth. Adjacent to it there was a crenelated single storey building and a two-storey octagon. At the top of the tower there was a platform on which a flag was flying.

'It was completed just last year,' the Captain said. 'The land formerly belonged to my uncle, Major General James d'Auvergne, who served in the Household Cavalry under your King George.'

'It's yours now, Captain?' Jean Marie asked.

'It is indeed, my lady. My uncle was good enough to leave the estate to me. There was only this mound of earth you see before you and several dilapidated chapels. I have kept the Chapel of Notre Dame intact but I have built my dining room on top of the ring crypt of the Jerusalem Chapel.'

'It is most impressive,' Jean Marie said.

'Thank you, my lady.'

The captain proffered his arm to Jean Marie, which she took, and he escorted the guests through the front entrance into the hallway. 'Our family's coat of arms,' the Captain said, pointing to an imposing heraldic shield on the stone wall in the hall. It depicted a silver tower and the family motto, 'we never change.'

'I am a staunch defender of our ancient codes and customs,' he said. 'I'm sure you'll agree, my lady, the age of chivalry is not over.'

'Those brute beasts in Paris have tried to stamp out the fire,' Jean Marie retorted. 'But the flames will never cease to burn.'

'That is indeed a *bon mot*,' the Captain replied, smiling at her.

265

'Come. Let me show you to the top of my tower before dinner is served.'

The Captain led the way through the library, proudly narrating that it had been built on the site of the Jerusalem Chapel. As they made their way to the first floor of the tower, they entered a drawing room. 'We shall retire here after dinner,' the Captain said.

Climbing the stairs to the second floor, the Captain pointed to the bedrooms. 'You will be sleeping here tonight. These rooms have the best beds in Jersey.'

'You are too kind,' Jean Marie said.

'And here is the *pièce de résistance*,' the Captain said as they walked up a small stair turret on the west side of the tower and passed through an oak door. Four men in naval uniform turned towards them and stood to attention.

'At ease,' the Captain said. 'Back to your duties, if you please.'

The men returned to their look-out stations, drawing telescopes out to their full extension and studying the landscape from every angle.

'The view, my friends, is unparalleled. The sun is going down now but on a fine day you can see not only the whole of Jersey but the west coast of France.'

'Jean Marie,' Eloise gasped.

'See there. We are situated between St Helier and Gorey. You can observe the entire island from this platform.'

'This is an observation point then,' Pryce said.

'That is its purpose. I have had ten such towers built around the island on the highest points I could find. They are all manned by a lieutenant, a midshipman and two seamen. Should the French Republican Army be foolish enough to attempt an invasion, their impertinence will be detected well in advance and the Jersey militia will be called out to send them back with their tails between their legs.'

'So this is in effect a system of signalling stations,' Pryce said.

'It is, my friend, and the Prince's Tower is the tallest of them all as well as the headquarters for the entire network.'

'And the mound of earth on which this is built,' Pryce said. 'What is it?'

'It is an ancient Armorican grave, the largest of its kind anywhere in Europe, the most spectacular of any found, or so I am told.'

The Captain turned to his men on the platform. 'Keep a careful look-out. We have just given the Republican soldiers a terrible mauling. If word leaks out, they will want revenge.'

'Were you followed back to Jersey, sir?' the Lieutenant asked.

'No. We were careful to leave no evidence of our invasion. But it would be prudent to be vigilant nonetheless.'

'Yes, sir.'

The Captain saluted his men and led his three guests back through the oak door and down the stone stair case towards the drawing room.

'Do you think our enemies will ever find the bodies of their massacred comrades?' Eloise asked.

'It is most unlikely. We left no trace. The two companies of French infantry will be to them like the lost legion of the ninth. The mystery of it all will stir up no small amount of fear in their ranks.'

As they entered the drawing room a footman in red livery was standing at the far entrance. 'Dinner is served,' he said.

'Ah, capital,' the Captain exclaimed. 'Follow me.'

The Captain led the way through a small library into a dining room in the single storey building on the north side of the Tower. He showed everyone to their seats. 'Would you do us the honour?' the Captain asked Pryce.

As the four of them stood at their mahogany chairs, Pryce said grace.

'Amen,' the others echoed, at which sound the servants entered with dinner plates of steaming stew.

'Tell me, Captain,' Jean Marie said. 'What is the name of this place?'

'It goes by the name of La Houge Bie, although originally it was known as La Houge Hambye.'

'That name sounds familiar,' Jean Marie said.

'It is a name of chivalrous renown,' the Captain replied.

'Didn't Hambye kill a dragon?' Eloise asked.

'That's right, my dear. Seigneur de Hambye lived in Normandy many years ago, or so legend tells us. He heard of a ferocious dragon that was tormenting Jersey, destroying crops and killing many inhabitants of this fine island. The brave knight travelled over the sea to confront the beast. He eventually found it in the marshes of Saint Saviour and entered into mortal combat with it.'

'So he was killed?' Eloise asked.

'I'm afraid he was. But not before he had severed the dragon's head with a single blow.'

'What a sad tale,' Jean Marie sighed.

'It gets sadder.'

'How so?' Jean Marie asked.

'It was not the dragon that killed the Seigneur,' the Captain said gravely.

'What was it, then?' Jean Marie asked.

'Not what but who.'

'Who then?'

'The brave knight was not slain by the dragon but by his squire.'

'No!' Jean Marie gasped.

'It's true. The squire had long been jealous of his master's wife and his master's land, so when he saw him lying wounded in the marsh he took the Seigneur's own sword and thrust it into his master's heart.'

'What a vile traitor!' Jean Marie cried.

'But that is not the end of the story. The squire went back to the knight's castle and told his master's wife that he had killed the dragon after her husband had been mortally wounded.'

'Villain!' Jean Marie cried.

'It gets worse, I'm afraid.'

'What could be worse than that?'

'The squire told the lady that her husband's dying wish was that she should now marry him. Being a dutiful wife, that's what she did.'

'Bastard!' Eloise exclaimed.

The Captain laughed.

Pryce sighed.

'Is there no justice in this tale?' Jean Marie asked.

'But of course there is! One night the wicked squire began to talk in his sleep while he was lying next to the Seigneur's widow. She heard him divulge the wicked subterfuge and reported it.'

'I hope he was hanged,' Jean Marie muttered.

'He was indeed. The lady had him brought before the courts where he admitted his guilt and was condemned to death.'

'Oh, please tell me,' Jean Marie said. 'Tell me that the brave knight was buried here.'

The Captain grinned. 'The story goes that the lady came in search of her husband and found his body in the marsh. She moved his corpse to the highest ground she could find and piled more earth on top of it before bidding her husband farewell.'

'Why on high ground?' Jean Marie asked.

'This mound can be seen from Normandy.'

'Then she could keep watch over her husband's grave for the rest of her days,' Jean Marie whispered.

'It's true,' said the Captain, 'or as true as these tales can be.'

'So that's how this place became known as La Houge Hambye?' Jean Marie asked.

'And then shortened to La Houge Bie,' the Captain concluded.

'That's quite a story,' Pryce said.

'A story doesn't have to be factual to be true, Thomas,' Jean Marie said.

Pryce frowned.

'Are you a little cynical, my friend?' the Captain asked.

'I don't believe in dragons, I'm afraid.'

'But you do believe in the devil, known as the Ancient Serpent.'

'I do.'

'So translate the story into your own language, your own life.'

'What do you mean?'

'You're fighting against great evil, no?'

'We all are,' Pryce replied.

'Then we are all dragon slayers,' the Captain said boldly.

'And we are all on the lookout for suspicious squires,' Pryce added.

'Bravo,' the Captain exclaimed, 'another *bon mot*. My friend, I congratulate you.'

The Captain raised his glass of claret. Pryce raised his. And the four lifted the wine to their lips as the Captain proposed a toast to undying chivalry.

'This seafood is superb,' Jean Marie said after a pause. 'Where did you find your chef?'

'Ah, I was hoping you would ask me that. He was sent ahead of us on a bugalet from the beach where we crushed our enemies, while Mister Pryce was conducting the sad farewell for our friend on board the ship.'

'I did not observe that,' Pryce said.

'I am glad. It was meant to be a subterfuge.'

With that the Captain whispered an order into his footman's ear and waited. Every eye was on the Captain. And he was clearly relishing the moment. As the door into the dining room re-opened, the Captain stood. 'Ladies and gentlemen, may I introduce to you the innkeeper, Monsieur Henry.'

Jean Marie dropped her fork.

Pryce gasped.

The two of them stood, removing their napkins and making their way swiftly to the innkeeper. He looked pale and fragile but there was colour in his plump cheeks and even a twinkle in his tired eyes.

'My dear Monsieur Henry,' Jean Marie cried, stretching out her arms. 'I am so happy to see that you are alive.'

'And so am I,' Pryce added. 'I must say that I feared the worst when I saw you being led in chains. It looked as if you had been subjected you to the most horrible abuse.'

'They tortured me, sir,' the innkeeper said, extricating himself politely from Jean Marie's embrace. 'I am just so sorry that I gave your position away. It was more than anybody could bear. Those men were vicious.'

'No man could have withstood that kind of torment,' Jean Marie said.

'We forgive you unreservedly,' Pryce added.

'And it all turned out well in the end,' Jean Marie concluded.

'Thank you, madam. Thank you, Mister Pryce. I am in the debt of you both.'

'No, Mister Henry, we are in yours,' Jean Marie insisted.

The Captain placed his hand on Henry's shoulder and nodded to him and Henry returned to the kitchens.

'That was indeed a surprise,' Jean Marie said. 'A most welcome one as well.'

'But it is not the only surprise I have planned for you,' the Captain said.

'What do you mean?' Pryce asked.

'I have a surprise specifically for you, Mister Pryce.'

'What kind of surprise?'

'It is, how shall I say, a transport of delight.'

Just then the footman re-entered the dining room and whispered into his master's ear.

'Please stand,' the Captain said. 'We have a very special guest.'

Just then an immaculately dressed gentleman entered the room. He was about fifty years of age and wearing a jacket as red as the claret on the table. A wig in the style of the ancient regime was perched above his high forehead which rose from a glowing face, which seemed to be etched in a rather child-like grin. He was short in stature and slight of build but he bore himself with the elegance of a nobleman.

'Mister Pryce, may I present to you the man who will help you travel to London tomorrow at unimaginable speed.'

The Captain paused for dramatic effect.

'This is Jacques-Etienne Montgolfier,' he announced, 'inventor of the hot air balloon.'

CHAPTER 41

'Quick! In here!' Morgues whispered.

The doctor followed Morgues into a dark alleyway leading away from the illuminated street.

'Don't move,' he said as they hid behind a slim buttress that protruded no more than a foot from the side of the building behind them.

The doctor pressed his back as hard as he could against the cold wall and peered past Morgues' shoulder. A moment later two men dressed in top hats and capes appeared at the entrance of the narrow passageway and stopped. The doctor watched as they strained their eyes to peer down the pitch black corridor. He held his breath, masking for a moment the heavy smell of coal smoke, and then moved to seize his sword cane.

Morgues put his hand over the doctor's arm.

A bead of sweat made its way like a snake down the doctor's furrowed brow and across his cheek.

A heartbeat later the pursuers turned to the left and made off down the street.

'Wait,' Morgues whispered.

A moment later the two men were back again. They stared one more time down the path between the two buildings and then spoke to each other before they were gone.

The doctor waited for his friend's signal.

'Bow Street Runners,' Morgues whispered.

'They are onto us,' the doctor replied. 'We must take great care.'

Soot was falling with the rain and the doctor was now coughing and shivering.

'We cannot go back to the Sabonière Inn,' Morgues said as he picked up the doctor's bag.

'What about Citizen Stanhope's home here in London?'

'We cannot go there either. It's too dangerous, especially if they know we visited him at his house in Kent.'

'Where then?' the doctor asked, as he kicked a rat sniffing at his feet.

'There's a safe house near St James' Park. We can lie low there until Friday afternoon and then meet up with Citizen Stanhope outside the palace.'

'That's risky,' the doctor muttered.

'I'm afraid after last night's killings our options are now limited.'

'Then it is what it is,' the doctor said.

He watched Morgues as he moved furtively towards the street, hugging the wall as he neared the entrance to the alleyway. Morgues removed his hat and slowly leaned out. 'It's all clear,' he whispered.

'Look the other way too,' the doctor urged.

Morgues moved to the opposite wall. 'It's clear that way too.'

'Let's go, then.'

The two agents hurried off in the opposite direction taken by the Bow Street Runners and scurried towards a hackney coach standing outside a church.

'St James' Park,' Morgues barked.

'Right away, Guv.'

The men clambered in and sat back under the welcome cover of the cab.

Fifteen minutes later the men had been set down just outside the Park. They had walked through the gate guarded by a sentinel and managed to negotiate their way past several fallow deer and a handful of prostitutes, or 'Mollys' as Morgues called them. They were now standing underneath the boughs of a lime tree near Rosamund's Pond.

'See there,' Morgues said, pointing towards a row of townhouses illuminated by a mixture of streetlights and oil lamps.

'What is it?'

'That middle house, no.17, is owned by a friend of liberty. I have used it before. It belongs to an Englishman sympathetic to our cause and is looked after by one of our ablest agents, Citizen Aubriet.'

'Ah, I have heard of Aubriet,' the doctor said. 'He has been very clever in forming secret English clubs designed to conspire against the government.'

'Precisely. It's perfectly located, here near the palace, and it is a safe place for us to prepare for Friday's meeting with the king.'

'Excellent,' the doctor said.

The doctor followed Morgues as he walked towards the edge of the Park. Morgues looked to his left and his right, then across the street and in the direction from which they had just come.

'Act normally,' Morgues whispered.

The two men waited until a sedan chair had made its way past them and then they walked to the middle of the rutted street, making their way towards the door of a tall Georgian townhouse.

'Excuse me, Guvs,' a man shouted as he ran with the purpose of an errand boy between them.

Morgues climbed several stone steps and then took the wrought iron knocker. He pounded three times, then tapped twice. A moment later a man appeared in a tailless double-breasted jacket. He was wearing a square cut and skirt-less waistcoat and a white shirt with no ruffles. He had short, natural brown hair and bright blue eyes.

'Can I help you?' the man asked.

The two agents unbuttoned their shirts and revealed their passkeys.

The man's pupils dilated when he saw that the doctor's was made of solid, gleaming gold.

'May the Eye of Ra watch over you,' the doctor said.

'And Reason be your guide,' the man replied, as he revealed his own passkey.

The man ushered them in and closed the door. 'Citizen Aubriet, at your service,' he said.

'Thank you, Citizen,' Morgues replied. 'Let me introduce you to Citizen Marat.'

'Welcome, Citizen,' the man exclaimed. 'You are truly welcome here.'

'Thank you, Citizen,' the doctor said.

'What can I do for you?' the host asked.

'We are on a mission of the utmost secrecy and are in need of your hospitality until midday on Friday.'

'You will be safe here,' Aubriet replied. 'The master of the house is a loyal supporter of our cause.'

'Is he at home?' Morgues asked.

'He is in Paris, speaking to some of our friends in the Directory.'

'That is good,' the doctor said.

Aubriet took their coats and led them into a drawing room with a large gilded mirror above the fire place. The walls were covered in Chinese wallpaper that had been painted by hand and the ceiling was adorned with stucco ornaments. Everywhere the doctor looked there was mahogany - upholstered mahogany chairs, mahogany tables for writing and playing cards, even the wainscoting on the walls was made of mahogany. It was modest, comfortable and decorous.

'Are you hungry?' Aubriet asked.

'I'm ravenous,' Morgues quipped.

'You are perpetually hungry,' the doctor smiled.

'Only when I know there's French food on the menu,' Morgues laughed.

'I'll have something prepared for you, and I'll bring you some banyans and slippers so you can relax by the fire after dinner.'

'That is most civil,' the doctor sighed.

'Do you need fresh nightshirts?' Aubriet asked as he was leaving the room.

'If you please,' the doctor replied.

'Is there anything else I can do for you?'

'I will need a pen and ink and some paper to write my report after dinner,' the doctor replied, 'and an important letter.'

'I can do that.'

'Can you get my report back to our Master in Paris?' the doctor asked.

'I can.'

'You are indeed a useful asset, Citizen Aubriet.'

'Thank you, Citizen.'

Aubriet picked up the doctor's case. 'I will put your bag in your room on the first floor, directly above this room,' he said as he made his way to the door. 'And dinner will be served in a short while.'

The doctor sat down in an armchair, holding both its mahogany arms, testing its strength. He smiled as the expensive wood refused to yield to his pressure. 'This house is a most commodious place to prepare for our mission.'

'And our host is a most capable and resourceful man,' Morgues added.

'He seems to be.'

Two hours later the three men had eaten onion soup, followed by an entrée of sturgeon steaks, a main course of *vol au vents* with chicken breasts in Bechemel sauce, a salad of celery *en roumelade* and a fruit dessert, all washed down with a generous quantity of claret - French claret.

'You are noticeably less grumpy after eating, my friend,' the doctor commented as the men sat by the fire again in the drawing room, their cheeks flushed, their eyes glazed and their stomachs extended. Morgues patted his satisfied belly. 'It is not just necessary to eat in order to live,' he exclaimed.

'It is necessary to live in order to eat,' the doctor intoned in response.

'Ha!' Aubriet exclaimed, 'it is truly the French way!'

'The English way is the exact opposite,' Morgues remarked. 'In this country you'd be better off dying than eating what's put on most tables.'

The men laughed.

When their merriment had subsided, Morgues turned to Aubriet. 'That was revolutionary cuisine at its very best.'

'It is one of the Shadow's favourite meals. He told me that he and Citizen Barras often use this menu for hosting their friends. I gave it to him last summer, in this very house, and have made it my aim to have it ready for him should he call.'

'You hosted the Shadow here?' the doctor enquired.

'Yes, I did. He sometimes makes his way across the Channel and we are always ready to make him feel at home when he does.'

'Well, I appreciate it most sincerely,' Morgues said. 'It's a little bit of France in a pig sty of a country.'

Aubriet grunted.

'Are you alright, Citizen?' the doctor asked.

'I was hoping that by now there would be far more than just a little bit of France in this city and in this country.'

'From what I have heard,' Morgues said, 'you have been doing admirably here.'

'But I have not achieved what I'd planned. I had hoped that by last Christmas the vast majority of the population would have been wearing the bonnet of liberty.'

'What has been obstructing you?' the doctor asked.

'The single greatest hindrance was William Pitt pushing through the Alien Act at the start of this year. Many of us were arrested and thrown in prison and with the withdrawal of *habeas corpus* some of us found ourselves in very deep waters.'

'What did you do?' the doctor asked.

'I was fortunate to have friends in the Foreign Office, so I wrote to Lord Grenville whom I know has misgivings about the loss of the freedom of speech in this country. Had not some of his staff intervened on my behalf, I would most likely be rotting in Newgate Prison or some such piss hole.'

'Well, I am glad for our sakes and yours that you are not,' Morgues said.

'I am happy too,' Aubriet replied.

The doctor stood up and walked over to a writing table where his host had left a pen, ink and some paper.

'Citizen Aubriet,' he said. 'I am writing a letter to Citizen Stanhope. You know of him?'

'But of course.'

'Have you met him?' the doctor asked.

'I have been to his London residence. We have had a number of private conversations about the course of the revolution.'

277

'Ah, that is most felicitous. I was hoping you would know where Citizen Stanhope resides. I need you to go to his house tomorrow evening and bring him here. Give him this letter. He will know who we are but it will also be advantageous for him to have you verify our identities.'

'What would you like me to ask him?'

'It's in the letter,' the doctor said, 'but please emphasize that we need him to bring us the passes. He will know what that means.'

'And I presume that I don't need to know.'

'You do not,' the doctor said firmly, 'but whatever happens, you must make sure that he doesn't leave his house without the two passes otherwise our mission will be over before it has begun.'

'And now,' the doctor added, 'I need to write my report to our master. This will take some time as well as concentration so I would be grateful to have the room to myself and the fire kept burning.'

'Of course,' Aubriet said.

As the doctor began to write he became unaware of the two men leaving the drawing room. He composed his letter in a code made up entirely of the suits and numbers of a pack of playing cards. At the bottom of the page he drew a picture of the King of Spades. Then he blew out the candle and the lamps in the drawing room and stood for a moment before the fire, whose flames were still reaching up towards the flue, as if trying to escape into the unrestrained freedom of the night.

As the doctor walked towards the drawing room door, he turned around to look once again at the plain elegance of his surroundings. As he did, he was momentarily drawn towards the ceiling.

He rubbed his eyes.

Then he rubbed them again.

There, on the white plaster above him, was the shape of a large eye. It had clearly been formed by the shadows cast by the burning logs in the hearth. But it seemed to be looking... looking at him.

'The Eye of Ra!' he gasped, before scuttling like a carob beetle from the room.

CHAPTER 42

Pryce woke at dawn wrapped in the folds of his knitted eiderdown and in the arms of his wife.

'You were having nightmares, darling,' she whispered.

Pryce turned towards Eloise.

'I know.'

'What were they about?'

'The usual… guillotines and corpses, shadows and demons, dragons and fire.'

'You have seen awful things in France,' she said. 'It will take a while for those memories to heal.'

'They may never heal,' Pryce answered.

Eloise's eyes widened and then began to close. When she opened them again, several moments later, there was a look of hunger.

'I know something that may help you forget, if only for a moment,' she said, her lips extending a fraction to reveal the trace of a mischievous smile.

Eloise wrapped her left leg more tightly around Pryce and pulled him towards her. At first Pryce resisted.

'Darling!' he whispered.

But his darling was not to be so easily rebuffed. She continued her soothing and caressing overtures, stroking the thin hairs on his chest, letting her hand rest from time to time around and upon his heart.

'Do you feel the healing in my hand?' she asked.

Pryce didn't answer. He sank back into the mattress and looked into Eloise's eyes, stroking the waves of her chestnut hair with his left hand.

'I have missed you,' he whispered.

'And I,' she said more breathlessly, 'have certainly missed you.'

Eloise lifted herself from his side and moved with the stealth and speed of a huntress. Sitting upright she straddled him and looked down into his eyes and smiled.

Eloise lowered her nightdress to her waist and began to move her thighs in gentle thrusts at first, before increasing her speed in unimpeded unison with her desire. As she moved beyond desire to ecstasy, she threw her head back and opened her mouth to moan.

'Hush!' Pryce gasped. 'You'll awaken the Tower.'

Eloise looked down for a moment as she reached the summit of the first of her ascensions.

As her breathing began to slow and her involuntary tremors subside, each one accompanied by a gasp of satisfaction, she bent over Pryce and kissed him on the ear, licking his earlobe with the tip of her trembling tongue.

'You're too late,' she said.

'What do you mean?' Pryce asked.

'It seems to me, my love,' she whispered, 'the tower has already been awakened.'

Pryce laughed. 'You are the mistress of the *bon mot*.'

'I think Captain D'Auvergne regards himself as the champion on that score,' she replied.

'Let's not talk about him just now,' Pryce said.

With that he lost himself within his beloved, rising and falling with her undulations until he himself broke like a wave upon the shore of their desire.

After ten minutes lying spent upon his back, Pryce touched his wife's stomach. He gazed into her eyes.

'How's our little one?'

'Safe,' she replied.

'That's good.'

Pryce gazed into Eloise's eyes.

'You'll make a great mother.'

'And you, my darling, will make a fine father.'

'I hope so.'

'I know so.'

Eloise leaned forward and rested on Pryce's chest, her soft skin touching his, sending a frisson of renewed desire throughout his body.

'We'll need to go down to breakfast soon,' he said.

Eloise emitted a playful groan, then giggled and held him more tightly.

'Not just yet,' she interjected, sitting upright once again and pushing down upon Pryce's chest with her hands.

'Not just yet.'

CHAPTER 43

Pryce stood in an open field near the Prince's Tower, watching as Jack and his men pulled at twelve ropes which kept a balloon, sixty feet high and forty feet in diameter, from launching into the heavens. Underneath the gaping mouth at its base, a fire was raging, completely filling the balloon in eight minutes, transforming it from a conical to a circular shape and causing the ropes to groan as it nagged at the boatmen to let it go.

'Good morning Monsieur Pryce,' Etienne Montgolfier said, turning for a moment from instructing the men.

'Is it?'

'It's perfect,' Etienne said. 'At least as far as travelling back to London is concerned. The weather is clear, the air is cool and the wind is perfect. It is a most serene and propitious day.'

Pryce looked at Etienne for a moment. He was dressed immaculately in a tight fitting redingote partly covered by a great coat with large, wide collars. Under his left arm he was carrying a small white poodle that was shivering, more from fear than cold, it seemed to Pryce. In stark contrast, Etienne wore an expression of nonchalance and confidence as he prepared for the flight.

'Is it your first time?' Etienne asked.

'It is.'

'Then you are in for an adventure, Monsieur Pryce. The skies are today what the oceans once were - open to navigation and exploration. We are airborne Columbuses, exploring the new world of the heavens.'

Pryce frowned. 'Pride cometh before a fall,' he muttered.

Etienne grunted. 'In my hands, Monsieur Pryce, we will be descending, not falling.'

'I hope you're right, monsieur. I hope you're right.'

At that moment, Captain D'Auvergne appeared in full ceremonial dress uniform. 'Ah, Monsieur Pryce, I see you are almost ready to depart. I have come to bid you farewell.'

'But not adieu,' Pryce replied.

'To be sure, my friend, this is not adieu. The saints will look after you. See here!' The Captain pointed to his chest where he had pinned an impressive badge decorated with the green robed figure of a priest, fixed to an eight pointed gold cross against a white enamel background. 'I am one of the few to be admitted into the order of Saint Joachim, the patron saint of married couples,' he said. 'He will watch over you as you fly and also over your beautiful wife as she sails.'

Pryce was about to reply when he was interrupted by Etienne who had barked an order, whereupon a small balloon and a kite shot up into the blue sky to join a few clouds that were scudding in a north easterly direction.

'See there, Monsieur Pryce. See how my little Montgolfier flies towards your country. This is the perfect moment. Say your farewells.'

Pryce turned to Eloise and kissed her. They spoke no words to each other, just looked for a moment into each other's eyes. When Pryce turned back towards the balloon, he saw that a wicker basket had been attached to it by ropes.

'Come. Come,' Etienne insisted, beckoning Pryce with his free arm.

Pryce walked towards the aerial car and with a hefty lift from Jack, clambered inside.

'I'll look after Mrs Pryce,' Jack said.

'Get her and my mother-in-law safely back to Deal and I will be in your debt, Jack.'

'Consider it done, sir,' the boatman replied.

Etienne approached the balloon and gently dropped his frightened dog into the basket. 'Monsieur Pryce will guard you, Louis,' he said, pouting his lips.

Pryce looked at the dog and the dog, now cowering in the corner of the basket, looked back. Louis was already beginning to emit a soft, lamentable whine as he pressed further into the corner, eventually making his way between two anchors and a grapnel to some cork jackets. Pawing at them frantically, he managed to create a modicum of cover and hid his head beneath the corner of one of the garments.

Etienne climbed without assistance into the basket and began to check his instruments - a barometer, mariner's compass, thermometer, telescope and a golden timepiece. He lifted it and squinted, then turned to Pryce. 'There are extra clothes in the corner in case you get cold. And feel free to use my telescope at any time. It is an exceptionally fine one and there will be sights to see beyond your wildest imaginings.'

Etienne looked back towards the boatmen of Deal and issued another order. At once three men brought three large sacks of sand ballast, weighing about ten pounds each, and passed them to Pryce who placed them one by one in the bottom of the basket at his feet. On Etienne's signal, the twelve boatmen released the ropes and cords attached to the balloon. 'We're on our way!' Etienne shouted to Pryce.

Pryce uttered a silent prayer.

'Good luck, my two intrepid aeronauts!' the Captain shouted flamboyantly from the ground, as the great balloon soared into the sky.

'You see,' Etienne shouted, 'we are experiencing a perfect ascension, no?'

Pryce nodded as he looked down. The boatmen were becoming smaller now, more like toy soldiers than men, but he could still make out the distinctive silhouette of his wife, and the Captain talking to her.

'It is a strange sensation, no?' Etienne said, 'especially for those who have only been attached to the surface of the globe.'

Pryce nodded again as the figure of his wife grew smaller and smaller until only the outline of the Prince's Tower could be made out far below.

As Etienne fed the burner with straw and wool, the balloon continued to ascend until it rose above the few clouds in the limitless expanse of the azure sky. 'We are at three thousand feet now,' Etienne shouted.

Pryce looked down again, resting his arms against the rim of the basket, gripping its tiny wooden gunwales with his whitening hands. The sea off Jersey now looked like a shimmering sheet of glass below.

After several more minutes the balloon levelled out. 'We are two miles high!' Etienne cried.

An unusual silence impressed itself upon both men as they stood on either side of the basket, no longer looking out towards the sky but inwards towards each other. Only the occasional flapping of the garnished taffeta interrupted it, and the intermittent grunts of Etienne's dog.

'Oh Louis, Louis,' the Frenchman pouted, 'come to Papa.'

The dog, however, was not to be coaxed and remained defiantly in his corner, squinting at his master and forcing his chops into what looked like a wild grin.

'Oh, very well, Louis, here, this will encourage you to exercise more fortitude.'

Etienne reached down and pulled a chicken leg from a leather postbag and stretched it towards his canine companion. The dog's nose began to twitch. Little by little he ventured out from his corner until his jaw opened and his tiny teeth chomped down upon the bone. As soon as the bird's leg was his, he turned and hurried back to his hiding place.

'Our victuals are in this bag,' Etienne said to Pryce. 'Help yourself whenever you're hungry, otherwise you may find Louis will get there first.'

Pryce thanked the aeronaut and then sat down into the basket. Looking up, he began to speak to his companion in French. 'Forgive me for asking, but how on earth did you come upon the idea of a hot air balloon?'

'Ah, it is a long story,' he replied.

'But we have at least six hours,' Pryce answered.

'Yes, well, that is true,' Etienne said, sitting down next to Pryce.

'Well, how did you think of it?'

'My brother Joseph and I thought of it. It all stemmed originally from a stunt our father used to pull.'

'What was that?'

'He used to create a very small incision in the bottom of a chicken's egg, drain all of its contents and then wait for it to dry. He then would seal the aperture using hot wax and heat the empty shell over the stove. When it reached a certain temperature it would slowly float towards the ceiling, causing Joseph and I to squeal with wonder.'

'Was that your inspiration?'

'There were others. My brother saw an orphan girl blowing soap bubbles one day and that got him thinking. And then there was the time when I was drying my wife's lingerie over the fire and the sight of the clothes billowing got me thinking too.'

Etienne looked up and smiled at the burner pouring heat through the mouth of the balloon, which was about fifteen feet in diameter. 'As I looked at my wife's clothes in front of the fire, I thought to myself, surely it would be possible to harness the force that carries particles of smoke up the flue of a chimney. Surely it would be possible to use that energy to lift conveyances for men over the earth.'

'Profound ideas have simple beginnings,' Pryce remarked.

'That's very true, my friend. It was not long before Joseph and I were experimenting with what we called our ascending machines.'

'So what did you do?'

'Joseph set about creating a machine that could be made lighter than the air it displaced through the expansive power of heat. It was he who came up with the idea of inflating a balloon through the combination of atmospheric air and heat. The dilated gas that's formed in the process is more than just rarified air. It's a lighter substance altogether and it's that which causes this machine to ascend.'

'Brilliant!' Pryce exclaimed.

'If you look above, Monsieur Pryce, you'll see that our straw burner suspended underneath the orifice has displaced the 3000 pounds of air and replaced it with 1500 pounds of hot air. That hot air is far lighter.'

'Extraordinary!' Pryce exclaimed, before pointing to their conveyance and adding, 'why did you choose this kind of material to carry your passengers?'

'Wicker is incredibly light and extraordinarily strong.'

'Don't you ever feel like you're flying in a great big bread basket?' Pryce asked.

Etienne chuckled. 'I do sometimes feel like a complete loaf!'

'I must say,' Pryce exclaimed, when the two men had finished laughing, 'you and your brother have invented something unique.'

'We have had some competition. There were some fellow countrymen experimenting with hydrogen at the same time as us in the 1780s. We preferred to fill our balloons physically rather than chemically. Hot air is far less expensive for one thing. Hydrogen is very hard to get hold of for another.'

'Who got into the sky first, then?'

'I did,' Etienne said firmly.

'You were the first aeronaut?'

'I was. The first official flight was by Pilâtre de Rozier, but I conducted experiments before that and was the first man to go up in an ascending machine.'

'You must be very proud.'

'I am. So is my brother. Joseph invented it. I flew it. That's why these balloons are called Montgolfières.'

The two men continued to converse for several hours, during which time Etienne occasionally stood to check the height and direction of the balloon as it moved in long arcs towards the British Isles. Sometimes he would cause the balloon to descend until it came upon a stable wind that blew towards London. Then Etienne would level the balloon and let it float with the wind at fifteen miles an hour towards their downwind destination.

Each time Etienne would sit down satisfied and continue to converse with Pryce - until the balloon began a sudden and unanticipated drop.

Chapter 44

'Shit!' Etienne cried as he stood quickly to his feet, moving to the barometer.

'What's the matter?'

'The mercury is rising.'

'What does that mean?'

'It means we are losing height.'

'You mean we are falling.'

'We do not fall, monsieur. We descend.'

'Why are we descending, then?'

'I'm not sure.'

'You don't know?'

'It happens.'

'It happens?'

'Yes, it happens.'

Etienne took hold of a pitchfork and thrust some straw into the burner suspended beneath the gawping orifice, taking care that no sparks were released into the air towards the gaudy and inflammable fabric of the balloon.

Pryce looked down. There was no mistake. They were no longer an ascending machine. They were now very much a descending one.

Pryce shivered. His eyes were now filled with water and his ears were singing. He was shaking from the altitude and the cold, and the rotations of the falling basket were now beginning to make him feel queasy.

'I cannot stop it,' Etienne shouted.

'What shall we do?' Pryce asked.

'Throw one of the sandbags overboard.'

Pryce hauled one of the bags to his shoulder, pushed it to the edge of the basket, and let it drop. For a moment the basket jolted and the balloon's descent began to slow. But then it picked up speed again.

'Throw another!' Etienne shouted as he thrust more straw and wool into the burner.

Pryce repeated the manoeuvre with exactly the same results.

'The last one, throw it!'

Pryce picked up the sandbag and released it from the basket.

The balloon began to slow but they were still falling and Pryce could now see the whites of the waves below.

'We're going to crash!' Pryce cried.

'We are most certainly not!' Etienne retorted. 'Cast off some of the ballast!'

Pryce took hold of the formal drapery on the outside of the basket, then the inner lining. He took the moulinnette and its apparatus and the gouvernail, as well as various ornaments and items of clothes, bottles and bags, and hurled them overboard.

But they were still falling.

'Here!' Etienne shouted, passing one of two inflated bladders to Pryce.

'Piss in it and throw it overboard.'

Pryce stared in disbelief for a moment before unbuttoning his breeches and doing as he had been told.

But the balloon was still falling.

'Put on your cork jacket,' Etienne cried.

Pryce quickly donned his primitive life vest, alarming the already terrified dog.

It was when he looked down again that he saw them. They were now less than three hundred feet from the ocean and about six hundred yards to the west of their basket there were three heavily gunned sloops, all carrying the French colours.

'Shit!' Etienne cried.

'They won't fire on us will they?' Pryce asked. 'Surely they won't know we are enemies?'

Etienne shook his head and pointed upwards towards the balloon. Underneath all the rope netting around the circular shape of the balloon there were the unmistakable emblems of royalist sympathies. The balloon's dome was covered in golden zodiac signs and *fleurs de lis* symbols. At its waist were the royal initials of King Louis XVI which alternated with blazing suns. At its base eagles flew between elaborate festoons and garlands.

Pryce was on board a craft that carried the most graphic and brazen advertisements of loyalty to the Bourbon kings.

'If you are a man of prayer, now would be a good time,' Etienne shouted.

But Pryce didn't have time. As the basket neared the water, the guns of the brigs opened up. Great columns of water appeared near the basket, drenching the two men and their dog.

The balloon slowed to a halt, the basket hovering just above the water.

A second barrage opened up.

Plumes of water appeared just behind them and Pryce flinched as a cannon ball grazed the side of the basket, causing sparks to ignite one corner.

As the dog yelped and scurried to the opposite side, Pryce took the one remaining pitchfork and attached a sponge to its end. He lowered it in the sea and then mopped the burning wicker until it was fully doused.

'Well done, Monsieur Pryce!' Etienne shouted.

Pryce stared at Etienne who was doing everything in his power to protect the flames in the burner from the jets of water that were forming all around them.

The guns opened up again.

As two columns of water rose within twenty feet of the balloon, a gust of air blew the balloon and its basket up and away from the ocean and the blast of wind caused the fire in the burner to explode into a greater flame.

Their machine was now ascending again. And with most of the ballast in the sea, it was ascending rapidly.

'Hurrah!' Etienne shouted, wiping the seawater from his face.

Within minutes they had levelled out again at two miles high, the sloops invisible beneath the gathering clouds.

'That was close,' Pryce sighed.

'We were fortunate,' Etienne replied, gathering his saturated dog in his arms and soothing him.

For several minutes the three occupants shivered in silence, their near death experience uniting them in a wordless gratitude.

It was Etienne who spoke first. 'It's time to get you home.'

'Are we on course?' Pryce asked.

'We are heading towards the British coast but we cannot do so in a straight line. We have to travel there in long arcs, directed by winds that are favourable.'

'So we don't know where we'll land?'

'Travelling by hot air balloon is an inexact science.'

'What does that mean?'

'It means that I can guarantee to get you towards London provided our destination remains downwind. But I cannot put you down in an exact location.'

'Oh dear,' Pryce sighed.

'It's not like a boat that you can row with oars and direct with a rudder. We tried that. We put oars on our first Montgolfieres. It didn't work. It wasn't, how shall I put it, *dirigible.*'

'So the only thing that's going to get me to London,' Pryce said, 'is your knowledge of wind patterns.'

'Absolutely, my friend, and the good news for you is that no one in the world knows more about those than I do.'

Pryce sat down in the basket and put his head in his hands. As he did he became aware of a wet nose pressing into his. It was Louis. Pryce moved his arms and the dog jumped into his lap, hiding his nose in Pryce's chest. Within moments, both of them had closed their eyes. Soothed by the motion of the basket, and calmed by the other worldly silence of the heavens, they soon descended into the welcoming respite of a deep sleep.

CHAPTER 45

It was Louis who woke Pryce with the sound of his barking. An increase in the strength of the wind had caused his master to shout.

'We're going at nearly twenty miles an hour! That's more than three times the speed of the coach from Dover to London, Monsieur Pryce.'

Pryce rose to his feet and peered over the edge of the basket. They were now clearly approaching Dover. Even from this great height, Pryce could make out the formidable breakers crashing on the shores around the distinctive chalky cliffs just a few miles from his parish of Deal.

'The wind has changed in our favour!' Etienne exclaimed. 'It's blowing us towards London.'

As Pryce looked down the Kent countryside appeared to him like a flat map, with no impression of any elevation or inequality in its green surface.

'We only took four hours to get from Jersey to Dover!' Etienne shouted. 'God is smiling on us!'

The balloon continued to pick up speed, its netting straining as forceful gusts of wind propelled the three aeronauts towards the city of London. At twenty miles distance, Pryce saw the outline of the city and the dome of St Paul's Cathedral, suspended like an ornamental bell. They were flying lower now, at about three thousand feet over well populated villages and impressive villas. From time to time, people milling in the squares and streets looked up at the ascending machine passing overhead, their eyes as wide as their mouths.

In what seemed like no time at all they were over the Thames. Scores of British naval ships, including men-of-war, frigates, brigs and gunboats, congregated like small canoes within the Upper

Pool. As the balloon dropped to under 1000 feet, Pryce could see ships carrying rum, sugar, ginger, dyewoods, and pimento arriving from the West Indies and approaching the Thames port. Several thousand craft were jostling within the congested river below, including barges, yachts, lighters and pleasure craft, all competing for the spaces on the wharves and quays. This congestion was being further exacerbated by the number of boats carrying cargo from the wharves to the ships and back again.

'They'll need to build new docks soon,' he shouted to Etienne. 'See there, the Isle of Dogs would be ideal. Wapping too.'

'How much money does your country make from all this trade?' Etienne asked.

'It's doubled in the last twenty five years,' Pryce shouted. 'Last year imported goods accounted for £18 million, and exports £24 million. And London itself benefitted from over half of that.'

'They should use some of that money to make the city cleaner,' Etienne sighed, covering his nose with a handkerchief.

They were just above the tallest buildings now and Etienne was looking for a suitable landing place. As the balloon made its way over the metropolis it continued to descend as Etienne diminished the fire in the burner and removed every last trace of ballast from the basket. As the last item went over the side, the vehicle struck the top of a chimney pot.

'Pardon us!' Etienne shouted.

'Look, Hyde Park!' Pryce shouted as the balloon descended to a hundred feet.

The basket struck the top of a tree before an open and spacious field beckoned to them ahead. Then it struck the ground with so much force that Pryce toppled on top of the shivering dog.

'Cast out the anchor!' Etienne cried as Louis whined.

Pryce somehow climbed to his feet, grabbed the iron stock of the anchor and threw it to the ground. Etienne grasped the shank of his and did the same and both men watched as the flukes dug into the soil and the great globe above them, no longer filled with heat, collapsed into a mighty swatch of taffeta strewn on the earth before them.

After several moments brushing themselves down, the two men stood on terra firma once again.

'Thank you, my friend,' Pryce said. 'That was, well, an adventure.'

'It is always an adventure when you travel with Etienne Montgolfier.'

'I'm sure you are right.'

'I am always right. We must do it again soon.'

'What will you do now?' Pryce asked.

'I have friends here in London. They will help me to return to Jersey where I can continue to be of use to Captain D'Auvergne.'

Etienne picked up his dog then looked at Pryce. 'And you, my friend,' he said. 'What will you do?'

Pryce fumbled in his pocket and found Lady Hester's calling card. 'I'm going to pay a visit to the patriotic daughter of a treacherous father,' he replied.

CHAPTER 46

The doctor was aroused by the sound of three loud knocks on the front door. 'The British Jacobin is here,' he whispered to Morgues.

'I hope he wasn't followed,' Morgues whispered back.

'The fog is thick in London tonight,' the doctor replied. 'It would have tested the best of watchers.'

The doctor stood and adjusted the tricolor ribbon just above his breast pocket. The next moment the door to the drawing room opened and Aubriet appeared, followed closely by the unmistakable figure of Lord Charles Stanhope. As he entered it seemed to the doctor that his tall frame filled the entire space and that his mountainous forehead almost grazed the ceiling.

'This is an historic moment,' Stanhope said, stretching out his huge right hand.

'Indeed, it is, Citizen,' the doctor replied, as his small hand disappeared into Stanhope's grasp.

The doctor stepped back. 'You remember my colleague, Citizen Morgues?'

'Ah, yes, I do,' Stanhope said, turning to Morgues.

'Shall we sit?' the doctor asked.

As the three men relaxed into their cushioned chairs, Aubriet poured some claret.

'Very civil of you,' Stanhope replied.

'Dinner will be served in an hour,' Aubriet said, closing the door as he left.

'You will not be disappointed by the Revolutionary cuisine, Citizen Stanhope,' Morgues said. 'It is as good here as it is in Paris.'

'Capital,' Stanhope said.

The doctor turned to Stanhope. 'We are grateful to you for coming over here tonight, Citizen.'

'All other matters are secondary,' Stanhope said.

'France is grateful too,' the doctor added.

'Shall we cut to the chase?' Stanhope asked.

The doctor nodded and Stanhope reached into a pocket. 'I think these are what you need, Citizen,' he said, passing two cards to the doctor.

The doctor took them in his hands and studied them through the lenses of his spectacles. They were imprinted at the top with the title, 'ST JAMES PALACE', and at the bottom with the crest of King George. In the centre were the words, 'Audience with his Majesty King George III', followed by the date and time of the meeting and the words, 'Petitions to His Majesty by Men of Science and Invention.'

'This is excellent,' the doctor said, passing the invitations to Morgues.

'Look, gentlemen,' Stanhope said. 'All you need to ensure is that you have your identity papers and that these tally with the aliases that I've given to the Palace.'

'Perfect,' the doctor said. 'I will have Citizen Aubriet complete our new identity papers tonight.'

'How are the rest of your preparations?' Stanhope asked.

'We are lying low here until tomorrow afternoon.'

'That is prudent,' Stanhope said. 'There's an uncommon number of parish constables, runners and watchers out tonight.'

'Why?' Morgues asked.

'There was a double murder several nights ago and the culprits have yet to be detained,' Stanhope replied. 'It seems that two men were savagely killed in a half-built mansion just off the Strand.'

Morgues shuffled restlessly in his seat.

'I don't suppose you'd know anything about that, now.'

'We do not,' the doctor insisted.

'That's good,' Stanhope said, taking a sip of his wine. 'You know my feelings about the unnecessary use of violence.'

The doctor nodded before speaking. 'Do you think you were followed here?'

'I am certain I was not. I took every precaution and in any case the streets are covered by a thick fog tonight.'

'That is good, Citizen,' the doctor said.

'Now that you have the invitations,' Stanhope continued, 'all that remains is for us to agree on the course of action and our story for tomorrow.'

'We will meet at half past one tomorrow afternoon,' the doctor said. 'Outside the clock tower of Saint James' Palace, where we will present our invitations and our identity papers. Then we will proceed as planned up the stairs the far side of Colour Court and into the Tapestry Room where the audience is to be held.'

'I am told,' Stanhope interrupted, 'that the final number of people making petitions to the king is in fact twelve. So there will very likely be a maximum of fifteen of us in the room.'

'In case we are asked,' the doctor said, 'what is the subject of our petition?'

'I have been writing a treatise called *The Principles of Electricity*, inspired by my friend Benjamin Franklin,' Stanhope said. 'This has involved conducting experiments with lightning on my estate in Kent.'

'Why do you need the King's help?' Morgues asked.

'I have already spent thousands of pounds. I now need more funds to set up a large number of portable lightning conductors. You can pass off as my assistants and fellow petitioners.'

'What if the other scientists notice our accents or ask us questions?' Morgues asked.

'Then simply tell them you are scientists from Basel and that you've been with me at Chevening, waiting for thunder storms over Star Hill. You can say that we've been conducting all kinds of experiments.'

Stanhope rubbed his chalky chin and allowed himself a rare smile. 'On one occasion,' he said with a glint in his eye, 'I even strapped a conductor on the back of a cow. The poor beast was completely unsettled by this strange burden and ran off into a forest making a devilish noise.'

Morgues chuckled.

'I have another question,' the doctor said. 'When Morgues and I take the king from the chamber, what will you do when the incident is investigated? It won't look good that you've been the source of our invitations.'

'I shall of course deny any knowledge of your plans,' Stanhope replied, 'and I'll simply say that you visited Chevening because you'd heard of my experiments and that you were masquerading as scientists as a cover to get access to the Presence Chamber.'

'Do you think anyone will believe that?'

'I am not sure I care terribly. The cause is worth the inconvenience.'

Stanhope paused for a moment, rubbed his bald head, and then looked intently at the doctor. 'It is my turn to ask you a question, Citizen.'

'Anything,' the doctor answered.

'How will you escape from the palace? There will be guards everywhere.'

'We have a key for the door from the Tapestry Room to the room beyond,' the doctor replied.

'Where did you get that?'

'It is perhaps best if you don't know, Citizen.'

Stanhope frowned.

'Our plan is to remove the king, lock the door after we have left the room, and proceed via a secret passageway underneath the chapel out into the Park and then on to the Thames. We will be heading towards the Channel before anyone can stop us.'

'And what will you do at the end of your voyage?'

'We will have the king incarcerated in The Tower. We will compel him to abdicate and then denounce all forms of monarchy.'

'That might not be as easy as you think,' Stanhope said. 'These Hanoverians can be very proud and stubborn.'

'He will yield,' the doctor said. 'Of that I have no doubt.'

299

At that moment the drawing room door opened and Aubriet, his face flushed, re-entered.

'Dinner is served.'

As Aubriet left the room, the doctor stood and raised his glass. There was a thin line of blood-red wine at the bottom of the crystal vessel. 'Tomorrow lightning will strike St James' Palace,' he said. 'And when it does, there will be a new power in this nation.'

Stanhope and Morgues stood to their feet and lifted their glasses.

'To an unforgettable strike of lightning,' the doctor said.

'To an unforgettable strike,' Morgues whispered.

CHAPTER 47

'Thomas!' Lady Hester squealed. 'What a delightful surprise!'

Pryce stood to his feet and kissed Lady Hester's hand. 'I am most grateful to you for allowing this unexpected intrusion,' Pryce said.

'Oh nonsense. I am alone in this great barn of a house tonight, as bored as it's possible to be. You are a most pleasant diversion.'

'Thank you, my lady.'

'Stuff and nonsense! You call me Hetty, as we agreed.'

'Very well, Hetty.'

Hester led Pryce by the hand up a staircase into a drawing room on the first floor. 'Sit here,' she insisted, tapping the space next to her on a chaise longue.

Pryce sat and Hester turned towards him, her face as close as it was decent to be. 'Now then, Thomas, tell me why you're here. You have clearly come in something of a rush. What's the matter? Are you in trouble?'

'Forgive me for my appearance,' Pryce said, sweeping his hand over his long black dishevelled hair. 'There is indeed trouble. I need your help.'

Hester placed her hand on Pryce's arm. 'Whatever you need me to do, Thomas.'

'I fear you may not so readily agree when you hear.'

Pryce took a deep breath as Hester rang a small copper bell. 'Two glasses of whiskey, Giles,' she said to her footman. 'Then please make sure we're not disturbed.'

'Very well, my lady.'

A few moments later Pryce had taken a large gulp and was ready to speak. 'It's a long story, and there isn't much time.'

Pryce told Hester of his covert journey to the French coast and then his coach ride to Paris, the tragic death of his father-in-law at the guillotine in the Place de la Révolution and the dangerous quest for Jean Marie in Brittany. When he told of Jean Marie's rescue Hester jumped in her seat with undisguised pleasure. But when he gravely narrated his discovery of the plot to assassinate their king, she fell quiet.

'So you see, Hetty, it appears that there are French agents intent on killing the king.' Pryce paused. 'And it also appears that I am now the only person in London who knows this and who might be able to prevent it.'

Hester took Pryce's hand and looked gravely into his eyes. 'Not the only person,' she whispered.

'What do you mean?'

'I mean that your visit here is at the very least propitious and at best providential.'

'Why, Hetty?'

Hester stood up and walked towards a window, gazing out at the illuminated street. 'I think I know what's about to happen.'

'What do you know?'

Hester turned back towards Pryce. 'Thomas, I think my father may be involved.' There were tears in her eyes now.

'Your father – are you sure?'

'I'm as sure as I am that you are sitting right in front of me.'

'What do you know?'

Hester walked over to Pryce and held out her hand. 'Come with me.'

She pulled Pryce to his feet and ran out of the drawing room, up a flight of stairs, into a room with a desk covered in papers and walls lined with leather-bound books. 'Here,' she said, 'look at this.'

Hester pulled a white card from its resting place above a piece of ink stained blotting paper. 'It's an invitation to Saint James' Palace.'

Pryce studied the writing. 'It's for tomorrow,' he said.

'Father told me that he was going to petition the king for funds to support his research into electricity.'

'And what is so unusual about that?'

'I have had two reasons to doubt this explanation.'

'And what are they?'

'The first is that my father hates the monarchy and despises the king. If there's one thing I know he wouldn't do, it's satirize him in one breath and petition him in another. It simply doesn't ring true.'

'And the other?'

'This is more serious,' Hester said, sitting in her father's chair. 'I was at Chevening a few days ago when two French gentlemen arrived to speak to my father.'

'What did they want?'

'They were asking for help.'

'What kind of help?'

'I'm not sure.'

'Hetty, please think carefully. What were they doing there?'

'I am convinced that they were planning something with my father.'

'Do you know where your father is now?'

'He said he was going out to deliver some papers.'

'Are you thinking what I'm thinking?'

'He went to deliver invitations to the two French agents,' Hester cried.

'Precisely, and that means we may already be too late.'

Hester slumped back in the chair. 'What if we go to Mister Wickham and share our suspicions?' He was at that dinner at Walmer Castle where we met. This is his line of work. Won't he be able to help?'

'We would waste valuable time trying,' Pryce replied. 'And I'm pretty sure he wouldn't believe us. I'm just a Vicar and you, Hetty, well forgive me, but you are Lord Stanhope's daughter.'

'Then we must come up with a plan ourselves,' Hester cried. 'And quickly...'

CHAPTER 48

'In here,' Hester whispered as she opened a door in the chilly basement of the house. 'This is where he keeps it.'

'Are you sure about this, Hetty?'

'Yes, Thomas, come on.'

Pryce entered the room and held his lamp in front of him, waving it from side to side, spying his surroundings. There were glass receptacles and tubes everywhere.

'Father's laboratory,' Hester whispered.

'What are we doing here?'

'Desperate times call for desperate measures,' she replied.

Hester walked over to a dresser in the far right corner of the room and opened the glass door of a cabinet resting on it. Its shelves were heavily laden with apothecary's pots, glasses and jugs with labels on them.

'Here it is,' she cried.

'What?'

'Chloroform.'

Pryce gasped. 'What are you projecting?'

Hester led Pryce out of the laboratory to the bottom of the stairs leading to the ground floor. Having locked the door behind her, she turned to him before ascending.

'We only have one choice,' she said.

'And that is?'

'We must incapacitate my father tonight and confine him to this house tomorrow.'

'Are you sure?'

'Yes,' Hester replied. 'And that's not all. You're going to have to go to the palace in my father's place.'

'But that won't work. I don't look anything like your father, Hetty.'

'That's not a problem.'

'I'm afraid it is.'

'No, Thomas, I can spend the morning making you look as close to my father as it's possible to be.'

'But he's over twice my age and completely bald.'

'That may be so, Thomas, but it's amazing what a razor and some make up can do. And besides, you're as tall as my father and you will easily fit into his clothes. It won't take much to make the deception convincing.'

'I don't know, Hetty. I'm not a vain man, but the thought of you making me as bald as your father is not exactly a flattering one.'

'This is for king and country, Thomas... for king and country.'

'Oh, very well,' Pryce sighed as Hester began to scuttle up the damp stone steps to the door above them.

As they reached the top step, Hester suddenly turned, her finger over her lips. The two froze. They could both clearly hear the sound of voices. 'Father's home,' she whispered.

Pryce strained to hear what was going on the far side of the basement door. He could make out two voices. 'Where is Lady Hester, Giles?'

'She had a visitor, my Lord, but she's now retired to bed, I believe.'

'Capital, capital, then I'll retire too.'

'Good night, my Lord.'

Pryce could hear the sound of footsteps departing. Someone was approaching the door in front of them. Hester grabbed Pryce and held him, her head buried into his chest. She was shaking. The door handle turned slowly. It turned again. Then it stopped. It retreated to its resting place. Outside, a man muttered. Then there were footsteps heading away from the basement door.

As the sound disappeared altogether, Hester pulled herself away.

'Calm yourself,' Pryce whispered. 'He's gone.'

Hester's breathing began to slow and her white cheeks throb with colour again. 'That was close,' she gasped.

'We must get out of here,' Pryce whispered.

'Come to my bedroom,' Hester insisted. 'We'll wait there till he's asleep and then use this.'

Hester lifted the tightly sealed bottle with the word 'chloroform' written in ink on a piece of white paper attached to it. 'We can knock him out and tie him up,' she said. 'Then you can go to the palace and save the king.'

CHAPTER 49

'What time is it?' Pryce whispered.

'It's time,' Hester replied from the four poster bed.

Pryce stood from the armchair beside the fireplace and brushed the creases out of his jacket. By the light of the dying fire, he saw Hester pull back the bed sheets and step out onto the cold floor, her lean and lithe figure just visible in the half light. She pulled a shawl over her pale shoulders and tiptoed towards Pryce.

'When we get to his room, you hold him down, Thomas. I'll apply the chloroform.'

Pryce nodded as Hester slowly and silently turned the ornate handle to her room and stepped out into the draughty corridor. She was holding the receptacle and a large white flannel in her hands.

Pryce followed behind her until the two reached a door further down the carpeted landing, next to a marble bust of Lord Stanhope.

Hester nodded to Pryce. He reached down to the handle and began to move it. The door opened several inches.

Pryce leaned again.

It opened further.

Hester slipped through first, as weightless as a phantom. She moved carefully, one step at a time, pausing to be sure of the floorboards beneath her feet.

Pryce mimicked every one of her movements, sensing more than seeing her body, responding to the strength and weakness of her perfume.

They moved in unison towards the bed at the far side of the room. Its curtained awning loomed above them like the giant wings of a bird of prey.

Hester stopped.

There was a sound from the bed.

A loud sigh.

Some words.

Movement.

Then silence.

Hester paused for a few moments and then took the jar, opened it carefully, and poured some of its contents onto the flannel.

Hester had been careful to cover the aperture of the container with the thick material of the cloth. Even so, a whiff of the anaesthetic filled Pryce's nostrils and he began to lose his balance.

He was now falling towards the bed.

He couldn't stop himself.

His limbs were as lifeless as a marionette's.

As Pryce slumped over the supine figure of the Earl, the impact aroused both men.

'Quick, Hetty, do it now!'

Pryce pinioned her father to the bed.

He was stirring now.

'What the hell...!'

The man angrily began to reach for the bell rope beside the bed.

Pryce struck his arm with a fist.

The Earl yowled like a wounded hound.

'Now Hetty!'

Pryce applied all his strength while Hester pressed the odorous cloth to her father's face.

Pryce buried his nose in the blankets.

The Earl was thrashing like a hooked fish.

But Pryce's grip held firm.

The man murmured.

Pryce could make out a muffled cry for help.

The limbs relaxed.

The tension in the body subsided.

Then silence.

'He's out cold,' Hester whispered as she removed the cloth and threw it away from their noses.

'Don't inhale any of it in, Thomas.'

'Bit too late for that,' Pryce murmured.

The two of them pulled the Earl by the feet from the bed, Hester cradling his head as the body slipped awkwardly onto the floor.

Within minutes they were back in the water closet leading off Hester's bedroom.

They propped Stanhope's back against a wooden wall and tied him tight with bed sheets, gagging him as he slept.

He was snoring now.

'I'll make his bed and tidy his room,' Hester whispered. 'The servants will think he's left early in the morning.'

'What if he's found in your rooms?'

'He won't be. I'll be here all the time to keep an eye on things tomorrow. I'll wait till after the audience with the king and then release him. He'll have a sore head but he'll be grateful when he learns about the treachery from which he's been rescued.'

'And what do you propose I do?' Pryce asked.

'Sleep in the guestroom next door. The bed's made up. I'll awaken you in the morning and after breakfast I'll apply my cosmetic skills to your head and face.'

Pryce sighed.

'Cheer up, Thomas,' she smiled. 'I'm about to promote you from a parson of the church into a peer of the realm.'

CHAPTER 50

Pryce stood before the full length mirror, observing Hester's handiwork. His thick black hair had disappeared altogether from his head, leaving his dome completely bald. The only remaining hair was around the sides and the back of his head but this had been reduced to the thinnest of crops and was now dyed grey. His face and forehead were lined and there were shadows under his eyes. The only concession to his former features was his nose. Hester had not attempted to change that into her father's more aquiline shape, arguing that this would have made him look like a character out of a pantomime, rendering the disguise obvious.

'What do you think?' Hester asked as she looked over Pryce's shoulder at the reflection.

'I think you've done a remarkable job. I look at least thirty years older.'

'You'll look even more the part when I've found my father's tails,' Hester said.

In a few minutes she returned with shirt, tails, trousers and shoes. 'I'll see how my father is doing. You get into these.'

Pryce quickly donned the Earl's outfit and stood in front of the mirror again.

Hester peered through the door of the water closet. 'That's perfect. From here you could easily pass off as my father. In fact, let's see what he thinks. Come over here, Thomas.'

Pryce walked to her. The moment the Earl clapped his eyes on him, he looked aghast. He tried to speak but the gag in his mouth held firm, as did the sheets around his body. The Earl looked at Hester with a plaintive expression, begging her to let him speak.

'No, father,' she said. 'In spite of appearances, my friend and I are here to help you. You have absolutely no idea how much trouble you're in or how much trouble you're about to be spared.'

Lord Stanhope wriggled frantically.

Hester knelt in front of him. 'Listen father, the two French agents you welcomed at Chevening are heading in several hours to Saint James' Palace. I do not know what they told you but whatever it was I cannot believe it was true because I know you would never have colluded with them had they been honest.'

Hester now drew closer. 'Father, we believe they intend to assassinate the king this afternoon.'

At this the Earl began to moan.

His daughter continued. 'The only person who can stop them is this gentleman here. His identity, I'm afraid, will have to be kept a secret for now but rest assured he is my friend and we can rely on him to do the right thing for our family.'

The Earl bowed his head. He looked defeated.

'I want you to stay here and be good until it's all over,' Hester said. 'Then I'll untie you.'

Hester stood to her feet and ushered Pryce out of the room.

'I know it's humiliating for him, but it's a lesson he'll never forget.'

Hester took Pryce by the hand and walked to the bed where his clothes were lying. 'Where's the pistol I gave you?'

Pryce fumbled in his jacket and removed the weapon and its accompanying bag.

'Good,' she said. 'Is it loaded?'

'No.'

'Then we need to load it now and test the weapon before sending you off to the palace.'

Hester took the pistol in her right hand. 'These weapons are prone to misfiring. So I'm going to replace the flint. See here. It's poorly napped. It's obviously taken a bit of punishment on your travels. I'll see to that now.'

Pryce watched as Hester adjusted the flint and checked the mizzen for moisture. She replaced the powder and then loaded the barrels with four bullets wrapped in paper, one in each of the barrels over and under the pistol. She rammed them into place with the short, extendable rod in the bag and then primed the flash pan and closed the frizzen.

'That should do it,' she said, handing the weapon to Pryce.

'What do you want me to do with this?'

'Hang on,' she replied.

Hester went to a large mahogany wardrobe with a drawer at its base. She pulled out the drawer using two brass ringed handles and withdrew an old doll dressed as a baby.

'I have never been fond of this.'

She placed the doll at the head of the bed, wedging it upright between two stacks of pillows. She then pulled Pryce's sleeve and drew him back towards the standing mirror about twelve feet from the doll.

'This is as good a target as any,' Hester said, shutting and locking her bedroom door.

Turning to Pryce, she winked at him. 'Right, Thomas, let's see if you can hit that ugly creature from here. The distances should be about right for this afternoon.'

'Are you saying I'm going to have to shoot those agents?'

'I think it almost certain,' Hester replied. 'If they do not submit, you will be faced with no alternative if they seek to do harm to His majesty.'

'In that case...'

Pryce raised the primed pistol. He pulled the hammer back and fired the first barrel.

A shower of sparks poured forwards from the mizzen and sideways from the flash hole. Pryce discharged the second barrel. Hester then directed his hand to a switch on the right hand side of the weapon. 'Turn it downwards and then fire the two remaining barrels,' she cried.

Pryce flicked the switch and marvelled as the chamber swivelled to make the powder available for the bottom two barrels. He aimed at the doll again and pulled the trigger twice.

With all the smoke from the discharged pistol, Pryce's vision was obscured. But even before the smoke had cleared, Hester was right in front of him presenting the doll. Its face was shattered and only half of its head remained. There was dark powder over the doll's white smock and clear evidence of two punctures in the body.

'Bulls eye with all four shots, Thomas! You're a marksman.'

'I owe it to my wife,' Pryce said. 'She taught me how to shoot.'

Suddenly there was a loud knocking on the door. 'Is everything all right, Lady Hester?'

A groan emerged from the water closet.

'Perfectly all right, Giles,' Hester shouted, shutting the water closet door. 'I'm just conducting an experiment with something my cousin Thomas bought for me.'

'Ah, very well, my lady.'

Hester breathed a sigh of relief. 'You clean and reload the weapon,' she said.

'While I'm doing that,' Pryce answered, 'I would be grateful if you could furnish me with a description of the two agents you saw at Chevening.'

'That's not difficult,' Hester said, clearing Pryce's clothes from her bed and concealing them in the wardrobe.

'The leader is a short man, about five feet five inches in height, with a completely bald scalp and a funny little nose. He wears silver rimmed spectacles and has cold and unfeeling eyes.'

'And the other man?'

'Slightly taller, I'd say, more cheerful, greying hair, chubby red cheeks, portly, obviously likes his food.'

'Is there anything else I need to remember?'

'Only this,' Hester said, handing him her father's invitation.

'I'll not get very far without that,' Pryce said, placing the card in an inside waist pocket.

He finished loading the pistol and secreted it in his inside breast pocket.

'I'll not need that,' he said to Hester as she handed him the pistol bag with the ram rod, powder and bullets.

'Really?' she asked.

'If I miss with the four bullets in these barrels, then my chance has gone forever.'

'Then you'd better not miss, Thomas,' Hester said, taking hold of his arm and staring into his eyes. 'Otherwise it won't be just the French who are playing chess without a king.'

CHAPTER 51

The doctor and his accomplice donned their capes, pocketed their papers and headed to the front door of their London safe house.

'I assume you don't need to return here after you've completed your mission,' Aubriet said as he stood on the doorstep.

'You assume correctly,' the doctor replied.

'Then I wish you good luck.'

The doctor peered into the road outside, looking left and right, before turning round. 'May the Eye of Ra watch over you,' he whispered.

'And Reason be your guide,' Aubriet whispered back.

The two agents marched away from the house, their shoes crunching the light snow. An icy wind blew about their faces so they drew their scarves over their numbing lips. As they marched towards Saint James' Palace, their top hats gathering flecks of snow, they passed a trio of Foot Guards underneath a lamp post.

'Gotta light, mister?' one of the redcoats asked.

The doctor shook his head and walked on by, the tip of his cane tapping the parts of the stone sidewalk that were yet to become stained by the ashen snow.

As the two men rounded the corner into Pall Mall, they could see the Tudor palace ahead of them. It was now early afternoon and the muddy lawns outside the gatehouse were crowded with people walking dogs and holding conversations. Hackney cabs and sedan chairs were offloading passengers and children were larking about in the snow.

As the doctor approached the gate he looked up at the clock face and then down at his timepiece. 'The two agree. It's half past one. Thirty minutes more, that's all.'

315

As the doctor approached the entrance to the palace, two guardsmen stood in their way. The doctor and his accomplice drew their invitations and their counterfeited papers from within their cloaks and presented them. A porter dressed in black emerged from a door within the entrance and studied them. He then looked at a paper with names written in black ink.

'You are part of Lord Stanhope's delegation?' the porter enquired.

The doctor and his associate nodded.

'The Earl has not arrived yet,' the porter said. 'I am afraid I will need to detain you here in the guard room until he does.'

'That won't be necessary.'

The voice came from behind the porter.

'I'll look after these men,' Richard Moore said.

The Irishman was dressed in red livery and, from the authority in his voice, clearly outranked the porter who, moving aside, ushered the two men under the stone arches past the guards and into the first court.

'I'll show our guests around,' Moore said as he escorted the doctor and his friend.

'This is Colour Court,' he said, maintaining the charade, 'and on your right is the Chapel Royal, on your left the Queen's Chapel.'

As the grimy snow began to fall more heavily, the people in the courtyard began to pick up pace, accelerating towards the portals of offices and apartments that seemed to surround them on every side.

'This way, gentlemen,' Moore urged.

The three men increased their speed as the cold and gusty wind began to whip the showering snowflakes down and up and to and fro.

'Through here,' Moore said.

The three men stepped through a door. They were under cover now. The doctor removed his hat and scarf as they ascended a double staircase.

At the top, Moore stopped. 'Ahead of us are the royal apartments,' he said.

The doctor followed the king's secretary to a door that was

guarded by two soldiers carrying muskets. Their shoes, buckles, buttons and blades were twinkling in the light of a chandelier above.

Moore presented the yeomen with the invitations and identity papers. One of them knocked on a door to his right and an officer appeared from the guard room. He took the papers, examined them, and then nodded.

He opened another door.

They were in.

Moore led them into a room whose walls were adorned with swords, pikes, muskets and pistols of every description and era. They were arranged in the shape of shields – some tall, others circular. Four soldiers stood underneath a golden hanging lamp suspended by an iron chain.

'The armoury,' More said.

At the far end of the room, Moore led them towards another door.

'I'll need to take your coats and hats here, gentlemen,' a footman said.

The two men obliged.

'I'll need to take that too, please sir,' he said, pointing to the doctor's cane.

'He needs his stick,' Moore interjected. 'He can't walk without it. I can vouch for him.'

The man paused for a moment, scrutinising the visitor from head to foot.

'Very well, sir,' he said.

The footman ushered them through the door behind him. The doctor limped into the entrée corridor beyond. Ten yards later and they were in the tapestry room.

The doctor drew a deep breath.

There were enormous tapestries depicting scenes from Greek mythology hanging from the walls to his right and left and at the far end of the room. On the left hand side of the chamber, the doctor saw a marble fireplace and hearth where logs were crackling and spitting. It was being tended by a footman with an iron spike.

In the centre of the room was a gaggle of men dressed in black, speaking in an animated way to each other, unfolding and folding rolls of papers covered with intricate line drawings in ink.

'The scientists,' Moore said.

The three men stood about ten feet from the rest of the visitors, keeping their own company.

As he looked to his left, the doctor saw an enormous red canopy that jutted out from the wall at the armoury end of the chamber. It stuck out several feet and was fixed just beneath the pale and unembellished ceiling. A red banner ran all the way down from the canopy, ending just above three chairs, the centre of which was designed like a throne. Just above this chair was the royal coat of arms, extending three feet high and three feet wide.

'His Majesty will be seated here when you are presented to him by name,' Moore said. 'Then the petitioners will form a circle in the centre of the room and the king will ask each one of you about your research. I will be with him, recording the details.'

The doctor turned away from the canopied wall for a moment. He looked past the other guests to the opposite end of the room. 'Is that the exit?' he asked.

Moore reached into his pocket. 'It is,' he said, revealing an iron key. 'Take this.'

The doctor seized the key and thrust it into the pocket of his short coat.

'All we need now,' Moore said, 'is our friend, Lord Stanhope.'

'He's late,' the doctor said, taking out his timepiece. 'He has only ten minutes.'

'I'll go and see where he's got to,' Moore said. 'You stay here.'

Moore left the way he had entered as the two agents stood before the freshly stoked fire. They warmed their hands for a moment.

As the doctor gazed at the leaping flames, Morgues spoke. 'What's that?'

'What's what?'

'That wood carving above the fireplace?'

As the doctor raised his eyes, he saw a diamond shaped frame painted in gold. Within the frame was what appeared to be a four leafed clover and in the centre of that an engraving of a lover's knot. Either side of that were two letters – H and A.

'What irony,' the doctor whispered.

'What do you mean?'

'H stands for Henry, as in Henry VIII.'

'Who was this A?'

'Anne Boleyn, one of his six queens.'

'He must have loved her very much,' Morgues said.

'Not that much,' the doctor grunted.

'Why do you say that?'

'She was decapitated.'

Morgues gasped.

The doctor raised his cane and pointed it towards the flames. 'And pretty soon,' he whispered, 'they will need to carve another name here.'

CHAPTER 52

'What's the hold up, man?' Pryce shouted.

The coach driver pointed to the road ahead. 'A cart full of claret, sir,' he shouted back. 'The whole thing's slipped on the ice and gone over.'

As Pryce leant out of the window, he could see the commotion ahead. The street was milling with people cupping their hands at cracks in the barrels that had spilled out of the upturned cart, sipping and gulping what they could of the wine. Some were even lying prostrate on the icy street, licking at red rivulets with tongues that were now scarlet. The whole road had come to a standstill, with cabs and carts unable either to reverse or move forward. Not even solitary riders and sedan chairs seemed able to navigate their way through the accident.

'How far is it to Saint James' Palace from here?' Pryce asked.

'Ten minutes.'

Pryce clambered out of the cab and paid his fare. 'I'll run it.'

Pryce sprinted past the offending cart and its driver. The man was nursing a bandage on his head, pressed down over a livid cut by a passing physician.

Pryce ran and ran, his hand over his chest where the pistol lay, keeping the weapon as still as possible as he puffed clouds of his breath into the freezing air.

On and on he raced, his heart pumping faster and faster, his hands marble with cold, his eyes stinging with the motes of soot as they dropped from the sullen sky.

Just as his legs were beginning to tire, Pryce rounded a corner and entered Pall Mall. The clock tower of Saint James' Palace was now in sight.

Three minutes to the hour.

He was within a musket's range now.

Two minutes to the hour.

He was at the portal, a soldier inspecting his papers.

'Let him pass!'

Pryce heard the man – a royal secretary in red livery, as bright as the claret he had seen on the road.

'Come this way, my lord,' the man cried.

Pryce followed him through a court, skidding on the ice near an archway, almost falling. Somehow he kept his footing and hurtled up a double staircase on the far side of the courtyard.

'This is Lord Stanhope!' the secretary said, causing several yeomen at the top of the stairs to part before him. Then he was in the armoury, passing his coat and hat hurriedly to a startled royal servant.

One minute to the hour.

Pryce was in the entrée corridor now. The latticed windows on his right were misting but he could make out the Park to the south of the royal apartments and the lines of trees that stood in ranks into the distance.

Then he was at the door to the Tapestry Room.

'Our friends are in here already,' the secretary whispered to him.

The secretary took hold of Pryce's sleeve and pointed towards the fireplace.

'There they are!' he whispered.

Two men in front of the blazing hearth turned. One was totally bald, wore spectacles and was leaning on a cane. The other was taller, sporting a pendulous belly, his face rosy from the heat of the fire.

As they saw Pryce enter, the bald man seemed to squint. He was about to say something to his companion, when the palace clock struck twice and the far door leading to the King's chambers opened.

'His Majesty, the king!' a man shouted.

The petitioners in the centre moved towards the edge of the room and bowed. Pryce moved to the wall opposite the fireplace. The two men he had spied were now watching the King intently as he entered the room, marched through the middle, and sat underneath the canopy next to the door leading to the armoury.

The secretary who had escorted Pryce walked towards the King, bowed and then sat down on the chair on his right. An equerry sat on the seat to his left. The doors both ends of the long chamber were closed loudly.

The equerry stood. 'His Majesty invites his honoured guests to stand in a circle in the centre of the room.'

The petitioners obeyed and Pryce joined the circle, positioning himself directly opposite the two men. The shorter man was leering at him. He was now cleaning his glasses. He placed them back on his nose. He stared again at Pryce. A look of confusion spread across his leaden face. He turned to the man next to him and whispered. The man looked horrified. Pryce reached into his pocket for the pistol. His hand was trembling but his eyes were fixed on the two men the other side of the room.

And they were now also trained on the secretary.

CHAPTER 53

As the King and his equerry rose and walked to the centre of the chamber, Pryce spied the secretary stepping to his right and inserting a cast iron key in the lock of the door leading to the armoury. He turned it swiftly and then joined the King who was now embarking on a conversation with the first petitioner in the circle, asking him about his invention and the benefit it would bring. The secretary, feigning interest, took out a pen and began to write down what the man was saying.

Pryce wiped a bead of sweat from his forehead with his left hand, noticing the dark stain of Lady Hester's make-up as he looked at his fingers. With his right hand, he cocked the four-barrelled pistol in the inside left pocket of his tails. The king would be conversing with the two interlopers within seconds.

As the conversation ended with the petitioner next to the two agents, Pryce gripped the butt of the pistol. The King moved two steps to his right and stood in front of the bald man. The man's head was gleaming, and so were his eyes.

Pryce gasped.

With the speed of a snake, the bald man took his cane and withdrew a long blade. 'Go!' he shouted. He thrust the blade into the equerry, who moaned, tilted backwards and fell to the floor, his head cracking on the wooden floorboards.

The secretary took a swift step to one side and grabbed the startled King from behind, holding him in an armlock.

'Release the King!' Pryce shouted, raising the pistol. 'Release him now!'

The secretary, surprised, turned his head. Enraged, he let go of his captive, who was now shouting with indignation, and made to run towards Pryce. A deep roar rose from the man's throat. Pryce hesitated for a moment then fired the first barrel before his adversary was a yard from him. Sparks and smoke flew from the front and the side of the weapon. A small black dot appeared in the secretary's forehead, no larger than a thimble head, and he fell to the floor, coming to rest next to the writhing body of the equerry.

'Oh my God!' Pryce cried, as he looked at the dead man.

But he had no time for remorse.

The bald man took hold of the long and glinting blade again.

'Put it down!' Pryce shouted.

But the swordsman took no notice. He raised the blade high above the King's head, preparing a death blow. Pryce took aim and fired the second upper barrel. More sparks. More smoke. The man dropped the sword. He yelped, clasping his hand.

There was banging and shouting at the armoury door now.

'Call out the guard!'

'Open the door!'

'In the name of the King, open the door!'

The bald man's accomplice ran to the blade and picked it up. He started to run towards Pryce. Pryce flicked the switch on his weapon, activating the two lower barrels. Again he hesitated.

'Halt!' he shouted.

But the man came on.

Pryce shook his head, as one whose options had deserted him, and pulled the trigger.

The man was hit in his considerable belly which he now clutched, desperately trying to stem the blood flowing from a powdery wound just above his belly button. His body hit the floor with a thud. He groaned.

There was shouting from the armoury. An axe was pounding the door. A musket was fired into the lock, sending a shower of sparks and splinters through the hole and into the Tapestry Room.

In the commotion, Pryce saw the bald man running to the door to the private chambers on his right. He tried to shoot the fleeing assassin but one of the petitioners was in his line of fire.

'Stop!' Pryce exclaimed.

But the man was moving with a speed born of a primeval need for survival. He was already at the door, turning the handle with his able, left hand. And before Pryce could discharge a round, he had sped from the room, leaving a trickle of blood and one of his fingers on the floor.

CHAPTER 54

'Protect the King and let the guardsmen in,' Pryce shouted as he sprinted to the door to the King's private chambers.

Pryce dashed from the Tapestry Room and turned right into a drawing room and then into a large bedroom.

'Make way!' he shouted at two grooms.

They retreated when they saw Pryce's pistol, their faces aghast.

Pryce chased through the royal water closet and on to a stone stair case. He descended at speed, observing the trail of the fleeing agent's blood upon the worn, grey steps. He passed through a disused kitchen and into an ancient wine vault. He could still make out the tell-tale spatters of blood leading to a door at the far corner.

He opened it. There was a gasp of air. Ahead of him he could see a candle. The fugitive had found illumination.

Pryce sped along the wet floor, following the glimmering light of the guttering candle that was now about one hundred feet ahead of him. He kept his pistol in front of his chest, the fourth and final barrel cocked, ready to be discharged should the bald man turn and attack him. He took deep breaths in the dank corridor and followed hard on the man's trail, his nostrils puffing, his chest heaving.

Suddenly the light ahead of him was gone.

Pryce stopped. He felt his way in the darkness with his free hand, touching the dripping side of the tunnel, until it ran into a facing wall and stopped him in his tracks. He turned to his right, following the course of the wall. Another door. He pushed it open.

Pryce was now in a huge cavernous chamber, some ancient and draughty underground hall with a musty odour of rotting faeces. As he groped in the darkness, fissures in the wall above cast a dim light into the hall and Pryce spied a sarcophagus on the far side of the room. A sister of the church had clearly been buried there. Her stone-carved body lay in everlasting repose on top of a rectangular chest, her hands together in prayer above her heart, her eyes closed in a fixed serenity.

As Pryce approached it, he saw that her face and her hands had scars and sores and open pores.

Leprosy.

Pryce made his way past statues of other leprous sisters and a lopsided gravestone with the words *Momento Mori*.

He was at the far corner of the hall now, his eyes straining for vision, his heart pumping.

The light ahead was flickering. The flame had nearly become a smouldering wick. Pryce increased his speed, his hand gripping the pistol as the light disappeared altogether.

The temperature dropped. An icy wind blew upon Pryce's face. He was up to his ankles in freezing water. Then up to his knees. He waded, keeping the pistol high above his head, its mechanism free from the water, until he came to the end of the tunnel. He pushed past some torn iron grating and through the shaggy branches of a willow tree.

The water was splashing around his waist. But the level was decreasing. Soon it was below his knees. Then it barely covered his buckled shoes. He was on dry land. Then he was on a bank, climbing upwards. He could see a white shape in some reeds a few feet to his right. Swans. He swung to his left. He was on a path now, running adjacent to the large pond he had just left. Ahead of him he could just make out the scalp of the bald man, as bright as a cast in the light of the moon. The man was running through Horse Guards Parade, clutching his wounded hand.

Within minutes Pryce had raced past Scotland Yard and through Whitehall and was now only fifty feet behind his quarry.

The bald man turned. He saw Pryce's pistol. He frowned and then hurried on to the edge of some stairs leading from street level to the littoral water of the Thames. He began to descend, calling out to a group of men in a jolly boat.

Pryce could hear the men's voices. Irish voices.

'Stop him!' Pryce shouted.

But the fugitive ignored him. He was nearing the bottom of the stairs.

Pryce raised the pistol.

He aimed.

Fired.

The last bullet hit the water beyond the boat.

Vacher stood on the deck of the boat and looked at Pryce.

'Perhaps next time you will have better luck, Monsieur.'

Vacher continued to mock him as the oarsmen rowed swiftly towards a sloop whose anchor was already being raised.

'Next time I will not miss!' Pryce shouted as the cold mist swirled across the water.

CHAPTER 55

'Excuse the state of my scalp, Prime Minister,' Pryce said as he and Eloise entered the dining room of Walmer Castle two days later. 'My wife decided that it would be better to be completely shaven, and to grow all my hair back evenly.'

'He looks most threatening, do you not think?' Eloise chuckled. 'Although I do miss his black hair.'

Pryce and Eloise bowed as they approached William Pitt, who was sitting at the head of the table, in front of an alcove where coffee was being poured by a footman.

'I heard from Lady Hester about your clever deception,' Pitt said. 'It was very cunning to assume Stanhope's identity.'

Pitt bid his guests sit at the table, opposite two men, dressed in tails. 'My, what a gathering of clever and clandestine souls is here!' Pitt said.

When the laughter subsided, Pryce turned to his host. 'What has happened to Lord Stanhope, Prime Minister?'

'He is in quite a pickle,' Pitt answered. 'As far as everyone in the palace is concerned, he is responsible for saving the King's life. They are convinced that it was he who thwarted the assassination. Your disguise, Mister Pryce, was convincing, and Lord Stanhope is languishing in the depths of a great irony.'

Pryce suppressed a laugh and said, 'that will cause him no end of misery if the news reaches his friends in France.'

'Precisely, and if he proves to be a nuisance to me again, I will release the details to the newspapers, along with the eyewitness testimonies of the scientists at St James. That should keep him reined in for a while.'

Pryce smiled.

'Now, then, to business,' Pitt said. 'Let me make some introductions.' He turned to face the two other men at the table.

'William Wickham, you know.'

Pryce nodded. 'My wife and I had the pleasure of meeting Mister Wickham and his wife here at this table.'

'This gentleman needs no introduction,' Pitt continued.

'Dean Jackson,' Pryce smiled. 'It is a surprise and a delight to see you again.'

'I like to keep an eye on my most outstanding former students,' the Dean said, peering at Pryce from underneath his wild, grey eyebrows. 'Your doctoral dissertation on Egypt in the time of Moses was a fine piece of work.'

The footman handed coffee to Pryce.

'We are here on behalf of the King,' Pitt said once the footman had left the room. 'His Majesty is in your debt and has offered you a considerable reward for saving his life.'

'You did well,' Wickham added.

'Astonishingly well,' the Dean whispered.

Pryce was silent for a moment. 'I was in extremis,' he said, his eyes staring at the liquid trembling in the China cup in front of him.

'And you proved to be most resourceful,' the Prime Minister said. 'And it is because of that Mister Wickham would like to offer you a proposal.'

'What kind of proposal?'

'These are perilous times,' Wickham took over. 'And we have urgent need of exceptional men.'

'And you are an exceptional man,' the Dean added. 'You showed extraordinary courage and capability in rescuing your mother-in-law from the most ruthless of enemy agents in Brittany.'

'By the bye, how is your mother, Mrs Pryce?' Pitt asked.

'She is living with us and recovering well,' Eloise replied. 'She will be a great help when our child is born.'

'Ah, I see congratulations are in order,' Pitt exclaimed.

'In the midst of death,' Eloise said, 'we see some signs of life at least.'

Pitt nodded then looked to his right again, signalling with a raised eyebrow for the conversation to accelerate.

'I would like to issue you an invitation,' Wickham said.

'What kind of invitation?' Eloise asked.

'We have urgent need of men like your husband who are brave and clever, especially ones who can speak French fluently.'

'To what end?' Eloise asked.

'I have been ordered by the Prime Minister to establish a formal secret service to protect our King and country. I am to train new agents for missions both home and abroad. You, Mister Pryce, would be a most welcome and resourceful addition.'

'But I'm a Vicar!'

'No ordinary Vicar,' the Dean murmured.

'Precisely,' Wickham said. 'We have very few men whose command of the French language is as perfect as yours and you know France intimately, especially Brittany.'

'We lost a very good man last month,' Pitt said. 'We have a pressing need to replace him with someone equally as able, if not more so.'

'That does not inspire me with confidence!' Eloise interrupted.

'These are desperate times, my dear,' Pitt said. 'So desperate indeed that I have now asked Mister Wickham to transform Walmer Castle into a secret base of operations, accountable to Evan Nepean, undersecretary at the Home Office.'

Pryce frowned. 'You're going to train spies here?'

'Yes, these grounds are ideal and the location, so close to the French coast, could not be more suitable.'

Pitt nodded to the Dean.

'I have some concrete suggestions to make,' the Dean said. 'I have been given permission to set up something called the 'CCC'.'

'CCC?'

'The Christ Church Correspondence, a network of old boys from our beloved college who have demonstrated, let me say, a particular aptitude for work in the field or for administrative undertakings.'

'And you want me to a member of this Correspondence?'

'We believe you are going to become one of our most able agents,' Pitt said.

'In the field or in the office?' Eloise asked.

'In the field,' the Dean answered. 'A foreign field, indeed.'

Eloise shook her head and sighed.

'I have been watching you since your curacy in Whitehall,' Wickham said. 'Your credentials, shall we say, are impeccable.'

'But do you not see the contradiction?' Pryce asked.

'Explain,' Pitt said.

'The contradiction between being a spy and being a vicar... I am already horribly compromised by what I've done.'

Pitt sat back in his chair and looked out of the window to the cannons outside. 'What if we all took that view? If all of us yielded to passivity there would be a guillotine in Hyde Park and His Majesty's head would be the first to fall from it.'

'You have already seen what we are up against,' Wickham added, 'the darkness, thick darkness, spreading from France to these shores.'

'What is it you said at this dinner table?' Pitt whispered. 'Our inaction will be the seedbed for evil to grow and flourish.'

'But that was with respect to my wife's mother!'

'Then what about all the other mothers, fathers, sons and brothers, daughters and sisters? What is the difference between defending them and defending your own? They may not be related by family ties but they are by human ones.'

'And you think being a Vicar and a spy can work?'

'It's the perfect cover,' Pitt replied. 'No one would suspect a man of God.'

'What about St Leonard's Church? I have only been the Vicar three weeks and already I have missed a Sunday.'

'We have that organized,' the Dean replied. 'If you say yes, the Archbishop will grant you a curate - a man who will know nothing about your work for the government but who will be a support in your parochial duties.'

'And what other support do you propose?'

'Are you saying yes?' Pitt interjected.

Pryce paused and looked at Eloise. Her eyes were filling with tears but somehow, from deep within her heaving chest, she summoned up the courage to nod.

Pryce turned to the Prime Minister. 'I suppose I am.'

'Then yes, there will be plenty of support.'

Pitt rang a small bell on the table and a tall man with a moustache appeared at the doorway.

'Jack!' Pryce cried.

'Good morning Prime Minister, my lady, gentlemen,' Jack said.

'What are you doing here?'

Jack looked at the Prime Minister, who nodded. 'We were Hardy's men,' Jack said. 'The spy who was killed last month in Brittany.'

Pryce gasped.

'Now they are your men,' the Prime Minister said.

'And what about that blessing I performed on your boat?' Pryce asked. 'Was that a subterfuge?'

Jack looked to Pitt.

'Don't answer that,' Pitt said.

'You see, there is my problem,' Pryce said. 'I am used to a world of truth and falsehood, a world where the boundaries are clearly demarcated, where duplicity is forbidden and dissembling is condemned.'

'So?' Pitt asked.

'So my public profession as a clergyman means that I am committed to navigating by the north star of truth. Yet my secret life as a spy will mean sailing in a sea of contradictions, where lying and even killing will be a grim necessity.'

'That may be the price you have to pay,' Pitt said. 'But the preservation of our national freedom will be the reward.'

'I feel as if I have no choice,' Pryce sighed.

'We all have choices,' Wickham said, 'but sometimes they are not susceptible to evangelical simplicities.'

Pryce turned to Eloise, whose face had settled somewhere between smiling and sadness.

'Very well.'

'Bravo!' the Prime Minister cried, shaking Pryce's hand.

'Excellent!' Wickham said, standing to his feet.

'Well done, my boy,' Dean Jackson said, placing his hand on Pryce's shoulder. 'I will always be here for you.'

'As will I,' said Jake, 'and the boatmen of Deal.'

'And I,' Eloise said, holding tightly to his arm.

As Pryce put his arm around his wife and looked into her eyes, Pitt poured five crystal glasses in the alcove behind his chair.

'To the Christ Church Correspondence,' he cried as he raised the blood-red port.

AKNOWLEDGEMENTS

We have used a number of historical sources that have proved invaluable in the research for this first adventure in the *Chronicles of Thomas Pryce*.

Most importantly, we must pay tribute to Elizabeth Sparrow and her ground-breaking book published in 1999, *Secret Service: British Agents in France 1792-1815*. Elizabeth advances the compelling thesis that the British Secret Service began not in the 20th century, before the outbreak of the First World War, but in the 18th century, as the British government sought to cope with the mass immigration of French fugitives from the Revolution, some of whom were not genuine refugees from terror but secret agents sent from the government in France - something that has remarkable parallels with our own times. To Elizabeth Sparrow we owe a huge debt of thanks.

Elizabeth Sparrow highlighted what we already knew, that a certain William Wickham was the first British Spy Master. Little had been written about Wickham however until 2009, when Michael Durey published *William Wickham, Master Spy: The Secret War against the French Revolution*. This has proved to be a goldmine of information not only about Wickham himself but also about the Alien Act, the Alien Office, and the nascent Secret Service in the 1790s. All of these figure prominently in *The Fate of Kings* and we owe a great debt of thanks to Michael for his meticulous research.

We would also like to pay tribute to Hubert Cole's 1971 book *Fouché: the Unprincipled Patriot*. This unearthed the multi-layered complexities of the man. Fouché's personality was indeed a mass of contradictions and this study very ably exposes these. The name which we give him, 'The Shadow of Death', is our own invention, created for symbolic purposes, but some of the other details are based on fact not fiction. He was, and is, a fascinating if sometimes disturbing object of historical study.

Being fans of period dramas, it was a joy to be able to include scenes in and around castles and country houses in England. Walmer Castle - a mile from Deal - straight away suggested itself as a more than suitable and indeed logical location. Perhaps the most intriguing visitor to the castle in the late eighteenth and early nineteenth century was Lady Hester Stanhope, an independent and courageous woman ahead of her time. In our research about her we have been indebted to Kirsten Ellis for her excellent book, *Star of the Morning: the Extraordinary Life of Lady Hester Stanhope*.

One source book that we couldn't have done without is David Darrah's *Conspiracy in Paris: the Strange Career of Joseph Picot de Limoelan* (1953). Without this detailed and readable study we would never have known anything like as much about the Limoelan family and their chateau in Brittany. David's information about Michel Alain and Jean Marie Picot proved invaluable, as did his material about Michel Alain's brother, the Abbé de la Clorivieres. The only detail we changed was the name of one of their daughters who in our story becomes Thomas Pryce's wife and is now called Eloise.

Another author we'd like to thank is Christopher Hibbert for his fascinating and brilliantly written *King George III: A Personal History*. The King was an unusual character. Although he has only a secondary part in our drama, Hibbert's book helped greatly. The same goes for William Pitt. William Hague's biography was useful in helping us to catch a glimpse of his character.

For our research into matters related to Jersey we have found the following books to be immensely helpful: *In the English Service: The Life of Philippe D'Auvergne* by Jane Ashelford (2008) and *The Battle of Jersey* by Richard Mayne (1981).

For the technicalities of hot air ballooning in the late eighteenth century we couldn't have done without *A Narrative of the Two Aerial Voyages of Doctor Jeffries with Mons Blanchard* (first published in 1786) and *The Montgolfier Brothers* by Charles Coulston Gillispie (1983).

We would like to thank Cate Bentley of Verbsmith for her excellent advice and meticulous copy-editing, and also Malcolm Down and Sarah Grace Griggs for their support and friendship as our publishers.

Finally, we would like to give heartfelt thanks to the current Lord Warden of the Cinque Ports, the Admiral of the Fleet the Lord Mike Boyce, as well as the supervisor at Walmer Castle, Sally Mewton-Hynds, and archivist Rowena Willard-Wright, for giving us unique access to the grounds and the rooms of the castle during the research phase, and also to Lieutenant Colonel Giles Stibbe O.B.E for giving us access to St James' Palace and its grounds.